Christy Reece grew up in a small, quiet community in Alabama. For her, books were an entrance into faraway worlds, wild adventures and fantastical journeys. If she wasn't reading, then the characters in her head entertained her, telling about their lives and amazing adventures. It wasn't until much later in life that she started writing their stories down. Now, she and her characters are thrilled to share those adventures with the world. Christy is the author of the *New York Times* bestselling *Last Chance Rescue* romantic suspense series. She also writes steamy, southern suspense under the pen name Ella Grace. Christy lives in Alabama with her husband, five precocious fur-kids and one incredibly shy turtle.

Praise for Christy Reece:

'Sizzling romance and fraught suspense fill the pages as the novel races toward its intensely riveting conclusion' *Publishers Weekly, Starred Review*

'Romantic suspense has a major new star!' *Romantic Times*

'A passionate and vivacious thrill-ride! . . . I feel like I've been on an epic journey after finishing it . . . Exquisite' *Joyfully Reviewed*

'A very compelling romantic suspense. The romance is sensuous, and the story moves along at an excellent pace with a lot of drama and violence. The characters are distinctly drawn, and the pages are filled with intrigue and emotional intensity' *Romance Reviews Today*

'Steamy sex scenes, intense fighting scenes, the sensation of struggling to survive, edge-of-your-seat feelings, and finding your true self make this mind-blowing book a must read story!' *Coffee Time Romance & More*

'A heart-racing tale from start to finish . . . I loved every minute of it!' *The Romance Reader's Connection*

'[A] brilliantly plotted book. The love story, as always, is hot and emotive and balanced well with the exciting and well-crafted mystery. Her main characters are vulnerable yet strong, and even the villains a[illegible] delicate brush strokes haur[illegible] *Fiction*

By Christy Reece

Last Chance Rescue Series

Rescue Me
Return to Me
Run to Me
No Chance
Second Chance
Last Chance
Sweet Justice
Sweet Revenge
Sweet Reward

No Chance

CHRISTY REECE

First published in the United States of America in 2010
by Ballantine Books, an imprint of
The Random House Publishing Group,
a division of Random House, Inc.

First published in Great Britain in 2013
by ETERNAL ROMANCE,
an imprint of HEADLINE PUBLISHING GROUP

1

Cataloguing in Publication Data is available from the British Library

ISBN 978 0 7553 9795 2

Offset in Sabon by Avon DataSet Ltd, Bidford-on-Avon, Warwickshire

Printed and bound by CPI Group (UK) Ltd, Croydon, CR0 4YY

Headline's policy is to use papers that are natural, renewable and recyclable products and made from wood grown in sustainable forests. The logging and manufacturing processes are expected to conform to the environmental regulations of the country of origin.

HEADLINE PUBLISHING GROUP
An Hachette UK Company
338 Euston Road
London NW1 3BH

www.eternalromancebooks.co.uk
www.headline.co.uk
www.hachette.co.uk

To Jim, who never lost faith

one

Kalamina Island
South Pacific
Eight years ago

"You do know there's more where that came from, don't you?" a softly teasing female voice asked.

Hunched over his plate, engrossed in stuffing himself with the feast before him, Gabe Maddox jerked his head up to glare. At the sight of the vision in front of him, his irritation at being interrupted and possibly mocked disappeared, along with his mouthful of food. Choking and gasping for breath, Gabe made a grab for his napkin.

"Oh, hey, I'm sorry. Are you okay?" She rushed behind him and pounded on his back.

A hot wave of embarrassment flooded through him. Only half of the food had gone down the wrong way. The other half he'd spewed out. Thankfully, the woman seemed too concerned with his health to notice the half-chewed piece of steak glistening on the table.

Finally catching his breath, Gabe wiped his mouth and eyes and looked at her as she came around to stand in front of him. Breath left him all over again. Beauty as he'd never imagined gazed down at him.

Long, thick mahogany hair, pulled back in a ponytail, drew attention to exotic cheekbones, skin the color of cream satin, full, beautiful lips, and eyes the color of a spring sky. He could do nothing but stare at the vision.

Her eyes darkened with concern. "Uh-oh, are you in some kind of shock or something? Should I call a doctor?"

Pulling in a wheezing breath, Gabe shook his head. "I'm fine. You just startled me."

He told himself she couldn't be real. She was an apparition. A figment of his overactive imagination brought on by starvation and torture. No one could be so beautiful. No way in hell could this woman be real.

And then she smiled. Suddenly, Gabe didn't care if she was a fantasy. Her smile was the kind poets wrote sonnets about. The exotic sky blue of her eyes was so clear he felt as if he could float away in them. Words he hadn't thought of since his college literature class burst into his mind. *Breathtaking. Mesmerizing. Unforgettable.*

Her smile tilted down a bit as she grimaced. "Sorry about sneaking up on you. I have a tendency to do that to people. My dad tells me I'm like a cat."

She stood for a few seconds as if waiting for something. Gabe still couldn't speak. Had no idea what to say. After a year of seeing only a handful of people, all of whom spoke a different language, his conversation skills were close to zero.

White teeth chewed delicately at her plump lips as if she were nervous. "Well, I guess I'll be going. Sorry to interrupt your meal. And, uh . . . sorry for almost killing you."

Before she could take another step, Gabe jumped to his feet. The movement, awkward and clumsy, almost knocked his chair over. He still had no idea what he was going to say to this beautiful creature. He only knew that if he allowed her to leave, he'd regret it for the rest of his life.

His abrupt move apparently startled her, because her eyes widened, but she didn't back away.

He finally forced words from his frozen mouth. "Would you like to join me?"

Though still thin from his year of deprivation, he was almost a foot taller than her and felt like a skinny, scraggly pine tree towering over an exotic, delicate flower. He was also known more for his hard, grim looks than his charm, so when she took several steps toward him, he was astounded. Stupid, really, but for some reason, he almost backed away. She was just that beautiful.

Her eyes examined and questioned; Gabe got the feeling she was searching for something. Finally she held out her hand and said, "I'm Skylar James. What's your name?"

Gabe's hand engulfed hers as he said, "Gabriel Maddox."

"Nice to meet you, Gabriel."

"Call me Gabe." He paused for half a second to swallow nervously, then added, "Nice to meet you . . . Skye."

Something odd flickered in her face and then that smile returned. "I'd love to join you. I've had dinner but was seriously contemplating the hot fudge sundae for dessert."

Remembering his manners wasn't easy. Where he'd been for the last year, humanity, even in its lowest forms, hadn't existed. However, his stepmother's soft instructions from years before finally kicked in and he held out a chair for her.

Skye sat down. Then, without missing a beat, she took the napkin in front of her and scooped up the food Gabe had spit on the table when he'd been choking. Placing it on the edge of the table for the waiter to pick up, she leaned forward and whispered as if she had a secret to share, "I heard if you compliment the chef, he'll put extra ice cream in the sundae. Want to try it?"

The innocence and sheer love of life shining in those unbelievable eyes melted every defense Gabe had erected over the last few years. The darkness that had enveloped him for so long began to evaporate and a new hope, a new beginning, emerged.

Skylar could feel Gabe's midnight blue gaze on her face as she ordered two hot fudge sundaes. Flashing a smile of thanks to the waiter, she turned back to look at the man across from her. Her heart began an unusually loud thumping in her chest. She'd never seen anyone like Gabe Maddox before. Only fierce determination and the mountain of pride etched in his face overshadowed his gaunt, half-starved appearance. Despite his thinness, he was attractive, even handsome, but that wasn't what drew her to him. There was something in his eyes, his expression, that made her want to know more about him.

She hadn't meant to embarrass him about gobbling his food. When she'd seen him hunched over his plate so protectively, as if someone might remove it at any moment, she'd blurted out her thoughts. One of her failings was her tendency to say whatever popped into her head. It had gotten her in hot water countless times. And poor Gabe had almost choked to death.

The instant he'd raised his head, she'd regretted her words. He'd thought she was mocking him. Instead, she'd almost killed him.

Now Gabe continued to stare at her without any indication that he would say anything soon. She'd been making small talk since her preteen days, but that intense blue gaze made her forget every conversation starter she'd ever heard. She felt nervous and all fluttery inside. Not a normal feeling for her at all.

Clearing her throat, she said, "Are you here on vacation?"

"Sort of. You?"

"Yes, just got here a couple of days ago." She frowned at the odd phrasing of his words. "What do you mean, 'sort of'?"

His thin shoulders lifted. "Kind of recovering."

"From what?" she blurted out and then winced. When would she learn to control her mouth?

"I—"

Mario, the young waiter who always flirted with her when she visited, set two giant sundaes in front of them and winked at her.

She smiled her thanks and then looked at Gabe, wondering if he'd seen the wink. He hadn't. His eyes were almost as large as their sundaes as he stared at the mounds of ice cream like he'd never seen anything so beautiful. Deciding conversation could wait until they finished, she dipped her spoon into the ice cream and took a small bite. Gabe dug into his, overloading his spoon and shoveling it into his mouth. It was a humbling experience to realize that the dessert in front of Gabe was more enticing to him than she was. For a girl who'd had more guys ask her out than the population of a small city, it was both intriguing and exciting. Gabe had no idea who she was.

As he scooped gobs of ice cream into his mouth, Skylar continued to spoon small amounts into hers and watched him, fascinated. She'd never seen anyone eat like that before.

The instant she head him scraping the bottom of his bowl, she pushed hers toward him. "That was delicious, but I'm stuffed. Can you finish mine for me?"

He eyed her for several seconds. "Are you sure?"

"Absolutely."

Gabe needed no second urging. He grabbed her bowl and proceeded to devour it until, once again, he was scraping the bottom of the bowl.

Skylar swallowed past the lump that had developed in her throat. Gabe wasn't just enjoying his food; he was relishing it as if he had never had anything like that in his life.

"You said you're sort of on vacation. What does that mean?"

Wiping his mouth, he gave her a look that did something to her insides. Her heart took a flip and her breathing increased. She'd never had that kind of reaction to a guy before. She'd kissed a few and had even thought about going all the way with a couple of them, but never had she felt all these tingly, achy feelings.

"I've been in prison."

Skylar couldn't control the gasp that left her mouth. If anyone else had said those words to her, she would have gotten up and run. Her reaction to Gabe's announcement was telling. By the solemn, desolate expression on his face, she knew whatever had happened had hurt him deeply. She also knew that she had nothing to fear from him.

"Can you talk about it?"

He glanced around at the open-air restaurant. Other than a few waiters, the place was almost empty. "We probably need to leave so they can close up."

Disappointed and slightly hurt at his obvious ignoring of her question, Skylar pushed back her chair to stand. Gabe was there before she could move, pulling her chair out farther for her and then holding his hand out.

Skylar looked down at the hand. Though his skin was tanned, he didn't look like he'd spent a lot of time outside. The hand was large but bony, like the rest of his body. Placing her hand in his, she was surprised at how small and dainty it looked enveloped in his.

He pulled her to stand but didn't move away, causing her to look up at him. Those deep blue eyes drew her as nothing ever had before. Surprising herself probably even more than Gabe, she rose up on her toes and pressed a soft kiss to his grim, unsmiling mouth.

"Why did you do that?"

"I don't know."

He held her gaze for the longest time and Skylar felt frozen, unable to do anything but return the stare. It was as if he were delving into the deepest part of her soul. Then that stern mouth moved up slightly. "It was nice."

And Skylar's heart did a triple flip.

Gabe drew in a deep, appreciative breath as they meandered along the brick walkway. The air was scented with the sweetness of flowers, freshly mowed grass, and the ocean. Breathing clean, open air was a gift he would never take for granted.

He eyed the young girl who walked so quietly beside him. She couldn't be real. Girls like that—beautiful but with an innocent exuberance and naturalness he found enchanting—didn't really exist outside of fantasies. Gabe inwardly cursed his fascination. How many times did he have to get kicked in the teeth before he learned his lesson?

"Can you talk about it?"

He knew she was referring to his bald statement in the restaurant. Most girls would have gotten up and left. Skye's expression had held a myriad of emotions; not one of them had been fear.

And because of the lack of judgment in her eyes, he found himself telling her everything.

She listened intently, her eyes wide with horror, then

soft with compassion. "So the entire village was decimated?"

He clenched his jaw. The pain had faded somewhat, but he would never forget the bloody horror and smells of the massacre. "Everything was destroyed. The huts, the houses we built. The clinic. The schoolhouse. They even burned the fields."

"But why?"

He shrugged. That kind of question had been asked for centuries. "Why does anyone attempt to conquer and destroy? Power? Ego? The sheer enjoyment of destruction and death? The villages had once been allies, but had a disagreement and grew apart. Then one man decided he wanted them together again so he could control them both. They were already at war when I arrived, but it was only the occasional raid, nothing major."

"What changed?"

Gabe looked out into the black night and saw her face. The face of betrayal. Pretty but not beautiful. Seemingly innocent but as deceitful and manipulative as the devil himself.

"One of the missionaries had a daughter. She wanted to go back home but didn't have the funds to get there. She helped them sneak into the village during a celebration when she knew security would be at its weakest. They attacked them at their most vulnerable time. About a hundred people were killed. Most escaped with whatever they had on their backs. Some were captured and imprisoned."

"Like you?"

"Like me."

He heard her swallow and it touched him unlike anything had in a long time. She barely knew him and yet her compassion seemed deeper and truer than the majority of people he'd met in his life.

"But aren't you an American citizen? How could they do that to you?"

How many nights had he lain in his hole of a cell, looked up at the stars, and wondered the same thing?

"Turns out no one knew about us for a long time. The village was burned to the ground. Funds were low so it took a while before the bodies could be identified. Then it took time for them to ferret out that we were being held and where. After that, it took months to free us."

"How many were there with you?"

"Eight. Only two of us were Americans. Not that I ever saw the other guy. They kept us as far away from each other as possible. That was part of their punishment. No one else spoke English."

"They punished you?"

"Mostly just worked us from dusk till dawn. Gave us little food and no freedom."

"Worked you how?"

"Anything they wanted done, we were their slaves to do it. Building . . . tearing down. Whatever they needed."

"How did you get out?"

"Group called Free Makers. They negotiated our release."

"How did you end up here . . . at this resort?"

"The group is funded by several philanthropists. After they checked me out, gave me a clean bill of health, I was offered a month of recovery at a resort. They gave me ten choices. This one sounded the best to me. So here I am."

"I'm glad you chose this one."

His mouth curved up again. "Me too."

"So where do you go from here?"

"Not really sure. I have a few weeks left to make a decision."

"What about your family?"

Gabe drew in a breath. He should be used to the stabbing pain in his chest by now. It'd been almost four years. At some point, the hurt had to stop, didn't it?

"My family's gone," he said.

"Gone? How?"

Spotting a bench along the sidewalk, Gabe headed toward it. Odd. He'd never talked to anyone about the accident that took his father and brother, but for some reason, he wanted to tell Skye.

"My dad and brother were killed in a mining accident."

She dropped down beside him and put her hand on his arm. "I'm so sorry. What happened?"

The vast ocean was before him but all Gabe saw was the darkness of that day. The darkest day of his life. "We'd just started work when it happened."

"You were there, too?"

He swallowed hard. "Yeah, there were nine of us."

"And your brother and father were killed?"

"Everyone was . . . but me."

"You feel guilty about that, don't you?"

He jerked at her perception, surprised someone so young could understand his feelings so accurately when so many others never had. "Hard not to feel guilty. Sons, fathers, brothers. They all died. I was spared and their loved ones died. They had a right to be resentful."

"They resented that you lived?"

"It's a normal—"

He was surprised when she jumped to her feet and stood in front of him. "That's not normal at all. They should have been happy that you lived."

A small smile lifted his lips at her indignation. He'd probably smiled more tonight, since meeting Skye, than he had in years. But he couldn't help himself. He'd known this girl less than an hour and she was happier that he was alive than the people he'd known all his life.

"I understood their feelings. It hurt but I understood."

"What about your mother?"

"My mom took off when I was a baby. Divorced my dad. I don't know where she is. My dad married my stepmom when I was four. She was a widow with a son a couple of years younger than me."

"And that was your brother . . . the one who died?"

"Yeah." The tightness in his chest grew more painful as he allowed himself to think about the bright, funny kid that became his brother the instant he met him. "He was never my 'step' anything, though."

"But your stepmom. She's still alive?"

He stared into the night again. "I believe so."

"She was one of the ones, wasn't she?"

He looked back up at her. "One of the ones what?"

"That resented you for being alive?"

He shrugged. "She lost both her son and her husband."

"And one of her sons survived."

Gabe swallowed. Dammit, he hadn't allowed himself to think about that hurt in years. Even though he'd understood the grief his stepmother was feeling, it had torn him apart to see the questions in her eyes. Why had he survived? What made him so damn special that he had lived when everyone else had died? He had never been able to answer that question. Admittedly, before his capture, when he'd worked tirelessly beside the villagers, he'd believed he had discovered the answer. Then that theory got blown all to hell.

Aware she was still waiting for an answer, he said, "It's all water under the bridge now. I'm sure she's made a new life for herself. She's probably got another family now."

Her body trembling with anger, Skylar clenched her fist to hold in her emotions. Gabe was acting as if it were completely normal to have people resent his survival. Instead of celebrating that he had lived, apparently they'd begrudged him for it. She might be able to understand strangers feeling that way. But people who knew him? And his stepmother? A woman who'd raised him, supposedly loved him? Not only was it inconceivable, it was indefensible.

She wanted to stomp her foot and tell him he should get mad, too. But she could see it in his expression—he had long ago accepted their treatment.

"You know, it suddenly occurs to me that you now know everything about me and I know nothing other than your name."

Skylar tensed for a new reason. Now that he'd explained where he'd been the last few years, she knew why he didn't know who she was. Her parents had only started allowing her to model when she was seventeen. Any photographs of her before that were published only in the society pages of the local papers and magazines. The modeling was still only occasional, but she'd quickly become a celebrity.

She had a choice to make. Tell Gabe and see his expression change to one of wariness. He would treat her differently. See her differently. Might even end their brief acquaintance immediately.

Or she could allow him to think she was just an average American college girl taking a vacation on her own. The resort staff wouldn't out her. Most of the guests were here for the very same reasons she was. Escape. An opportunity to be themselves. She'd already spotted a couple of actors and a musician. They'd barely looked her way, as she had them. This place was all about privacy.

Could she take this time and be a different Skylar James? The lure of being treated like a normal person as opposed to the American princess the media liked to dub her was just too enticing to resist.

Holding out her hand, she smiled and said, "Let's walk and I'll tell you all about Skye James."

two

"Oh wow, Skye. Did you see that?"

Leaning back against the hard chest behind her, Skylar looked up at Gabe. "Yes. They're beautiful."

Concern furrowed his brow. "Are you okay? You've hardly said anything since we got on the boat."

She forced a smile, hoping it didn't look as fake as it felt. "I'm fine. I think I had too much lunch. I'm kind of sleepy."

Midnight blue eyes darkened as they roamed her face. "I kept you up too late last night."

Skylar shivered. When he looked at her like that, it felt like bolts of electricity were running through her. How had she fallen in love so deeply, so quickly?

Gabe lowered his head and pressed a soft kiss to her mouth. "I can never resist that look."

"What look?"

"The one that says 'Kiss me.' "

She couldn't keep the smile from her face. This time a real one. "I'll have to keep that look on my face all the time then."

"Look at that one!" a voice shouted.

They turned to see another whale soaring through the water. Gabe wrapped his arms around her and Skylar looked out into the sea. It was a spectacular sight, but she couldn't keep her mind on anything other than what she had to do. She had to tell him the truth.

Almost two weeks had passed and she still hadn't told him that one small secret. She couldn't keep it from him any longer. When she'd first made the decision not to tell, it had been the lure of being treated no differently from anyone else. Falling in love with him had never been in her plan.

Gabe was everything she could want in a man. Kind. Considerate. Sweet. He treated her with the utmost respect. Listened when she talked, as if what she said was important. She had never been treated like what she thought really mattered. Oh, she knew her family loved her, but other people had never acted as if she had a brain in her head. She was pretty. She had money. She was photogenic. That's all they saw, all she was to most of the people in the world. Gabe saw beneath the surface. He knew who she was. He just didn't know *who* she was.

And Gabe made her see herself differently, too. He was twenty-three years old and had done wonderful, exciting, useful things with his life. Skylar couldn't think of anything useful she had accomplished. Gabe made her realize she had been drifting, allowing others to control her destiny. She'd never really thought about her place in the world till she met him.

He had changed, too. Every day they were together, he grew less grim. His thin body was filling out and he no longer looked malnourished. Occasionally she would see that dark sadness reemerge, but she was usually able to bring him out of it quickly with a kiss or a joke.

How would he react when she confessed? Would it make a difference to him? She would still be the same person. So what if she had a little more money than the average person? Did a few extra bucks mean that much? Okay, a few million extra bucks. But it was still just money.

Gabe knew her family was wealthy. She hadn't been able to hide that. Not many college-aged girls could afford a vacation on a remote luxury resort in the South Pacific. When she'd told him that her father owned some companies, he'd asked a few questions, but hadn't seemed that interested or impressed. Money didn't seem to mean anything to him.

Gabe bit her earlobe gently and whispered, "You ready to go back?"

Skylar shivered. That growly voice, those deep blue eyes, delicious, soul-deep kisses. They just did it for her every time. Pulling away from his arms, she turned to gaze up at him. Unable to keep one other secret from him any longer, she said, "I love you."

An amazing transformation took place. The last of those shadows lifted and his mouth curved into the most beautiful smile she'd ever seen. "I love you, too."

Determined to ignore the blaze of the searing sun, Gabe squinted his eyes against the brightness as he lobbed the ball toward Skye, his mind on something other than playing tennis.

She yelled, "Out!" and ran toward him, a little frown scrunched on her pretty face. "Are you sure you want to play?"

Dropping his racket below his waist, Gabe nodded. Speaking at a time like this was impossible. They'd done everything he could think to stay out of his bungalow. Tennis had never been his favorite game, but if it achieved his goal, he'd play all day.

Skye had no idea what he was going through. And that innocence was the very reason he was standing in almost-one-hundred-degree heat playing a game he not only sucked at, but also disliked. Doing what he really wanted to do was out of the question.

"Are you okay?"

"Fine. Just kind of hot." And he meant that sincerely.

"Want to go for a swim?"

Skye in a swimsuit was a torturous vision beyond his imaginings, but maybe if he swam two or three miles, he'd be able to think of something other than how much he wanted to remove her suit and make love to her until they dropped in satiated exhaustion.

Aware that she was looking even more concerned since he hadn't answered her question, Gabe did the only thing he could do. He swallowed hard and said, "Sure, a swim sounds good."

She took his racket from him. "I'll drop these off on the way to my bungalow and meet you back here in fifteen minutes. How does that sound?"

Gabe managed a grimaced smile and watched as she ran off the tennis court. She was driving him crazy and he could do nothing about it. Skye was as innocent as he'd first thought . . . a virgin. The last thing he wanted to do was make her do something she wasn't ready for.

Shoving his fingers through his hair, he stared out into the vivid blue water, the color reminding him of Skye's eyes when she wanted him to kiss her.

He'd never been in love before. Hadn't even known this type of love existed. He'd had a couple of girlfriends in high school he'd really liked but hadn't loved. And the girl in Africa who had betrayed so many . . . he'd had many feelings for her, but they hadn't been love. Now that he'd met Skye, he was certain of that.

His dad had once told him that when that special someone comes along, you just know it deep in your gut. He'd been right.

Skye was special in every way possible. The purity he'd seen in her eyes when they first met had been confirmed the first time he kissed her. She'd been sweet and eager, but also inexperienced. Her eagerness to learn and Gabe's willingness to teach had led to some of the steamiest make-out sessions he'd ever experienced, but he couldn't take it further. Skye wasn't ready, and until she was, neither was he.

That this beautiful woman, who could probably get any guy in existence, loved him humbled and amazed Gabe. And because of that love, he knew she wouldn't stop him if he asked for more than just hot kisses. He couldn't do that to her. When they made love, it would be her choice . . . not because she felt pressured but because it was something she was sure she wanted. Until that happened, he would continue his daily regimen of cold showers and extreme exhaustion.

"Gabe, are you coming?"

He jerked around to see Skye waiting for him outside the gate. Hell, he'd been standing here under the hot blaze of the sun without any concept of time.

Taking a breath, he ran toward her and held out his hand. "I'll swim in these shorts."

Her sweet smile assured Gabe she knew nothing of his struggles to keep his hands to himself. When Skye was ready, she would let him know. He just hoped to hell he could still walk.

They were halfway down the sidewalk, headed to the beach, when the first clap of thunder rumbled.

Skye shot him a disappointed glance. "Looks like that swim will have to wait."

Pressing a kiss to her palm, Gabe spoke his mind before he considered the words. "Wonder what we can do instead?"

Guilt hit him at the flash of apprehension in Skye's expression. Dammit, and after he'd told himself it had to be her decision. If those words didn't sound like pressure, he didn't know what did.

He was about to suggest they find shelter somewhere and play cards, when Skye surprised him by pulling her hand from his. Shooting him a smile he felt to his soul, she shouted, "Race you home!" and started running.

Loving her spontaneity and sheer exuberance, he erupted in laughter as he ran behind her. With the enticing sight of her beautiful bottom and gorgeous legs, Gabe was content to let her stay several feet ahead of him.

Another loud clap of thunder boomed, warning them a downpour was imminent. In the next instant, as if a dam burst open, rain gushed down, pummeling hard.

Increasing his speed, Gabe caught up with Skye, wrapped his arms around her, and picked her up without breaking his stride. With a soft little laugh, Skye put her arms around his neck and pressed her face against his chest.

At the bungalow, he took the steps two at a time and kicked open the door with his foot. He looked down at the drenched woman in his arms and swallowed hard. If there was anything sexier than Skye in a bathing suit, it was Skye in a wet bathing suit revealing everything that swimsuit had covered. Her beautiful breasts and hard nipples pressed against the wet material.

Dropping her feet to the floor, Gabe could barely catch his breath as he growled, "I'll get us some towels," and stomped into the bathroom. If she stayed one more moment in his arms, he would break every promise he'd made to himself.

He pulled off his rain-soaked shirt, grabbed a towel, and roughly dried his chest, all the while giving himself a stinging lecture on self-discipline and self-denial. In his mind, he repeated his reasons: Skye was too young. Too inexperienced. Wasn't ready. He loved her too much to pressure her. When she was ready, she would tell him.

His mind set on keeping his hands to himself, Gabe

grabbed another towel and headed back to the bedroom. He jerked to a stop at the door. Shock and sheer wonder punched him in the gut at the vision before him.

A nude Skye.

Apparently hearing him, she whirled around, her beautiful hair swirling and then landing around her shoulders like a dark, silken cloud.

Gripping the towel in his hands, Gabe stopped breathing, his eyes hungrily devouring every luscious inch of her creamy flesh. He had seen her in various stages of nudity while they were making out, but had never imagined how incredible she would be. Gently sloping shoulders, full plump breasts a goddess would envy, flat, taut stomach, lovely hips curved into the shapeliest bottom imaginable, long legs, lightly tanned and toned to perfection.

Gabe's eyes inventoried every beautiful feature and then went back to her face. His heart almost cracked. While he'd been staring, she'd been standing in nervous uncertainty. How could anyone who looked like Skye be unsure about her body? She was perfect in every way. That vulnerable, innocent expression grounded him. Whether he understood her need for reassurance or not, her expression told him she did need it. Forcing his stiff legs to move, he walked slowly toward her, unable to keep his eyes from roaming down her body. Heat zoomed, settled low, and throbbed unrepentantly.

Within inches of her, under the roaring of lust in his head, he heard himself say, "You're even more beautiful than I imagined you would be."

Uncertainty disappeared and she gave him a look of such relief and happiness, it was all he could do not to grab her and devour every inch of her sweet body.

Reaching out, Gabe touched a jutting nipple with his finger, somewhat surprised his hand wasn't shaking. He felt as though small earthquakes were erupting inside him. This woman was the loveliest, most wondrous creature in the universe.

At his touch on her nipple, Skye moaned and closed her eyes.

"Your nipples want my mouth on them, don't they?"

Her eyes flew open, but Gabe's gaze stayed on her nipples, fascinated to see them harden even more. It was almost as if just by staring at them, he made her even more aroused.

"Please, Gabe."

"What, Skye baby?"

"Put your mouth on me."

Throbbing with a need so great he could barely speak, Gabe managed to breathe out "With pleasure" as he lowered his head and put his tongue on her nipple. Coherent thought vanished; the sweet, hard bud against his tongue tasted more delicious than the sweetest of candies.

His hands had a will of their own as one held her closer and the other caressed the silken flesh of her stomach. When he reached the soft, springy curls at her mound, he stopped and whispered, "Open your legs for me, Skye."

Gabe watched her face for any kind of hesitation or fear. He saw none as Skye spread her legs so he could move his hand between them. Fingers touching her softly, he opened the soft folds at her sex and gently pressed a finger against her hard bud. When he felt the hot, sweet moisture of her arousal, Gabe whispered, "You're soft and so wet down there. So hot and sweet."

Her eyes fluttering closed, she shuddered and opened her legs more. Gabe pressed deeper and almost lost it when she moved sensuously against him, sweetly riding his finger. A burning haze of lust swamped him; Gabe fought the almost overwhelming need to lay her on the floor and push inside her immediately.

She wanted him, he knew she did, but he had to make

sure. Her first time should be something special. Gabe wanted this experience to be something she would look back on with pleasure, not regret.

"Are you sure, Skye?"

"I've never been more sure of anything in my entire life."

"There's no rush, no hurry. There's never a time you tell me to stop and I won't. Okay?"

"I love you so much, Gabe."

Control on the edge of shattering, Gabe said, "Let's get on the bed."

Locking his eyes with hers, he pushed her backward into the bedroom and stopped her at the edge of the bed. Skye sat on the edge; Gabe went to his knees before her.

Never had he seen anything more beautiful or more precious than Skye. Love, acceptance, arousal, and surrender were all there in her eyes. Unable to hold back the words that had been hammering at him for days, Gabe whispered, "Marry me."

Her smile was unlike any she'd ever given him before, and her words, "Yes, Gabe. Yes," told him exactly what he needed to hear. She was completely and totally his forever.

Sealing their commitment with a soft kiss to her mouth, he whispered a heartfelt vow against her lips, "I'm going to love you past forever."

No longer able to hold back, Gabe pulled her legs apart, spread the moist, pink folds of her sex, lowered his head and devoured her sweetness. Under the roaring need inside him, he heard a screaming gasp, felt her body tense beneath him, and then Skye, his sweet, beautiful Skye, exploded against his mouth.

Groaning at her taste, Gabe suckled and thrust gently with his tongue, bringing her softly and slowly back to earth. At the last soft throb, he raised his head to look at her. Lovely face flushed, her blue eyes glittered with a combination of satisfaction and hunger.

"You're delicious everywhere."

Unable to stop himself, Gabe went back for seconds. He thrusted deeper, harder this time as Skye's hands gripped his head, holding him in place, her screams of pleasure urging him on.

Aroused to the point of explosion, Gabe surged to his feet and ripped off his clothes. About to grab a condom, he had a brief moment of shyness as he looked down at his body. He'd gained weight but was still skinny. Skye's soft, beautiful body and his were so opposite they almost didn't belong in the same species. He dared a glance at her face to see if she agreed. His heart hitched at her expression. Desire and heat . . . unbelievable acceptance. A multitude of emotions scrambled inside him . . . he felt humbled and invincible, powerful and awed. He was the most fortunate man in the universe. Skye loved him, was about to make love with him and was going to marry him. No man had ever been so blessed.

He came to his senses when he heard a gasp. Following her wide gaze, his eyes went to his erection. Hard and throbbing, it stood out like a sturdy tree limb and probably scared the hell out of her.

"Remember, Skye. If you get scared at any time, just tell me to stop."

The small sexy smile that lifted her mouth almost caused immediate eruption. But when she moved to the middle of the bed and held out her hand in obvious invitation, Gabe went into action.

His entire body shook as he slid a condom on, groaning at how sensitive he was to just that thin layer. What would it be like when he got inside Skye's heat? He crawled onto the bed and covered her, pressing his mouth against hers until she opened up, allowing his tongue to plunge deep. With a soft gasp, Skye's tongue met and tangled with his, sucking at him, pulling him deeper and deeper into a realm Gabe had never known.

Pulling away from her sweet mouth, he watched for any sign of fear or pain as he pushed inside. Tight, hot heat clasped and sucked at him as he slid deeper. Gabe gritted his teeth, his body stiff and tense as he fought the need to bury himself to the hilt. Though she flinched and her breath hitched slightly, he saw no hesitation, no fear . . . only love and acceptance.

His body shouting at him to let go and take her hard and fast, Gabe forced words from his grimacing mouth, hoping he didn't scare her again. "Let's stay still, just for a moment, so you can get used to it."

Her heart in her eyes, Skye nodded and held him close.

Filled with as much love as lust for the precious gift in his arms, Gabe felt her tension ease. Willing himself self-control and patience, Gabe moved inside her slightly and heard a small, soft sound. He looked into Skye's face and saw everything he wanted and so much more. *Paradise.* Gabe pulled back and then thrust hard . . . deep. With a gasping moan, Skye wrapped her legs tighter around him.

Bracing himself on his elbows, Gabe watched her face as he settled into a rhythm of shallow thrusts, retreat, and then deep, hard plunges. No fear, no hesitation . . . only hot desire and a bright shining love. Covering her mouth with his again, Gabe surrendered himself completely to Skye's beauty. Perhaps this was why he'd survived, to love and treasure Skye for all eternity.

Eyes closed in ecstasy, Gabe finally found peace.

Five days later
New York City

"Daddy, please don't be mad. I'll bring him here to meet you. I know you'll love him just as much as I do."

Jeremiah James shook his head as if he couldn't believe what he was hearing. Perhaps blurting out that she had gotten married wasn't the best way to break the news to her overprotective father. Would she ever learn to control her tongue?

"I just can't believe you would do something like this without telling me first."

"We didn't plan it, but it was exactly the kind of wedding I wanted. If we'd gotten married here, it would have been a media circus."

"Why isn't he here with you now?"

Hoping to disguise her nervousness, Skylar dropped down onto the sofa and held her hands clenched in her lap. He had to accept Gabe into the family. He just had to.

"I wanted to tell you first before you met him."

"Did he not have enough guts to face me?"

She was on her feet in an instant, hands on her hips. "He's one of the most courageous people I've ever known. He just—"

"He just what?"

"The truth is, he doesn't know about me." She bit her lip. "I mean the famous part and stuff."

He snorted. "Believe me, Skylar, the man knows who you are. Why do you think he married you without your family around?"

"I wanted it like that. Not him. He wanted to wait. And you're wrong. He doesn't know who I am. At least not the part the world sees."

He was furious and not bothering to hide it, his face

almost purple with fury. Skylar tried hard not to put her father in a temper. Not that he would be abusive, she just never liked to see him angry or upset. But now it couldn't be helped. She was a married woman and he was just going to have to deal with it.

"I wanted to tell you, let you get used to the idea. Then you can come to the island in a few days. Or we'll come here."

The tic in his jaw told her he was working to control his anger. "Tell me about him."

She blew out a breath, knowing the next few minutes were crucial. If she got her father on board, everyone else would follow suit. The entire world would accept Gabe as her husband. But she had to convince Jeremiah James first. She had to help him understand what an amazing man her new husband was.

As she described Gabe, told about his family dying, how he'd worked in Africa to build homes for a small village and how he'd been held captive, she could see something shift in his eyes. Her heart thudded in an optimistic beat. Yes, she was getting through to him.

"You should have seen him, Dad. . . . When I first met him, he was almost malnourished. And so very sad. He's been through so much but he's almost completely recovered now. Just the occasional nightmare. And he has a thing about enclosed spaces. Which is understandable after what he's been through." She held out her hands as she strove to describe the man she'd come to admire so much. "He's done so much with his life. And he's got such a good heart. I know you're going to love him."

"He sounds like a fine man."

Okay, so the words were a bit stiff and insincere and his eyes were still burning with anger, but it was a start.

"He's the finest, Daddy. Just you wait and see."

"What does he do?"

"What do you mean?"

"Does he have a career?"

"Well, he's been recovering from his ordeal in Africa, so he's not really had a chance to make any plans. He's talked about going back to school and getting his degree."

"He doesn't even have a degree?"

Skylar bit her lip to keep from snapping out her anger at his obvious condescension. It would do no good to shout that what Gabe had done was more important than having a piece of paper. Yes, college was important, but what he had accomplished was so much more. If she expected her father to be reasonable, then she had to behave reasonably as well.

"He's only twenty-three, Dad. He's got lots of time."

"Maybe he'd like something with one of my companies."

Though she couldn't see Gabe wearing a suit every day and working in an office, now was not the time to mention that. The fact that her father had even had that thought was encouraging, though.

"You can talk to him about it when you meet him," she said.

"When will that be?"

Skylar glanced at her watch. "I'm flying back there in a couple of hours." She couldn't keep the smile from her face. "We kind of wanted to continue our honeymoon for a few more days. Then, if you want, I'll bring him here. I promise."

His brows met as he frowned. "You're leaving now? You just got here."

"I promised him I'd be back as soon as I could. We'll be back in a few days. A week, tops."

Her father stood. "Then I guess you'd better be on your way."

Knowing she'd disappointed him, Skylar ran into his arms the way she used to do when she was a little girl. "I'm sorry, Dad. I know you're angry with me, but I promise, I swear, you'll love him."

Holding her close, he whispered in her ear, "I'm sure I will, sweetie. Now, go on before you miss your flight."

Giving him one last hug and a kiss on the cheek, Skylar ran out the door. She'd asked the taxi to wait for her. Though she could have asked her father's chauffeur to take her to the airport, she wanted to start living like a regular person. Chauffeurs were for rich people. She and Gabe would have to live on a budget until they both decided what they were going to do.

Modeling and endorsements had produced a nice income over the last couple of years, but it wasn't something she wanted to do for much longer. After meeting Gabe . . . seeing what he had accomplished, she realized how fruitless her life had been. She and Gabe could do wonderful things together. Working together, they could make a real difference in the world.

She ignored the soft little voice that reminded her that most people couldn't ask a taxi to wait for forty-five minutes. The fare would be enormous. But this was a special occasion. Sometimes you had to splurge.

The cellphone in her purse jingled. The sound jarred her ears. This was the first time she'd even had the phone on since she'd left over two weeks ago. She pulled it out and checked the readout. *Oh no.*

Holding it to her ear, Skylar tried to sound happy. "Hello, Mother."

"It's about time you answered your phone. I've been calling you for days."

"You knew I was on vacation."

"But what if I needed to tell you something important?"

"Do you?"

"Well, no, but I could have."

Rolling her eyes, she asked, "What did you need?"

"I want to see you. Your father says you're back, but only for a few hours."

"You already talked to Daddy?"

"Yes. He said you had news. I assumed you were coming here to tell me, but he says that's not the case."

Making her mother angry at a time like this was not a good idea. Though her parents had been divorced for years, if there was one area where Carole James still had influence over her former husband, it was Skylar. If her mother thought Gabe was good for Skylar, chances are her father would, too. Maybe she should have gone to her mother first. Overoptimism was another flaw of hers. She'd been silly to think her dad would just jump on board about her marriage to man he'd never met.

Biting her lip, Skylar glanced at her watch again. She would miss her plane if she didn't get to the airport within the next hour. There was another one tomorrow night, but she'd wanted to get back to Gabe as soon as she could. However, getting her mother's approval would make everything else so much easier.

"How about I delay my plans for another day and drop by to see you?"

"That sounds wonderful, darling. I'll have Henri make something special for dinner."

"I'll see you in about an hour then." Skylar closed the phone, then leaned forward. "Can you take me into midtown Manhattan? Twelve Sutton Place South."

"Yes, ma'am."

Blowing out a long sigh, she slumped back into the seat. She desperately wanted to call Gabe. She'd told him she would be back as soon as she could, but she hadn't given him a definite time frame. Just told him probably no more than two or three days. She'd said she needed to take care of some family business. He hadn't asked her any questions but she'd seen them in his eyes.

Suddenly exhausted, Skylar closed her eyes. First she had to make her mother promise to talk with her dad to accept Gabe into the family. Then she had to go back and do the hardest job of all. Apologize to Gabe for not telling him the truth. She only hoped he loved her enough to forgive her.

For the tenth time in as many minutes, Gabe checked his watch and then looked at the clock on the bedside table. She'd said she might not make it back today. He should have gone with her, but she'd looked so nervous and upset when he'd made the suggestion he'd backed down.

Unable to stay in the small room and just pace, Gabe went out onto the balcony. It was still small, but at least it was outdoors and he'd didn't feel as though he were smothering. He wished he could take a run on the beach, but he wanted to be here in case Skye surprised him and came in tonight.

She was telling her family about him. He knew she was. She hadn't said, but she'd made mention more than once that her father was ultra-protective of her. Since Gabe felt very protective of her himself, he couldn't fault the man for wanting to take care of her. Skye was special.

It was still hard to believe they were actually married. If he'd been told three weeks ago that he'd leave the island a married man, he would've laughed. No way in hell did he figure he'd ever marry. But now he couldn't wait to start married life. They had so many things to talk about. Lots of important decisions to make. For the first time in years, he was actually glad to be alive.

Skye had not only made him fall in love with her, she'd given him his life back.

How he had found the one perfect woman for him, he didn't even bother to question. Maybe after all his bad luck, fate had finally given him a break. Only, he didn't feel like this was a break. This was beyond anything he'd ever fantasized about. Skye was everything he could have wanted and so much more.

A knock at the door had him back in the room in a second. She was back!

Gabe swung the door open, his smile of welcome freezing on his face as he looked at the hard-faced middle-aged man glaring at him.

"Can I help you, sir?"

"Yes. You can damn well leave my daughter alone."

Skylar perched on the edge of the worn-out taxi seat. She just couldn't seem to relax or stop worrying. The ride from the airport back to the resort had never seemed so long before. An odd anxiousness had built up inside her, and the only thing that could calm her was being back in Gabe's arms again.

Getting back to him had been a nightmare. First the flight had been delayed for bad weather. Then customs had been short-staffed, slowing everyone down. She had considered using her name to get special treatment but couldn't make herself do it. It was time she started behaving as if she meant to go forward.

But the wait was killing her. For some reason, the minute she'd stepped out of the cab in front of her mother's apartment building, she had felt the need to turn around and get back to Gabe as soon as possible. She just had the oddest thought that he needed her.

She had forced herself to keep going. Getting her mother on board was crucial. Unfortunately, it hadn't worked out the way she'd hoped. Not only was her mother appalled that she'd married without telling the family, she couldn't believe Skylar had married a man with no money or social standing. She'd acted as if her daughter had committed a major crime.

After an explosive exchange of words, Skylar had ended up leaving the apartment in tears and going to the airport, hoping to get a connecting flight somewhere that would get her back to the island sooner. She had failed. Instead, she'd spent a miserable night at an airport hotel.

She could have called Gabe. Stupid not to, but if she did, she would cry. And then he would be upset, too. Though she wasn't usually an overemotional person, being in love had brought all sorts of tumultuous feelings to the surface. Breaking down over the phone with her new husband wasn't something she wanted to put either of them through.

Besides, she still had her number one major worry to deal with. What would Gabe say when she told him who she was? It couldn't change his feelings for her. He might be disappointed in her for not being entirely truthful, but Gabe loved the real Skylar James. Not the fake one she showed the world.

"Here we are, ma'am."

Grateful that the interminable trip was finally over, Skylar grabbed the door handle before the driver had a chance to open it. She bounded out of the car, handed the man more than enough to cover the fare, along with a giant tip, and then, moving as fast as her feet would carry her, headed to Gabe's bungalow.

Skylar ran up onto the small porch, burst through the door, and faced an empty room. She blew out a half sigh, half sob. After all that worry, he wasn't even here. He must have gone for a swim or run.

She turned to go outside to look for him when a movement out of the corner of her eye caught her attention. A small piece of paper on the dresser fluttered from the breeze of the open door. An odd sort of dread filled her, turning her legs to lead, as she made her way slowly to pick up the note.

Her hands shaking, she read the scribbled words.

By the time you read this, I'll be gone.

Clutching the note in her hand, Skylar whirled around and ran for the door. Her heart, her very being, crying in denial, she stopped on the porch and screamed, "Gabe!"

three

New York City
Present day

By the time you read this, I'll be gone.

Skylar James sank down onto the edge of her chair. The last time she'd read these words, her world had fallen apart. An ominous darkness . . . that feeling of dread she knew all too well . . . swept over her. Something dire was about to happen.

Most people would laugh if they knew one of the wealthiest and most photographed women in the world relied on such mumbo jumbo to make decisions for her. She didn't care. These feelings had never failed her. She'd ignored them once and had paid an enormous price.

Her eyes went back to the email.

I know you don't think this is the right thing for me, but this might be my only chance for something this wonderful. Don't be mad. I'll call you as soon as I have some news.

Love,

Kendra—soon to be supermodel—Carson

Skylar told herself to ignore the feeling of impending doom. Kendra was twenty-one years old. Not a child. She could make decisions for herself, and any mistakes she made, she would learn from them and grow stronger, just like every adult. So why did she feel that this was something she absolutely had to stop? Skylar pressed her fingers to her suddenly burning eyes. She knew the answer to that. Had lived with the knowledge for years.

Quite often mistakes could cause massive regret and major heartbreak. But in some cases, they could take everything you had.

Kendra Carson squinted down at the wrinkled piece of paper where she'd scribbled the address. Why hadn't she at least brought her glasses with her? Vanity, of course. When you were auditioning to be a fashion model, you didn't want to look like the town librarian. She'd worn glasses for so long, she often forgot that she had them on. To ensure she wouldn't wear them at her audition, she'd simply left them on her bedroom dresser.

But this address had to be correct. She'd shown the cabdriver the piece of paper.

Perspiration under her arms trickled down her sides, and she wriggled at the clammy, uncomfortable feeling. When she got nervous, she perspired . . . a lot. Hopefully, the dampness wouldn't show.

She caught a glance at herself in the window. Even through the dusty and smudged glass, the reflection pleased her. Her shoulder-length, honey-blond hair had just the right amount of golden highlights. The new, shorter style accentuated her cheekbones and flattered her heart-shaped face. The simple navy dress, one Skylar had helped her pick out last year, darkened her hazel eyes, giving them a hint of mystery. The fitted waist and tiny pleats at her hips emphasized her long legs and slender body. Yes, she looked fashionable and very pretty . . . and not a sign of sweat.

Skylar would be upset with her for not telling her until after the fact that she was going on the interview. She insisted that Kendra wouldn't enjoy being a model, that it wasn't as glamorous as it appeared. Easy for a woman like Skylar to say—beautiful, confident, and famous before she was even born. Kendra had to work every day for that beauty, had zero confidence most days, and craved to see her name and face on billboards and magazines all over the world. And now it could very well happen.

Skylar wasn't even really the right size to be a model, yet she'd been on the cover of almost every magazine in existence numerous times. Though slender, Skylar wasn't pencil-thin like most models and was only about five-seven—four inches shorter than Kendra's own five feet eleven inches. But with Skylar's beauty, not to mention the James money and influence, little things like that got ignored.

Okay, so she wasn't being exactly fair to her friend. Not only was Skylar gorgeous, she was also incredibly photogenic. And once she realized how badly Kendra wanted to be a model, she offered to make introductions for her. Skylar had even paid for her first photo shoot. But this opportunity seemed too good to pass up.

Even though someone had directed Kendra to the ad, getting the job would be up to her. If they hired her, it would be because Kendra had earned it herself. No one would have given it to her . . . she would be able to say she'd done it all on her own.

Her mother would be impressed. How often had she told Kendra she'd never amount to anything? And Calvin, with his snide innuendos that she didn't have the kind of looks it takes to make it big, would have to admit he was wrong. Her snotty roommates, who giggled every time she mentioned modeling . . . they'd eat their words, too.

She'd show them all.

Gathering her courage, Kendra stiffened her spine, prepared to fake the confidence until she actually owned it.

Her head tilted with just the right amount of aloof arrogance she'd seen Skylar adopt on occasion, she opened the door and walked through.

The ad had given little information. Just the height, age, and weight requirements. But it had emphasized that it was a start-up agency. That must be why they had to meet in an older building, to save money. She kind of liked that they would grow famous together.

"Well, hello there."

Kendra whipped around at the sound of a friendly male voice. A young, very attractive man stood a few feet from her. She flashed the confident, sexy smile she'd been practicing. "Hello."

"Are you here for the modeling job?"

Her heart picked up a beat in anticipation. "Why, yes I am."

The look in his eyes as his gaze slid down her body told her he was impressed. The smile he gave her was equally encouraging, but his words were what she longed to hear. "I can already see you on the runway in Milan."

"Really?"

"Absolutely. Come this way. The interviews are about to get started."

Kendra followed him to a door. He stood aside and allowed her to enter, giving her a look that thrilled her down to the stiletto heels pinching her feet. This was it. She was about to become famous!

"Over here, Skylar!"

"Look here, Skylar!"

"Smile, Skylar!"

Lights exploded as cameras flashed. Photographers shouted and shoved at one another to get the shot of the day.

"Where are you going?"

"Are you meeting Benjamin?

"When are you two getting married?"

"Did you know he was seen with Lauren Miles at Benito's the other night? How do you feel about that?"

"Any truth to the rumor that you and Benjamin are just friends and are faking a real relationship to throw people off?"

As usual, the instant she walked out of her apartment building, she was swamped with reporters shouting inane questions and photographers clicking their cameras, hoping for that one brilliant shot.

Maintaining her world-famous and oh-so-practiced smile, Skylar made her way down the sidewalk toward the waiting limousine. She ignored the clicking cameras in her face and pretended that the questions being thrown at her didn't irritate the hell out of her. As annoying as the incessant questions about Benjamin were, at least they focused on something she didn't care about. Which was the biggest reason she'd entered into this strange agreement with Benjamin in the first place. Their mutual using of each other satisfied the gossips and tabloids and gave them the opportunity to actually have a life.

One day, though, she'd love to be able to answer their stupid questions with the truth. She fantasized what their expressions would be if she said, "Yes! It's all fake . . . every bit of it. We're using each other and have nothing in common other than a shared antipathy for nosey reporters. Now, go find some real news for a change."

But she wouldn't do that. By projecting one image, she could protect another one. If they knew the real Skylar, she'd have no life. So as ridiculous and irritating as it was sometimes, she allowed them in to see this façade of glamour and uselessness so she could enjoy the other part. The part known only to her and a few trusted friends.

"Did you see the photos of Benjamin with Lauren Miles? Are you jealous?"

"How do you feel about being two-timed?"

"Are you two breaking up?"

These questions, meant to entice her to say something inappropriate and therefore newsworthy, were actually her favorite kind. She'd much rather have her relationship with Ben questioned than her feelings on politics, world hunger, or the alarming rate of teen suicides. Those issues meant too much to her to throw out glib replies.

Skylar smiled, waved . . . blew a kiss at one photographer who'd done his best to follow her on her last secret visit. She'd enjoyed losing him on the subway.

Finally able to get into the limo, she sank into the comfortable leather seats with a long sigh. "They're ravenous today. Must be a slow news day."

Adjusting his mirror, Malcolm pulled out onto the street, honking at one persistent photographer who refused to get out of the way. "It's summertime. Buzzards always come out in hot weather."

Skylar chuckled. Malcolm, her chauffeur/bodyguard, had been with her for years and knew almost every secret. Not for the first time, Skylar felt a deep appreciation that she'd been able to secure this man on her own and could trust him, unlike all the others her father had hired before him.

"That's true. And being summertime, there are less people here to photograph."

Skylar smiled at Malcolm's snort. They both knew that no matter who was in town, Skylar James would get press attention. His eyes on the road and the taxis behind them filled with photographers, he asked, "So where to?"

She fingered the gold bands she kept on a chain she

wore around her neck. They were always hidden beneath her clothes, because any question about them was something she'd never be prepared to answer. Still, the bands always gave her comfort, especially when worry hammered at her, as it did now.

Two days had passed since she'd received that email from Kendra and still no word from her. As soon as Skylar read the message, she'd called her and gotten no answer. She'd left messages with Kendra's roommates and on her cellphone. Yesterday she'd gone to her apartment. Her roommates hadn't heard from her and as usual didn't seem to care. Her mother claimed to have not heard from her in over a month, which Skylar believed.

Kendra was no doubt at her sometimes-boyfriend-and-all-the-time-creep's apartment. As much as Skylar hated it, she was going to have to go there.

"Let's head to Calvin's apartment in the Village. Kendra hasn't answered any of my calls."

There was little Malcolm didn't know. "When is Kendra going to give up on that slug?"

Skylar chuckled at the apt description of Calvin. "I'm not sure who uses the other more. Unfortunately for both of them, it doesn't look like it's going to end anytime soon."

"Any preferences on what direction we should take?"

She was famous for mapping out her strategies for getting around and avoiding as much press as possible. "I'll leave it up to you. Just try to lose as many of them as you can."

"Yes, ma'am."

Trusting Malcolm to get her there safely with the minimum of exposure, Skylar settled back into her seat and tried to figure out a way to help Kendra without her young friend resenting her interference. She'd known

Kendra for over three years. Had met her just after Kendra's mother had thrown her daughter out of the house for the last time.

The young, impressionable Kendra had been at first belligerent, embarrassed by her circumstances, distrusting of everyone and quite hostile, especially to Skylar. Thankfully, that had changed and she and Kendra had developed a friendship.

Though Kendra had hinted occasionally that she'd love to be a model, Skylar had encouraged her to return to high school and graduate first. And she had. Kendra ended up doing very well her last year of school, making excellent grades, giving her an opportunity to be accepted into some well-respected universities. Unfortunately, getting her degree didn't interest her as much as becoming a model and all the fame and money that went with it.

Money. Skylar huffed out a tired sigh. It could solve so many problems and could create just as many more. Those who had it wanted more. People who didn't have it fantasized about what their life would be like if they had all the money they needed. Problem was, no one ever seemed satisfied. What exactly was the right amount?

Some might roll their eyes and say it was easy to dislike money when you had plenty of it. Skylar wasn't a hypocrite. She enjoyed what money could buy, but she also knew the most precious things were free and freely given.

Giving herself a mental shake, she stared sightlessly out the window. Why was she so melancholy today? It had been years since she'd allowed herself to think about those perfect weeks. Eighteen days of bliss. Of lying in her lover's arms, listening to his deep, even breaths, and cherishing what they'd discovered . . . a true and perfect love.

"Are you okay?"

Skylar jerked around. "Yes, why?"

Malcolm's compassionate eyes searched her face, but all he said was "We're here, ma'am."

It wasn't until a teardrop fell on her hand that she realized she'd been crying. How very odd. The last time she'd cried over Gabe . . . She shook her head. She couldn't even remember the last time. Those days were gone and could never be reclaimed. Now all she could do was keep the promise she'd made to herself. Whenever, wherever, whoever, she would never ignore a cry for help. She'd failed Gabe and they had both paid the price. That would never happen again.

Skylar hurriedly dried her eyes and then flashed a grateful smile at Malcolm as he opened the car door for her. "I'll be back in a few minutes."

"Sure you don't want me to go with you?"

"No. This is one twerp I can handle all by myself."

Out of habit, she ignored the elevator and headed for the stairs. One of the few things that hadn't changed from all those years ago. She'd never questioned Gabe's need to take the stairs. Had thought she knew the reasons . . . thought she knew everything she needed to know about him. If only she had questioned him more, would that have changed the outcome? She'd stupidly thought she was the only one keeping secrets.

She gave herself another mental shake. Did any of that matter now? What had happened had happened.

As she walked up the five flights to Calvin's apartment, she wondered about Kendra's silence. Perhaps they'd turned her down for the job and she'd been too embarrassed to tell Skylar. Hopefully, that was the case as opposed to it being the shady organization Skylar feared it might be. There were way too many unscrupulous creeps out to take advantage of unsuspecting, impressionable young people. And when the dust settled, the creeps had moved on and the kids were left penniless.

Reaching Calvin's apartment door, she took a breath and then knocked. No answer. She waited a few seconds and then knocked again. "Kendra, are you here?"

"Who's there?" a young masculine voice asked.

"Calvin? It's Skylar. I'm here to see Kendra."

"Just a minute."

Several minutes later, just when she was beginning to think he'd forgotten about her, the door opened.

"Hey, baby, you here to see me?"

Calvin Henderson didn't even crack her revulsion meter. He wasn't worth it. "I'm here to see Kendra."

"Haven't seen the bitch in almost a week." He took a draw off the offensive-smelling cigarette in his hand. "Why don't you come on in and wait for her? I just got some damn good weed."

"No thanks. Have you talked with her in the last few days?"

"Yeah, a couple of days ago. Said she was going on some kind of interview and would come by afterward." He lifted a bony shoulder. "Guess she changed her mind."

"Have you tried calling her?"

"No." His smile revealed teeth that were already becoming tobacco stained. "Why don't you come in and we'll call her together? Maybe we can have ourselves a little party."

"Are you not worried about her?"

"I'm not her daddy. She's taken off plenty of times. I figure when she runs out of money, she'll come back."

Calvin Henderson was a kid who'd had it way too easy his entire life and didn't give a damn about anything other than partying and getting high. What did Kendra see in him? His lank, dark brown hair hung in his thin, pale face, and his body was almost emaciated, reminding her of an anemic vampire.

Sadly, Skylar knew what Calvin's biggest attraction for Kendra was—his money. Something Calvin never seemed to run out of. Kendra's mother had cut off her funds, hoping she'd grow up and get a job. Calvin's money kept Kendra coming back to him.

Her worry shot up when his words registered. Kendra's roommates hadn't seen her and now Calvin hadn't seen her. Making a decision, she pulled her cellphone from her purse. "I'm calling the police."

"Hell, don't bring those bastards here. I got shit they don't need to be seeing."

"Then perhaps you should get rid of it."

He grabbed her arm. "Now, listen, bitch."

She glanced down at his hand and back at his face. "If you want to keep that hand attached to your body, I suggest you remove it from my arm."

He snorted and tightened his grip.

Skylar swung her arm up, knocking his hand away. Then, grabbing his arm, she twisted it behind his back.

"Hey, that hurts!"

Turning her face away to avoid the stale, vile breath he huffed out, Skylar said, "Good. Now, let's get back to Kendra. Do you know where her interview was?"

"No, and I don't care."

Skylar jerked his arm tighter. "Do you care if I break your arm?"

He yelped again. "Okay, dammit. She said the interview was on Highland Avenue . . . some old building that used to be a button factory or something."

"That's more like it." Skylar released his arm and backed away. "I'm going to find her, and once I do, I'm going to suggest she move on to someone much better."

He sneered. "She can't get any better than me."

Rolling her eyes, she turned and headed to the elevators. Time was too precious to waste on the stairs. If Kendra had interviewed with these people and they were still there, she should be able to get information on what happened.

And even though she wanted to call the police, sadly it wouldn't ignite the concern it would for most people who might have gone missing. Kendra had run away so many times, even her mother had stopped reporting it.

If the people Kendra had interviewed with couldn't shed light on her whereabouts, then she would call the police and convince them that something was wrong. They hadn't seen the changes in her like Skylar had. If Kendra couldn't be found, there was reason to worry.

Twenty minutes later, Skylar stood in a deserted parking lot in front of the dilapidated building. Her dread increased to a nauseating pitch. No legitimate agency, modeling or otherwise, would have conducted interviews here.

She'd been worried that Kendra might get her feelings crushed or be taken advantage of financially. Now she only hoped that was what happened. There were other, more hideous, things that could happen to a young, naïve girl. Until now, she hadn't considered them.

"I don't like the looks of this place," Malcolm grumbled beside her.

"Neither do I." She looked down at the response to the text message she'd sent on her BlackBerry. "The listing company said the ad only ran for a week and wasn't renewed. They did verify that this was the address listed on the ad, though."

"Then let me go in and check it out."

Skylar glanced down at her four-inch heels and short, straight skirt. Not exactly the best outfit for clomping around in an old abandoned building. She shot a look at Malcolm's attire. Though his shirt and pants were nice, his shoes were sensible. Since time was of the most import, she nodded. He could check things out much quicker without her.

"I'll stay here. If you see anything suspicious at all, call me on my cell and I'll call the police."

His expression was more grim than she'd seen it in years, and that ominous feeling inside her grew larger. Placing her hand on his arm, she said, "Wait. Let me call the police first."

"And tell them what?"

"That a friend of mine has disappeared and I'm at the last place she was seen."

"And the minute you tell them who it is, they'll assume she's taken off again." He shot another grim look at the building. "Give me a minute. I'm just going to have a quick look around."

Already recognizing the stubborn set of his jaw, Skylar nodded and put her finger on the key, ready to call 911 in an instant. Malcolm wouldn't change his mind, but if they needed help, she'd do her best to make sure they had it as quickly as possible.

Malcolm Marshall didn't like the situation one bit. If he had a brain in his head, he'd tell his "far too compassionate for her own good" charge that Kendra Carson didn't deserve the concern Skylar was constantly giving her. The young woman had caused nothing but problems for her. Everything Skylar did, Kendra never appeared to appreciate and just seemed to expect more.

Pulling out his gun, he approached the front of the

building warily. His years of experience as a bodyguard and security specialist had taught him to listen with his gut. Something was definitely not right. Putting Skylar at risk wasn't something he took lightly. Not only was she his responsibility, he'd been in love with her from the moment he met her. Just like most men who took one look at her were. Not that he, or anyone else for that matter, would ever be able to do anything about it.

Skylar thought of him as her employee and had a tendency to try to take care of him instead of the other way around. Not exactly the best setup for a romantic relationship. Besides, there were other, bigger issues. One being that he, along with her parents and several of her father's closest advisors, were keeping extraordinary secrets from her. If she ever discovered the truth, there would be hell to pay for all of them. No less than they deserved.

Skylar's worried gaze burned a hole in his back as he pushed open the door and stepped into the building. He probably should have told her to stay in the car. But he didn't really expect any trouble or he would've waited for backup. Putting Skylar in danger was the last thing he wanted.

He stopped in the middle of the bare lobby. At one time, the building had housed some kind of fabric business. There were still scraps of dusty cloth and a few rusted pieces of machinery lying about. But based upon the broken windows and filth on the floor, it'd been years since anything legitimate had happened here.

That giant pit in his stomach just grew larger, thicker, darker. *Hell!*

Malcolm turned around and started running. He was at the front entrance of the building when he heard Skylar scream. Gun at the ready, he dashed out the door.

His heart went through his throat. A man was dragging Skylar to a car. Shouting “Stop!” Malcolm ran toward them.

Out of the corner of his eye, he saw a movement. Before he could react, a searing pain hit his chest. His arm. His head. And then there was nothing.

four

A hard hand bit into her shoulder and pulled her up. "Sit up so we can take this hood off. We know you're awake."

Her heart pounding, her body shuddered as much from shock as it did from fear. Skylar felt the tug on the hood over her head. Seconds ago, she'd woken to darkness and a throbbing headache. She'd kept as quiet as possible, hoping whoever had her would believe she was still unconscious and talk freely. Apparently she wasn't very good at pretending unconsciousness.

The hood disappeared and Skylar found herself looking up at two young men . . . about Kendra's age. One had long blond hair and wore glasses. The other was clean-cut and looked like he'd just gotten out of prep school. They both scared the hell out of her.

The long-haired one shot at glance at his companion. "Damn, Aaron. She's about the best-looking one we ever caught."

Instead of answering, Aaron grabbed a handful of her hair and jerked her face up to the light. "Hell, Joey . . . don't she look familiar to you?"

Joey took off his glasses and bent down to inspect her closer. Skylar pulled as far away from him as she could get. With her hands tied behind her back and the pain from the man tugging on her hair, she barely moved more than an inch or so.

"I don't know. I guess she kind of looks familiar. Who do you think she is?"

"She looks like that rich bitch that's always in the magazines and on television. My sister's always talking about wanting to look like her." He raised horrified eyes to Joey. "We're in deep shit."

"Hell, we didn't have a choice. Styx told us to clean up and get rid of any evidence. There's no way we could've known this bitch and her bodyguard would've been there."

Malcolm. Memory slammed into Skylar and she let out a whimper. He was dead. They'd shot him three times. . . . The last bullet had hit him between his eyes. *Dear God, Malcolm was dead.*

Fury overwhelmed fear. In one swift movement, Skylar shot up from the floor and butted Joey in the gut with her head. With her hands tied behind her, it was the best she could do.

Breath whooshed from Joey as he fell backward. Her legs wobbly and weak, she was unable to keep her balance and collapsed on top of him.

"She's a live one, isn't she?" Aaron chortled behind them.

"Get her off me!" Joey shouted.

Skylar rolled over, onto the floor. Sobs built up in her chest, but she couldn't release them. "You're going to pay for this. Both of you."

Aaron grabbed her by the shoulders and pulled her to her feet. "Don't do that again."

Still on the floor, Joey snarled, "I don't care who the bitch is, she's going to pay for that."

"We need to wait and see what Styx says."

Joey pulled himself up to stand. His pale face was mottled with red blotches, and his eyes gleamed behind his glasses. "Hold her for me."

"Back off, Joey. We can't sell or ransom a dead bitch."

"I'm not going to kill her. I'm just going to show her who's boss."

With a long-suffering sigh, Aaron wrapped his arms around her chest and held her tight. Using his arms as leverage, Skylar picked up her feet and kicked behind her. She'd lost her shoes at some point, but her bare heels made a nice, hard *thud* as they hit both of his shins.

Aaron shook her hard. "Stop it, bitch. Or I'll let him *really* hurt you. You earned this punishment. So stand still."

Twisting and jerking against the arms that held her, she shouted at the man coming toward her, "You lowlife sleaze, you lay one hand on me and I'll—"

Pain exploded in her left jaw as Joey backhanded her. Her legs crumbling beneath her, Skylar slumped.

A hand yanked her hair. She slammed against Aaron's shoulder again as he held her tighter. "Okay. One more and that's it, Joey. Better make it count."

"No," she whispered.

Her eyes swimming with tears, she saw Joey's grinning face waver before her and then pain exploded in her face again. Agony and darkness swirled as she slumped into the arms that held her. Despite the intense desire to just let go and lose herself in unconsciousness, Skylar took long, controlled breaths, fighting it. She would not let these bastards defeat her. Kendra might be somewhere around here. She needed to find out as much as she could.

"That'll teach her a lesson she won't soon forget."

Joey's smug comment brought her head up again. One eye already swelling and the other filled with tears, she could barely make out his shadowed image. Everything within her told her to give him the response he deserved, but she held on to that anger. If she said anything, he'd hit her again and she doubted she'd be able to stay conscious. Let him think he'd won. She'd soon show him what she was made of.

Aaron chuckled as he threw her in the corner. "Guess you learned who's boss."

Skylar raised her head and glared. She might not say anything to them, but damned if she'd cower in the corner. She heard a rip and watched as Aaron tore a piece of duct tape off a roll.

He dropped to his knees in front of her and pulled her to sit up. Pressing the tape to her mouth, he offered her some advice. "Better be careful. Joey's got a nasty temper. You say anything else and there won't be much left of you." He twisted around and grabbed the hood they'd dropped on the floor. "Let's cover that face up, too. You're not that good-looking anymore."

Her head once more covered, Skylar leaned against the wall and waited. She would stay still and listen. At some point, one of them would say something that would help her figure out how to find Kendra and get them both out of this mess alive.

The distant sound of a door opening and closing caught her attention. She tensed as heavy footsteps clomped closer.

"That's Styx. We'll let him decide what we need to do with her."

Joey snorted. "I already know what my vote will be. I vote we fuck her and kill her."

Ice went through her veins as she waited for Aaron's response.

"Hell, Joey. That don't get us any money. You can grab a fuck from one of the other girls."

Before Joey could answer, a door opened and a cold, emotionless voice said, "Who's in the corner?"

"We picked up some trouble when we went back to clean up. Shot a man and grabbed this bitch."

"You killed someone?" Styx's tone stayed flat; the emotionless way he talked about killing made Skylar shiver.

"We cleaned it up. Dumped him where nobody'll ever find him. Dropped his car off at a chop shop. That's one bastard no one will ever hear from again."

Skylar choked back a sob. *Oh, Malcolm, I'm so sorry.*

"What were they doing there?"

"Don't know. Didn't have time to ask questions. We figured they were there looking for the girl."

Her ears perked up; she held her breath. Were they talking about Kendra?

Footsteps drew closer to where she sat. All the muscles in her body froze.

"Is this one as good-looking as the others?"

"Better . . . or at least she used to be," Aaron said.

"Whaddya mean?"

"Joey got a little carried away."

"Hey," Joey's defensive voice broke in, "I couldn't let her get away with what she did. Bitch needed to learn a lesson."

"One day that temper's going to get you in real trouble, Joey," Styx said. "She too messed up to sell?"

"No, she'll heal." There was an audible swallow. "We got a bigger problem."

"What?"

"The bitch is famous."

"Whaddya mean, she's famous?"

"That James bitch that's always in the news."

"Skylar James?" For the first time, Styx's voice changed tone. He sounded both incredulous and intrigued.

"Yeah."

"Hell, we can't sell her like the others. There'll be cops

everywhere looking for her. She ain't like the other girls."

"Yeah, that's what we were thinking," Aaron said. "You got any ideas about what we can do with her?"

"I got an idea." Joey's slimy voice made no secret as to what he wanted to do.

"Maybe," Styx said. "Let me make a call."

"While you do that, we're going to play a little more."

Aaron's voice. Funny, she'd figured he was the least of her worries. Two shadowed figures approached her; Skylar readied herself. They thought she couldn't fight them, but she'd show them.

Instead of picking her up, she felt a sting in her neck. The tape over her mouth muffled her terrified scream. Drugs! She jerked away.

"Settle down, baby," Aaron said. "We're not killing you. Just want you a little more docile."

Using her tied hands behind her, she pushed herself to her feet and started to run. She didn't know where she was going . . . couldn't see anything in front of her, but she had to get away from them. No one tried to stop her. Laughter, wild, uninhibited, and evil, followed behind her. With the suddenness of a dropping hammer, lethargy swamped her and she felt herself falling. Someone caught her and held her upright.

Skylar swayed as her mind blurred and spun. She could not lose consciousness. She had to find Kendra.

"Let's play catch."

Her mind muddled with terror and whatever they'd given her, she no longer recognized their voices. Hands threw her from one man to the other. She hit, bounced, and then was pushed again. Sobs built inside her with no place to go. Her legs were weak, but every time she felt herself falling, she was caught and then thrown again.

Bile rushed up her esophagus and she gagged.

"Hell, she's puking."

Someone ripped off the hood and tore the tape from her mouth. Unable to control it, Skylar spewed vomit all over the man who held her. He cursed and let her go.

"Damn, she puked all over me."

As she swayed on her feet, a smile formed on her wet, swollen lips. *Joey.* She hoped the bastard smelled like sour vomit into eternity.

A vicious hand pushed her again, shoving her toward the corner. Unable to catch herself, she fell face-first onto the floor. Pain exploded in her forehead . . . her shoulder . . . dull and distant . . . almost as if it happened to someone else.

A door opened and closed again. "Shit. What's that smell?"

"She puked."

"Clean her up. We got a buyer and I ain't taking her like that."

"You ransomed her?"

"Hell no. The bitch is too hot for that. I called somebody who handles stuff like this. He's paying us a hundred thousand."

"Bet we'd get a million times more if we ransomed her ourselves."

"That ain't our job, Aaron. Shit like that takes time and will bring us attention we can't afford. The man pays us to get girls. Not kidnap them for ransom. He'll be pissed if he finds out about this. With his connections, he might even know the bitch."

An explosive sigh. "I guess you're right." Hands picked her up again. "Come here, baby. Let's get you cleaned up."

Skylar felt herself being lifted. She sat up and looked around her. Three men were looking at her. Though she had only one good eye and her brain could barely function, she stared hard and committed their faces to memory. These men would pay for what they had done. But she still needed to know about Kendra.

She waited until Aaron brought a clean wet cloth and wiped at her face. Though it stung, the cold dampness woke her a little. Swallowing past the vile taste in her mouth, she whispered, "What did you do with Kendra?"

Aaron stopped abruptly. "Huh?"

"Kendra. The girl you took a few days ago. What did you do with her?"

The cloth covered her face again. "Stop asking questions."

"Please, tell me—"

A dry towel replaced the wet cloth as he wiped the moisture from her face. Before she could ask anything else, he slapped a fresh piece of tape on her mouth. "I told you to stop asking questions. The bitch is spoken for. Might as well forget her. She's got a sweet setup . . . hell of a lot better than most of them get."

Unable to give up, she tried to form words beneath the tape. Only muffled sounds escaped.

Standing behind Aaron, Joey guffawed as he wiped vomit off his shirt. "I wish I could get a picture of that. It'd probably sell for a million on its own."

"No," Styx said. "We can't have any evidence that we were involved in this." He paused for a second and peered down at her. "She ready?"

"Yeah."

"Good. Stand back. I always wanted to hit a rich bitch."

Aaron backed away and Styx stood in front of her. Skylar saw the ham-sized fist headed toward her face and jerked her head to dodge it. Pain slammed through her and darkness descended once more.

five

The Florida Keys

Gabe Maddox jerked awake. Breath wheezed, coming in desperate pants; his heart pounded with a too familiar panic and dread. In one fluid movement, he grabbed his gun and sprang to his knees. His eyes roamed the room, searched for a threat. Saw nothing wrong. Nothing out of place. No unusual sounds. No smothering darkness, chains, or bars. The light he'd left on in the bathroom still shone brightly. The small oak bureau in the corner still had one drawer slightly open from the day before when he'd been searching for a clean pair of pants.

Daylight was just now coming through skylight over the bed, telling him it was around five-thirty. About his usual time to wake up. It'd just been his semiweekly nightmare. Nothing more. Thankfully, he had woken before the grim climax.

Yawning widely, Gabe dropped his feet to the floor, stood, and gave an all over body stretch. He winced. Damn, he was sounding more like a Rice Krispies commercial every day—the snap, crackle, and pop a reminder of a body that'd seen too much abuse.

He padded barefoot to the bathroom, and as he performed his morning routine, he reviewed the day ahead of him. He'd been putting it off for too long. His boss, Noah McCall, wasn't going to like it, because it meant he'd be out of the circuit for a few days, but it was hell and damn past time to get this over and done with. Time to move on and allow Skye to do the same. He owed her that; she owed him that, too. This time he was going to see her and damn well going to convince her. He didn't care whose ass he had to kick to get to her. He would not be put off again.

Even once he got past her guard dogs, seeing her wouldn't be easy. A man didn't forget a woman like Skylar James, no matter how deceitful and self-absorbed she was. It'd been five years since he'd seen her in person—if standing on a street corner a hundred yards away counted as seeing her. Eight years since he'd talked to her . . . on the freaking phone. Eight years and four days since he'd been stupid enough to marry her.

It was time to get on with the rest of his life. The yearlong job he'd been on was almost at an end—the search for Rosemount's people was almost over. Some very bad people had been put away, and fellow LCR operative Cole Mathison was close to getting the vengeance he deserved.

Rosemount's other victims were receiving the medical care they needed to overcome the abuse they'd suffered. Only one man still eluded them—the doctor responsible for the mind-destroying drug. Cole wouldn't give up until the doctor was caught. He didn't need Gabe for that. Cole was one of LCR's best trackers. He could do this on his own, then call in reinforcements when the deal went down.

Seeing Cole be able to close the door on that hellacious event and Ethan Bishop finally put his life back on track with Shea made Gabe realize he'd put off his own inevitable ending for too long. It was way past time to end what never should have happened in the first place.

Barely paying attention to the hard-edged, grim-faced

man in the mirror, Gabe shaved and slapped on some cooling gel. Returning to the bedroom, he slid into a pair of faded jeans and a black T-shirt. When he was on assignment, he dressed the way he had to, to fit the role. Given a choice, jeans and a T-shirt were what he preferred. It took him back to his simple roots, and as much as he liked to escape many of the memories, he couldn't deny that dressing down was much more his personality than anything else.

He pulled his duffel from the closet and threw in some clothes and toiletries. He didn't know how long he'd be gone, but if he needed anything else, he'd buy it there. Traveling with the bare minimum was his preferred way. He wasn't a man who needed much. The more you had, the more you had to lose. He'd learned that the hard way.

Gabe grabbed his duffel and stalked out the door. He'd call Noah on the way to the airport. Not that McCall would be surprised. His boss had mentioned more than once that every LCR operative at some point had to deal with their past. Some sooner than others. The man knew what he was talking about—McCall had dealt with his own past a couple of years back.

The sun glinted off the windshield of his mini–cabin cruiser tied to the dock—his home while he'd built his house. As usual, he stood and surveyed the area. Not that he expected intruders or any trouble, but life had taught him wariness at an early age. Other than the dead branches from a downed tree beating against the side of the dock, he saw nothing out of place. Satisfied, he jumped in, slipped on his sunglasses, and started the engine.

Living on a tiny, remote island out in the middle of nowhere had several advantages. No neighbors, other than gators and snakes. The only interruption was the occasional boat looking for a bit of privacy or a good fishing spot. Gabe could handle a hungry gator or wayward boat a hell of a lot better than he could handle living in a large city. The smothering effect of thousands of people living on top of one another was his vision of hell. Revulsion shuddered through him.

Salt-filled wind, scented with a hint of the coming rain, blasted into his face. He took long, cleansing breaths, appreciating, as always, the sheer luxury of fresh air and freedom, something he would never take for granted again.

As he sped toward the island of Key West, he mentally reviewed his itinerary. Once he landed in New York, he'd head to her apartment. Since this was July and the wealthiest of New Yorkers summered elsewhere, he figured if he couldn't catch her in the city, he'd find her at her family's estate in the Hamptons.

It wouldn't be easy to get to her. Years ago, he'd given up trying to contact her. For someone who was on the news weekly, shown going to one party or another, she was one of the most untouchable people he'd ever known. So different from the young woman he thought he'd married. Seeing her on the television and in magazines, he found it hard to believe they were the same person. But she was excellent at pretend. Another lesson learned.

Gabe puttered into the marina and nodded a thank-you to the tanned, sandy-haired kid who tied his boat to the dock. Grabbing his helmet, he jumped onto the dock and headed to his Harley. Parking at the marina wasn't cheap, but with their tight security, it was perfect for him.

He straddled the seat, but before he could put his helmet on, his cellphone vibrated in his pocket. Pulling the phone out, he checked the readout. Not surprised that it was Noah.

"I was just about to call you."

"Where are you?" McCall asked.

"Headed to the airport. There's something I need to take care of."

"I need to see you."

"You're in town?"

"Yeah . . . meet me at the Marriott on Fielding Avenue . . . room 1213."

Gabe didn't know what surprised him more—that his boss was in Florida or the hard-edged tone to his voice. It'd been a while since he'd heard that iron control. "What's up?"

"We'll talk when you get here."

"If this is about a case, give it to someone else. I've been putting this off too long."

"Get here and we'll talk. Ring me when you're on your way up."

Noah ended the call before Gabe could respond.

McCall's abruptness didn't concern him. When the man was in mission mode, politeness got put on the back burner. It was the oddity of his tone that intrigued Gabe; there was an edginess to it that Gabe couldn't quite fathom.

Taking time off shouldn't be a concern. LCR operatives were free agents and could take off whenever they liked, though most of them were dedicated enough that taking vacation was a rarity. This was probably the first time in two or three years that he'd taken more than a day off. And even then, if McCall needed him back, he knew he only had to pick up the phone. Gabe, like almost every LCR employee, owed Noah his life. Besides, Gabe believed in this cause too much not to be available if need be.

He didn't like having to turn down a job, but this thing with Skye had been festering too long. It was way past time for it to end.

* * *

Noah McCall leaned back in his chair and studied the man across from him. He knew quite a bit about Jeremiah James. There were few people in the civilized world who hadn't heard the man's name—one of the movers and shakers in the business world, with more money than most people could fathom.

"He's on his way," Noah said.

The silver-headed man shook his head, the furrows around his mouth deepening with his frown. "Why can't you do it? You're supposed to be the best. I want you on the case."

"This man will get the job done better than anyone."

"Better than you?"

"Yes."

"Why?"

"You'll see."

The man raised a shaky hand to wipe at his pale, damp forehead. "I don't know. She's too important—"

"All of our clients are of utmost importance to us. And this man is one of my most valued operatives. He's saved a hell of a lot of lives."

"Will he understand the need for discretion? If this news gets out . . . it would be a nightmare."

Noah examined the man closer. Few people could surprise him anymore, but for some reason, James did. He wasn't an easy person to read. On the one hand, he seemed genuinely concerned; on the other hand, he was worried about the press. Question was, which concerned him more?

"Media attention isn't something LCR wants either," Noah said.

"But she's one of the most recognizable people in the world. Are you sure he—"

"Our operatives rescue people from all backgrounds,

all economic levels. The wealthiest of victims and the poorest of victims receive the same professional treatment. We have no interest in personalities, famous or otherwise. And this man is better at ignoring things like that than most."

"You make him sound like a machine. Everyone cares about things like that to a certain extent . . . some more than others."

Noah's mouth tilted in a cool smile. "He's as human as the next person. He just understands his priorities better than most."

James dabbed at his damp forehead again. Though he was known to be ruthless in the boardroom and heartless when it came to his competitors, the older man's dilated eyes and perspiration indicated that where his daughter was concerned, he appeared to have genuine affection. Noah would soon know for sure. Seeing Gabe would either make the man balk or reveal that his daughter's welfare was the most important factor, no matter who the rescuer was.

Noah had no compunction about surprising James. The man's reaction would be key to the mission. However, he did suffer a blip of conscience that Gabe would be caught off guard also. While that couldn't be helped, Noah had a small amount of regret that one of his best men would soon be getting some disturbing news and it would be delivered by a man Noah knew Gabe despised.

The soft buzz of his phone alerted him. Gabe's signal that he was on his way up.

Jeremiah James heard the sound and stood, his anxiousness at meeting the man who would save his daughter apparent.

Noah remained slumped in his chair, unmoving. When several minutes passed and Gabe still hadn't come through the door, James dropped back into his chair and snapped, "Why is it taking so long?"

Noah didn't answer. His operative's need to take the stairs was Gabe's business and no one else's. Gabe didn't owe anyone an explanation, least of all this man.

A soft knock and then the door swung open.

Gabe closed the door behind him and headed toward Noah, who stood waiting for him. Though reading Noah McCall was like trying to read a brick wall, Gabe could tell he was disturbed about something. "What's up, you sounded—"

Halfway across the room, Gabe jerked to a halt as the silver-haired man sitting in front of Noah stood and turned. A man he knew all too well. And one he'd hoped never to see again. He was older . . . his hair now completely silver as opposed to the salt and pepper it'd been eight years ago. The lines on his face had increased and his posture was more stooped, but he would recognize him anywhere. Hard to forget the man who'd had a hand in destroying the last of his dreams. Jeremiah James, his father-in-law.

Gabe shot a glare at his boss. "What the hell's going on?"

McCall didn't bother to prevaricate. "I believe you and Mr. James know each other."

James frowned in concentration. His confusion obvious, he slowly walked toward Gabe. The instant he recognized him, shock replaced the arrogant look Gabe remembered all too well.

Though his father-in-law might look eight years older, between the two of them, Gabe knew he'd changed the most. Gone was the idealistic young man who'd felt he had the world at his feet when he was with the woman he loved. A cold, hardened man stood in his place.

James stopped a couple of feet from Gabe and said, "Maddox?"

"The one and the same," Gabe answered softly.

James whirled around and snapped, "What the hell's going on here?"

McCall's enigmatic expression never changed. "This is the man we spoke of."

"No." His head shook violently. "No way is this man going to save my daughter."

Gabe stiffened. "What are you talking about? Something's happened to Skye?"

James jerked his head to glare at Gabe. "She doesn't like to be called Skye." Turning back to Noah, James barked, "Get me somebody else. I don't want this man anywhere near my daughter."

Grabbing the older man's shoulder, Gabe twisted him around. "What's happened to Skye?"

James continued to glare and pressed his lips together, making it clear he didn't want to give Gabe any answers.

Noah answered for him. "Skylar's been kidnapped, Gabe. Mr. James has come to LCR for help."

"When? How?"

Jeremiah James had been a tough, mean bastard the one time he met him, and Gabe could tell the man hadn't gotten any nicer. But to put his daughter's life on the line because of his prejudice seemed extreme even for him.

Noah growled at the man being so stubbornly silent. "James, Gabe's the best man to save your daughter. Are you going to let your personal differences get in the way of saving Skylar's life?"

James swallowed audibly; the look he gave both men was almost panicked. "There's got to be someone else."

Gabe glared at his father-in-law. "I'm going to give you

one warning and that's it. Tell me what's happened to Skye."

Arrogance returned to James's expression. "Or what?"

Gabe moved, putting his face inches from his father-in-law's. "You really going to stand there and preen while your little girl's in trouble?"

Faded blue eyes examined Gabe. Though they were dulled with age and grief, Gabe saw in them Skylar's eyes. Finally, James's shoulders drooped. "Are you sure you can get her?"

Without even knowing the details, Gabe didn't hesitate in answering, "There's no one more qualified."

His sigh full of weary resignation, James walked back to his chair and dropped into it. "Eight days ago, Skylar didn't show up for a benefit dinner. One she attends every year. I became concerned . . . went to her apartment. It was empty. Her chauffeur, who's also her bodyguard, had disappeared, too. I wasn't too worried, because she does that sometimes."

"Does what?" Gabe asked.

His shoulders raised in a tired shrug. "Disappears from time to time . . . to get away from the media frenzy that always surrounds her. She cuts off all communication."

"And now you think it's something else?"

"I left numerous voice messages. Again that didn't worry me too much." His eyes darted away briefly. "Sometimes she ignores my calls."

Why Skylar avoided her father was her own business, so he didn't question the man's guilty look. He had only one priority.

"What makes you think this is different?"

"Two days ago she missed another benefit dinner. The cause not only meant a lot to her, she was one of the honorees and is on the board of directors. She never would have missed it unless something had happened."

The visible shudder that went through James's body worried Gabe a hell of a lot more than his words. Something else had happened.

"What?" Gabe asked softly.

Noah handed Gabe a piece of paper from his desk. "Mr. James found this folded in his newspaper yesterday morning."

Refusing to acknowledge the alarm clamoring toward explosion inside him, Gabe read the printed words:

We have your daughter. If you ever want to see her alive again, deposit ten million dollars into account 39482894J, Mid-Central Bank, by ten A.M. Friday. Tell the police and she dies. Tell anyone, she dies. Once we have the money, we'll be in touch on where you can retrieve your daughter. Whether you retrieve her alive or dead is entirely up to you.

Gabe tore his eyes away from the note to glance at his watch. Today was Monday. Two questions sprang to his mind. Why give James almost a week to come up with the money? And how the hell was Gabe going to find her in such a short amount of time?

"I barely had time to comprehend the note when a package was delivered to the door." James nodded toward the television set in the corner. "McCall, would you play it again?"

Noah picked up a remote and pressed play.

The picture was dark and wobbly, as if whoever held the camera was either nervous or an amateur. For several seconds, the image was out of focus, but then it became heart-stoppingly clear.

A woman sat slumped in a chair with a gag over her mouth. Long strands of mahogany hair hanging in her face hid her identity, until one of the men grabbed a handful of hair and jerked her face up for the camera. Normally creamy skin, mottled with bruises and cuts, was starkly white. Two men stood on either side of her, their faces covered with hoods. Each man held a Glock in his hand, pointed at the woman's head. Not just any woman, though. *Skye.* Skylar James . . . Maddox. His wife.

Gabe wasn't one to panic or give in to fear. That kind of emotion had been smothered out of him years ago. He was known for his cold, calculating analysis of an operation. Everything around him might be in a frenzy, but that never fazed Gabe.

Skye hadn't been a part of his life for a long time. She was no longer the woman he'd married. Hell, she'd never been the woman he thought he married. This was just another case. Another missing person that he'd been assigned to rescue. Nothing more.

The fact that the woman's face was bruised and swollen and the one eye that wasn't swollen shut was dilated and glazed, indicating she'd been drugged, didn't matter. *Couldn't matter.*

He shot a glance at James. "Any reason to believe they're targeting you for another reason besides the money?"

"You mean, does someone have a grudge against me?"

Gabe nodded. He had a major grudge against this man and was willing to bet he wasn't the only one.

"I have business acquaintances who may hate me, but not enough to use my daughter as a pawn."

"You've told no one?"

"No."

He studied the older man. James was wealthy beyond most people's imaginings. In his world, money fixed problems. "So why take the chance with us? Why not just pay the ransom?"

When he seemed to hesitate to answer, Gabe felt a punch to his gut. "You don't want to have to pay the money?"

James's eyes blazed with fury. "I'll pay everything I have to get her back, Maddox. More than anything, I need to know that Skylar will be safe. If I just wire the money, with no assurance, I have no leverage."

Gabe couldn't argue with him. The man might well be right. Paying the money didn't necessarily mean these people would return Skye alive.

"Keep your damn money." He turned to Noah. "I'll head to New York tonight."

The older man made a frantic gesture. "You have to be discreet. If they get a hint that I've hired you, they could kill her."

"No one will ever know."

There was something else in James's face. Something he didn't want Gabe to know. He'd been around too many slimy bastards not to recognize the symptoms.

"If you got more information you're not telling, you're only risking your daughter's life."

Again those faded blue eyes skittered away from Gabe's direct gaze, but he shook his head and said, "No. There's nothing else."

"You're lying."

James chewed on his lip. The man was definitely hiding something.

"Tell me."

"It's been years since she's seen you. She'll be . . . surprised."

"Of course she'll be surprised, she has no idea who I work for. Besides that, we didn't exactly end things on the very best terms."

James continued to chew his lip.

"Dammit, spit it out. Skye's life is on the line here."

"I just hate to cause her more trauma." He looked at Noah. "Are you sure there's no one else?"

"James," Gabe said softly, "we are not going to do this. You came to LCR for a reason . . . we're the best. And I'm going after her. Deal with it."

His shoulders slumped in defeat. "Bring her back, Maddox. I'll pay you whatever I—"

Hot blood surged through Gabe and then boiled over. Grabbing the older man by his shoulders, Gabe literally picked him up, carried him across the room, and pressed him hard against the door. "I told you the first time you tried to buy me, I'm not for sale. You try it again and you'll be talking from your ass for the rest of your life. You got that?"

The minute he saw the weary sadness in the man's eyes, Gabe regretted his temper. At least in this, Jeremiah James was no different from any other parent who would pay whatever they could to have their child rescued. Just because he'd tried to buy Gabe off years ago didn't correlate to this situation.

Dropping his hands, Gabe moved away and shot a knowing glance at his boss. "You need to talk."

McCall's eyes gave an infinitesimal flicker, acknowledging Gabe's unspoken question. Yeah, there was definitely more to this. Something his boss didn't want Skye's father to know.

Noah turned his black eyes to James. "Go back to your hotel room. I'll contact you in a couple of hours to give you an update."

James nodded and turned to go out the door. He stopped suddenly and gave what Gabe could only describe as an apprehensive look. "Don't be cruel to her, Maddox. She doesn't deserve it."

Gabe didn't have an answer for that. He'd never been cruel to any woman, even the ones who'd betrayed him.

He waited until James left and then turned to McCall. "You know who's got her?"

Noah's grim expression shot an electric surge of adrenaline through Gabe.

"How bad?" Gabe asked quietly.

"Bad." Noah switched the television set back on. "The guy on the left . . . see the tattoo on his wrist?"

Gabe focused on the man's wrist, not allowing himself to look at the terrified woman in the chair. If he was going to save Skye, he had to think of her as another victim. Not as someone he'd once loved.

"I see the tattoo. I don't recognize it, though."

"Few people have seen it and lived to describe its meaning."

"Who are these guys?"

"I don't know the other man. I only know the one with the tattoo. Goes by the name Victor Lymes. He's been responsible for some of the highest-profile cases in the last few years. He's a loner . . . hires his people as he moves around. His MO is different than most. One of the reasons he's been so hard to catch."

"Different how?"

"He's rarely responsible for the actual abduction, but he somehow ends up with the victim and demands the money."

"He abducts them from the kidnapper?"

"On occasion. Most of the time, he buys them, then asks for more money."

"So he buys them at a bargain and sells them for a profit."

"Yeah."

"So Skye was possibly kidnapped by someone else and then Lymes got hold of her?"

"Either that or he found a way to snatch her himself."

That information wasn't the cause of McCall's grim look.

"There's something else. What?" Gabe asked.

"He has a reputation of not returning them in good condition."

"Like what?"

"Beatings. Occasionally rape. Mutilation is his favorite type of torture. He likes to cut off body parts—toes, ears, tongues—and sends them with the ransom note. I was surprised he sent only the note and not something else with it."

Noah turned his attention back to the frozen horror on the screen. "Another thing that's different. Still shots of his victims are his usual thing. The video is very unusual for him."

Gabe nodded. "He knows what he's got."

"Yeah. As high profile as Skylar James is, if he just sold the video and did nothing else, he'd still make a bundle."

"Any idea where he works from?"

"He's worked all over Europe, but his last few jobs were in South America. Most of his work is underground. That's how he learns about the abductions. Then he makes a contact. If they won't sell the victim, he'll take them by force if he thinks the prize is worth it."

"How do we know so much about him?"

"We've been fortunate to have someone who's worked with him in the past."

"Worked?"

"Undercover."

"Who?"

Noah's grim look lightened for a second. "I think you call her Ghost."

"McKenna?"

"Yeah."

"She's worked with the bastard?"

Noah nodded. "She's managed to rescue two victims."

"How'd she get away with it?"

"That's something I don't even bother to ask anymore."

Gabe looked at the screen again. McKenna was one of the most elusive operatives LCR had. Gabe had worked with her on several cases before he even knew her first name. He still didn't know her last. Wasn't sure anyone did other than Noah. Since Gabe had felt the need to call her something, he'd nicknamed her Ghost, mostly because she was a slender wisp of a girl who appeared without warning, did her job, and then disappeared just as quickly. The name had stuck, because now she got called Ghost more times than she was called McKenna.

"Can you get in touch with her?"

Noah shook his head. "No need. She's already contacted me. She's hoping to go in this afternoon."

He stiffened at the news. "She knows where they are?"

"No, but she heard the chatter. Got in touch with Victor on her own . . . told him she was looking for a job. He's been impressed with her work before." Noah jerked his head toward the screen. "These guys are obviously amateurs. He's going to want someone with experience to handle Skylar till the ransom's paid. McKenna will go in, make an assessment, and then get back with us."

Gabe was already shaking his head. No way in hell was he going to just wait around while Skye could very well be being tortured, raped, or worse. "And I'm just supposed to sit on my ass and wait?"

McCall swallowed a snort. "Sitting on your ass and

waiting are barely in your vocabulary, much less your skill set. Victor's last two victims were brought to Brazil to await ransom. Though he hasn't confirmed it yet, she thinks that's where he's got Skylar. McKenna suggested you get to Rio. She'll find you."

"I'm assuming, working together, we're going to get rid of the bastard once and for all."

McCall shrugged. "That would be best-case scenario. Might not happen this time."

He wanted the bastard who dared touch Skye dead. "Why the hell not?"

"Victor's been a busy boy. Around the time of Skylar's abduction, another one took place. Almost as high profile. Businessman from England . . . Lucas Kane."

"The billionaire?"

"Yeah. And a good friend of the prime minister's son. McKenna thinks Victor was directly responsible for Kane's abduction. Since she believes Victor's in Rio, she's going to work with you on getting Skylar. Then she'll stay behind and grab Kane."

"By herself?"

Noah shrugged again, but his darkened expression showed his disapproval. "She's the only one with the contact, so I'll allow her some slack. I'm keeping three operatives on standby just in case. Cole's at loose ends since he lost contact with the doctor he's tracking. He'll watch your back until you get Skylar back home."

Gabe nodded. There was no one he'd rather have watching his back than Cole. He worried about McKenna, though. Her "I can do it by myself" attitude had gotten her in hot water more than once. The woman often acted as if she were a one-person army.

"So once Kane is safe, we're going in after Victor."

Noah shook his head. "Your priority has to be Skylar."

"I know what my priority is, McCall," Gabe snapped.

"But if you think I'm going to let him get away with what he did, you're wrong."

"I don't expect that. I do, however, expect you to take care of your wife."

For the first time ever, Gabe saw a bit of censure in his boss's eyes. He stiffened at the implication of Noah's words but knew he couldn't argue. Hell, how many men would stay married but separated from their wives for eight years with no chance of reconciliation? Gabe knew of only one man who could be that stupid. Him.

Hell of a note that just as he decided he could no longer put off their inevitable divorce, Fate would step in. Gabe no longer questioned the cruel little bitch called Fate. When she wanted to grab you by the balls, sometimes it was just best to grit your teeth and take the pain.

And as much as he hated to admit it, Noah's thoughts mirrored his own. He owed it to Skye to protect and care for her . . . even if she wanted nothing to do with him.

"Has McKenna tried to get rid of Victor before?"

"Of course . . . several times. The guy's shrewd and damn dangerous. McKenna's one of the few who's worked with him more than once and lived to tell about it."

"How'd she survive?"

Sadness flickered on his face. "I'm not sure she did."

Gabe didn't bother to ask him what he meant. Most of the time, LCR operatives could escape the worst of the effects of their chosen profession by remembering the good they'd done. Rescuing victims was a high like none other. But occasionally, when an op went bad or the operative had to go too deep for too long, the aftereffects could be devastating.

McKenna had a reputation of going deeper than just about any other operative LCR employed. She'd seen too much and sometimes that took everything you had left.

"I'll head to Rio tonight."

"I'll have a jet waiting for you."

He ignored the flash of compassion on his boss's face. Not many knew about his difficulty with enclosed places. Which was a good thing. When people were depending on you to save their lives, learning that your protector could almost disintegrate under certain conditions didn't exactly inspire confidence.

Noah placed a hand on Gabe's shoulder. "Sorry I couldn't warn you ahead of time. I needed to see James's reaction."

"I'm glad you didn't. It would have given me too much time to think about the things I wanted to say to him. Focusing on saving Skye is the most important thing. My antipathy for the man can't come into play."

"Be safe, Gabe. Check in when you can."

Gabe turned and stalked out the door. Acid churned in his gut. He had less than ten hours to prepare. He didn't bother castigating himself for his weakness. After living with it for so long, it was just something he dealt with. However, knowing that Skye's life depended upon him dealing with his problem without the slightest impact on the operation gave him extra incentive. He might no longer love her, but she was still his wife. He would do whatever he had to do to make sure Skye was set free.

And then, he'd set both of them free.

six

Kendra swallowed the sob building inside her. They were on water now. Though her head was covered with some kind of hood, making it impossible to see anything, she recognized the dip and surge. At some point, while she was unconscious, they'd taken her even farther from home.

Oh God, they had Skylar, too. She'd been in the next room, tied up and gagged, and heard them boasting about getting someone so famous. Had heard the things they said and did to Skylar. Had listened to them beating her and Skylar's screams of pain and rage. And she'd been unable to do anything but lie there and weep for her.

And then, like a piece of property or an animal, they'd sold Skylar. They'd been laughing, bragging about what they were going to do with their extra money, as they carried her limp body out the door. They'd passed by where Kendra could see them. One of them—Joey—had grinned and winked at her.

Someone had bought Skylar? Why? What would they do with her?

Her friend, her only true friend, had no doubt come looking for her and had been taken, too.

Tears filled Kendra's gritty eyes and poured down her face. It was all her fault. If she hadn't had this stupid, blind ambition to be rich and famous, this never would have happened. And now, not only was she probably going to be raped and killed, the same thing might happen to Skylar.

Kendra sniffed and tried to wipe her face on her shoulder. Her hands were tied behind her back, so she couldn't use them. Where were they taking her? Her life since she'd been taken had become a daily regimen of terror. They hadn't raped her, hadn't even physically hurt her except for giving her some kind of drug that knocked her out every few hours. No one would tell her why, or what their plans were.

Did anyone know she was missing? Did anyone even care?

Skylar! No one but Skylar would care about Kendra. Everyone else had given up on her. But people, lots of wealthy, important people, cared about Skylar. In her email to Skylar, she had promised to call her as soon as she returned from her interview. Would Skylar have shared that information with anyone?

A harsh sob escaped her. Then she heard a sound. One she suddenly realized had been in the background and she hadn't comprehended its meaning. Someone else was crying. She heard whispering and talking. Were there other girls like her? Or was she wrong . . . was Skylar here, too?

"Skylar?" Kendra said.

She heard a few sniffles but Skylar didn't answer.

"Who's there?" Kendra asked.

"My name is Lacey . . . what's yours?"

"Kendra." She paused for a second and then said, "Are there more of us?"

"I think so . . . I just woke up."

Kendra took a breath and called out as loudly as her

dry throat would allow, "Okay, one by one, can you say your name?"

Slowly and haltingly at first, and then more quickly and firmly, as if each girl gained confidence by realizing she wasn't alone, each one said her name. When there were several seconds after the last name was said, Kendra figured all girls had identified themselves. And then a revolting chill swept through her. Seven girls, including Kendra, were on the boat. Dear God, what were these bastards planning?

A frightened young voice interrupted her terror. "Can anyone see anything?"

A chorus of no's followed.

Kendra closed her eyes and took several long breaths, forcing her careening thoughts to calm down. From the sound of the other girls' voices, they were all very young . . . maybe late teens. Kendra knew she might well be the oldest of them. That meant she needed to be their protector. Was she up to the job? Weariness washed over her. She'd never had to fend for herself; how could she be expected to protect anyone else?

A soft voice that sounded a lot like Skylar's whispered inside her head. It told her she was stronger than she gave herself credit for. And that it was time to take charge of her life. Something unfamiliar sprouted, bloomed, and then settled inside her. If Skylar were here, she would take charge and show these bastards they couldn't treat people this way. Since Skylar wasn't here, it was up to Kendra.

She had to help these young girls escape and then she needed to figure out a way to save Skylar, too. She would do what she had to do. Skylar would expect that of her. And, no matter what she'd been told most of her life, it was what she should expect out of herself.

Rio de Janeiro, Brazil

"Get your hands off of me!"

Mean, sherry-brown eyes glinted in amusement as he rapped out an order to the woman behind him: "Put her on the bed. Untie her, then cuff her to the bed rail. I think I'll take a few . . . more-*graphic* photos of our famous captive, to convince her father just how serious I am." His smile grew wider. "In fact, I bet I could make a little extra by selling some of those pictures." A slimy gaze slithered over her body. "Lots of people would love to see what's beneath all those expensive clothes."

Hands shoved Skylar toward the filthy-looking cot. "Do what he says . . . get on the bed."

Her hands tied at her back, Skylar whirled and tried to butt heads with the woman. Her cold, expressionless face never changed as she easily pushed Skylar away.

"You're going to pay for this." Skylar didn't care that she had been reduced to throwing out cheap threats that sounded like she was in a cheesy late-night TV movie. She meant them. These people would pay for everything they'd done. She would make sure of it.

At the door, the man she'd heard them call Victor stopped and smiled. "Actually, *you're* going to pay for it. Or at least your daddy will. Now, do what she says or I'll mark up that pretty face even more."

When the door closed, Skylar swung around and connected her head with the woman's cheek.

"Dammit." The woman jerked back and snarled, "If you don't behave, I'm going to knock you out again." Grabbing Skylar's arm, she pushed her onto the bed. "Understand?"

Landing on her side on the mattress, Skylar glared up at the woman. Damned if she'd answer her.

Her hands on her hips, she frowned at Skylar. "Look, just do what he says, whenever he says it. You'll be fine."

"I'll pay you to help me get away."

"Thanks, but I'd like to keep all of my parts exactly where they are."

Before Skylar could react, the woman flipped her over onto her stomach and untied her hands. Holding them tight, giving Skylar no time to move, she wrapped handcuffs around her wrists and locked them to the railing of the bed. "Now, behave. It'll be over soon."

Skylar rolled around for a more comfortable position. Settling her head against the bed rail, she looked up at her female captor. "Why are you doing this?"

A catlike smile curved her lips. "It pays the rent."

"Do you know anything about Kendra?"

For an instant, Skye saw confusion. "Who?"

"The girl abducted earlier."

"I don't know a Kendra. You're the only one here."

Sorrow filled Skylar. "Oh God, I'll never find her. She might even be dead."

"Victor doesn't kill unless there's money in it."

"Not Victor . . . the other men. The first ones who took me. They took her, too, but wouldn't tell me anything about her."

"Those kind of men don't kidnap to kill either."

"Then for what?"

A fleeting shadow darkened her face. "I don't know." Her eyes narrowed as they examined Skylar. "You know, you've got some nasty bruises on your face and you've been drugged. Maybe you're just imagining it."

"No. I went to the warehouse to look for Kendra, and that's when I was taken."

Another odd look flickered across the woman's face. "Well, we don't have her." She glanced down at her watch and then at the door as though distracted. Then, as if realizing she'd lost her meanness momentarily, she gave Skylar an ice-cold smile. "Just pray your papa loves you as much as you think he does."

Skylar examined the woman more closely. Beneath the thick makeup, she saw skin that was unbelievably clear and youthful-looking. This woman couldn't be more than twenty-two or so, if that, though it was obvious she tried to age herself with the harsh makeup and brassy bleached hair color.

Coming from a world where everyone tried to appear as youthful and attractive as possible, Skylar was intrigued by fact that this woman tried to do the exact opposite.

"How old are you?"

The woman snorted. "Older than you think or none of your damn business. Take your pick."

Her wrist aching from the cuff, Skylar rubbed her skin. "Why—"

"Listen, I'm sure you'd love to have a girl chat, but it's not really my thing. And I don't get paid enough to waste my time on it. Just stay out of Victor's way. Keep your mouth shut. Do whatever he tells you to do. And do not even try to get out of here on your own. I promise, you'll regret it. When your daddy pays the money, you can go. Till then—"

"Can I at least have some water?"

With an exasperated sigh, the woman turned her back to look around. "I don't see—"

Using her shoulders for balance, Skylar raised a long leg and made a hard swipe at the woman with her foot, knocking her backward. On the way to the floor, the woman's head thumped the edge of the bedside table. Her glazing eyes wide with surprise, she muttered, "He didn't mention how much trouble you'd be."

Skylar knew she had only a few seconds to act. The woman was unconscious, but there was no way to know how long she'd stay that way. Stretching her leg, grateful for her long, slender toes, Skylar eased her foot into the woman's pocket. She'd seen her drop the keys there after she'd cuffed Skylar.

Tension pounded through her, followed by overwhelming relief when her toes touched the keys and slid them from the pocket. Twelve years of dance classes were finally paying off. Her body supple and limber, she brought her foot to her hands and grabbed on to the key. Fingers shaking with exhilaration and fear, she inserted the key into the hole. A click indicated the sweet sound of freedom.

Swinging her feet to the floor, she bounced from the bed. Her eyes fixed on the unconscious woman, Skylar skirted her body and skulked to the door. Hand on the knob, she took a bracing breath and twisted. The door burst open. Skylar fell back and swallowed a scream. One of Victor's men—the one who'd made some of the most offensive remarks—stood before her. Hair cut in a buzz and almost no eyebrows, the man looked as though he'd just escaped from an insane asylum. The almost maniacal laugh that burst from him told Skylar she might well be right.

"Going for a walk, little girl?"

Skylar backed away and glanced around for a weapon. Dammit, why hadn't she thought to look for one before? There was nothing to grab on to, nothing to throw. She braced herself as he came toward her. Two years of self-defense classes and a lifetime of living in New York City—she could defend herself. She'd been caught by surprise before, and there had been two of them. Handling this one bastard should be no problem.

Knees slightly apart, arms at her side, she waited. An

instant before he grabbed for her, Skylar shot her fist into his throat. Then the side of her foot flew to his knee. He clutched his throat, gagging.

Triumph soared. Agony followed a second later as his fist slammed into her jaw. Her legs went out from under her. She barely comprehended the pain of slamming backward onto the floor before he threw himself on top of her, wrapped his hands around her neck, and started to squeeze.

Her vision rapidly blurring, she recognized a killing hatred in his expression, along with the erection he was grinding against her.

Her savior came from an unlikely source.

She dimly heard the woman's voice. "Edmond! What the hell are you doing?"

Her vision full of black spots, Skylar gurgled, gasping. Underneath the deafening roar in her head, she heard the satisfying clunk when the woman bashed her gun against the man's head.

He snarled, "The bitch hurt me. She's going to find out what real hurt is."

"I don't care if she killed you. Get off her."

When he continued to squeeze, Skylar closed her eyes against the ugly, vicious face above her. With one last desperate move, she forced her knee up and rammed him in the balls. Just as unconsciousness blacked out her vision and blanked her mind, she felt the pressure around her neck disappear. Unable to hold on, Skylar passed out.

McKenna glared at the man she'd just knocked the hell out of as she checked Skylar's pulse. She didn't know who she was more angry with—Skylar James for trying to escape, Edmond Fritz for trying to rape the girl, or herself for letting her guard down. If Victor found out, there would be hell to pay.

"What the hell's going on?"

Oh shit. McKenna sprang to her feet and whirled around to face Victor. The rage in his cold, mean eyes wasn't something she hadn't seen before, but she didn't like it when it was directed at her or her charge. "Edmond got carried away."

They both looked down at the unconscious man lying beside the unconscious Skylar.

"How she'd get unlocked?"

Hell, she hated this part. "Edmond unlocked her . . . said he wanted to get a taste before you let her go."

"Fucking bastard. I knew he wouldn't be able to keep his dick in his pants. Get rid of him."

Ignoring the nausea in her stomach, she nodded. When she'd told the lie, she'd known what it would lead to. Getting rid of Edmond meant one less man she had to worry about. That didn't mean that she would enjoy the deed. Even though she knew Edmond had murdered and raped most of his adult life, killing never came easy to her. She figured when it did, the soul that had been shrinking for years would finally dissolve forever.

Victor picked Skylar up and dumped her back on the bed. McKenna turned to see him pull out a small bottle of liquid and a needle from his pocket.

"What are you doing?"

"Just ensuring she won't cause any more problems. With the right amount of this stuff, she'll sleep through Armageddon."

As McKenna tugged Edmond's still-unconscious body from the room, a thought came to her that if Gabe Maddox got hold of him, Victor would be wondering if Armageddon really had happened.

McKenna had worked with Gabe on several ops, and if there was one man she figured she never wanted to piss off, it'd be Gabe. More the type to beat the hell out of a person first and ask questions later, Gabe didn't shrink away from the hard stuff.

Unlike her.

Gritting her teeth and holding her breath, McKenna squeezed the trigger and ended the worthless life of Edmond Fritz. Then, doing what she always did, she ran to the bathroom and threw her guts up.

Turning to the sink, she cupped water in her hands to rinse the vile taste from her mouth. Not seeing a towel, she pulled her shirt up and, ignoring the deathly pale face in the mirror in front of her, wiped her mouth. Then, taking a deep breath, McKenna straightened her spine and opened the door. "I'm taking the garbage out, be back in a few minutes."

Victor came to the door. "Lester and I will load him in your car. My other prize is stashed just a few miles down the road, so I'm headed over there. Lester and Stan will stay here till you get back."

They both glanced down at Edmond, who looked no different really, other than his eyes were closed and he had a neat little hole in the middle of his forehead. "Take Eddy boy over to the morgue on Sixty-first Street. Wait for payment. I'll call and let them know you're coming and how much I want. Fresh, young body like that ought to bring in more than that old geezer I sold them last year."

McKenna swallowed a shudder. She didn't want to know what these people would want a dead body for, other than burial. She had more important things to worry about. Two people who were still very much alive and she could do something for. Unfortunately for Edmond, she'd done all she could do for him.

She heard soft grunts and some curses as Victor and Lester carried Edmond to her car. The trunk squeaked open and Edmond's body made a loud thud when they threw him inside. She was glad she'd lined the car with plastic right after she'd picked it up from the rental company. Explaining massive amounts of blood when she returned it wasn't something she wanted to deal with.

With a nod to Victor, she jumped in the car and headed to the morgue. She'd give Victor about five minutes before she called Gabe. The last thing she wanted was for Victor and Gabe to have a confrontation. Lucas Kane was somewhere close by. Until she knew where, Victor had to stay alive.

For the first time in a long time, McKenna thought she might not mind having to kill when the time came. She could think of only one other man who deserved death more than Victor.

Like a caged panther, Gabe paced back and forth in his hotel room. Even after years of freedom, staying locked up in a room for more than a few hours still drove him crazy. The fact that he hadn't heard from McKenna sure as hell wasn't helping. What was taking her so long?

Ever since he'd learned of Skye's kidnapping, he'd done his best not to think about what she was going through. For years, he'd been angry with her. Only recently had he realized the anger no longer existed. They'd both been young and foolish—reckless. After the hell he'd just come from, Skye had seemed like a godsend. An innocent, beautiful angel. He had projected onto her so many qualities she'd never possessed. His blindness and naïveté had led to the destruction of his dreams. Not Skye.

For the first time in a long time, Gabe allowed himself to think about the vivacious, seemingly wholesome beauty he'd met all those years ago.

Eight years ago
Kalamina Island, South Pacific

"What do you think?"

Gabe turned from the mirror he'd been grimacing into. Wearing a tie felt as foreign to him as shoes would to a dog. It was almost unnatural.

He caught his breath on a gasp, his discomfort completely forgotten. Never had he seen a more beautiful sight in his life. At any time, Skye was beautiful, but today she went beyond into a sphere he didn't know existed. The short, white satin dress lovingly hugged every beautiful curve. The only time he'd ever seen her more exquisite was last night, when he'd seen her nude for the first time. He hardened at the sweet memory.

"Uh-oh, you don't like it?"

Hard to believe that someone with Skye's looks could sound so uncertain and vulnerable. One of the many reasons he loved her so much.

Gabe shook his head as he slowly walked toward her. "I just can't believe how incredible you look. You do know you're the most beautiful woman in the world, don't you?"

Her smile tightened for an instant, her eyes revealing that vulnerability even more. "You're the only one I care about thinking that. You know that, don't you?"

Stopping within inches of her, he gazed down at the beauty before him. In just a few short hours, she would become his wife. How the hell had he gotten so lucky? After the past few years, Gabe had figured any happiness in his life he'd already received. And then, the instant he met Skye, all of that had changed.

"Are you sure you wouldn't rather wait and have a larger wedding with your family?"

She scrunched her pretty nose into a cute grimace.

"Trust me. Having a big wedding doesn't interest me in the least. My mother would turn it into a circus. This way, we get to have the wedding we want." Her hands grasped his shoulders as her lips lifted in a sexy curve. "And we can have the honeymoon we want, too."

Dipping his head, his mouth covered hers, devouring her sweetness. Skye groaned and pressed deeper into him. Memories of the night before appeared in his mind. Skye's beauty. Her passion. And the never-ending want he had for this woman. The instant they'd made love, he'd wanted her again.

Gabe abruptly pulled away. One more second in her arms and he'd say to hell with the marriage vows and head straight into the honeymoon. He wanted her like nothing he'd ever wanted in his life, but he wanted her permanently. Legally and forever. An unbreakable bond.

Giving him that oh-so-sexy, satisfied look, she whispered, "Let's go get married."

The cellphone in his pocket vibrated, jerking Gabe back into the present. He grabbed the phone, eager to get to the job he'd come here for. Thinking about the clueless idiot he'd been back then served no purpose other than to make him angrier at himself.

Now it was time to go rescue the girl who'd started it all.

seven

The dream started as it always did. Gabe was lying beside her in bed, whispering soft, sexy words as he caressed her face. She loved this part of the dream. The part where he was so warm and dear. The part where there was still hope. Soon the nightmare would begin. *No.* She wanted to hang on to the good part as long as possible. "Stay," she whispered. "Please stay. Don't leave me."

"Skye, wake up . . . we've got to get out of here."

"Don't leave me."

"I'm not about to leave you, but if you don't get up, we're going to be in big trouble."

Skylar tried to lift her heavy eyelids, realized she couldn't and decided not to bother. Besides, if she woke up, the dream would end. She would give anything to stay in this dream forever.

Two hard hands bit into her shoulders. "Dammit, Skylar. Wake up."

"No." She heard the childish tone of her voice and giggled.

Fingers pried one of her lids open. Someone cursed.

"What'd they give her?" a harsh, masculine voice asked.

A female voice said, "I don't know. Nothing too bad . . . he wouldn't want her dead. Just said it would put her out for a while."

"Hell, I'm going to have to carry her out of here. That means you've got no backup."

"I don't need backup. I just need you gone before he comes back. I've got to get out of here and get back to my car. He needs to be the one to find Lester and Stan. Not me."

"I'll come back."

"No. I have to find where he's holding Kane first. Just go before he comes back."

Skylar moaned and tried to turn away from the loud voices. Did they realize how loudly they were speaking? Didn't they know she was trying to sleep? She wanted to return to her dreams. When her body suddenly moved, she realized she was being lifted off the bed. How fun . . . she felt like she was floating. Giggling again, she snuggled up against the hard chest.

A man growled, "Skye, either stay asleep or wake up and help me out."

Skye. No one called her Skye except Gabe. She'd always hated being called Skye, but when Gabe said it in that growling, sexy way of his, she loved it. Moaning again, she snuggled deeper against him. The dream was back. This was the best one she'd had in years.

"Is she waking up?"

Skylar frowned. Why was a woman speaking in her dream? That was odd.

Forcing her eyes open, Skylar squinted up at Gabe. He looked different from the usual dreams. Older. He had lines around his mouth and eyes; his hair, still thick and black, was shorter; and anger sparkled in his dark blue gaze.

Doing what she always did when she dreamed of him, Skylar reached out and touched Gabe's face. She always met with empty air but it never stopped her from trying. When she felt the warm, solid face, she pressed her fingers against him and caressed a crease at his mouth. *Oh, this was definitely the best dream yet.*

"Skye."

The voice sounded different, too. Deeper, more mature, but still gravelly and full of emotion. Her fingers moved over his face again, but when a hand grabbed her wrist and pulled it away, she jerked and opened her eyes wide.

Hallucinations. The drug she'd been given was causing this. Why else would she be seeing the man she'd once been married to? Oh God, what kind of hideous, cruel drug had she been given?

Pulling in a long breath, Skylar opened her mouth to scream.

Gabe slapped a hand over her mouth before she could release a sound. What the hell was wrong with her?

Her eyes were wide with horror as she stared up at him. Hell, had he shocked her that badly?

She struggled for barely an instant before her eyes closed and she went limp. His heart in his throat, Gabe checked her pulse. Slow and steady. The trauma of the last few days, along with whatever drug Victor had given her, had taken its toll. This was best anyway. Rescuing people was a hell of a lot easier when they weren't screaming and struggling to get loose.

"Go, Gabe," McKenna's urgent voice whispered behind him. "He'll be back any minute."

Gabe turned to glare at her. Hell, he didn't want to leave her to face Victor alone. "Come with me and we'll come back and get Kane together."

Her mouth lifted in a slight smile. "What's wrong with you, Maddox? You getting soft in your old age? Get out of here, before I have to kick you in the ass for trying to be a gentleman. I'll be fine. I know how to handle Victor."

Her eyes, dark and haunted, belied her brave words. Gabe didn't even want to speculate on how she planned to handle what was sure to be a violent confrontation with Victor.

But right now, Skye was his priority. Knowing he had no other choice, Gabe clamped his mouth shut against further protest, held Skye more securely in his arms, and stalked out the door.

McKenna allowed herself one second of regret as she watched Gabe place his wife in the backseat of his car. Just her luck. Gabe Maddox was the first man she'd been attracted to in years. One look at his face when he'd seen his wife lying on the bed had squelched any hope of anything coming of that attraction. Never had she seen such stark, absolute love. Unfortunately for both Skylar and Gabe, a look of denial had quickly followed. She could recognize denial faster than anything. It was her forte.

Not that Gabe had ever indicated he felt an ounce of attraction for McKenna. Most times when he looked at her, she expected a pat on her head. Maddox had a reputation for being overly protective of those he cared for. Which seemed odd since the woman he'd just had to rescue was a wife McKenna hadn't even known he had. That was a can of worms she needed to stay out of.

Relieved to see his taillights disappear around the corner, McKenna jumped into her car and went in the opposite direction. Victor would be returning any minute now.

Once he found out his prize trophy had escaped, she'd have a hell of a time calming him down. Victor wasn't one to forgive and forget. Even though it had been Stan and Lester's responsibility to watch their charge, they were dead and wouldn't be able to give the bastard what he would want. An outlet for his special kind of vengeance. When she returned, she'd have to pay a hefty price for this failed job.

Damned if she would die, especially by Victor's hand. Besides, Lucas Kane needed rescuing. She'd read about him. Knew what kind of man he was. A good one. She might pay a high price, but she would save one more before she and Victor had their final confrontation.

Rounding another corner, she parked herself in front of the building she'd left a few moments before. Victor's shouting could be heard all the way out in the street. She tensed in spite of her bravado. Pain wasn't a big thrill for her . . . but it had been a part of her life for so long, it had become commonplace.

Besides, she'd chosen this life. A punishment for an unforgivable act. She had nothing to whine about. At least she was alive. Those she had betrayed hadn't been so lucky.

The need to get Skye to a safe house was foremost in Gabe's mind. No telling how many people Victor had on his payroll. Once he realized his victim had been taken, he'd most likely have all of them on the lookout for her, roaming the streets and hotels.

Despite his knowledge that Skye was his main priority, leaving McKenna to Victor's wrath hadn't been easy. No one knew how old McKenna was, but he'd once seen her without the heavy makeup she insisted on caking on her face. She'd looked about sixteen. Gabe knew she was older than that, but he figured not a whole lot older.

As he maneuvered through the busy streets of Rio, dodging cyclists, taxis, and buses, he shot a quick glance back at Skye. She had changed a lot in the last eight years. Beneath the cuts and bruises on her face, he knew she was still beautiful. Maybe even more so. He'd seen her occasionally on television, but not on purpose. The few times he did, he quickly changed the channel. Seeing her always stirred up those gut-wrenching emotions he thought he'd successfully killed years ago.

His eyes on his surroundings, Gabe saw nothing to indicate they were being followed. He turned in to an alleyway, made two more sharp turns, and then stopped in front of a seedy-looking building—their hideout until it was safe to get Skye out of the country.

Gabe jumped out of the car, looked around again, and then pulled the back door open. Skye was still unconscious. He didn't know if it was from the drug she'd been given, the trauma she'd experienced, or both.

Lifting her into his arms, Gabe kicked the car door closed and then shoved open the door to the building. His teeth ground together; he ignored the knots developing in his stomach as he stalked into the elevator and pressed the button for the fourth floor. If he hadn't needed to get Skylar to safety as soon as possible, he'd have taken the stairs. Unfortunately, that wasn't an option. Gabe was a pragmatist. He did what he had to do. No matter how it churned his guts. And, of course, this being an old building, the elevator was ancient and as slow as molasses. Setting his shoulders straight and gritting his teeth, Gabe held Skye and endured.

Skylar felt as if she were floating. She opened heavy eyelids and looked up at the man above her, who was sweating profusely. Funny, he looked so much like Gabe . . . but not. And he looked so pale, almost sick.

Unable to keep her eyes opened any longer, she closed them and continued to dwell in that comfortable limbo between consciousness and dreaminess.

Her body jerked a bit and the sensation of floating ended. Too sleepy and content to try to wake up, she pressed her cheek against the hard chest. The harsh rasps of breath disturbed her. Why was he breathing like that?

She heard keys jingling. A door opened and then

closed. The warms arms disappeared and a cool, fresh-smelling pillow met her cheek. Skylar smiled.

"Skye, are you awake?"

Gabe's voice again. *Oh good, another Gabe dream.* She snuggled deeper into her pillow, enjoying the luxury of another dream. She was usually allowed only one a night. This extra one was a treat.

Hard hands shook her shoulders. "Skye, I need you to wake and talk to me."

"No," she muttered. "Don't want to."

She heard the thud of feet move away from her. Good. Now she would get back to her dream.

A cold, wet feeling hit her face. Someone was wiping at her face . . . she moved away from the sensation.

"Dammit, Skye. Wake up."

Skylar huffed in irritation. Apparently she had no choice but to confront this person and tell him to leave her alone. She only prayed her dream would be waiting for her when she slept again. Forcing her eyes open, she blinked her heavy lids. A face wavered in front of her. She brought her hands up to her eyes and rubbed them hard. The pain in her bruised eye brought reality crashing down around her. Opening her eyes again, she stared into the face that had haunted her dreams and caused endless nightmares for years. *No. It couldn't be.*

Her mouth frozen, shock and denial zoomed through her. She finally opened her mouth but only a gasping sound emerged. She was unable to say his name. If she said it, would he disappear?

"Don't look so terrified, Skye. You're safe now. I'm going to get you back home as soon as possible."

Skylar felt her head shaking in tiny, rapid movements. No, this couldn't be happening. This wasn't real. It was the drug that bastard had given her. It had to be.

A warm, calloused hand touched her face. "Everything's going to be all right."

Skylar no longer cared if it was a dream or not. Gabe was in front of her. If this was just a hallucination, pray God she never recovered. With a small sob, Skylar threw herself at Gabe. His hard arms caught and held her tight.

Sobs of agony, joy . . . the sheer wonder of the miracle that had been granted her burst from Skylar's throat. She cried against the hard, masculine chest. Breathed in the familiar scent of masculine sweat and musk. How could this be a dream or a hallucination? It seemed so real. He smelled just like Gabe. Yet, how could it be anything but a hallucination?

Forcing herself to face reality, Skylar pulled away and looked up at the man who obviously was either a fantasy or trying to pretend to be Gabriel Maddox.

"Feel better?" the fake Gabe asked.

Unable to stop herself, Skylar raised a trembling hand and touched his face again. Beard stubble stung the tips of her fingers as she caressed his jaw.

"Skye, you're scaring me. I know you can get drunk on a half of a glass of wine. Did the drug that bastard gave you knock you out that bad?"

How would anyone but Gabe know that she couldn't drink but a small amount of alcohol before she was completely tipsy?

She pulled her hand away and let her eyes roam over the face she'd just caressed. Older. Harsher. Tougher. But it was Gabe's face. *Gabe!*

Disbelief mingled with joy; Skylar threw her arms around him again for a whole new reason. It was Gabe. Dear God, Gabe! As she pressed kisses to his face and his neck, sobs of happiness built up and exploded. He was really here!

"I'm glad you're so happy to see me, honey. But we really need to talk."

The sardonic tone jerked her back to reality. Skylar pulled away so abruptly, she fell from the bed onto the floor.

"Damn. Are you all right?"

Ignoring the hand that reached for her, she pulled herself to her feet. Her head shaking once more in denial, Skylar pointed a trembling finger at him. Fury pounded through her but was consumed by a hurt so intense, so devastating, she knew if she didn't get away from him, she wouldn't be responsible for her actions.

Whirling, Skylar spotted a door across the room. Saw the edge of a sink. She ran toward the bathroom. Her legs wobbling like a newborn calf's, she staggered but couldn't stop. Anguished sobs were rising to a crescendo inside her and she needed to get away from him before they burst out again. Gabe would never, ever see that again. He'd lost the right to see anything other than her wrath and hatred.

Slamming the door behind her, Skylar collapsed onto the floor and covered her face with her hands. How could he? Sweet God, how could he have betrayed her like that?

Frozen with shock, Gabe watched a seemingly devastated Skye stumble out of the room. He was tempted to follow her but her look of pure hatred stopped him. What the hell had happened?

Sure, she was probably surprised to see him. They hadn't seen each other in over eight years. And it hadn't exactly been a good parting. Terminating a marriage by phone wouldn't be anyone's idea of a good ending. But the choice had been hers, not his. Admittedly, getting married had been a crazy, impulsive thing to do in the first place, and the marriage probably wouldn't have lasted more than a few weeks more. Nevertheless the call had been a shock.

Jeremiah James had at least tried to warn him. He had to give the bastard credit for that. Finding him on his doorstep instead of Skye had been a rude awakening . . . but that had only been the beginning. Out of the blue, or more like out of hell, Jeremiah had introduced himself and explained not only who he was, but who his incredibly famous daughter was also.

Since Gabe had been out of the country for over three years and had never read a gossip magazine in his life, he hadn't known that Skylar James was the only daughter of the famous Jeremiah James and heiress to a multi-billion-dollar fortune. Sometime model, all-the-time playgirl. Jeremiah had made sure he knew all the facts.

Why Skylar hadn't told him wasn't hard to figure out. She'd enjoyed playing house with a clueless country hick. Why she'd taken it as far as to marry him had puzzled him. Then, after all her little machinations had played out, Gabe realized that to Skylar James, little things like wedding vows and till-death-do-you-parts were meaningless words and phrases. Nothing more. The Jameses of this world were apparently above such things.

Gabe turned when he heard water running in the basin. Hopefully, she was about to come out and explain her bizarre behavior. Then they needed to discuss the information McKenna had given him. Another girl had been abducted?

The door opened and he was glad to see she'd regained her composure. However, the hollow, lost look in her eyes still bothered him. The bruises on her face stood out in stark relief against her pale skin. He knew she'd been through hell . . . but had something more happened to her? McKenna had told him about the bastard who'd tried to choke Skye—was that the reason she seemed so disturbed? Or had something else happened, maybe before Victor took her? Had she been sexually assaulted by the first bastards who snatched her?

Gabe stiffened his legs to keep from going to her. His natural instinct was to comfort someone so obviously upset. With Skye, it just wasn't that simple. He asked gruffly, "You all right?"

Instead of answering, she walked slowly toward him, her eyes locking with his. Without conscious will, Gabe took a step toward her, suddenly feeling as if eight years had never passed. Skye stopped within inches of him. His heart kicked up, pounding with what felt like anticipation. Gabe waited.

Giving him no warning, she drew her hand back and slapped him full across the face. "You bastard!"

His jaw stinging, Gabe grabbed the hand that was headed toward his face again. "Damn, woman, are you crazy?"

"Why, Gabe, why?"

"What the hell are you talking about?"

"You know exactly what I'm talking about."

The anger and bitterness he'd thought were long gone suddenly emerged full force inside him. "Actually, I don't, babe. I suggest you either explain yourself or back away before you get more than you bargained for."

As if she hadn't heard him, she moved closer. Her eyes were still dilated and he wondered if the drug was causing this bizarre behavior.

"Why didn't you just tell me you didn't want to be married to me? Wouldn't that have been easier?"

"I still have no idea what you're talking about."

"Damn you, Gabriel Maddox." Her voice, though cold and hard, shook with emotion. "If you didn't want to be married to me, why didn't you just tell me that instead of faking your death?"

Gabe dropped the arm he'd been holding and jerked back. "What the hell are you talking about?"

"Stop asking me that question, dammit. You fake your own death and then show up eight years later as if nothing ever happened. What the hell kind of man are you?"

"Skye, those drugs must've screwed up your brain or something. You'd better lie down."

Her look one of pure loathing, she turned around and started toward the front door.

"Where the hell do you think you're going?"

"Getting away from you."

Gabe was on her in a second, pulling her around to face him. "You little idiot. Victor's probably got his hounds out there sniffing every street. You're staying here until I can get you out of Brazil."

She glanced up at him, obviously startled. "I'm in Brazil?"

"Yeah. Rio to be exact."

"I didn't know . . . no one ever told me." She glanced around the room and then back at him. "Maybe you should tell me what's going on. And the truth this time, please."

Determined to get back to her ridiculous claim that he'd faked his own death to get out of their marriage, Gabe explained how her father had contacted LCR.

As if her legs were no longer able to hold her up, Skye dropped into the nearest chair. "So my father is the only one who knows about my abduction?"

"As far as we know."

"And you work for Last Chance Rescue?"

"Yes. You've heard of it?"

"Of course. Who hasn't? Did my father see you?"

"Yes, he was surprised."

"Of course he was surprised. He thought you were dead."

Gabe gritted his teeth. "We'll get back to that in a minute."

"Yes, we will. Until then, I need to know something. There's a young girl missing. Kendra Carson. I think she must have been abducted at the same place I was."

Gabe nodded. "McKenna said you were concerned about a young girl."

"McKenna?"

"The blond girl working with Victor. She's an LCR operative, working undercover."

Seeing her wince, he said, "What's wrong?"

"Now I feel guilty for knocking her out."

Gabe swallowed a surprised chuckle. "You knocked McKenna out? Hell, no wonder she looked so pissed."

Skylar shrugged. "I was trying to escape. She was in the way."

Gabe looked at Skye with newfound respect. Few people could get the jump on McKenna. She had the reputation of having eyes in the back of her head. He wasn't surprised that McKenna hadn't told him about the incident. The operative was also known for her pride in being able to see her opponent coming.

"Tell me about Kendra," Gabe said.

"She's twenty-one years old. From a wealthy family . . . not that they pay any attention to her. She sent me a message that she was interviewing for a modeling job. When I didn't hear from her, I checked with her boyfriend. He hadn't heard from her either and didn't give a damn. I went to the address in the ad. My bodyguard . . ."

She closed her eyes for a second and took a trembling breath. When she opened them, he saw pain. "Malcolm insisted on going in to check things out. He was only in the building for a couple of minutes before I saw him at the door. Then, someone made a running leap toward me and started pulling me to a car. At the same time, Malcolm ran toward me. They shot him . . . three times . . . once in the head." She swallowed hard and whispered, "There's no way he could have survived."

"Your father mentioned that no one had heard from you or your bodyguard."

Skylar nodded. "They claimed to have put his body where no one would ever find it."

Gabe didn't bother to try to lie to her. Hiding a body forever wasn't that hard to do. Malcolm most likely would never be found.

"Did he have a family?"

She shuddered out a sigh and shook her head. "No. His wife was killed in a car wreck a year or so after they married. They didn't have children." She swallowed. "I think I was the closest thing to a family he had."

"I'm sorry, Skye."

Shuddering out another breath, she straightened her shoulders. "We need to find Kendra. There's no telling what those bastards have done with her."

"I've already contacted LCR. They're assigning a couple of operatives to search for her."

Gabe watched the blood drain from her face as if everything was hitting her at once. "This is such a nightmare," she muttered, then covered her face with her hands and shook her head. "I can't believe all of this is happening."

Recognizing shock, along with the normal exhaustion after an adrenaline surge, he said, "Why don't you lie down for a while? I've got someone arranging safe passage for you. Till then, there's nothing we can do."

She rose and walked with a sad, weary gait toward the bed. Curling up on her side, she whispered something that would have broken his heart if he still had one to break. "I really believed you loved me." Her eyes fluttered closed and he saw her breath become even and shallow.

While he still had the willpower, Gabe turned away. Everything inside him wanted to lie down with her, hold her, and relive for just a few moments what they'd once had. But he couldn't act on that instinct. . . . Stupid, foolish, and crazy didn't even begin to describe what those actions would be. Besides, he had to figure out what she was talking about. She'd thought he was dead? Where the hell had that come from?

eight

Setting her chin with grim determination, McKenna ran into the building. Victor's booming, furious voice would soon attract more attention than they could afford.

Her expression one of surprise and concern, she shoved open the door and shouted, "What the hell happened?"

Victor whirled around, his arm swinging toward her. McKenna jumped back but not before he got in a glancing slug to her right eye. *Shit, that hurt.*

Blinking rapidly to avoid the natural tears that sprang to her eyes, McKenna focused on her role. "What the hell's the matter, V?"

His face purple with fury, Victor reached for her. McKenna jumped out of his way again. Damned if she'd make it that easy for him.

"Somebody stole the bitch."

"What?" Her eyes searched the room. The two men she and Gabe had left on the floor were still there . . . still not breathing. "Who would've done that?"

"You tell me." Victor's smooth, slimy voice didn't fool her. This would be the third victim he'd lost when she was conveniently not around. The man might be crazy mean; that didn't mean he was stupid.

She swung her hands out, all innocence. "I dumped Edmond at the morgue like you told me to. Just got back."

Victor's eyes roamed all over her. She knew what he saw. A smallish, not too bright woman with a half-ton of makeup on her face and short, bleached-blond hair. McKenna maintained her "I don't have the sense of a dung beetle" act with little difficulty. Victor would be quite surprised to know how high her IQ really was. She'd always maintained that it took a true genius to act as dumb as she did and get away with it.

"Get over here. Now."

His face still purple, veins bulged in his forehead. Having seen his uncontrollable anger before, McKenna knew she had two choices. There were only two ways to appease him. Take the beating from hell or the screwing from hell. Both would hurt, but she needed to be able to function after his punishment had passed. She had to go along with Victor until she found Lucas Kane. Then and only then would she be able to make him pay.

Closing down her mind for what lay ahead, McKenna moved closer. "Baby, I'm sorry I wasn't here." She rubbed her hand up and down his arm in a rough caress. "Let's go find her. Maybe she's still around."

"No. She's long gone. Their bodies are almost cold."

"But—"

Her head and back thudded as he pushed her against the wall. McKenna controlled the wince—seeing her hurting would only turn him on more. His hand encircled her throat and tightened. "If you hadn't killed Edmond, you would've been here. This never would have happened."

She knew how to play the game. Knew what he wanted. Reminding him that he'd been the one to order the killing wouldn't do anything but piss him off more. "You're right, baby, I'm sorry. Isn't there anything I can do to make it up to you?"

Keeping one hand around her neck, he slid the other one down to her crotch and squeezed hard, intentionally inflicting pain. "Oh, I think there might be something."

Torn between wanting to scream at how much he was hurting her and the even greater desire to kill the freak, she closed her eyes and moaned as if she loved what he was doing.

His mouth smashed down on hers and McKenna made her mind go blank. The only thing she needed to do was survive . . . just this one more time and then, she swore, after Lucas Kane was safe, she would make sure Victor paid for every vile thing he'd done to her and countless others.

Skylar snuggled up against the warm, hard body next to her. Another dream. They were coming more frequently now and seemed so much more real than before. At the sound of a soft snore, her eyes flew open. It wasn't a dream. Gabe was really here . . . he was alive.

She pulled away from him and sat up. The agonizing hurt she'd managed to suppress earlier returned full force. All these years she'd been grieving for a man who'd been alive and well. She'd been consumed with guilt for not seeing his emotional problems earlier. Had blamed herself for leaving him alone. Thought that if she'd stayed with him, he never would have killed himself.

And now here he was, lying beside her. He'd acted shocked at her words. Like she was going to believe anything he said. But why, after all these years, would he suddenly appear in her life to help her out? Was it just because he worked for Last Chance Rescue? She was a job? Nothing more? How ironic.

His breathing changed; he was waking up. She needed to be on her feet when that happened. Lying beside him like this, she felt vulnerable. Unable to handle the confrontation she was determined they have.

Throwing her legs over the side, she placed her feet on

the floor. Before she could stand, a hand wrapped around her waist and Gabe growled behind her, "Stay here."

"No, I need—"

"And I need this. Please, Skye. Just for a minute." She felt his hot breath at her back and then gasped as he lifted her blouse and nuzzled the small of her back, pressing a kiss against her skin. "Just for a minute." He pressed another soft kiss and then his tongue licked along her spine . . . a secret erogenous zone she hadn't known she had until Gabe had revealed it. A hot throbbing sensation and heated moisture pooled between her legs. That easy . . . she'd always been that easy for Gabe.

Her eyes closed at the sweetly erotic sensation of his scruffy beard on her skin. Even after all these years, he could still turn her on. Without permission, her body took control of her resistance and she leaned back against him.

Gabe pulled her down beside him. Before she could speak, work up any kind of protest, his mouth was on hers, hot and sexy, but oh so soft and tender.

Skylar groaned against his lips and, unable to stop herself, opened her mouth and let him in. He tasted wonderful. Better than she remembered. With another groan of surrender, she wrapped her arms around his shoulders and pulled him closer and deeper into the kiss.

This was the way it had always been for them. Within hours of meeting, they'd kissed. And though they hadn't made love until right before they married, they'd struggled to keep their hands off each other. Gabe's natural tendency to be a gentleman and her innocence had inhibited going all the way . . . but it had created some hot, steamy make-out sessions. And when they'd finally made love, it had been wild . . . explosive.

A desire that hot and potent was destined to die out. She should have known that.

Realizing if she didn't stop him now it would be too late for both of them, she pressed her hands against his shoulders.

He resisted briefly and then, as if he knew this had been a stupid thing to do, he pulled away with a heavy sigh.

Skylar rose up to get out of bed, but his arm stopped her. "No. I'll keep my hands to myself. Promise."

She shook her head and pushed him away. "I think we both need some distance." She stood and walked the few feet to the ragged, cloth-covered chair in the corner.

Sitting up, Gabe blew out a long breath and leaned against the headboard. "Okay. Out with it. Tell me why the hell you think I faked my death."

She raised her brows. "Uh, well . . . maybe because you did?"

"Hell, Skye. This isn't getting us anywhere. Tell me what happened."

Skylar ground her teeth. He wanted to dig that deep into the past, then fine. That's what she'd do. He was the shithead who'd betrayed her. She looked forward to his explanation. Not that there would be one she'd accept.

"I'm waiting, Skye."

"Don't call me Skye."

Black brows drew together in a furious frown. "Why the hell not?"

"Because I don't like people calling me Skye. I never have."

"You didn't object to it before."

"That was different."

"Why?"

"Because . . . you were . . . I thought . . ." She shook her head. "Never mind. Just don't call me that again."

"Fine. *Skylar,*" he said with sarcastic emphasis on her name. "Now, tell me why you think I faked my death."

In an effort to give a cool, unemotional account of those dark days of hell, she drew in a breath and straightened her spine. "I came back to the island from visiting my family. You'd left a note on the dresser." She repeated those hated words. " 'By the time you read this, I'll be gone.' You said you'd been filled with sadness, and though being with me had helped, you couldn't escape it completely. You said the darkness was closing in on you."

Skylar swallowed the lump in her throat. She never talked about that time with anyone anymore. Her family had tried to be sympathetic but deep down she knew they'd been more relieved than anything. Having her marry a stranger at the age of twenty hadn't been something they had approved of. Especially since the groom had no connections and no money.

"Skylar?"

Gabe's hard, cold voice jerked her back to the present. "I went looking for you." She swallowed again to rid herself of the thickness in her voice. "That's when I learned that you had rented a boat but hadn't returned. I rented another boat and we went looking for you. We found the boat . . . about a mile and a half from shore . . . you weren't on it. You'd left your wedding ring and another note on the driver's seat."

His voice concrete hard, he said, "What did that note say?"

Fighting the urge to scream at him that he knew damn well what it said, she recited the most hurtful part first, " 'I thought you could save me, but no one can.' " She swallowed again to clear her husky voice and continued, " 'I'm not the man you thought I was.' " Her eyes swam with tears. How ridiculous. She was once again grieving over that horrific note, and it had all been a lie.

Gabe's feet hit the floor with a loud thud. His expression was unfathomable as he stared across the room at her. Skylar held her breath. Even though she told herself there was nothing he could do to make up for faking his death, somehow she wanted him to have an explanation. Something other than he hadn't wanted to be married to her and just hadn't had the courage to tell her in person.

When he spoke, she barely recognized his voice. The tone was low, almost like the sound of a wild animal bent on attack . . . and it was full of fury. "Two days after you left, I opened the door to find your father on the doorstep. He told me who he was . . . who you were. First he tried to bribe me. Promised me money, a job . . . anything if I would just get the hell out of your life. When I refused, he showed me magazine after magazine, filled with photographs of your smiling, very famous face. He explained that you fell in love easily and fell out of love just as easily. That he was always fixing your messes and I was just one more."

Skylar sat in stunned silence. This was the best he could do? Blame it on her father? "That's the biggest pile of bullshit I've ever heard. You expect me to believe that my father convinced you to fake your death?"

Through clenched teeth, he gritted out the words, "For the last fucking time . . . I did not fake my death. I told your father to get the hell away from me. That you might be famous, but I knew you loved me."

No. That didn't make any sense. Still not believing him, she decided to play along. "Okay . . . say my father did show up, that still doesn't explain why you faked—" She stopped when she saw his look of furious denial. "Okay, fine. So why did you leave?"

If possible, he looked even angrier. "Because you called and told me you didn't want to be married to me anymore, Skye. That's why I left."

In an instant, Skylar was on her feet and marching

toward him. "You're crazy! I never did that." Stopping in front of him, her hands on her hips, she challenged, "Come up with a better lie, Gabe. That one doesn't fly."

"It's the truth. You apologized for not being able to break it off in person, but you couldn't come back. There was some sort of party or something you had to attend. You said you hoped I didn't hold any grudges and that—" She saw his jaw work furiously as if he could barely contain his rage.

"What?"

"You offered to send me money." He glared at her. "As you'll recall, I refused."

"I never called you, Gabe. I came back . . . found that note. Divers searched for days for your body."

Gabe shook his head. "I left you a letter—though not the one you referred to—along with the ring. Stupid really, but what you said on the phone shocked me so much, I barely said anything at all to you. I gave it to the manager at the resort. He promised to forward it to you. And then I left."

Skylar could feel her head shaking, but her body was so numb, she had no control to make the shaking stop. What he said had to be a lie. But she saw in his eyes . . . he was telling the truth. But who would do this? Who would create such an elaborate ploy to keep them apart?

Apparently seeing the question in her face, he gave an answer she absolutely could not accept.

"Your father," Gabe said.

"No. He wouldn't do anything like that. He wouldn't."

"Did you know he was coming to the island?"

"No." Then, realizing she needed to remember every moment to prove her father had nothing to do with such a hideous cover-up, she paced back and forth in front of him as she recited what she remembered. "I went home to tell him I'd gotten married. He wasn't happy about it.

I knew he wouldn't be . . . he thought I was too young to know my own heart. But he said he would reserve judgment until he met you."

She waved a hand as she explained. "I knew it would take some time for him to accept it. He's always been so protective. I had planned to come back to the island after I talked to him, but my mom called and asked to see me, so I went. I'm not as close to my mom as I am my dad—that's the biggest reason I went to see him first, instead of her. I wanted to get back to you as soon as I could, but I changed my mind when she called. If there was one area my mom still had influence over him with, it was about me. I figured if I could convince her how happy I was, she would convince him."

"Tell me about the phone call, Skye."

"I didn't call you, Gabe. At any time. I knew if I did, I'd start crying. I was so emotional during that time and I didn't want to upset you. I wanted to get my family on board before I came back to you. I still hadn't told you who I was. I mean . . . well, you know what I mean."

"Then who called me?"

"I have no idea. I—" She halted abruptly at a hideous thought.

"What?"

The memory of girlish laughter skittered in her mind. Her cousin Lisa had always mimicked her. They were close in age and spent every summer together as kids. Lisa had studied acting and prided herself on being able to mimic just about anyone. She did Skylar's voice perfectly.

"My cousin Lisa used to mimic me . . . can sound just like me."

"So your father had her call, pretend to be you, and break off the marriage."

She still wasn't ready to believe that the father she'd

known, loved, and trusted all these years had done something so incredibly cruel. After he'd seen what she'd gone through? What Gabe's suicide had done to her? How could he have not told her the truth?

Skylar took a bracing breath. She could only deal with the here and now. She needed an answer to a very important question. "Why didn't you ever try to get in touch with me? My God, Gabe. We're still married."

"Hell, Skye, I tried, numerous times, with little luck. Every letter I sent you was sent back."

"I never got one letter."

"Your dad didn't want you to be married, so he apparently kept them from you."

"Just because he didn't want me to be married didn't mean I wasn't."

"I sent divorce papers more than once. They were returned, too, with no explanation. After a while, I gave up. Since I never planned to marry again, I figured if you were interested in a divorce you could find me."

Despite the knowledge that he had every reason to believe she had wanted to end the marriage, Skylar couldn't deny the deep hurt. All it had taken was one lousy phone call from someone who sounded like her and he'd been gone.

Sinking down on the chair again, she wrapped her arms around herself. "I still can't believe my father would do anything like this. What if I had wanted to get married again? I thought I was a widow."

"You'll have to ask the bastard when you see him again." He stood and grabbed his keys. "And I plan to be right there with you." He stalked to the door. "I've got some things to take care of. There's food in the minifridge if you're hungry. Don't answer the door for anyone. There's a gun on the nightstand. You know how to use it?"

He barely waited for her small nod before he added, “Use it if anyone tries to break in. Understand?”

In too much shock to do anything but nod again, she watched Gabe go through the door and heard the click of the lock.

And in her mind, two things whirled around and around like a spinning top. *Gabe was alive! They were still married!*

nine

Gabe closed the door to the apartment and then slumped against it. A wave of killing fury, like a volcanic eruption, surged through him. Gritting his teeth, he fought as it tried to control and devour him. He was known for his focus while on a mission, but it took every bit of willpower he possessed not to throw Skylar on a plane and go to New York to beat the shit out of Jeremiah James. The man's prejudice and arrogance had almost destroyed two lives.

And dammit, how stupid he'd been. How fucking stupid he'd been.

Pulling in rasping breaths, Gabe knew he had to get out of the building into open air. His claustrophobia didn't usually hit him unless he'd been indoors too long, but the crushing pressure in his chest told him if he didn't get outside soon, implosion was imminent.

His long legs eating the distance like a cheetah's, Gabe ran down four flights of stairs at a record-breaking speed. Shoving open the door to the outside, he drew in deep breaths. Air, thick and heavy with humidity and promising a thunderstorm, was like a healing nectar coating his tortured lungs.

The vibration of his cellphone in his pocket reminded him that other issues were more important than his need for revenge. Once Skylar was safe and the creeps who'd kidnapped her stopped, he'd deal with his bastard of a father-in-law. For now, his priorities were set.

"Yeah?" he answered.

"Mr. Grump?"

Despite his anger, Gabe couldn't prevent a small quirk to his lips at Angela's favorite name for him.

"Yes, this is Mr. Grump."

"Sir, there will be a slight delay in your package pickup. We won't be able to arrange for delivery until Monday."

Knowing it'd do no good to question why Skylar couldn't be flown out until four days from now, Gabe didn't bother to argue. The heat must be high for it to take so long to get her out.

"Please bring the package to your usual slot. Also, please be sure to wrap the package appropriately. And be prepared to show the appropriate documentation."

Meaning disguise Skye beyond any possible recognition, be prepared with every document imaginable, and be ready if sugar went to shit.

"Sounds good, Peaches."

He heard a snicker as she ended the call.

Gabe's eyes swept the area as he pressed a button for another incoming call.

"You okay?"

Cole Mathison's gruff words broke LCR protocol, telling Gabe that he needed to get his act together. Standing on a street corner and staring into space might look normal in some neighborhoods, but not here. Attracting attention of any kind was a risk he couldn't take.

"Yeah. Fine. Delivery's set for Monday."

"Need anything?"

"No. I'll handle the details."

"I'll be around," Cole answered, and ended the call.

Gabe didn't bother to look for the man, but he knew he was there. Hard to disappear when you're six-five and weigh about two-thirty. Somehow Cole could do it. And there was no one else he'd rather have watching his back than Cole.

Taking one last breath of open air, Gabe turned around and headed back inside. He felt only marginally less murderous than he had before. His only priority right now had to be getting Skye out of Brazil. Then, when this job was over, he would hunt Jeremiah James down and beat the ever-living shit out of him.

Skylar wrapped the towel around her. After Gabe left, she'd had the intense desire to get clean. It had been more than a week since she'd taken a bath and those men had put their filthy hands on her. Now her body tingled and felt almost raw from the scrubbing, but she had to get their prints off of her.

Exhaustion from her ordeal, worry for Kendra, and the shock of seeing Gabe alive were taking their toll. Her limbs felt as if every bit of blood had been drained from her body. If she didn't get into a chair soon, Gabe would find her on the floor when he returned.

But first, she had to find some clothes to put on. She might technically still be married to the man, but he was now a stranger to her. Having him see her without clothes wasn't something she could deal with right now.

She pulled open the closet door and released a ragged breath. Nothing but hangers. Turning, she headed for the dresser against the wall. If nothing else, maybe Gabe had some underwear she could put on until he could find something suitable for her.

She pulled the drawer open and found a pair of jeans. Her size! She pulled them out and then her heart almost stopped at the sight of what was underneath the jeans.

With trembling fingers, she withdrew the white cotton T-shirt with the big colorful fish on the front. It had been her favorite shirt to wear on the island.

And even after all these years, the sweet memory lingered.

Eight years ago
Kalamina Island, South Pacific

Sitting on the sandy beach, the early morning sun blazing down on her, Skylar gave a deep, appreciative sigh. Had she ever felt so alive? So free? She glanced at the man lying beside her. Or so much in love? Unable to be next to him and not touch him, she leaned over and pressed a kiss to Gabe's ear. "Let's go to the other side of the island today and pretend we're tourists."

"Should be easy . . . we *are* tourists." His face buried in his towel, the muffled, sleepy tone of his voice told Skylar he was almost asleep.

"No we're not. You've been here three weeks. I've been here almost two weeks. We're practically natives."

Gabe rolled over on his back and looked at her. Despite the heat of the sun searing her skin, Skylar couldn't help but shiver. Those midnight blue eyes just did it for her. Every time. When he turned them on her, she felt as if her insides were turning to mush. And he knew it, too. A glimmer of satisfaction entered his expression when he saw her shiver.

"You want me to kiss you, don't you?"

That gravelly, sexy voice did it for her, too. Skylar could only nod her head.

"Then come down here."

Resisting the urge to throw herself on him, she slowly leaned down. When she was inches from him, he pulled her to meet him and pressed a quick, very unromantic kiss to her mouth. Then he pushed her away and sat up.

"If we're going to look like tourists, we have to dress like tourists." He stood and held out his hand. "Come with me. I have the perfect outfit in mind for you."

Ten minutes later, they left the gift shop with Skylar giggling like a ten-year-old girl. Gabe had bought her the silliest-looking T-shirt, with a bright, colorful fish on the front. And he'd bought himself a wide-brimmed straw hat and thick sunglasses with a plastic nose attachment. Every time she looked at him, she burst into laughter.

"I see you've found your clothes."

Gabe's deep voice jerked her from the past. Skylar whirled around with a gasp. The anger she'd seen in his eyes was gone, and while that should have made her feel better, it didn't. Now there was no emotion at all. The look reminded her of when they'd first met. Each day they'd been together, it had faded just a little more. But this grim, hollow expression had a granite-like permanency.

Keeping a tight grip on the towel wrapped around her, she held up the fish T-shirt. "You kept my shirt."

He shrugged. "After you called me and broke it off . . . or after someone called me and broke it off, I left. Since you said you weren't coming back, I figured that meant you didn't care what happened to your clothes."

She clutched the shirt to her chest. "I left the island . . . after you . . . after I . . ." Swallowing hard, she closed her eyes briefly. *Don't think about it.* "I didn't ask what happened to my clothes—or yours—for a long time. When I did ask, I was told they were donated."

If possible, his face went harder, more remote.

"Why keep my shirt . . . after all this time?"

Another shrug, this one with a sarcastic edge. "A reminder of how stupid I'd been."

The words shouldn't hurt. It had been eight years. They were different people now. Didn't love each other anymore. And maybe he never had loved her.

Unable to respond with any kind of appropriate zinger, she nodded and said, "I'll go change and then I guess we need to talk."

His eyes swept down her body and for the life of her she couldn't control that damn shiver that only he had ever been able to create.

Before he could comment on it, she took the shirt and jeans, marched into the bathroom, closed and locked the door. Damned if she was going to give him the satisfaction of knowing that even after all these years he could still turn her on with one small look.

His heart pounding like he'd been running sprints, Gabe watched Skye disappear into the bathroom. He knew that look. Hell, how many times had he fantasized about it over the years? When her eyes turned the blue of a sky right before a storm, and her breathing increased to tiny, sexy pants, she wanted one thing. Skye had wanted to kiss him. And damned if he didn't want that, too.

That one taste he'd had earlier hadn't satisfied the craving. A stupid move he'd told himself not to make . . . a weakness he couldn't afford to repeat again. The ache had only increased. Hell, he knew better than anyone, nothing could satisfy his craving for Skye. Even back then, the moment he'd had her, he'd wanted her again, and then again.

Gritting his teeth, Gabe ignored the hard-on from hell and cursed inwardly. Wouldn't be the first time he'd had to ignore what he couldn't have. The phone on the bedside table rang, effectively dousing a need he could do nothing about.

He grabbed the phone. "Yeah?"

"Get someplace secure. We need to talk." Noah's hard voice slammed Gabe back to reality. Something was very wrong if Noah was calling him here.

"Five minutes."

Gabe hung up the phone and turned around. Skye stood at the door. He ignored how the blue in the colorful fish on the shirt enhanced the color of her eyes. It had been the reason he'd bought the shirt for her. That and the way it emphasized her beautiful breasts. His eyes lowered to the luscious mounds and that familiar gut punch slammed into him again. *Shit.*

"I've got to go out for a few minutes. Someone's watching the building. You're safe, but know where the gun is and use it if you have to."

Her eyes were wide with the knowledge of what he'd been thinking. She knew what turned him on, how he liked it, what he liked. Swallowing another curse, Gabe stalked out the door again.

Three minutes later, he was in the back of a greasy, run-down restaurant dialing Noah. Valenti's had been a friend to LCR for years. This was one of the few locations in South America that Gabe knew was secure.

"What's up?" he asked as soon as Noah answered.

"We started searching for Kendra Carson, Skylar's friend. Looks like we've got bigger problems than just one missing girl."

"What do you mean?"

"Ten girls from various states have disappeared over the last year, six in just the last two months. The modeling scam was a new one, but all the disappearances sound too similar not to be related. All were interviewing for some kind of seemingly glamorous job. All between the ages of seventeen and twenty-five."

"A ring?"

"That's my guess. Most of the girls are from broken families. All have been runaways."

"Vulnerable," Gabe muttered.

"Yeah . . . and impressionable."

"You want me to work it?"

"Yes. You and Cole. Bring Skylar here before you take her home. Maybe she can shed some light on Kendra that'll help us."

Gabe refused to acknowledge the relief that Skye would be with him for a few more days. He was setting himself up for another stupid disappointment. One he was pretty damn sure he wouldn't recover from this time.

He forced his mind to the business at hand. "You still in Florida?"

"Yes."

"We'll be there on Monday."

"Sounds good. In the meantime, get what you can from Skylar. We'll put the rest of the pieces together when you get here."

Gabe hung up the phone and headed back to the place he'd stashed Skye. So what if he spent another few days with her? It wouldn't change the outcome. When they returned to New York, they'd both get a chance to confront her father. Then she'd go see her lawyer and finally they could both put the past to rest.

It was what he wanted. And he was sure it was what Skye wanted, too. He ignored the tightening of his chest at that thought. A few days ago, he'd been prepared to find her and end their marriage. This situation only made it easier. So why the hell did he suddenly feel as though he'd just jumped off a cliff and all he saw below him was a gaping black hole of nothingness?

* * *

McKenna rolled out from under Victor's naked, sweating body. She had to get away from him before she barfed all over both of them.

"Where're you going?"

"Bathroom."

"Bring me a beer when you come back."

Without answering, she scooped her clothes off the floor and walked on shaky legs to the bathroom. Turning on the shower to the hottest setting, McKenna almost threw herself into the shower. Why this experience today bothered her more than other times she couldn't say. She only knew that this man would never touch her again. Using her body as a sexual weapon wasn't something she did on a regular basis, but if she deemed it necessary to save a life, she did it. But never again with this bastard.

Hot water poured down on McKenna as she scrubbed every place Victor had touched. She ignored the sting of soap on the bite marks and scratches. Sanitizing herself was worth the pain it caused. Besides, she'd had worse.

She couldn't stay in the shower as long as she would've liked. Not only had she not immediately returned with his beer; once was never enough for Victor. Which was one of the reasons she hadn't carried the beer to him. He would have kept at her for hours—she'd learned that the hard way.

She jerked as Victor pounded on the door. "Hey, bitch. I didn't tell you that you could come in here and take a shower. And what's the idea of locking the door? I gotta piss."

"I'm coming." As her mind scrambled for the best way to handle the next few minutes, she grabbed a towel and wrapped it around her soaking body. If Victor saw her naked, saw the bruises and bites he'd marked her with, that would turn him on faster than anything. Another mistake she'd never repeat.

She unlocked the door and stood back as he pushed it open. Giving her a glare, he went to the toilet, kicked the lid up with his foot, and urinated.

McKenna took advantage of those few seconds to dry as much of her body as she could, then quickly pulled her jeans and T-shirt over her still-damp body. Bra and panties would just have to wait.

"What're you doing?"

She whirled around to see a naked Victor caressing his hardening penis. Just as she figured, he was getting ready for round two. Damned if that appendage would get near her ever again.

"I figured you needed to get back to your other job."

Cold eyes assessed her. McKenna kept the "too stupid to live" expression on her face. It always served her well with these kinds of bastards.

Finally he nodded. "You're right. Can't afford to lose this one. I'm going to make another little movie. I'll have to double the ransom to make up for losing the bitch. I paid a shitload of money for her and got nothing."

His mind lightning quick, Victor had no problem jumping from one evil thought to another. The malevolent grin on his thin lips said it all. "The bastard's got the most proper British accent you ever heard, on top of having balls of steel. He's pissed me off more than once. I'm going to film cutting his tongue out and send it along with the tape. That'll earn me some extra dough . . . and it'll keep the bastard quiet, too."

McKenna swallowed the nausea that surged at the image in her mind. The thought of that happening to anyone was bad enough. But she'd seen Lucas Kane on television. Tall, golden perfection. And he had the most beautifully cultured British accent. The first time she'd heard him speak, she'd felt such odd tingles all over her. Victor's words only made her determination greater. She would make sure he never got a chance to harm him.

Running a towel through her short, damp hair, she giggled like the insane idiot he thought her. "I took Edmond's knife before those mortuary people got him. It's got the sweetest edge . . . perfect for slicing off a tongue."

Victor grinned his approval as he continued to stroke himself. "That's why we make such a good team, baby. You are one fucked-up bitch."

Funny, that was the first time she'd ever agreed with Victor.

A hand on her shoulder jerked Skylar from a restless sleep. She blinked up at the man looking down at her. It was still such a surreal thing to see Gabe's face. She was incredibly grateful that he was alive, but the awfulness of what had happened tempered that joy. Her father . . . dear sweet heaven . . . her father had betrayed her in the worst way.

"Skye? You okay?"

"I'm fine. Just a bit groggy. What's up?"

"You feel up to talking?"

Wariness hit her. "About Kendra?"

"Yes . . . and about your abduction. I need to know everything you remember."

She sat up and stretched out the stiffness. "Okay. What do you need to know?"

"You said they knocked you out when they took you. What do you remember from after you woke?"

She rubbed her forehead and tried to recall. The drugs she'd been given blurred a lot of those memories. "I remember being cold. I thought it was dark . . . but I think that's because I had a hood over my head."

"How many of them were there?"

"Two . . . at the beginning. One grabbed me around my neck. I managed to scream and kick behind me. Then, just as Malcolm ran out of the building, he was shot. The man who held me had both of his hands on me, so he couldn't have shot a gun. The other man did it."

"What happened after Malcolm was shot?"

"That's when they knocked me out."

"And then, once you woke up?"

She remembered their voices and her terror. "Three . . . all males . . . two were young . . . early twenties. The other one was late thirties . . . early forties."

"Do you remember what they looked like?"

She squeezed her eyes shut. "One was tall and skinny, with long blond hair and glasses. Early twenties. He had a small goatee, and a really prominent Adam's apple that jerked a lot when he talked. His name was Joey." Excitement zoomed through her as she realized she'd remembered everything. She knew she'd wanted to commit their faces to memory but wasn't sure she'd been able to.

"That's great. What about the other two?"

"There was a guy named Aaron. He was about five-ten. Short, dark brown hair, hazel eyes . . . maybe about twenty-two. Clean-cut. I remember thinking he looked like an average, normal guy."

"What about the third man?"

She shivered. The other two had scared her, but the third man had terrified her. "They called him Styx. He was the older one. Almost completely bald. Had a large gut and yellowed teeth, except for a big gold tooth on the upper front."

"Hell, how long did you see these guys?"

She shrugged, feeling an odd sort of victory at being able to give such apt descriptions. "A couple of minutes here and there."

"Anything else?"

Her eyes shut tighter as she tried to force another memory. Blowing out a disappointed breath, she opened her eyes and shook her head. "That's all."

The admiration gleaming in Gabe's eyes sent a thrill through her, easing her somehow.

"That was damn good. With those detailed descriptions, we should be able to get a good composite. Anything else you remember?"

She swallowed hard. "They enjoy their work. The two of them, Aaron and Joey, threw me around the room, playing with me. You know, kind of like a cat plays with its prey?"

Gabe's eyes went flinty hard and his jaw worked, but all he said was "What else?"

"They kept mentioning 'the man.' "

" 'The man'?"

"Yes. Apparently the man who was in charge. They said he wouldn't like that they'd grabbed someone so well known." Her eyes widened as a memory hit her.

"What, Skye?"

"One of them . . . it was Styx . . . he said that with 'the man's' connections, he might even know me."

"He used those exact words?"

Skylar nodded. "I didn't really pay attention to it then, but do you think it means something?"

Gabe shrugged. "Wouldn't be the first time a respectable citizen was involved in something like this."

Skylar shivered at the thought of actually knowing someone who could be involved in such a disgusting trade.

"What else . . . did you ask them any questions?"

"I asked about Kendra. They didn't want to tell me anything. Finally one of them said that she'd already been spoken for . . . that she had it good. Better than most."

"They said those words—she was already spoken for? And had it better than most?"

She jerked her head up. "Yes. Why? Do you think that means something?"

His expression revealed nothing. "Maybe. What else do you remember?"

"They were all excited about who I was. Joey wanted to—" She swallowed hard. "Joey said he wanted to fuck me and kill me. Aaron wanted to wait and see what Styx said first. Styx was the one who knew someone they could sell me to."

"What else?"

She was noticing something interesting about Gabe. The angrier he became, the quieter his voice was. Though rage glinted in his eyes, his words had become softer, more controlled.

"Styx hit me . . . knocked me out. The next thing I knew, I was lying on a bed and that horrid man named Victor was taking pictures of me."

"Was it Styx that caused those bruises all over your face and gave you the black eye?"

"No." She shivered at the memory of how she'd received each bruise. "I knocked Joey down . . . rammed my head into his stomach. It made him mad. As punishment, Aaron held me up while Joey hit me."

Gabe's jaw clenched, but he said softly, "What else?"

"They'd put tape on my mouth and were throwing me around. I started to vomit and began to choke. They pulled the tape from my mouth and it went all over Joey."

Skylar stopped when she saw the anger in Gabe's eyes increase tenfold.

"Go on, Skye."

She shrugged. "They threw me in the corner, kicked me a couple of times."

"And?"

"And then Styx hit me . . . said he'd always wanted to hit a rich bitch." Without realizing it, she was almost lying down again. The retelling of her abduction had taken a toll she hadn't expected. Exhaustion slammed in on her. "That's all I remember."

Gabe's face was a mixture of controlled emotions she was too tired to fathom. Her eyes fluttered as she tried to blink back exhaustion.

With the old gentleness that she remembered so well, Gabe pushed her all the way down to her pillow and whispered, "Sleep, Skye."

Skylar closed her eyes and felt a soft kiss on her forehead. She told herself she was probably dreaming, but she didn't care. Gabe was here, and for the first time in eight years, she felt whole.

Gabe made it out to the street again without shouting with rage. Seeing Skye's horror through her eyes made him want to find the bastards and beat every one of them to death.

After several controlled breaths, he pulled his cell out and called Cole.

"Make a call for me. Sounds like her friend might have been targeted from the beginning. Also, the main man might be wealthy and well connected. Maybe from her neck of the woods."

"Will do. You okay?"

"Fine," Gabe lied.

Cole snorted. "Yeah. Sure."

"I will be once we find the bastards."

"I'll make the call. See you on Monday."

Gabe closed the phone and looked out at the busy milling streets of the giant city. This was one of the few large cities he didn't mind spending extra time in. Even though there was plenty of poverty and sadness, the people were always friendly and filled with the joy of being alive. He admired their ability to find happiness in the simple things.

Today none of that joy penetrated the coldness of his thoughts. Seeing Skye again had reopened some old wounds he'd thought long healed. And it had reignited feelings he'd thought were smothered years ago.

Not that any of that mattered. It couldn't matter. He wouldn't let it matter.

Pulling in one last deep breath, Gabe turned to go back inside. By the time he returned Skye to New York, he was sure he would have convinced himself that these feelings were just an illusion. He ignored the little gremlin inside his head that laughingly taunted him with *Yeah, right*.

ten

Three days later

"Skye, it's time to go."

Skylar jerked awake and sat up in bed. "Okay."

Her bleary eyes gazed around the room she'd been incarcerated in for the last few days. She wouldn't miss it, that was for sure. She'd been by herself ninety percent of the time. Where Gabe went, and what he did, was a mystery.

At first she'd thought he hadn't wanted to be near her so he'd gone somewhere else to sleep. But she didn't think so. He may well not have wanted to be near her, but he wasn't getting sleep somewhere else. The dark shadows under his eyes and the paleness of his face beneath his tan proved that. But for some reason, he couldn't stay for more than a few minutes at a time in this room. When he was here, he paced constantly. She knew his dislike of enclosed spaces had something to do with it, but this seemed to be much worse. Had his condition worsened over the years?

"I brought you some coffee, a roll, and some fruit. Eat it, because our transportation is not as deluxe as what you're used to. No first-class food service or free drinks. You'll actually be treated like a regular person, not a princess."

This wasn't the first time he'd made a snide remark

about her wealth. Though the remarks stung, they also grounded her. This was exactly the attitude she'd expected years ago when they'd first met. One of the biggest reasons she hadn't told him who she was. She had wanted to be seen as just another young girl on vacation. Having him see her as nothing more than that had given her a freedom she'd never experienced. It had also created a deception she sorely regretted.

Unwilling to get into an argument neither of them would win, she took the coffee from the bedside table and headed to the bathroom. No use trying to defend herself against his remarks. He was right. When was the last time she'd flown like a normal person? Of course, she really couldn't fly like a normal person because of the media frenzy that always surrounded her, but what he said was true. She was used to the best.

Closing the door, Skylar sipped her coffee and proceeded to get ready for what lay ahead. Gabe had given her few details about who they thought had Kendra. But she was glad he didn't just plan to send her back home without at least letting her try to help in any way she could. He'd told her they were going to Florida to meet with Noah McCall. She just hoped she could find a way to help more.

Yesterday she'd made the dreadful mistake of offering LCR a large reward to find Kendra. That hadn't gone over well with Gabe. The money hadn't been offered to him personally, but with his hang-up about her wealth, he'd been the wrong person to say it to.

When she met Noah McCall, she planned to offer what help she could, including money. And if Gabe didn't like it . . . that was his problem, not hers.

Gabe glanced over at Skye in the seat next to him. When he'd told her their accommodations wouldn't be what she was used to, he wondered if she knew how right he was. Even though she wore a black wig and sunglasses and he'd provided her some stage makeup to add some fullness to her face, he wasn't willing to take chances. So here they sat in what could be called an airplane only in the broadest sense of the word—it had an engine, propeller, two wings, and a few ratty seats. Thankfully, it would take only a couple of hours to get them to São Paulo. Then they'd trade for a more accommodating ride.

"Are you all right?" Skye's soft, concerned voice pulled him away from the misery he always suffered from. Stupid to think she wouldn't notice how sweat beaded on his face, his breath rasped from his tight chest, and he continually swallowed to abate the nausea rising to his throat.

"Yeah. Fine." He shot her a look. "You?"

He hadn't intentionally sounded condescending, but he couldn't blame her for flinching. Hell, in the four days since he'd rescued her, he'd done nothing other than try to avoid or demean her when she'd been close. It was a wonder she hadn't slapped him upside the head half a dozen times. It was no less than he deserved.

His only defense—and a piss-poor one at that—was he literally couldn't be around her and act naturally. If he went on those natural instincts, then he'd kiss her until they both passed out from pleasure. It had been eight years. Eight cold, damn lonely years.

His cellphone vibrated. Gabe grabbed it, eager to think about anything other than this crazy desire that could never be met. "Yeah?"

McCall's voice growled back, "Kane is safe. He's already back home."

"And McKenna?"

"She's alive."

Gabe closed his eyes in regret. How he hated those grim words. Yes, any time an LCR operative was successful in rescuing a victim and managed to stay alive in the process was a good thing. But the term "alive" meant something more. It meant there had been a cost. If it had been a clean rescue, without cost to the operative, Noah would have answered with "She's good."

"Alive" meant still breathing but hurting . . . and not necessarily hurting in the physical sense.

"She take off?" Gabe asked.

"Yeah. Not sure we'll see her for a while."

For some reason, maybe because the pain he saw in McKenna's eyes was a reflection of his own, he always felt a bit more protective of her than he did of most LCR employees. She was young . . . probably about the age he was when he met Skye.

"Victor taken care of?"

"Permanently."

Noah's grim voice held a tinge of satisfaction. A satisfaction Gabe shared. Still, there was a downside. Despite the fact that he was glad that the bastard who'd dared touch Skye was no longer living, McKenna had no doubt done the deed. That was never easy, no matter how lowlife the bastard had been.

"We should be there sometime early morning," Gabe said.

"You don't want to get a room or take Skylar to your house . . . let her relax a day before bringing her in?"

Skylar in his house? *Hell no*. Once she left, he'd never get her out of his mind. Out of his house. He'd have to move and it'd taken years to find a place he actually liked living.

"No. We'll head to the office as soon as we land."

"See you then."

Gabe hung up the phone and glanced over at Skye,

who was pretending to stare out the window, even though he knew she'd heard every word he'd said.

She turned to look at him. Figuring she was about to ask him about his phone call, he was caught off guard with her question.

"When are we going to talk about the gorilla in the room?"

She didn't have to explain what she meant. They'd yet to address the fact that they were still married. Of course, he'd known that for years. She had just learned about it.

"What's there to talk about?"

"We're still married, Gabe."

"I realize that, Skye. Known it for a long time."

Her eyes flickered with hurt. Yeah, she knew he was a prick, but seeing her hurt tore at him. He'd much rather have her spitting fire at him. Pissing her off would accomplish that. "What's the matter? You worried some of your society friends are going to find out you're married to a former coal miner? Too bad, princess. We've got a young girl to find. That's our priority. If the cat gets out of the bag, you can always say I was one of your charity cases."

Her eyes narrowed into an icy glare. "I am sick of your thinly veiled innuendos about my wealth. I know exactly what the priorities are. You, however, seem to be able to pick and choose yours whenever the mood hits you."

"What the hell's that supposed to mean?"

She stood. "You figure it out . . . you're so damned smart. I'm going to the ladies' room."

Skylar stalked toward the tiny closet masquerading as a minuscule bathroom. She'd already visited it twice. She didn't have a choice. If she stayed sitting beside Gabe, she'd find something heavy and exceedingly lethal to hit him with. How in the hell could she ever have thought she loved him? He was such a jerk.

The tiny mirror attached to the wall showed a distorted image of her face. The blur was from the tears filling her eyes. Dammit, she hated to cry. The makeup Gabe had made her put on would run and she'd look even more ridiculous. Not that it mattered. The only man she cared about could barely even stand the sight of her.

How different things were now. They had both changed so much. Not only in looks, but in attitudes. Eight years ago, Gabe had been such a gentleman. Though he'd talked little of his childhood, she always figured his father and stepmother must have been exceptional at instilling good manners in him. He'd treated her with respect; had been wonderfully kind. And he'd been so gentle. The first time they'd made love had been her first time. It had been somewhat awkward . . . and absolutely beautiful. He'd been so sweet. So loving. She'd loved him before they made love. And had loved him a thousand times more after.

"Skye?"

Skylar jumped as Gabe called her name through the thin door.

"Yes?"

"You okay?"

"Yes, I'll be out in a minute."

Without asking permission, Gabe pushed the door open. Damn door didn't even have a lock.

Skylar turned away from him and snapped, "I said I'll be out in a minute."

Gentle hands landed on her shoulders as he turned her around. Skylar kept her eyes focused on his broad chest. She would not let him see how much he'd hurt her. He would think she still cared. She didn't.

"I'm sorry, sweetheart. I've been behaving like a bear with a sore paw. You've been through hell and I'm not making it any better."

Oh hell. Now why did he have to go and be nice? Sobs built up and suddenly she couldn't hold them back.

Muttering another apology, Gabe pulled her against his chest. Skylar buried her face against him and let go. She cried for so many things. Kendra. Malcolm. The trauma she'd gone through. Her father's cruel betrayal. And Gabe . . . what they had lost . . . what no longer existed.

Gabe held her for several more seconds and then, when she felt him about to pull away, she pulled away first. "Sorry about that. It's just been a few rough days."

He stared down at her for the longest time, and if his face hadn't looked so much older and harder, she could almost believe that it was years ago. His eyes held the old tenderness. In the next second, the ice-cold look returned. And with it, harsh reality.

"We should be landing soon. You should go back to your seat till we do."

Skylar nodded. Had she imagined those few tender seconds? Wishful thinking that somewhere inside that grim exterior the young, idealistic Gabe still lived? His cool, watchful eyes confirmed her fears. The man she'd fallen in love with no longer existed. He might not have died in the physical sense as she had thought, but the man she had married was dead.

Holding her arms stiff at her sides, careful to keep from touching him, Skylar walked past him and back to her seat.

Kendra sat on the bed, shivering with shock and cold. How long had she been here? Days? Weeks? She'd lost count.

They'd pumped some kind of drug into her again and

taken her from the boat. The other girls . . . where were they? She had gotten to know them. Had learned their names, ages, how they were abducted. It had all been a ruse. Every one of them had been snared in a similar fashion. How incredibly stupid they'd been. What had terrified her most, and what she hadn't told them, was one common bond they all shared. They had all been runaways. Had been in trouble with the law . . . with the authorities.

Kendra hadn't told them her theory. Why kill their hope? It was all they had left. But she knew the truth. How many people wouldn't just assume these girls had simply run away once again? How much time would be spent on trying to find girls who apparently wanted to disappear? Whoever planned this had done their homework.

"You cold?"

Kendra looked up at her current tormentor. Big, mean-looking, and flabby. And he always smelled like onions. His name was Styx and she hated him.

Today he'd come in with a camera and taken pictures. That was it. Nothing more. She'd covered herself with her hands and he hadn't stopped her. Hadn't even acted as if she were alive . . . didn't speak to her, just took pictures. And then he'd gone over to the corner, leaned back against the wall . . . and stared.

No one had touched her yet. Not really. When she'd first arrived, they'd ripped her clothes off and thrown her in a tub of ice water. Then they'd given her a towel to dry off with, a toothbrush, and a small tube of toothpaste. And that was it. The towel had been taken from her and she'd been forced into a room with a bed, a mattress, and a naked pillow. Nothing else. She had nothing to cover herself with and she was cold . . . so very cold.

But then the real torture had begun. Each day, she was

given two glasses of water and a small piece of bread. Bread and water . . . nothing more. The stomach cramps from hunger had finally stopped. Now she was just weak . . . and still so very cold.

"Why are you doing this?"

She wouldn't get an answer. It was the same question she'd been asking since she'd been here. What was the purpose? She wasn't raped, wasn't physically violated. She was merely being starved to death.

This time her question elicited more of an answer than she'd been given before. He grinned, the giant gold front tooth gleaming. "You'll soon see."

So that meant they had a plan?

"I need to go to the bathroom."

"You know the rules. You piss in the morning and at night."

Fury gave her a zap of energy. She sat up and screamed, "I'm not a dog, you freak! I want to go to the bathroom and I want to go now!"

The gold tooth gleamed brighter as he approached her. Kendra forced her weak body not to collapse. She knew almost nothing about self-defense, but knew enough to kick him in the balls if he came close enough.

"That's enough, Styx. Time for another lesson."

A voice spoke from the ceiling. Kendra jerked her head up and stared at what she'd assumed was a security monitor. Now she wasn't so sure. Was it a camera? Was someone watching her all the time? Why? What kind of pleasure would someone get from watching her starve to death?

Styx stopped in his tracks and winked at her. "Your lucky day." He turned around and went through the door. And once more she was alone—she shot a glare up to the camera—or as alone as she'd been since she had been here.

Determined not to cower down to these animals, Kendra gathered her strength and stood. She was naked; she didn't care. If they wanted to get their rocks off by looking at a skinny, terrified girl, then let them. She was going to tell them what she thought.

She stalked to the middle of the room and began to shout. Calling them every obscenity she'd ever heard and some she made up, she told them exactly what they were.

How long she did that, she didn't know. At least an hour, maybe more. She was thirsty and so very hungry. Her legs suddenly dropped out beneath her and she fell. Landing on her knees, she began to cry. And then the begging started. She pleaded. She begged. And she cried some more.

When that brought no answers, Kendra crawled back to her bed. Huddling on the bare mattress, she sank into an exhausted slumber.

Sometime later, a masculine voice, thick with emotion, whispered in her ear, "You're almost there, my jewel. You're almost there."

She tried to open her eyes. Was it a dream? Or was someone actually in the room with her? Too exhausted and weak to care, Kendra escaped back into unconsciousness.

Key West, Florida

Noah McCall wasn't a man who refrained from giving his opinion. Arrogant enough to believe his opinion mattered, he was also wise enough to know when to keep his mouth shut.

Being married to Samara had tempered his arrogance somewhat. Hard to maintain that kind of attitude when his beautiful wife got it into her head to tell him exactly why he shouldn't be arrogant. Especially when he found himself agreeing with her most of the time.

Therefore, despite his desire to tell both Gabe and Skylar that they were behaving like idiots, he maintained his silence and watched as they tried to pretend they cared nothing for each other.

"So you believe Kendra might have been targeted?" Skylar asked.

Not looking at her, Gabe answered before Noah could speak. "Hard to say, since there have been similar disappearances. The only reason I think so is what you remembered. The comment that she's already been chosen."

"Spoken for," Skylar corrected.

Gabe shrugged. "Spoken for . . . chosen. Thing is, if she was targeted, it might mean it was someone she knew."

"What kind of circles does Kendra run in?" Noah asked.

"Typical young crowd. She's settled down in the last year or so, but her boyfriend is still a sleaze."

"A wealthy sleaze?" Noah asked.

"Yes, but not bright enough to devise this. Besides, why would he?"

"Perhaps to make money?"

"That's possible. He never seems to run out. His parents are dead, so he's not getting it from home."

Noah gave a quick nod. "That's an angle we can work. I'll have him checked out. And this 'man' they spoke of . . . they only indicated he had connections?"

For a second, Skylar's eyes went unfocused as she tried to remember. Then she shook her head and said, "That's all they said . . . that with his connections he might even know me."

Noah jotted a note, then looked back at Skylar. "Any boyfriends other than Calvin or acquaintances that you know of?"

Her brow furrowed slightly in concentration. "She shares an apartment with two girls, Andrea Partow and Maleah Bramford. They're not friends, though."

"Any reason to believe they would be involved?"

Skylar shook her head. "No. They might be a bit self-absorbed, but I can't see them getting involved in something like this. They tend to treat Kendra as if she doesn't exist."

"So you're basically all she's got."

Noah's comment caused an interesting reaction. Skylar's eyes filled with tears as she nodded. Gabe's reaction when he saw those tears was a steely-eyed glare at his boss.

Swallowing a chuckle, Noah leaned toward Skylar and gave Gabe a gift he knew the man wouldn't take for himself. "Tell me about yourself."

Noah didn't know who looked the most surprised—though for different reasons. Skylar probably thought he was being nosy. Gabe would know otherwise. Would realize exactly what he was doing. Didn't matter. He was still going to do it.

"What sorts of things do you want to know, Mr. McCall?"

Known for his subtly in most situations, Noah didn't see a need for it here. Never underestimate the value of shocking the truth out of people. "Tell me about Benjamin Bradford."

First reactions were often the most telling. Skylar shot a glance at Gabe, a look of both guilt and defiance. Gabe's expression was even more interesting. A half second of vulnerability and then an even harder glare. That famous Maddox control had a tiny fracture. About damn time.

Skylar cleared her throat. "Well . . . Ben and I are very good friends."

"Any reason to believe he might be involved in this?"

"Of course not. Why would you even ask such a question? Ben is—"

"What?"

Gabe's growling word startled Skylar so much she jumped and revealed probably more than she intended. "He's one of the most sought-after bachelors in the country. On top of being enormously wealthy, he's also one of the most committed and decently moral men I know."

"Committed to what?"

This time Gabe's question caused a spark of irritation instead of surprise. "To his girlfriend," she snapped.

Noah recognized something that Gabe, in his anger and jealousy, had obviously missed. The relationship between Skylar and Benjamin Bradford wasn't romantic. What was going on, he didn't know. Didn't really want to know. At some point, though, once Gabe stopped being so damned stubborn, he'd definitely want to know more.

"And Kendra . . . how did you two meet?"

Another interesting look. Not guilt . . . more like defenselessness or fear.

"She was having trouble . . . we became friends." An awkward shrug and then, "Is this really pertinent?"

"Might be," Noah said.

She took a breath and answered with intriguing brevity. "I was introduced to her . . . related to her problems. I tried to help her."

Noah leaned forward. "You're involved in a lot of charity work, aren't you? On a lot of committees, boards of directors?"

"A few. Why?"

He shrugged. He could tell her he'd done some background work on her in the last few days. Her charity work was unique and quite interesting. Much of it was done behind the scenes, where she would get no recognition or credit. And he was willing to bet she used her name only if she thought it would be useful. The woman had secrets. Something he hoped Gabe would take the time to delve into . . . once he got his head out of his ass.

Feeling a bit guilty for making her answer questions she was obviously not comfortable answering, Noah let her off the hook. Hopefully, what she had shared would penetrate Gabe's thick head at some point.

He shot a look at her stubborn husband. "Take Skylar back home. In the meantime, I'll do some background work on this Calvin creep."

"Gabe's coming to New York?"

"You got a problem with that, princess?"

Blue eyes flashed annoyance. "No, I don't have a problem with that, Gabe. I asked a question."

Gabe stood. "And there's your answer. Don't worry. I'll make sure to use the back entrance to your home so no one will see me."

Skylar stood and moved within inches of him. Since she was several inches shorter, only coming to his shoulder in height, she stood on her toes and leaned closer. "Make sure you wipe your feet before you come in, too."

She whirled around to Noah. "It was nice to meet you, Mr. McCall. Please accept my sincerest appreciation for your help in my rescue and for taking on Kendra's case." She shot a scathing glance at her husband before adding, "As you know, I have money and influence. I'm ready to offer a substantial reward, if you think that will help. And if there's anything at all I can do, please don't hesitate to call on me."

With a dignity Noah figured she'd been born with, she marched toward the door and then turned around to hurl one final insult at her husband: "If you're coming to New York with me, be kind enough to leave that giant chip on your shoulder here. I'm getting damned tired of you lugging it around everywhere you go."

The door closed behind her, leaving Gabe glaring and Noah swallowing laughter.

Then Gabe turned around and Noah felt heartened at the liveliness of Gabe's expression. His words were even more encouraging. "Damn, she's a piece of work, isn't she?"

Noah couldn't contain his smile. Seeing a different expression on his operative's normally grim, stoic face gave him a certain kind of hope. About time Gabe Maddox got a life.

eleven

New York City

William Harrington III tossed the newspaper into the small trashcan beside his desk. He barely glanced at the financial papers any longer, since they usually only depressed or confused him. Everything that had seemed so safe and solid a year or so ago had experienced a meltdown. Many of his friends were now living on the fringe of bankruptcy. Others had already toppled. Some would make a comeback; others would disappear into obscurity.

And so it goes.

Leaning back into his leather chair, William released a satisfied sigh of complete fulfillment. Not that he had to worry about such things. He had the perfect life.

As a young man, he'd been the Harrington everyone said wouldn't make it through Harvard. The Harrington destined to have to marry well because he wouldn't be able to comprehend the business world well enough to maintain his family's wealth. The Harrington who would have to rely on his looks because his intelligence was below par. They'd expected him to fail and he'd proven them wrong. So what if he'd had to buy off a couple of professors in college to get his degree? He wasn't the first or the last to use his creativity to achieve his goals.

Now some of those very same naysayers who'd been

sure he would never make it were coming to him, begging for money, begging for his help. Begging for his financial wisdom.

If they knew how he'd been able to maintain his fortune when so many around him had lost theirs, they'd be shocked. But how many would secretly envy his ambition? His ingenuity? Want to share in his little diversions? Most likely a few of them would love to partner with him. Not that he'd let that happen, since he trusted few of them. Besides, he had never really liked to share.

Being the head of his secret little enterprise gave him the opportunity to taste the merchandise and choose the best of the lot. In the ten years he'd been doing this venture, he'd enjoyed some of the tastiest treats ever created.

Some in the trade criticized him for enjoying the fruits of his labor. They chose to keep their hands off the merchandise and benefit only from the profits. To hell with them. *Impotent idiots.*

To William, not sampling the merchandise would be like owning an ice cream business and never tasting the variety of flavors his company offered. If he didn't taste the product, how would he know how good the quality was? It was only good business sense.

Besides, it wasn't like he indulged frequently. When he found a flavor he liked, he glutted himself on it until it no longer satisfied him. And with his exquisite taste, the ones he chose were able to keep him quite happy for a very long time. When it was time for a new flavor, he was extremely selective—quality over quantity was most definitely his motto.

William flipped a switch on his desk that controlled all the doors and windows connected to his office. His family had a tendency to barge in on him at inopportune moments. Most of the time, they were welcome to come in. Occasionally, it was inconvenient.

Standing, William went to the bar and poured himself a generous amount of his favorite brandy. As the amber liquid swirled around the glass, he allowed the momentum to build. Sometimes this was his favorite part . . . anticipating. His palms heating the liquor to just the right temperature, he inhaled the subtle but heady fragrance. He took a long swallow and sighed with enjoyment as the heat and flavors blended on his tongue.

Anticipation soared higher. His body now hard with the need to do what he'd thought about all day, William pressed a small latch, then uncovered and opened the door to his secret treasure trove. Turning on the lights, he took a moment to delight in what he thought of as his vault of pleasure. Magazines catalogued and stacked neatly sat on a long narrow table against one wall. Above the table were shelves filled with hardcover and paperback books detailing some of the most interesting and enlightening sexual techniques and experiences known to man. Another wall had a floor-to-ceiling shelf filled with some of the finest adult films ever made.

A third wall was filled with personal memorabilia. Photographs of the few precious jewels he'd collected over the years. Along with a few of his favorite tools of pleasure, the ones he used only on his most prized acquisitions. Such as the one being prepared for him now.

Pulling out a drawer, William withdrew a folder. It had arrived by special delivery two days ago. Self-discipline to the extreme. He'd had it for two days and had waited. Now it was time.

He dropped into his soft leather chair and took another sip of brandy, just to add to the anticipation. Then he flipped open the file. And there she was . . . his newest jewel. She was special; he already knew that. He was taking a big chance with her. She was a local girl and he rarely liked to keep the local ones. Not only was it too dangerous, William generally preferred the more exotic variety.

But he'd picked her out, chosen her specifically. Usually the merchandise found its way to him. After making his selection, he would enjoy the product until he tired of it and would send it on its way. That method had always pleased him in the past. But he personally knew this one, had met her on several occasions, had cultivated their relationship, and had led her to him. He'd seen her, wanted her, and had arranged for this very special meeting. Yes, she was unique in every way.

Very soon he would officially introduce himself and their new relationship would begin. Right now she was being prepped . . . seasoned. When they met, she would be so happy, glad to see him. Grateful. He would be her hero, her savior.

Anticipation thrummed to a fever pitch. His fingers shaking with the need to touch, he pressed a fingertip to her face. Traced the single teardrop rolling down her cheek. He could almost feel the wetness. Feel her shaking beneath him. Feel the sobs of terror that would give way to gratitude. And then, in those pretty hazel eyes, he would see the culmination of his hard work and patience . . . pure submission. Whatever he wanted, whenever he wanted it, she would submit and be grateful. A shudder went through him as his hand went to his crotch.

A knock on the door of his office had him slamming the file closed, almost crying out his disappointment. Couldn't a man enjoy some peace and quiet even in his own home?

"Daddy?"

William huffed a long-suffering sigh. No doubt another preteen crisis . . . another dramatic event in his youngest daughter's life.

Closing the file on his beauty wasn't easy, but he had no choice. He got up and hurriedly left the vault.

"Daddy? Are you in there?"

"Yes. Just a moment."

The door handle rattled. "Can I talk to you?"

"Give me a moment, Leanne."

William prided himself on being a good father, always being available for his children. Assuring himself that his secret treasure was safely hidden, he took several breaths to compose himself. Just one look at that young, supple body and he'd been consumed by lust. How would he feel when he touched her for the first time? He groaned . . . his hand went back to his crotch.

"Daddy!"

Jerked back to reality, William turned the knob of the office door. His daughter and her sisters and brothers were his priority. That's why he'd gone into his side business in the first place. Sampling and enjoying his product was just an added benefit. Admittedly a very pleasurable added benefit.

Pulling open the door, he looked down with fatherly indulgence at his youngest daughter . . . the face of innocence.

"What's wrong, sweetie?"

Skylar curled up on her side and stared at the bare wall of the hotel room. Gabe had dropped her off an hour or so ago. At least he'd shown some semblance of concern by checking the entire suite of rooms, waiting until her food arrived from room service, and giving her the stern warning "Don't let anyone in this room for any reason." And then, "I'll see you in the morning." And he'd left.

Rolling over on her back, she stared up at the ceiling. She really should get some sleep. Her body still ached from the rough handling she'd endured, not to mention the dull headache she'd had since being given those damned drugs. Tomorrow would be a long day. Flying always exhausted her, even when she wasn't recovering from a trauma.

She closed her suddenly stinging eyes. Trauma? What a riot. More like an avalanche of horrendous events.

Where was Kendra? Was she even alive? If only Skylar herself hadn't been sold to someone else. Her damnable fame had finally paid off, but she resented it. If they had kept her, would she have been put with Kendra? Could she have saved them both?

What was done was done. The most important thing was to find her now. Gabe would work the case until Kendra was found. She knew very little about her husband anymore, but she'd seen the determination. She trusted him to find Kendra.

Gabe.

She was still married to him. She'd thought herself a widow. Only a few people even knew about him—her family of course, and a few close friends. And Benjamin Bradford. They'd entered into a mutually satisfying arrangement. Neither wanted a relationship with the other, but they'd wanted a private life. Though he hadn't asked, Skylar had felt compelled to tell him the truth. She knew he wouldn't tell anyone. Ben had his own secrets.

Learning that she was a widow had surprised him. But what shocked him even more were her reasons for wanting a pretend romance. Ben's reasons had been his need to keep the identity of his girlfriend private. Skylar wanted a pretend romance because she wanted no romance at all. Ever again.

A year after Gabe's supposed death, she had tried dating. Admittedly, most of them had been men her father had introduced to her, but she'd never found anyone she wanted a second date with. She'd even tried kissing one or two of them, but had never been able to take it further. The desire just wasn't there. Not like it had been with Gabe.

An unwelcome and unexpected flush of heat enveloped her as she remembered Gabe's lovemaking. It had been so wonderful, felt so good. Perfect. Closing her eyes, Skylar allowed herself to remember the most beautiful event in her life. Her first time with Gabe.

Eight years ago
Kalamina Island, South Pacific

An earth-shattering boom of thunder alerted the island that the daily rainstorm had come a bit early.

Strolling beside Gabe on the pathway toward the beach, she shot him a glance. "Looks like that swim will have to wait."

He grabbed her hand and pressed a kiss to her palm. "Wonder what we can do instead?"

Shivers went through her body, a blend of excitement, anticipation, and apprehension. They hadn't gone all the way yet, but she knew that soon neither one of them would be able to stop. Suddenly, Skylar was tired of waiting. Tired of her fear of the unknown.

Pulling her hand from his, she took a forward leap and shouted, "Race you home!"

Gabe's laughter followed her as she ran toward his

bungalow. His long legs could easily outrun hers, but he stayed several steps behind her. A hundred yards from his door, the heavens exploded and torrents of water washed over them.

Before she knew what was happening, Gabe came up beside her, scooped her up in one fluid movement, and kept on running. Skylar wrapped her arms around his neck and hung on.

At the bungalow, he took the steps two at a time and burst through the door. Dropping her to her feet, he said, "I'll get us some towels."

Skylar looked down at her swimsuit and grimaced. She was soaked. Making a quick decision she sincerely hoped she wouldn't regret, she unhooked her swimsuit top, then pulled down her bottoms, dropping everything on the floor. Completely naked, she waited for Gabe.

Hearing a gasp, she whirled around. He stood at the bathroom door. He'd taken his shirt off and was holding a towel. As he walked slowly toward her, his eyes roamed over her body in a scorching caress Skylar felt to her core. She was already throbbing, aching for his touch.

"You're even more beautiful than I imagined you would be."

Though she had never posed nude, she'd had numerous photographs of her taken in swimsuits, but had never known uncertainty and vulnerability as she did now. Gabe's words were a balm to an ego she hadn't even known needed stroking.

As if he were touching something precious and fragile, his hand reached out and his finger barely touched her jutting nipple. Moaning at the delicate, erotic sensation, Skylar closed her eyes.

"Your nipples want my mouth on them, don't they?"

Opening her eyes, she saw him staring at her nipple and it grew harder under his gaze.

"Please, Gabe."

"What, Skye baby?"

"Put your mouth on me."

"With pleasure."

In an instant, hot breath bathed her nipple and then his mouth clamped down. A hard, delicious throb answered in her sex. Skylar weaved her fingers through his hair and held him against her breast. Three nights ago, he'd kissed her breasts for the first time, but it had felt nothing like this. A gasping sob escaped her as she felt one of his hands slowly caress her stomach and then stop at the top of her sex.

Gabe pulled away slightly. His breath hot against her skin, he whispered, "Open your legs for me, Skye."

Her mind was no longer in control of her body; Gabe's voice was. She felt her legs separate and then his hand was there, on her. His fingers, gentle and exploring, opened her folds and then a finger touched, caressed the part that throbbed, ached. Wanted.

"You're soft and so wet down there. So hot and sweet."

Those gravelly, sexy words caused shudders throughout her body. She opened her legs more and undulated against his probing fingers. Warm moisture seeped from her, easing his fingers deeper inside.

Gabe pulled from the breast he'd been nibbling and looked down at her. "Are you sure, Skye?"

"I've never been more sure of anything in my entire life."

Though hunger as she'd never imagined was etched on his face, his words sought to reassure her, causing Skylar to love him all the more. "There's no rush, no hurry. There's never a time you tell me to stop and I won't. Okay?"

"I love you so much, Gabe."

Pressing a soft kiss to her mouth, he whispered, "Let's get on the bed." He nudged her gently into the bedroom, never taking his eyes from hers. When Skylar felt the edge of the bed against the back of her legs, she sat down. And before she knew it, Gabe was on his knees before her.

His expression one of awe, as though he was staring at the most beautiful sight in the world, he whispered, "Marry me."

Her heart leaped for joy, and tears filled her eyes. "Yes, Gabe. Yes."

A smile lifted his lips as he pulled her down and pressed a soft kiss to her mouth. "I'm going to love you past forever." Then, pulling away from her, he parted her legs, spread her sex with his thumbs, and put his mouth on her. Skylar screamed. And then she came.

Gabe groaned and continued to devour until every drop of wetness was consumed and every throb had stopped. He pulled away slowly and looked up at her. Face flushed, eyes glittering hot, he whispered, "You're delicious everywhere."

Those growling words caused a deep, answering throb inside her. Eyes falling closed, she groaned at the sensation. And then she felt him there again. Nuzzling, nibbling, and then a deep, opened-mouth tongue thrust.

Swallowing screams of pleasure, Skylar held his head against her and endured ecstasy. After one last long slide of his tongue, Gabe rose to his feet and stripped off the rest of his clothes. Wishing she had energy to get up and help, Skylar could only lie there and enjoy watching him. His body was still thin, but had filled out quite a bit since she'd met him. Broad shoulders and a hard, slightly furred chest tapered to a narrow waist and a taut abdomen. Her eyes lowered farther and she let out a half gasp. She knew what a penis looked like—she wasn't that clueless—but she'd never seen one aroused.

Gabe must have thought he'd scared her, because he said, "Remember, Skye. If you get scared at any time, just tell me to stop."

Stop? She almost laughed, but figured that wasn't the appropriate response. But there was no way in the world she would ever want him to stop. Get scared? With Gabe? It wasn't possible.

Skylar pulled herself farther up on the bed and watched fascinated as he slid a condom over his hard length. Then he came over her and covered her mouth with his. She tasted herself on his tongue and she tasted Gabe; their flavors intermingled as their mouths devoured each other. And then she felt his hot, hard flesh probing at her. He pulled away and stared into her eyes as he eased into her.

A shaky gasp escaped her. It hurt . . . she couldn't deny the sting, but it was the most beautiful, exciting pain in the world. When he was fully inside her, he whispered, "Let's stay still, just for a moment, so you can get used to it."

Her emotions overflowing with love for this beautiful, sexy, giving man, she could only nod. And then, when they were both close to explosion, Gabe began to move. Skylar threw her arms around him, wrapped her legs around his hips, and let herself go.

They'd made love three times that night and had married the next day. And never, ever had another man made her want to do anything remotely similar. Was she odd? Crazy? Undersexed? She didn't know; didn't care.

Swallowing a half snort, half sob, Skylar rolled over onto her stomach. Good thing, that. Since she would have been committing adultery if she had found someone else. And her father knew this. Knew she was still married. Had that even crossed his mind? Concerned him at all? His betrayal hurt almost more than anything. How could he have done this to her? To them?

Even after all these years, she still remembered the moment she read the suicide note she'd thought Gabe had left. She had been consumed not only with grief but also with guilt. How had she not seen his mental illness? Yes, there were days he'd had a darkness about him she found hard to penetrate, but she had never anticipated or guessed that darkness would consume him. Turned out it hadn't.

The darkness had almost consumed her, though. And her father had been right there with her, comforting her, encouraging her. She'd thought him the most wonderfully compassionate man in the world. Had thought how fortunate she was to have such a loving, supportive family. Their love had sustained her, kept her sane when she had wanted to just give up.

And all the while, they'd had this knowledge. All the while, they could have given her the truth and allowed her peace. Instead, because of some sort of elitism or just pure, selfish arrogance, they'd decided Gabe wasn't good enough for her. It had been easier for them to see her almost lose her mind . . . almost die . . . than to allow him into their family.

Just what kind of sick, screwed-up family did she have?

The sun had barely risen in the sky when Gabe ran up the stairs three at a time. Skye wasn't answering the cellphone he'd given her or the phone in the room. He told himself she was most likely in the shower. After all, an

LCR operative had watched her door all night and had reported nothing wrong. Still, he worried. He'd just now found her, damned if he would lose her again.

That thought almost pulled him to a halt. Worry overrode shock, so he kept going, but that didn't stop the self-castigation. Lose her again? Hell, he'd never really had her. He'd married a young girl never knowing who she was. Their marriage had been a huge mistake. One that they would rectify very soon. Skye most assuredly felt the same way.

Reaching her door, he pounded hard.

When there wasn't an immediate response, he cursed and pounded again. Dammit, why hadn't he got an extra key? Ignoring the doors opening around him and heads peeking out to see what the noise was all about, Gabe backed up, preparing to ram the door. When it opened about an inch, he stalked toward it.

"Skye, are you all right?"

She pulled the door open with one hand while holding a towel around her naked, wet body. *Holy hell.*

"I'm fine. I was in the shower."

"I've called you ten times in the last half hour."

Her mouth tightened. "I take long showers."

Gabe took in what he hadn't noticed before. Puffy red eyes. She looked as though she'd been crying for hours.

"What's wrong?"

"What's right?"

Someone snickered behind him. He'd been so focused on Skye, he'd forgotten they had an audience. "Let me in."

She backed away and allowed him inside. He closed the door and looked around the room.

She huffed out a breath. "There's no one here but me."

Gabe shrugged. "Habit."

As if just realizing she wore nothing but a minuscule towel, she glanced down at herself and flushed. "I'll get dressed."

His tongue seemingly stuck to the roof of his mouth, Gabe could only nod as he watched her walk away. Every time he looked at her, he wanted to kiss her and hold her. The fact that they were married made it perfectly all right and absolutely not all right. A piece of paper did not a marriage make.

He took a quick inventory. Dishes from last night's dinner still sat on the table. From the looks of it, she hadn't eaten but a few bites. He checked his watch. They still had about forty-five minutes before they had to leave for the airport. Time enough for her to eat breakfast.

He picked up the phone and dialed room service. Assured they'd put a rush on the meal, Gabe turned when he heard the bathroom door open.

Angela had missed her calling. She might be Noah's receptionist but she was also damned good at selecting clothes for beautiful women. The midnight blue pantsuit hugged Skye's slender frame, emphasizing every delicate curve to its best advantage. Eight years ago, Skye had been a lovely twenty-year-old, on the cusp of breathtaking beauty. She had achieved that promise of beauty and surpassed it. Today, she was a stunningly gorgeous, confident woman. Gabe swallowed hard. She was also sexy as hell.

"Who's Ben?"

"What?"

Those blue eyes that had deepened to the color of her pantsuit flashed with confusion.

"Noah mentioned you'd been dating some guy named Ben."

Her eyes went brighter. This time with temper. "Are you telling me you haven't seen pictures of us together?"

"I don't read stuff about you."

"Why?"

He shrugged. "None of my business."

For barely a second, he saw hurt reflected in her face. He hadn't meant to be mean; it was just the truth. He did his dead-level best not to know who she was seeing, what she was doing. He hadn't needed any more evidence that Skye didn't give a damn that she was still a married woman.

When they'd first split, he'd bought every magazine and read every newspaper article he could get his hands on. Each one had only reconfirmed what he'd believed. What her father had perpetuated. Their marriage had been a mistake. Finally, after glutting himself on her extravagant lifestyle for three months, he'd avoided any kind of mention of her. Damn hard to do, since she seemed to be everywhere. She'd said she was devastated that he'd committed suicide. Her lifestyle sure as shit didn't bear that out.

Gabe shut those dark memories down. The art of pain avoidance was an acquired skill . . . one he'd learned a long time ago.

A polite mask of indifference firmly in place, she took a step toward him. "I'm ready when you are."

"We've got some time. I ordered breakfast."

"Thanks. I'm not hungry."

"Tough. You're going to eat anyway."

"You can't make me eat, Gabe."

"Stop acting like a child. You'll make yourself sick if you don't eat."

That mutinous look tightened her mouth once more, but she nodded. Before he could say anything else, someone knocked on the door.

Gabe pulled his gun and said quietly, "Go to the bathroom and shut the door. Don't come out until I tell you to."

Her eyes widened at the gun but she thankfully didn't argue. He waited until she had closed the door.

Gabe stalked to the door and looked through the peephole. Room service. Keeping his gun behind him, he unlocked the door. Before the young man could push the food trolley in, Gabe slammed a twenty into his hand and said, "I'll take it." He grabbed the cart and shut the door.

"Skye," Gabe called.

She came back into the room, her eyes darting immediately to the gun he slid back into his ankle holster. "You're very comfortable with guns, aren't you?"

"Stupid to have one and not be."

Taking the tray of food from the cart, he lifted the dome and took an appreciative sniff. Then he poured two cups of coffee, pulled out a chair for Skye, and looked at her. "Come eat."

Her face a study in the myriad of questions she obviously wanted to ask, Skye sat down, placed the napkin on her lap, and took a sip of the coffee. If she wanted to question him while she ate, that was fine. Years ago, she'd been soft, curvy. Now she was so slender, a good stiff wind would knock her down. And since he'd rescued her, she hadn't eaten enough to keep a baby alive.

"Eat and we'll talk."

Widened eyes revealed her surprise. "You'll answer my questions?"

He lifted a shoulder. "I don't have any secrets."

She snorted softly. "You work for an agency filled with secrets."

"LCR has to keep secrets to save lives." He shrugged. "I don't have any. Ask away."

"When did you start working with LCR?"

"I started about a year after I left the island."

"How did you get started?"

"How're your eggs?"

"What?"

"Clean your plate and ask me anything you want."

"That's blackmail."

"That's the deal. Take it or leave it."

She scooped up a forkful of eggs and put it in her mouth. As she chewed, she shot him a look that would have had him laughing if there was anything left to laugh at.

Satisfied to see her eating, Gabe said, "I heard about LCR from the people who helped secure my release. They'd worked with them before. I contacted Noah, interviewed with him, and then he hired me."

"So you've been with them for over seven years now?"

"Yes."

"What about your family?"

Gabe stiffened. Okay, so maybe a few areas were off-limits. Talking about his family wasn't something he did very often. Actually not at all, except eight years ago with Skye.

"I don't have a family, Skye. You know that."

"Is your stepmother gone?"

"No. As far as I know, she's still alive."

"Then she's still your family. Why haven't you gone to see her? Remember, we talked about it?"

"I never went back to see her."

"Why not?"

"She has another life. She married again, has other children. She didn't need me bringing back bad memories."

"They weren't all bad, Gabe."

Hell, he thought she was going to talk about his job. Not his past. She knew it all anyway. What was the point in talking more about it?

"There's a reason memories are in the past, Skye. They have no relationship to the here and now."

"Don't you think she'd like to know how you are?" When he didn't answer, she leaned forward to catch his gaze. "She raised you from the time you were four. You were her child."

Gabe stood. "This isn't getting us anywhere."

"You need to stop blaming yourself for living, Gabe. The mining accident wasn't your fault. Do you think your father or stepbrother would have wanted you to carry that burden?"

"You haven't seen me in eight years, Skylar. And we knew each other barely three weeks, most of which was spent doing things that didn't require talking. So don't try to psychoanalyze me. You don't know me."

Skylar watched Gabe fight every human emotion he had. Sometimes she wondered if those who felt too deeply were the ones who, when hurt, shut down their emotions even tighter than others.

Just in the few weeks they were together, she'd recognized that Gabe had deep-seated core values of loyalty, honor, and devotion to family. However, his experiences had severely bruised those beliefs.

Funny. Even eight years later, she still felt such a connection to Gabe, and such a deep understanding of him. Not that he'd allow her to get that close ever again. It had taken her two weeks to get him to share his deepest thoughts.

But almost from the minute she'd met him, she'd lied to him, betrayed him. Was it any wonder he didn't trust anyone?

Gabe might be surprised to know that other than that one small bit of information, everything else had been the truth. She'd never been able to share her deepest feelings, her true self, with anyone until Gabe. She'd kept her fame out of their conversation deliberately, but not for the reasons he probably believed.

"Did you ever wonder why I didn't tell you who I was?"

The loosening of his granite-hard jaw told her he was relieved that she'd dropped the subject of his stepmother. She would revisit it at some point, but not now.

He took a long swallow of coffee. "I figured you told me what you wanted me to know."

"That's not it, at all, Gabe. I—"

She stopped abruptly when he rose from his chair and pressed a finger to his mouth for her to be quiet. He went quietly to the door and looked in the peephole. The relaxing of his shoulders indicated there was no danger.

He cracked opened the door and asked, "When'd you get back?"

Skylar heard a man's deep voice answer, "Just got in. I'm flying with you."

Gabe backed away and Skylar watched a man come through the door. Reasoning that he was also an LCR operative, she immediately wondered if LCR had certain requirements about hiring tall, dark, and handsome men. This man, though more muscular than most male models, had the bone structure and good looks to be on the cover of any top magazine.

She watched as Gabe and the stranger spoke quietly to each other. Though the stranger might look more like the eye candy she was used to seeing in her world, she greatly preferred Gabe's rugged masculinity. There was just something about Gabe that caused all sorts of flutters inside her. It had happened the moment she met him, and now, eight years later, those flutters had been rekindled and seemed stronger than ever.

"Skye, this is Cole Mathison."

Skylar stood and held out her hand. "You're with LCR also?"

"Yes, ma'am."

Skylar couldn't prevent a smile at his beautiful Texas drawl. "What part of Texas are you from?"

"I've lived in most of the major cities, ma'am."

"Call me Skylar."

Cole Mathison gave a brief nod and looked at Gabe. "You about ready?"

Gabe turned those piercing eyes on her and then looked at her still-full plate. "You hardly ate anything."

"I'll eat when I get home."

"This is a private jet. We'll get you some food there."

What was the big deal about her eating?

Cole glanced around the room. "You have luggage?"

Skylar shook her head. "No. Just the things Gabe gave me yesterday."

"I'll bring the car to the back entrance."

She waited until Cole walked out the door, and then asked, "What's the deal with all this secrecy? We're thousands of miles away from the creep who had me."

"Doesn't hurt to be careful. Besides, you're known all over the world, not just New York. I figured you'd want to avoid any press until you got home."

He was right about that. She shuddered at the thought of having reporters ask questions about her bruises and how she got them.

"I'll wait for you in the hallway," Gabe said.

Skylar watched him leave the room and felt an enormous sense of loss. Great, he was right outside the door and she already missed him. How was she going to feel when he left for good?

Sighing, she began to gather up the few garments and toiletries she had been given. That was a thought she didn't even want to contemplate right now. The most important thing was to find Kendra. Then she'd worry about what she would do for the rest of her life knowing that Gabe was still in this world but didn't want to be part of hers.

twelve

"Lick your lips like you can't wait to taste it."

Her mouth dehydrated from fear and lack of water, the best Kendra could manage was a sweep of her dry tongue over her even drier mouth. Maybe if her lips didn't glisten enough, they'd take her out and shoot her. Which would be a hell of a lot better than what she had endured since she'd been here.

"Come on, baby. You can do better than that. Remember, this is what you wanted . . . to be a model. So do it already." The photographer from hell, her current torturer, turned around and shouted, "Get me some Vaseline. Her lips are all dried and cracked."

Kendra stiffened as he approached her with a jar of petroleum jelly. She had two choices. Let the bastard touch her, which meant giving him enjoyment, or comply and put it on herself. She didn't want to obey these perverts in anything, but she couldn't bear having this creep's hands on her again.

Slicked-back hair matched the slimy look in his eyes; his expression told her he knew exactly what she was thinking as he held the jar out to her. "I'll be glad to stick it in every opening you've got. Your choice."

Kendra grabbed the jar from his hands, careful not to touch him. With a grin, he backed away.

Her trembling finger barely touched the jelly, then she

touched her lips. They were dry and chapped just as he said. Going days with almost no water or food would do that to a person. Not that they gave a shit.

"Now, let's see those pretty lips pucker up. Think of that steak dinner we promised you tonight."

As he knew it would, her mouth began to water. She'd had only the barest amount of food for days. The thought of eating a full meal filled her entire being with excitement.

"Oh, baby, yeah. You want that steak real bad, don't you?"

The flash of his camera startled her. Dammit, she'd been thinking about food and he'd gotten the shot he wanted.

"Okay, let's try it with a little less clothes on. Pull your panties off and show us just a little muff. Like those pictures I showed you of the other girls."

The allure of the fantasy meal vanished under a wave of nausea. He'd made her look at picture after picture of provocative photographs. Young, scantily clad women showing off various body parts, and all the girls had one major thing in common—their eyes had been glazed with drugs. If she didn't comply, these creeps would do the same thing to her.

"Get that look off your face or we'll have to bring in someone to convince you."

Kendra shuddered at his reminder that they could do much worse than shoot her with drugs. What she had witnessed yesterday went beyond any kind of torture she could imagine.

Biting her lips to keep from crying, Kendra pulled off her panties. She closed her eyes and tried to pretend she was somewhere else. Anywhere that she wasn't being kept captive by crazy people who said and did hideous things for their own amusement.

"Okay, love. On your back. One leg up, the other bent sideways."

Fighting tears, Kendra arranged her legs so she could show the pervert just enough to satisfy him.

After several flashes, he put his camera down and smiled. "You can relax now. That should be enough to satisfy him."

This wasn't the first time another man had been mentioned. She'd learned to hold her tongue, though. After having been forced to watch the beating and rape of a young girl, she knew not to say anything. The girl's eyes had been filled with pain, fear, and accusation.

Kendra had screamed for them to stop. Kicked, punched, and bit at them. She'd fought for the girl and for herself. She'd lost. When it was over, she'd been told that if she ever questioned anyone or fought them again, the punishment would be worse, much worse.

Kendra believed them.

Stretching his long legs out in front of him, Cole settled into the leather seat of the private jet, prepared to be entertained. The coming attractions had already been fascinating. Watching both Gabe and Skylar pretend they weren't completely aware of each other was a study in subtlety.

As soon as they'd boarded the plane, Gabe had held a long conversation with the flight attendant. Cole had wondered about that. Gabe wasn't the type to initiate conversation with anyone unless he was asking questions about a case. Skylar had tried to pretend she hadn't cared that her husband seemed to be chatting up the attractive attendant, but Cole had seen the tightening of her mouth. She'd cared a lot.

Then, as soon as the plane leveled out, Cole figured out what Gabe had been doing. A steaming plate of fluffy eggs, along with toast, orange juice, and coffee, was delivered to Skylar. It had been nothing more than Gabe taking care of his wife.

Cole felt a slight movement of his mouth and put his fingers to his lips. After almost a year of having no emotions at all, he was still surprised when they occurred.

"Something amusing?" Gabe asked.

Cole felt his mouth tilt upward even more but resisted the urge to feel the change. Instead he shrugged at his friend. "Just nice to see you turn your attention to someone else for a change."

"What's that supposed to mean?"

"You've been big-brothering me since we've been working together. Good to see you use those skills on someone else."

Gabe snorted. "You're the one who walked into that mansion without a weapon, ready to kick ass."

"I don't need a weapon to kiss ass."

"No, but when somebody's shooting at you, kicking bullets doesn't work."

"Bastard wasn't there anyway."

"We'll get him."

Cole turned his head and stared blindly out the window. Not getting the monster who'd created the drug that had almost destroyed him wasn't something he dared contemplate. Though he would never be able to atone for what he had done while under the influence of the drug, he would damn well find the man who'd been responsible for making it. And he would pay.

Forcing back the darkness, Cole turned back to Gabe. "Jeremiah James called Noah again. Threatened him if we didn't produce Skylar soon."

Gabe snorted again. Before he could say anything, Skylar spoke up. "I hope he didn't cause problems for Noah."

"McCall can take care of himself," Gabe said.

Skylar looked down at the food she'd been pushing around on her plate, her expression one of deep thought. Then she gave Gabe a sideways, wary glance. "We haven't really talked about my father . . . what we're going to say to him."

"You mean before or after I beat the shit out of him?" Gabe asked.

"Stop it, Gabe. He hurt both of us, but I want to hear his explanation."

"Now, just what kind of explanation do you think he's going to give, princess?"

Her eyes flashed. "Stop calling me 'princess.' "

Gabe turned away to look out the window and Skylar continued to play with her food. Cole slouched deeper into his seat, crossed his arms, and enjoyed the main event.

"There's got to be more to this than him lying. I mean, what if either one of us wanted to get married again?"

"I'm sure with your daddy's money, he could have bought off some judges. Better yet, maybe he could've had me killed. Gotten rid of me altogether."

"My father's not like that."

"Your father's a whole lot more capable of things like that than you think. How can you keep defending the man?"

"Because he's my father."

"Oh, and that makes what he did all right?"

"Of course it doesn't."

Tears flooded her eyes and Cole checked his impulse to comfort her. It wasn't his place . . . she wasn't his wife. But judging by Gabe's hard, stubborn expression, he wasn't going to do anything about it either.

"Excuse me." Cole stood and stalked down the aisle to the bathroom. He pulled tissues from a box on the counter and then, because he knew Gabe so well, changed his mind and picked up the entire box.

Cole returned to see Skylar rummaging through her purse and Gabe's granite jaw even harder.

"Here." Cole handed the box to Skylar. "I brought you the box. From the looks of it, you're going to need it."

Skylar thanked him with a small smile and Gabe glared.

Cole returned to his seat. It'd been a long while, a very long while, since he'd felt any kind of enjoyment. Though this case was as serious as they came—rescuing a young girl—he found himself looking forward to the future fireworks that were apparently going to happen often between Gabe Maddox and his beautiful wife.

New York City

Gabe took another glance at Skye before they got out of the taxi. It was a little before midnight and since no one other than Jeremiah James knew they were coming, their arrival should go unnoticed. Just in case a stray photographer or reporter was hanging out, he'd given her sunglasses and a scarf to put over her head. He didn't figure she was ready to answer questions about him or the bruises she still wore on her face.

Dressed this way, she reminded him of one of those beautiful movie stars from the past. Anything Skylar wore, she wore with glamour and style. It was just part of who she was. And the part he wanted nothing to do with.

She cast a worried look around. "Do you think my father will be at my apartment?"

"Doubtful. Noah told him you were coming home, but two hours later than our arrival time. That'll give you an opportunity to freshen up. And prepare."

He did his damnedest to ignore the gratitude in her expressive face. Those kinds of looks were unguarded and real and made him want to touch her. He had done nothing more than press his fingers to her elbow since they'd left Florida.

Taking one more glance around, Gabe put his hand on the door handle. He turned back to issue final instructions. "Cole will go in front of us. Keep your eyes straight ahead. No looking around. Okay?"

Skye nodded, and Gabe opened the door. At Cole's hand signal of an all-clear, Gabe took Skye's hand and helped her out of the car.

Pleased to see her staring straight ahead, Gabe made a sweeping glance of the perimeter as he walked beside her to the giant glass double doors. Cole went ahead of them and said something to the doorman, who took a quick glance at Skye and Gabe and then looked down, pretending he hadn't seen anything at all. *Good.*

When Skye made an abrupt stop in the middle of the large foyer, Gabe halted. Hand on his gun, his eyes searched for a threat. "What's wrong?"

As she turned to face him, her expression was an interesting blend of defensiveness and concern. "I live on the top floor . . . the penthouse."

Aw, hell. Of course she did.

Gabe clenched his jaw and said, "That's fine. Get on the elevator."

"We can take the stairs."

Torn between gratitude for her concern and anger at his damned weakness, Gabe shook his head. "Get on the elevator. I'll be fine."

Cole gave him a nod and pressed the button for the top floor. Gabe knew he could have let Skye travel up with Cole and taken the stairs. He trusted Cole with Skye's life. But for some stupid, idiotic, asinine reason, he couldn't let her out of his sight right now. Stupid, since in a very short while, he'd be leaving for good. And, unless he saw her on a magazine cover or on television, he planned never to see her again. But for now, he had to be by her side. Fuck his diseased brain that allowed the suffocating fear.

The elevator doors closed and his heart started the familiar pounding. Gritting his teeth, he concentrated on breathing slow, shallow breaths. He could do this . . . he could do this.

After what seemed like an eternity but was probably only a couple of minutes, the bell rang announcing their arrival at her penthouse. Resisting the urge to run out of the cage as soon as it opened, he touched Skylar's elbow, indicating she should go first.

The elevator door opened to the oversized foyer of her penthouse. Every mental image he'd ever had about what her kind of wealth would look like was confirmed, but not in the way he expected. Her apartment was large, airy, and obviously filled with expensive furnishings. But it was also comfortable-looking. As much as he hated being indoors for any length of time, Gabe was surprised to feel almost relieved to be inside her apartment.

Skylights above gave an open-air feeling. The furnishings were scattered around almost sparsely. Large green plants sat in different areas, giving the place not only color, but a sense of being outdoors. A large leather sofa in the living room invited an afternoon nap. And the fireplace in front of it made it even more inviting. The colors she'd chosen were warm, eclectic, and soothing.

Feeling unusually tense and uncertain about her home, Skylar watched Gabe as he stalked through each room. Those intelligent but wary blue eyes held an intense curiosity. When he looked back at her, her heart leaped to see a hint of approval. She told herself she didn't care if he liked her apartment or not. She liked it and that was all that mattered. Skylar also knew she was lying.

Cole made a sweeping glance around, much as Gabe had. Apparently satisfied, he turned to Gabe. "I'll go check in at the hotel."

Gabe nodded. "I'll give you a call when I get there. Let's plan on a quick review around seven A.M. Then we'll head out to see the boyfriend."

"Do you want me to go with you?" Skylar asked.

Both Gabe and Cole turned their eyes to her and said "No" in unison.

"Why not?"

Gabe growled an answer. "You don't need to be involved."

Cole was nice enough to add, "If he sees you, he might mention it to others. Not something LCR would want. Besides, having two big bruisers like Gabe and me show up will get answers faster."

She believed him. If she didn't know they were two of the good guys, she'd be terrified if they showed up at her door. Her heart lifted at the thought of Calvin getting the hell scared out of him. Couldn't happen to a more deserving person.

Cole gave her a slight nod and headed to the door. The instant she heard it close, she tensed. Every time she and Gabe were alone, they seemed to end up arguing. Since she needed to save all of her energy for the upcoming confrontation with her father, she sincerely hoped to avoid another argument.

"Why don't you take a shower and relax?"

Skylar shot him a surprised glance at the gruff concern in his voice. Of course, after the last few days, she probably looked like hell. And Gabe probably wanted to avoid talking with her. When they'd been together those few short weeks, they'd never argued or had a disagreement. Another stark reminder of the difference between then and now.

She shook her head and headed toward the bar in the living room. "Would you like a drink?"

"Yeah. Fine. Whatever you're having."

Skylar opened the door to her wine cooler and stared at the bottles intently, as if it was of utmost importance to choose the correct one.

"If you want me to, I'll call your father and put off seeing him until you can get some rest."

She hid a grimace as she turned back to look at him. She must look worse than she thought. "No, I need to get it over with . . . we both do."

She chose a bottle of merlot, opened it, and poured two glasses. Taking a breath, she turned and handed him a glass, not looking at him directly. Sometimes it was just so hard to look at him at all, knowing what had happened, what could have been. If she weren't so worried about Kendra, she knew she'd be a puddle of an emotional mess. Her father had a lot to answer for.

A buzzer sounded, alerting her she had a visitor.

Gabe huffed out a disgusted breath. As he stalked to the speaker, he said, "The doorman was told to turn everyone away, with the exception of your father. Looks like he couldn't wait to get here."

Before he pressed the button to talk to the doorman, he glanced back at her. "You want me to tell him to wait until you've had your bath?"

She almost smiled. Few people would have had the guts to tell Jeremiah James to do anything. Which was probably one of the reasons her father hadn't liked him. Gabe's protectiveness had an arrogant edge. One of the many reasons she'd fallen in love with him. Skylar squelched that thought. It had been eight years. That love was gone.

And that Gabe no longer existed. She needed to remember that.

Aware that he was waiting for her answer, Skylar shook her head. "Let him come up. I'd like to get it over with so you can concentrate on finding Kendra."

Gabe barked into the speaker, "Let the bastard up."

Skylar winced. Her father would have heard that. Fireworks were about to erupt.

Gabe tried to keep the concern off his face as he waited with Skye for Jeremiah James to come through the door. She looked like death. This was probably not the best time to be having this meeting with her father. After the trauma of the last few days, she needed peace and quiet and someone to take care of her. But though her skin was milk white from exhaustion, he recognized the stubborn tilt to her chin. One he'd become very acquainted with over the last few days. The young, naïve Skye he'd married had grown into a strong, determined woman.

Since she was set on seeing this through right now, the best he could do was stand beside her and not go with his natural instinct, which was to beat the hell out of her father.

The elevator doors opened and there stood Jeremiah James. Gabe fully expected arrogance, denial, even anger. That wasn't what he got.

"Skylar!" Jeremiah ran for his daughter and scooped her up in his arms. As he whirled her around, Gabe heard choked sobs coming from the man many considered one of the coldest, most ruthless men in the world.

"I'm fine, Dad. Really. Put me down."

Skye's eyes were filled with tears as she flashed a somewhat helpless look at Gabe.

He pulled himself from his deep freeze of surprise and gently but firmly pulled Skye away from her father.

Jeremiah stood still for several seconds, as if trying to

control the mass of emotions inside him. Finally, after releasing a harsh breath, he said, "Thank God you're okay. Oh, baby, they hurt you, didn't they?" His hand trembled as he touched the bruises on her cheek.

"Not bad. Not like it could have been." She shot a look at Gabe. "Thanks to Gabe."

Jeremiah glanced over at him and suddenly seemed to remember he was in deep shit. A flash of guilt on the older man's face was quickly followed by arrogance. Ah yes, that's the look Gabe expected.

"I suppose you want an explanation about some things," James said.

Skye shook her head and whispered, "How could you, Dad?"

"I did it for you, baby."

"Don't give me that. You almost destroyed two lives. Don't tell me it was for my own good."

"It wouldn't have lasted, sweetie. I thought he was only after your money . . . and besides, you're too different and—" He shot a look at Gabe. "No offense, but you're just not like us."

Gabe snorted. "Offense? Hell, James, you just paid me a compliment."

"Oh for heaven's sake, Dad. Gabe didn't even know who I was . . . much less anything about my finances. I told you he didn't. And if it hadn't lasted, at least it would have been our choice to end it—not yours."

Jeremiah reached out his hand and Skye jerked away. He flinched and said, "I'm sorry, baby. I never wanted to hurt you." His eyes swimming with tears, he looked at Gabe. "Even though I don't think it would have worked out, if I had known what would happen, I never would have done it."

Gabe had been holding his tongue with difficulty. Between the two of them, Skye deserved getting her wrath out. She'd been the one most betrayed. But James's words and the tortured look on his face had Gabe asking, "What do you mean? What happened?"

Skye waved a hand. "It's not important."

"We almost lost her," her father said.

Gabe stiffened. "You almost lost her . . . how?"

"Dad, stop it. It's not—"

Jeremiah's head shook vigorously. "You almost died, Skylar. And it would have been my fault."

"What the hell is he talking about, Skye?"

"It's nothing. Really."

Tears poured down James's face as he recounted the event. "She went out looking for you. After the divers gave up . . . she went out again, by herself. Rented a boat and dove on her own." He swallowed hard and added, "Over and over again, looking for your body."

Jeremiah drew in a shuddering breath. "When I found out, we went after her." He looked at his daughter, who had wrapped her arms around herself and turned away from both of them. "We saw her dive into the water. By the time we got to her, she'd gone deep. The divers went in after her and she fought them, tried to get away." He swallowed hard. "She almost drowned. She was so exhausted from diving, the rescuers said if we hadn't found her when we did, she would have died on that last dive."

A shaking began inside Gabe. Fury at her father. Fury at Skye for her careless disregard for her own welfare. And yes, fury at himself for allowing this to happen in the first place. One fake phone call and he'd given up on them. And Skye had almost died.

A soft hand pulled him from the brink. He looked down at Skye, who, unbelievably, looked almost apologetic. "It's not your fault, Gabe."

Yes it was, but that was between him and Skye.

Jeremiah James had interfered too much already. Damned if he'd say anything in front of him.

"Can you forgive me, Skylar?" Jeremiah asked.

She ignored his question and said, "The phone call Gabe got, breaking it off. It was Lisa, wasn't it?"

When she didn't answer his question, James flinched and nodded.

"Did everyone know? I mean, everyone in the family?"

Jeremiah chewed on his lip, obviously wanting to protect as many of Skye's relatives as possible.

"You might as well tell me. If you don't, I'll go to every one of them and make them confess."

"Your mother, Lisa, and I were the only ones in the family who knew."

"So when Mom called and asked me to come see her before I went back to the island . . . that's when all of this took place?"

At Jeremiah's nod, she continued, "How did you get all those people at the resort to go along with this?"

Gabe swallowed a humorless laugh. Even after all these years, she still didn't realize what money could buy?

"We'd been going there for years on vacation, Skylar. I helped pay for some new facilities, a college education here and there . . ." He broke off, obviously realizing the more he said, the worse it sounded.

"How did you know it would work? That I would believe Gabe had committed suicide?"

His shoulders hunched defensively. "You told me enough for me to realize that he had some problems. I made some calls. Found out what he'd been through. Figured that'd be the most believable story." He glared at Gabe. "If you had just done what I asked you to do, none of that would have been necessary."

Gabe ignored Skye's gasp as he grabbed James's collar. "You bastard, don't blame me for your lack of ethics."

"I was protecting my daughter."

A soft, delicate hand on his arm, pulling him away, was the only thing that kept Gabe from slugging the self-righteous son of a bitch.

Skye's voice trembled. "Both of you . . . please calm down." She turned back to her father. "You suddenly appeared when we were looking for Gabe . . . I thought it was because you had come to meet him. But you were there even before I arrived, weren't you?"

James nodded. "They told me as soon as you got there."

"How did you know Gabe wouldn't try to contact me?"

Gabe crossed his arms and waited, wondering if James would tell the truth. The flash of guilt on his face was telling. But would he tell all?

"I had people watching you night and day. They knew what Maddox looked like. They were to keep him from you at all costs."

Skye shot Gabe a questioning look.

Gabe nodded. He hadn't told her this before. Had wanted to see what James's reaction would be. "I came to New York twice to see you. Got my ass kicked twice, too."

A humiliating thing to admit. He'd been skinny and untrained. Clueless on how to defend himself. The bastards could have done more damage than they did; the mortification was almost worse than the bruises. However, the experience had actually had a positive effect. Gabe had not only dedicated himself to getting into peak condition, but had gotten himself trained. And no one had ever kicked his ass again.

James shook his head in denial. "I never told them to hurt you, Maddox. Just to keep you away."

Gabe swallowed a snort. Goliaths like that were rarely

into negotiating with words. Their type of persuasion was usually handled with their fists. And he'd worn the bruises for weeks.

As humiliating and hurtful as those experiences had been, that wasn't the reason he'd given up on seeing Skye. He'd been stupidly planning another trip to New York when he'd received what he thought was proof positive that Skye truly wanted to pretend they'd never married.

Gabe took a breath. Whether James planned to be truthful about everything or not no longer mattered. Everything needed to be exposed.

"You want to tell her about the letter or shall I?"

"Letter? You mean the suicide notes I thought you left?" Skye said.

His eyes not straying from the older man's face, Gabe shook his head.

James shrugged defensively. "It was the only way I knew to get him to stop trying to see you for good."

"What did you do, Dad?"

"I . . ." He shot an angry, helpless look at Gabe. "I'm sure you remember it better than I do."

Yeah. Almost verbatim.

Though hurting Skye more than she'd already been hurt was the last thing he wanted, he forced himself to continue. "I received a letter, supposedly from you. It was filled with certain facts that only you would have known."

"What kind of facts?"

Her voice was weak and shaky, telling him she was on the edge. Gabe summarized instead of repeating the words he remembered all too clearly. "You said it had been fun, but as far as you were concerned, it wasn't real. Our love, the marriage. Nothing. You made reference to my background, lack of education, my brother's death." He took a breath. Even knowing it hadn't come from her, he couldn't deny the sting. "And the fact that even my stepmother couldn't love me. Why should you?"

"Oh God, Gabe," she gasped. "No, I would never . . ." Her eyes wide with horror, she shook her head and glared at her father. "I told you those things because I was trying to make sense of everything . . . justify why Gabe had committed suicide. And you used them against me. Daddy, you used them against me? How could you?"

Exhaustion and shock were beginning to take its toll. Other than the green and brown bruises, she had no color in her face at all. Her eyes, usually a bright, sky blue, were glazed with tears and looked almost dull gray.

In a voice so thick it was almost unrecognizable, she asked, "How did you keep him away from me for eight years? Have you had someone watching me the entire time?"

Looking at least twenty years older than he had when he first arrived, James shook his head. "After I sent the letter, I had Maddox watched for a while longer. When he left the country, I figured it was over with." He shrugged. "Malcolm knew not to—"

"Malcolm? Oh God, he knew, too?"

"I'm sorry, baby. I did it—"

She held up a shaking hand, the pain in her voice almost more than Gabe could stand.

"If you tell me you did it for my own good one more time, I'm going to scream. You had no right to interfere in my life like that. What would have happened if I wanted to marry again? Would you have let me commit bigamy, just to protect yourself?"

"I worried about that every day."

She snorted softly.

"Believe me, I did." He held out his hand again. "Remember, baby, when I made you promise never to run off again like that and get married? I would have told you the truth . . . if you'd wanted to marry again. I wanted you to be happy . . . really I did. But you never seemed interested." He swallowed hard. "I've lived with this for eight years, but I never—"

"And you had eight years to tell me the truth."

"I'm so sorry."

Though the grief and regret in the older man's face seemed genuine, Gabe could find no sympathy for him. The man's arrogance and snobbery had almost gotten his daughter killed and most certainly destroyed a marriage. Whether their marriage would have made it or not should have been theirs to decide. Not James's.

Her body visibly trembling, Skye turned her back to her father. "Go away. Please, just go."

Nodding sadly, Jeremiah headed to the elevator door. Before he reached it, he twisted around and said, "Maddox, I still don't like you involved with my daughter, but I thank you from the bottom of my heart for saving her."

He turned, pressed the button for the elevator, and disappeared before Gabe could come up with just one phrase that didn't sound like a death threat. He didn't have one. Never in all the years he'd been chasing after the scum of the earth had he wanted to kill as he did now.

When he saw Skye stumble, his priorities were quickly adjusted. He grabbed her before she fell to the floor. Sobs tore through her and the only thing he could do was hold her and curse everyone who'd hurt her, especially himself.

thirteen

Skylar woke filled with purpose. The last couple of days she'd done nothing but sleep, cry, and then sleep some more. When she'd collapsed after her father left, Gabe had been so kind and tender. And he'd wanted to stay with her. She'd refused. She needed the time alone. She'd mourned her husband's death eight years ago. Now she needed to mourn her father's betrayal and the empty years she'd endured. Years she could never reclaim.

Silly really, but as unrealistic as it had been, despite all the evidence that proved otherwise, she'd somehow hoped that her father had not had a hand in the awful lie of Gabe's death. She'd held on to that hope, small though it was, until she saw his face. Guilt had been spread all over it.

After he left, she'd collapsed. She wasn't proud of that. Actually hadn't had that kind of meltdown since she thought Gabe had killed himself. But everything had been accumulating and her father's confession had been the last straw.

Gabe had held her until she calmed down and then put her to bed. Before she'd fallen into a deep, dreamless sleep, she'd felt his lips on her forehead. She'd carried that memory into her sleep. He'd called each day to check on her. She'd assured him she was fine. And today, somehow, she knew she was. She felt energized and ready to do what needed to be done. Kendra was somewhere out there and she needed to do something to help find her.

After giving herself a full-body stretch to work out the remaining kinks and stiffness, Skylar strode to the bathroom. Since she'd gotten home, she couldn't get enough showers. Even now, the thought of those men's hands on her body caused her to feel grimy and unclean.

As hot water blasted down on her, Skylar soaped her body with her favorite lavender soap and reviewed how she might help find Kendra. She hadn't asked but she assumed Gabe was still in the city. She didn't hold out much hope that he would feel obligated to say goodbye when he left, but she knew he was still working Kendra's case. Until he'd explored all avenues here, she figured he'd stay.

She stepped out of the shower and wrapped the towel around her body. Her mind on Gabe and the myriad of feelings he still stirred in her, she entered the bedroom and then stopped when she realized it was no longer empty. The man who occupied her thoughts now occupied her bedroom.

"How did you get in?"

He shrugged. "I know the doorman." His eyes roamed all over her body. "I somehow always enter either too late or too early."

"What do you mean?"

His eyes filled with a dangerous light. He said, "Seems every time I walk in, you've just gotten out of the shower and covered up."

Her heart picked up a beat as the meaning of his words hit. If he'd come in sooner, she would have been nude. Did he still have feelings for her? Everything inside her screamed for that to be true.

She was just about to say something—what she had

no idea, since all of a sudden her tongue seemed much too large for her mouth—when Gabe's face went blank.

"Is that Benjamin?"

Still reeling from his earlier words, it took Skylar a few seconds to realize he'd seen the photograph she kept by her bedside of Benjamin Bradford. How was he to know that she kept it there for the cleaning people to see? Maintaining the illusion of their relationship was of great importance to both of them.

"Yes, that's Ben . . . but he's not—"

Gabe turned and stalked to the door. "Get some clothes on and come out. We need to talk." He shut the door behind him.

She wanted to call him back, to explain, but stopped herself. What would be the point? Years ago, Gabe had allowed one phone call to end their marriage. Her father's interference had been the impetus, but it had been Gabe's decision to leave the island. He'd said he had tried to see her back then, and she believed him, but she couldn't help but wonder why he hadn't tried to see her in all these years since.

The letter he'd received had no doubt been the biggest reason. Her father's cruelty in using what she'd told him in her grief was almost more than she could comprehend. It had been the lowest kind of blow.

And she couldn't deny that it hurt that Gabe believed she could have been that cold and cruel. She had thought he knew her. She'd been wrong.

Skylar was a romantic at heart. If Gabe had loved her, really believed that their love was worth fighting for, he would have come after her. No matter if he had to fight her father and anyone else who got in the way to be with her. But one phone call and one letter had ended it.

Sighing, Skylar turned back to the bathroom and went about getting ready. What was done was done. The most important thing now was to find Kendra. Then she and Gabe could legally end a marriage that never should have happened to begin with. He could go back to his world and she would return to hers.

That's the way he obviously wanted it. And, at some point, she planned to feel the same way.

Gabe paced back and forth as he waited for Skylar to emerge from the bedroom. In between chasing leads that led nowhere in their search for Kendra, he'd been struggling with all sorts of feelings. He hadn't wanted to leave her after her collapse, but he'd seen the look on her face. She was on the edge. If he'd stayed . . . hell, if he had stayed, he would have tried making love to her and opened up a whole new set of problems. Problems neither of them needed.

But while he'd stayed away, he couldn't shut down his memories. He'd successfully held them back for years, but like a dam had been let loose they flooded him. Every tiny detail came into play as he thought about those days of bliss. Hot summer sun, soothing breezes, and Skye in his arms. No man could have asked more of heaven.

What would have happened if he hadn't left the island? If he had just waited . . . or come to New York, gotten past her bodyguards and confronted her. Had he tried hard enough to see her?

After that damn letter, he'd been numb for months. Then he'd hired a discreet attorney and pursued a divorce. After a couple of years of sending divorce papers that were returned unsigned, he'd given up. But what would have happened if he hadn't allowed his stupid insecurities full reign? If he had tried just one more time to see her?

Jeremiah James's taunting words had done exactly what he'd set out to do—created a doubt that Skye's love was real. That someone like Gabe, an awkward, dorky nobody from nowhere, West Virginia, could hold on to a woman like Skye. She was Skylar James, wealthy beyond his imaginings, known and revered by everyone.

The magazines and newspapers the man had thrown at him, showing exactly who Skylar James was, only added to those deep-seated insecurities he hadn't known existed. Gabe had never been ashamed of his humble background. Had never really considered himself that different from anyone else. But Jeremiah James had planted seeds of doubt.

When the call came from the woman who sounded identical to Skye, ending their marriage, those seeds had sprouted and taken off like kudzu. Gabe had left the island before she could hurt him any more.

And Skye had almost died. He couldn't get over that thought. She'd almost died because she'd been searching for him. Her love had been real . . . perhaps more so than his.

Those feelings he once had for her were reemerging and blending with newer ones. Especially after his conversation with Noah this morning. He and Skye had a hell of a lot to talk about.

Gabe had assumed her lifestyle of wealth and fame was the real Skye. And she hadn't tried to defend herself. Why should she? He was the prick who'd assumed the worst without asking questions. Well, no more.

The door opened and Skye emerged. She looked rested. The color had returned to her face, the bruises were still there but healing, and damn it all to hell, she had on a sleeveless white shirt and skin-tight jeans that emphasized every sleek curve . . . and he wanted her. Dammit all to hell, he wanted her.

She flashed him a wary, tentative smile. Most likely because he probably looked like the gruffest, grumpiest man on the planet. He was married to this woman and couldn't touch her . . . couldn't make love to her. Whoever said you had to die before you experienced hell hadn't walked in his shoes.

Apparently hoping to improve his mood, she headed for the kitchen. "I'll make some coffee. Would you like breakfast?"

Gabe pulled his head out of his ass and followed her. "I made coffee when I first arrived. Might be too strong. I also ate some cereal you had in the pantry."

She wrinkled her nose. "I haven't opened the refrigerator since I got back. Was the milk okay?"

Gabe shrugged. "Ate it dry. It was fine."

A full-fledged smile sprang to her lips and his heart gave a painful jerk. He remembered that smile.

"Why don't I make us a real breakfast? We'll think better and you can tell me what you've learned while I cook."

"You cook?"

The smile froze on her face for barely a second, but she regrouped and said, "Yes, amazing what a fortune can do. I took cooking lessons." She turned away from him and opened the refrigerator.

Hell, he'd hurt her feelings. But he couldn't deny his surprise. She could afford a chef to cook every meal for her, but she chose to learn how to do it on her own. Just in the last few hours, he'd learned several important things about Skye, and now Gabe wanted to know everything. He didn't care that it wasn't wise, smart, or even the proper timing. Skylar James had just become his number one interest.

And then, after their talk, after they had said what they needed to say, he would do what he should have done eight years ago. He'd say goodbye to her face. And walk away . . . this time for good.

Skylar grimaced as the egg she'd just cracked almost slipped from her hand. He made her nervous. Those blue eyes that had mesmerized her from their first meeting watched her like a hawk as she prepared a simple meal of eggs Benedict. His surprise that she could cook had hurt, but she understood. Because she had money and could hire a cook, why bother to learn? The fact that she enjoyed doing things for herself probably never entered his head.

To keep her mind off him and on their main priority, she said, "You said you wanted to talk. Did Calvin give you any information on Kendra?"

Disgust tightened his face. "Other than the kid needing a change of underwear and giving us his promise to get right with the Lord, going to see him was worthless."

Even though he hadn't been able to shed any light on Kendra's disappearance, she couldn't help but be glad Calvin had received a good scare. Maybe it would do him some good.

"And you were right. He's not bright enough to be involved, even on the most basic level. My guess is his money comes from drugs."

Nodding her agreement, she watched as Gabe took a sip of the fresh coffee she'd made. Would he notice she'd remembered how he liked his coffee? Black with two teaspoons of sugar? He took several appreciative sips but didn't mention it. She told herself it was stupid to be disappointed. She wasn't looking for his approval or appreciation.

"Noah faxed some stuff over this morning. Cole and I reviewed it before I came over."

Which reminded her that there was someone else in New York with him. Gabe's presence had a tendency to reduce everything and everyone around her to the background. And as handsome and appealing as Cole Mathison was, he wasn't Gabe.

"Where is Cole? Will he be here also?"

"No, he went back to Florida this morning."

Before she could question him further, Gabe turned and went toward her office. "I'll show you what we've got."

By the time he returned, she'd set breakfast on the table. Since she knew she wouldn't be able to eat once they started talking about Kendra, she allowed herself a few bites before she looked down at the papers Gabe slid toward her.

While she read through the information, she was comforted by the knowledge that Gabe was there with her. His quiet strength gave her hope. And from the looks of the reports, they were going to need all they could get.

She looked up at the grim-faced man across from her. "So Kendra could be in any one of these cities?" Her eyes dropped back to the papers in front of her. "My God, this spans the globe."

"Whoever is in charge of this operation has been doing it for quite some time."

"But how is it that they don't get caught? Advertising on such a popular list should have caught someone's attention before now."

Gabe shook his head. "That's not how they're all nabbed. Looks as though he or they use several different methods."

Skylar glanced down at the locations of the girls who'd disappeared. "And he's getting them from all over the world . . . not just New York . . . not just the U.S."

"No." Gabe's voice was grim. "Which means we have to find the bastard before we can find the missing girls."

"What about the police? And the FBI? Aren't they involved?"

"Yes and no. Every one of these girls has a history of running away. There's only one girl who's underage. The others are of legal consent. Most of them were either homeless or have no permanent address."

"So no one really believes they've been abducted?"

"We do."

"Why?"

"From what you've told us about Kendra, she wouldn't have run away. The other girls fit her profile. No real family to believe they haven't run away again. But each of them disappeared in a similar fashion."

"Will you keep the police informed?"

"LCR has a good working relationship with New York authorities. We have a couple of contacts we can call on, but for now it's LCR and a few civilians. Until we can do some digging, we'll keep it below the radar."

Skylar took another sip of coffee and said, "Okay, so what's our plan?"

"I need more information on Kendra."

"Like what?"

"Apparently you're the only one who's even aware she's missing. I want to know how a young girl with her connections could disappear and you be the only one who gives a damn."

"There are other people who care. They just believe she's run away again."

"They don't care . . . not like you do." He paused a second as if waiting for her to say something else. Then he said softly, "Tell me about your mentoring program, Skye."

Gabe watched a myriad of emotions cross her face, wariness being the most obvious. Did she think he was going to make light of what she'd done with her life? He was still reeling from the information Noah had given him. To most of the world, Skylar James might well be a social butterfly with nothing more on her mind than the next party or fashion accessory, but Skye had a secret life. One that few knew about.

"It's just something I got involved with a few years back."

"Don't minimize what you do, Skye. Mentoring high-risk teens is an admirable occupation. Why do you hide it?"

"Can you imagine what would happen if it was discovered? The press would follow me everywhere. Every time someone famous does something like that, people look for ulterior motives. They dig and dig until they come up with something that sounds even the slightest bit sleazy, and that's what they focus on. Those kids don't need that kind of attention. They need to feel safe. Not judged by society. Give reporters any kind of hint and they'd have a field day."

"How do you keep it a secret? Your life is spread out on newspapers, magazines, and television for all the world to see."

"The world sees what it wants to see. People see a beautiful, wealthy woman flaunting herself, seemingly enjoying all that her money has to offer, and they don't look for secrets. I give them what they want and I get to have a life."

That seemed too simplistic but also too complicated. "Why not just get out of the public eye? There are a lot of women who manage—"

"I've been in the limelight since I was born."

He shook his head. "I think part of it is that you enjoy it. You get a certain sense of satisfaction from fooling everyone."

Her lips tilted slightly. "Maybe."

"How many girls have you mentored?"

She shrugged. "Not that many . . . maybe a dozen or so."

"Do you still see them?"

A smile brightened her face and Gabe had to grip the table to keep from leaning over and capturing it with his mouth. He'd never forgotten Skye's smiles or what they could do to him.

"I don't see them as much as I used to. A few of them left the city and found jobs elsewhere. Four of them still live here. I get together with them every few months." She shrugged. "They have jobs . . . careers now." She beamed like a proud parent and said, "Gretchen, one of the first girls I mentored, passed the bar last year and is an assistant DA."

"You helped them turn their lives around."

She shook her head. "No, they did all the hard work. I was just there to listen to them. Encourage them."

"When did you start mentoring?"

A shadow flickered on her face. And Gabe suddenly understood. Not only what his supposed death had done to her, but also the remarkable strength Skye had inside her. Behind that incredible beauty the world saw and admired was a woman of depth and substance.

"It was after you thought I committed suicide, wasn't it?"

When her eyes glazed with tears, Gabe cursed himself for asking what he already knew.

"Seems so crazy talking about it with you." She swallowed a laughing sob. "I felt so guilty for what happened. Not recognizing that you needed help. That you had an illness I didn't see. When I finally reemerged from the grief, I knew I needed to do something." She shrugged. "It wasn't much but it was—"

"Do not even think about minimizing what you've

done, Skye. I'm just sorry you went through so much pain."

She waved her hand awkwardly as if embarrassed by his praise. "Kendra was my toughest nut to crack. And she was coming around." She shook her head and repeated softly, "She was coming around."

"So tell me about her."

She stood and began to clear the table. And as if they'd been doing it forever, Gabe stood up and began to help her.

As they cleaned and put breakfast dishes away, Skylar described Kendra Carson. "She's a good kid, but her parents split up when she was a young teen . . . thirteen, I think. Her mother got full custody, but spent most of her alimony and child support on herself. She left Kendra on her own too long. By the time she realized that her daughter was involved with the wrong crowd and seriously screwing up her life, it was too late. So she dropped the parental hammer and Kendra rebelled."

"What happened?"

"What usually happens when a parent starts parenting too late. She ran away . . . again and again. Last time, she was found in some slum for drug addicts and pimps. She was taken back to her mom, who didn't know how to handle her and was tired of trying. As part of her treatment, she had to have counseling. I'd done some work for the youth center . . . all very public, but then I became close to several of the girls."

"Kind of like a 'big sister' program?"

"Something like that, only not in any official capacity. Somehow I seemed able to relate to them."

"And they didn't rat you out to the press?"

"They had as much fun keeping it a secret as I did. Kendra wasn't the most pleasant person at first, but I saw the pain behind all that bluster."

"When she disappeared again . . . how did you know she hadn't run away again?"

"Because I trust her. And she sent me that email. There would be no reason for her to do that if she was going to just run away. Besides, I've seen how hard she's worked to get her life straightened out. After she finished high school, she wasn't interested in going to college, so I encouraged her to find a profession she liked. She worked a few jobs but never found her passion. Modeling was the only thing she could talk about."

She grimaced. "I tried to discourage her. Kendra's a lovely girl, but the modeling business is so competitive and isn't easy. I've done my share of it, and while it can be fun and looks glamorous, it's hard work. Few make it to the big time. And it's full of pain and rejection. For someone who's loaded with self-confidence, modeling can be hard. For someone who has low self-esteem already, it can be devastating."

"You were trying to protect her and she thought you were holding her back."

She lifted her shoulders in a sad little shrug. "We had a lot of arguments over it. Finally, I offered to introduce her to some people, paid for her first photo shoot. I thought if she could see how hard and unglamorous it really was, she would lose the bug."

"And she didn't?"

"She did for a while . . . at least I thought she had. Then I got her email that she was going on an interview for a start-up modeling agency."

"Only it was a scam to lure unsuspecting young women."

She drew in a shaky breath. "She's tough. I just hope she's tough enough."

Gabe didn't say the obvious, though he figured Skye knew. As hideous as it was, being sold into sexual slavery wasn't the worst thing that could happen to Kendra. He hoped to hell they could find her before that could happen.

He took a breath. Now came the hard part. "Since we believe several of these cases are related, each girl needs to be checked out in the city where she disappeared."

Skye nodded. "That makes sense."

Gabe took another breath and said, "I'm leaving. Depending on what I find out, I don't know when or if I'll be back. Noah will keep you updated on our progress."

There was a brief flash of pain and then her expression froze into one of polite interest, as if they were discussing something totally meaningless. She stood stiffly and held her hands clasped in front of her. "I know you'll do your best. Thank you for your help."

"Stop it, Skye."

"Stop what, Gabe? You've made it more than clear that we never should have married. Nothing's changed for you. You always knew you were married." Her shoulders straightened even more. "I'll have my lawyers draw up divorce papers."

Gabe fought every instinct he had. He couldn't touch her. If he did, he wouldn't stop. And that would create complications neither of them needed or had time for.

He took one last long look at her, memorizing her face. A memory he'd carry till the day he died. Turning, he stalked to the door. He had to get out of here.

At the entrance, he turned around again. There was one thing he could give her. Stupid really. If she believed him, it'd be the most telling thing about him. If she didn't believe him . . . then it didn't really matter.

Gabe cut open his heart and said, "For what's it worth. I haven't slept with another woman since we married."

She stared at him the longest time and then she asked quietly, "Why not?"

"Because I don't cheat."

His jaw clenched, he withstood her scrutiny. And then she gave him the words they both knew he deserved. "No, you just leave."

Gabe acknowledged her statement with a nod and proved her correct by walking out the door.

The minute the door closed, Skylar collapsed into the nearest chair. She couldn't cry. There were no tears left. She'd drained herself dry over the last few days, and all that was left was a gaping hole of nothingness.

She had known he would go eventually. Just hadn't expected it now . . . this soon. She had to give him credit, though. He'd done it fast and clean, like ripping tape off skin. Funny how that was supposed to hurt less.

At least this time he'd said goodbye to her face. So why didn't that make her feel better?

He claimed he hadn't slept with another woman since they married. She didn't know him anymore, but the Gabe from eight years ago wouldn't have cheated on her. Maybe it should make her feel better to know he'd at least kept that part of their vows. It didn't. She just felt sad for both of them. For the time they'd wasted and the future they would never have.

In the span of a week, she'd gone from widow, to a married woman, to a woman seeking a divorce. Even for someone who lived a seemingly exciting, glamorous life, this was a bit much.

Grim humor, but it was the best she could do today.

William locked the door and dashed to his desk. There it was . . . sitting there, waiting for him. He picked it up and held it to his face. Inhaling deeply, he imagined he could smell her essence on it. Arousal beat deep within him as he allowed the momentum to build.

Anticipation made his fingers into thumbs as he

ripped open the package. A special courier had delivered it over two hours ago, but he'd been tied up with family issues. He and his wife insisted on having the family together for dinner each night. He loved that tradition. Catching up on what his children were up to was an important daily event he tried not to miss. However, it sometimes put a kink in his extracurricular activities. The package had been sitting on his desk, just waiting for his attention. He'd most likely have indigestion later because he'd gobbled his meal.

Finally the package ripped and photographs spilled out onto his desk. He groaned at the sight. The photographer he'd hired had worked for some of the best porn places in the business. He knew exactly how to set a pose to make the most out of his subject.

She was beautiful.

His hand shook as he reached out to caress the smooth leg. He could just imagine the silk of her skin beneath his hands. Unable to hold back, one hand reached below the desk and caressed his hardening flesh. So long . . . it had been so long since he'd indulged in the secret delights he provided to others. He'd relinquished his last jewel over a year ago. And then he'd spotted this treasure. She was young and progressing so beautifully. If she continued as she was, he should be able to keep her for years.

His eyes moved over her body, pausing at certain areas he could almost taste, he wanted them so much. His mouth watered. He hardened as he rubbed himself faster. . . . His eyes continued to roam. Long, smooth legs, taut, flat tummy, the perfect amount of cleavage revealed . . . just a hint of the beauty he would soon see. His mouth watered even more. Long, slender neck and her face . . . Everything stopped. Her face! Rage bloomed. Passion dwindled, went limp in his hand. *A bruise.* She had a bruise on her face—someone had hit her.

His fury was so great, his hand shook as he grabbed the phone. Someone better damn well have an explanation for this.

"Foster?" he snapped.

"Yes." The voice held a wary tinge.

"You want to tell me why there's a bruise?"

The man gave an audible swallow. "She fought us. We had no choice but to restrain her. It wasn't our fault."

"I. Do. Not. Want. Her. Bruised. Do you understand me?"

"Yes, sir."

"No more photographs until she's healed. Got that?"

"Yes, sir."

William pulled in a calming breath. His voice still hard, but controlled, he said, "When she's healed, I'll want a short movie . . . perhaps twenty minutes in length. One man will be allowed to touch her to pose her, provide instructions, but nothing else." His voice hardened. "Is that understood?"

"Yes, sir."

William hung up the phone, unable to speak any further. Despite his anticipation of the upcoming movie, his day was still ruined. He had so looked forward to getting these photographs. Had fantasized about how she would look. How he would feel when he was with her for the first time. But seeing her skin marred, imperfect, had destroyed his pleasure.

His tastes were exact and specific. Beautiful. Young. Desperate. Unblemished. Not a mark on them. Until he made the marks himself.

fourteen

"Skylar, you have to come out of your apartment sometime." Carole James's voice held the petulant tone Skylar had grown up with.

"How do you know I've not been out?"

"Your father happened to mention it."

The slight hesitation before her mother answered was telling. So they had someone watching her . . . again.

"And Dad knows I've not been out of my apartment how?"

"Does it really matter, darling? That's not really the issue. You need—"

"I need you to leave me alone, Mother."

"Skylar!"

At one time, the shocked hurt in her mother's voice would have caused guilt. Not anymore. Her parents had controlled her life without her even knowing it. She refused to allow that to happen again.

"With Dad's help, you did something totally unforgivable. Do you even care about that?"

"But darling, we did it for your own good."

"Stop it. I'm a grown woman . . . a grown, married woman. I decide what's for my own good. Not anyone else. Understand?"

"Of course you're a grown woman, darling, but we love you and want what's best for you."

"What's best for me is to live my life as I please. Now,

either tell Dad to call off whoever is watching me or I'll call the police and report that my own father is stalking me. The paparazzi will love that."

"Darling, let me come over and visit with you. It's been so long and—"

"Call off the spies, Mom."

The sputter on the other end of the line almost caused Skylar to smile. Her mother hated to be called Mom.

"Fine. But when you're ready to stop acting like a spoiled brat, your family will be waiting for you . . . as we always are."

Rolling her eyes at the drama queen of the family, she said, "Goodbye, *Mom*."

After she hung up, she gazed around her apartment and wrinkled her nose at the mess. She hadn't left her apartment in over a week. There was no place she wanted to go, no one she wanted to see. Except the one man who didn't want to see her.

The press was having a field day with speculation on what had happened to her. Breast implants and a broken heart were the top two speculations. Though the broken heart was more apt, it wasn't for the man they thought. She hadn't seen Benjamin since she'd returned.

Other than the daily calls from her family, urging her to get back to her old life, Noah McCall had been her only connection to the outside world. He called every couple of days with an update on Kendra's case. Not that there was much to report.

Kendra had been missing for almost three weeks now. And still, other than LCR and herself, no one believed it wasn't voluntary. A bad case of crying wolf too often. Kendra had disappeared so many times, it barely caused a blip of alarm to anyone. Even Kendra's mother.

With effort, Skylar pulled herself up from the couch. Though she hated to admit it, her mother was right about one thing. She couldn't stay cooped up in this apartment forever. It was time to face the world again.

And it was time to do what she'd told Gabe she would do. The divorce that probably would have happened long ago needed to begin. It might not be what her heart really wanted, but her head told her different. Gabe obviously didn't want to be married to her. And damned if she wanted to be married to someone who didn't want her.

The more Skylar thought about it, the more anxious she was to get out of her apartment and get the process started. She hurried through her shower, blew-dry her hair, and put on the minimum of makeup. Wrapping a towel around her, she turned to go into her bedroom, contemplating her wardrobe. What did one wear to a meeting where your heart was to be ripped to shreds and demolished forever?

Skylar pushed opened the door and swallowed a scream.

"Sorry. I did knock this time."

"What are you doing here, Gabe?"

His eyes took on that brilliant blue glint, and once again she stood there and let him devour her with a look. Her nipples peaked and pressed against the towel. His eyes seemed to know as they zeroed in on them. He had loved her breasts. Had told her they were the most perfect mounds God had ever created.

"I need to talk to you."

She shuddered, returning to reality with a crash. Gabe had recovered quicker than she had.

"Is it Kendra?"

"Yes . . . and no." He gave her one last lustful glance and turned away. "Get dressed and let's talk."

As Gabe paced the living room, waiting for Skye to dress, he called himself every kind of fool for even being here. Someone else could have handled this . . . probably a hell of a lot better than he could. But he hadn't wanted anyone else with Skye. No one but him.

Not that he'd handled it that well with Noah. His boss had known exactly what he was asking of his operative. With a glint of barely concealed amusement, he'd delivered the details of Gabe's new assignment.

"You want me to do what?" Gabe shouted. "What the hell do you mean, I've got to go back to New York?"

"We got reliable sources telling us that a high-profile and very wealthy man is in charge. We used the information Skylar gave us about the man being well connected. That helped us narrow down the search . . . it paid off."

"You got a name?"

"Not yet."

Gabe was already getting that feeling in the pit of his stomach that told him the next words were ones he wouldn't want to hear.

"He's got wealth and power . . . and he's in New York."

High profile. Wealthy. "Hell, it's not Jeremiah James, is it?" Though Gabe hated the bastard, he didn't want Skye's father to be mixed up in this kind of shit. The man had already hurt her enough.

"No. Not James, but someone just as powerful."

Noah's silence after that statement was purposeful. He was waiting for Gabe to come to the conclusion he didn't want to come to.

Gabe sighed. "You want me to go undercover with Skye."

"You have the best inroad anyone does. Skylar knows everyone. They'd never suspect she would be bringing someone in to investigate them."

"You got me a cover?"

"We're working on one now. You got any suggestions?"

"Anything other than Skylar James's boy toy."

Gabe could still hear McCall's snort of laughter in his mind. When he'd been given the details of his cover, he'd balked again. Undercover wasn't his forte. Being bluntly honest and not one to put up with a lot of bullshit, he often ended up telling people exactly what he thought. Not the best way to stay undercover.

For a moment, he'd even contemplated suggesting Cole handle the job. But the thought of Cole or any man other than himself pretending an intimacy with Skye wasn't something he could stomach.

"So why are you here?"

Gabe whirled and swallowed hard at the vision before him. Dammit, why the hell did this one woman create such a clamoring of emotions inside him? Emotions he'd worked for years to suppress.

"LCR has uncovered information that someone in New York—someone wealthy, powerful, and connected—is involved in Kendra's disappearance, and the other girls', too."

"Someone I might know?"

"Most likely."

Wrapping her arms around herself, she dropped onto the sofa. "But how can you know this? I mean . . . if you know it's someone here . . . how can you not know his name?"

Explaining how McCall obtained information would take hours, only skim the surface, and probably be only halfway accurate. Gabe had long ago given up trying to figure out how his boss uncovered the information he did. He was just damn grateful McCall used his talents for the good.

"LCR's spent hundreds of man-hours on this. The

clue those bastards gave you about it being someone well connected helped narrow the search. They know he's wealthy, powerful, and from this area. And probably thinks he's either above the law or his reputation is so clean, no one would ever find out."

She drew in a breath. "So what's the plan?"

Since being blunt was his normal MO, Gabe said, "I'm going undercover . . . working with you. You'll take me around, introduce me. I'll find him."

She looked shocked but not overly so. "So what are we going to do? Tell people you're my long-lost husband? Or that we just got married?"

"Would that bother you, princess? Telling people we're married? You think they'll see a coal miner under the designer suits?"

"Stop it, Gabe. You know that's not how I feel, but—"

"Relax." He shoved a folder toward her. "Here's my cover. Should make you feel a little better."

Before she glanced down at the information he'd given her, she gave him a glare. "I told you to leave that chip on your shoulder behind. Looks like you travel everywhere with it."

Gabe nodded toward the folder. "Read the information, Skye."

As he waited for her to respond to what she was reading, he glanced around her apartment. It was cluttered and smelled musty, as if it'd been closed up for a while.

Finally she looked up. "So you're new money."

"Yeah. Think it'll fly?"

"New York society is a mixture of both. The old money will be more suspicious of you. Suddenly showing up and no one ever having heard of you will cause a certain amount of distrust."

Gabe shrugged. "Money new or otherwise spends just

as well. I'm a self-made man. That'll give me an opportunity to be a bit more flamboyant."

"But buying up foreclosed mortgages and selling them? You can't carry off—"

"You don't know what I can and can't carry off, princess."

"I'm sure you're very good at your job, Gabe. It's just these people . . ."

"What, Skye? These people can spot a fake? Hell, that's all these people are. Why shouldn't I be one more?" The smile Gabe gave her wasn't kind. "I'll make sure I don't embarrass you."

Skye's hand gesture indicated her exasperation. "You could never embarrass me, except when you're acting like a jerk, as you are now. Not everyone is a fake. That's just your prejudice showing."

Prejudice, hell. Gabe kept quiet. Arguing the point wouldn't get him anywhere.

Skye's continued to voice her concerns. "I'm just worried that whoever this man we're searching for is, he'll get suspicious."

"There's no reason anyone will get suspicious. My cover will be tight. I'll just be a new love interest for you. The only man you've been linked with in the last few years has been Benjamin Bradford." He watched her closely as he added, "There's speculation that your relationship is on the rocks."

"Ben and I date only casually. I tried to tell you that before. I can break it off."

Gabe lifted a broad shoulder in a careless shrug. "Don't do it on my account."

Seeing Skye's face freeze into a polite mask of indifference caused a major pang of guilt. Why the hell did he have to be such a prick around her?

"I'll call him and explain that we can't see each other for a while."

"Will he accept that?"

"Like I said . . . it's casual."

Her challenging look was a warning; Gabe took it as such and nodded. "Fine."

"So what do I need to do?"

This was the part where he would have his way. He leaned forward and locked his gaze with hers. "Absolutely nothing. You take me around . . . introduce me but you don't get involved. At all."

She waved a hand at him. "I can give—"

"Not. At. All. Skye. I'm not going to have you in danger again. If it looks like that's even a remote possibility, I'm pulling you out. Understand?"

Her full mouth pursed in disapproval. Gabe straightened and pulled away from her before he kissed that pretty pout.

"Do we need to go shopping?" she asked.

"No. Noah's receptionist is a closet fashion queen. She assured me that not even Skylar James herself could tell I wasn't born into high society." He smiled briefly. "Angela's a fan."

"You're not, though . . . are you, Gabe?"

How the hell was he supposed to answer that question? A fan? No, he could never be considered a fan or an admirer. The words were too weak . . . too common. The powerful feelings Skye brought out in him were more akin to words like "volcanic," "tumultuous," and "unrelenting."

Since he couldn't tell her that his feelings for her went well beyond simple admiration, he chose to change the subject, knowing it would definitely get her mind off their current conversation.

"So where do you want me to sleep?"

"You're staying here?"

"You've got reporters watching your apartment at all hours. They see me staying with you, they're likely to be more convinced. Besides, it'll just be easier to work together if I stay here."

The look on her expression-filled face was priceless. He read her perfectly. She was wondering if he was looking to create more than just a façade of intimacy. Would she be interested if he was? The instant that thought surfaced, Gabe squelched it. No way in hell was he going to start up something when they both knew where it would lead.

"You do have an extra bedroom, don't you?"

And again, he read her perfectly. She looked relieved. He ignored the stabbing pain in his gut. Stupid to think she'd want anything else. What was stupider was for him to want anything else. Grabbing his luggage he'd dropped on the floor, he turned around and headed to the guest bedroom. "I'm going to take a shower." With one last look at the beautiful woman he was married to but couldn't touch, Gabe closed the door.

A long shuddering breath escaping her, Skylar twisted around quickly in case Gabe opened the door again. If he saw her face, he'd know the truth. Know what she was thinking. Gabe was here. Staying with her. They would be together.

She told herself not to get her hopes up. The expression on his face told her he didn't want to be here. This was a job for him. She was merely assisting him, giving him access to information he otherwise would not be able to get. Nothing more.

Finding Kendra and the creep who had her was their main priority. She would never forget that. Ever. But when he'd asked about where he would sleep, she hadn't been able to hide her reaction. He'd scared the hell out of her. Stupid really, but she hadn't slept with a man in eight years. Gabe had been her one and only lover. And once again, she'd felt like the twenty-year-old virgin she'd been. As inexperienced and inept as she had been when they'd first made love. Only Gabe had ever been able to bring out these insecurities.

When he'd mentioned the guest bedroom, she had felt a moment of relief. Followed quickly by an overwhelming disappointment. Gabe wasn't here to reignite anything between them. She needed to remember that.

She also needed to forget that once her nervousness about intimacy with Gabe had disappeared, she'd been uninhibited and ravenous, enjoying his lovemaking unlike anything else she'd ever experienced.

Glancing down at her body, she knew forgetting how Gabe could make her feel would be a test in willpower. Her peaked nipples and the slow, sensuous throbbing between her legs was a clear indication that when it came to Gabe, forgetting his lovemaking . . . and not wanting it again . . . would be no easy task. Especially with him just a bedroom away.

fifteen

Gabe looked down at the invitations in his hand. Four parties in one night? How the hell could a person live like this? Why would anyone willingly live like this? Just attending one party was a sure prescription for a massive pain in the ass. Going to four in one night was something he wouldn't wish on his worst enemy. And it looked as though he'd be living this hell at least until they pinpointed the bastard they were looking for.

A sound behind him alerted him that he was no longer alone. He turned and had to wad the invitations in his hand to keep from dropping them. On a regular day, Skye was a beautiful woman. Tonight she stunned.

The shimmering gold dress clung to her as though it were a part of her . . . as if it were attached to her skin. It glittered and sparkled as she breathed, mesmerizing and exciting at the same time. Shoulders, bare and gleaming, reminded him of rich cream. His mouth watered as he remembered running his mouth over her warm, silky skin, gliding his tongue down her back, cupping her perfect ass in his hands. The memories were eight years old but as vivid as if they'd happened yesterday.

Swallowing a curse, Gabe looked back down at the wadded invitations, knowing if he continued to look at her, he wouldn't be able to keep his hands to himself. He'd wanted her years ago like nothing he'd ever wanted in his life. Why the hell had he thought that had changed?

He was still attracted . . . very attracted . . . to his wife. Hell, what was he thinking? Of course he was attracted to her. Skye was a beautiful woman and he was a man who'd gone without a woman for a long time. It was nothing more than that.

"Do I look okay?"

Her tentative question brought his head up and him back to earth. He was probably scowling—his usual expression.

"Yeah, you look real nice." He mentally rolled his eyes. Not only had he sounded like the country bumpkin he was, he also sounded like a dimwit.

Fortunately, she seemed to enjoy his lame response, since she gave him a smile that could light up New York. His heart and another body part responded the way they were designed to respond. *Dammit.*

"You look very handsome."

Tearing his eyes away from the vision in front of him, Gabe glanced down at his own garb. Wearing a tuxedo went against every natural instinct he possessed. Even though the fit was excellent and the designer one even he'd heard of, it still felt unnatural and strange.

And Skye looked as comfortable in her expensive clothing as if she'd been born in them. Which she practically had been.

"Did you look at the invitations I accepted?"

"Yeah."

As if she'd been doing it for years, she glided toward him with a smile and adjusted his tie. A very wifely thing to do. "It won't be as bad as you think."

Gabe breathed in her scent . . . lavender with a touch of spice. He jerked away from her hands before he did something supremely stupid.

Ignoring the little dip in her smile, he said, "Did you get in touch with your boyfriend?" Ah hell, he'd meant that to sound businesslike but it sounded more like a jealous teenager. Or jealous husband?

"Yes. I told him I needed to back off seeing him for a while. I told you the truth, though—there's really nothing going on between us. We're just good friends."

"That's not what the tabloids say."

She tilted her head in the flirty way he remembered all too well. "I thought you didn't read them."

He shrugged and turned away with the pretense of grabbing something from the desk. "I've seen them in the checkout counters at the grocery store. They're kind of hard to miss."

A full-throated laugh was her response.

Gabe whirled, ready to snarl some sarcastic comeback. He swallowed the words. Her eyes were glittering with amusement and sweetness. How the hell did a woman who'd been surrounded by the best of everything all of her life still look so sweetly innocent? That had been one of the biggest reasons he'd fallen in love with her. She'd been so natural . . . so real. At that thought, he shut down those memories. He didn't need them and neither did Skye. Besides, they had a job to do.

"You have any more questions about me or my cover before we head out?"

"Not you, but I'm still a little confused about Cole's cover. How is pretending to be my new chauffeur going to help us find the guy who has Kendra?"

"Chauffeurs know a hell of a lot about their employers. Cole's excellent at getting people to talk."

"So while we're inside, looking for the creep, he'll be with the other chauffeurs discussing secret liaisons and such."

"Something like that."

"Then I guess he's waiting downstairs for us, so we'd better go." She held out her hand to him. Before he knew it, he took it and walked hand in hand with her to the elevator.

Skylar kept a surreptitious eye on Gabe as they entered the small space. She'd never seen anyone look more uncomfortable in a tuxedo in her life, especially a Sebastian St. Claude. And the crazy part was, he looked gorgeous. "Tall, dark, and devastatingly handsome" might be the oldest cliché in existence, but it fit Gabe perfectly.

Eight years ago, Gabe had been just as tall and dark, but he'd been lanky, thin. He'd still been recovering from his ordeal and had look malnourished. And there had been an innocence about him . . . a naïveté. Even after all he'd been through. Skylar had fallen in love with a shy, handsome boy with a wicked sense of humor and a unique sense of adventure. He'd also been one of the kindest people she'd ever met.

The only resemblance between the young Gabe and this gorgeous man beside her was that he was still tall and dark. Everything else had changed. Broad, muscular shoulders tapered to a narrow waist and hips. His long legs looked like solid tree trunks beneath his clothing.

Years ago, she'd thought Gabe was handsome but had fallen in love with the man inside. Today, she was uncertain of the man inside, but the outside man made her mouth water.

They were only about two floors down when she heard the increase in his breathing. Dammit, why did she have to live forty floors up in a penthouse apartment anyway?

They were five floors down when his face began to perspire.

Odd, but when they'd come up a week or so ago, he hadn't had the same reaction. Then it hit her. He'd been concerned for her. His focus had been on her safety and well-being and not his.

Taking a chance that she wasn't doing something monumentally stupid that she'd live to regret, Skylar turned to stand in front of him. Placing her hands on his shoulders, she looked up at him and said softly, "You know, we never did get to finish our honeymoon. How about we continue it tonight?"

Deep blue eyes, which had been dilated and slightly out of focus, zeroed in on her. "Are you insane?"

Satisfied she had his attention, she moved even closer and whispered a soft kiss against that stubborn chin. Her lips moved softly back and forth, loving the slight stubble prickling at her mouth. "Remember how good it was, Gabe? How hot you could get me?" Her tongue flicked out and licked at the corner of his mouth. "Remember how I would scream when you pushed inside—"

His mouth slammed down on hers and Skylar forgot all about the reasons she'd started this distraction. Wrapping her arms around his shoulders, she pressed against his hard body and allowed him to eat at her lips. His tongue plunged and retreated over and over again and Skylar groaned as heat ignited, simmered, built, and then raged out of control.

Years. It had been years since she'd felt this arousal . . . this mind-blowing, body-exploding experience. Gabe's hands roamed all over her body; one hand stopped at her ass, where it kneaded, molded, and pinched; another hand moved up her torso and then stopped on a breast, where it caressed with just the right amount of pressure.

Skylar gasped against his mouth and moved into him, trying to fit her mound against the hard steel of his erection. She rubbed, she moaned. Dropping her hands to his hips, she pressed him deeper, grinding against the part of his body that had once given her so much pleasure.

Shattering, earth-pounding pleasure flooded through her. Yes, this is what she'd been missing. What she'd longed for. Heat flashed like lightning through her. She was throbbing, breaking apart . . . coming full force . . . life darkened, expanded . . . brightened . . . brilliant light flashed . . . the universe was exploding and then . . .

Ping! The elevator doors slid open.

Breathing heavily, Gabe dropped his hands and growled against her mouth, "Nice diversion, babe. Was it good for you?"

"Gabe, this is Jackson Harding. He's—"

"The owner and chairman of Harding Holdings . . . the premier investment firm in North America." As Gabe finished Skylar's sentence, he held out his hand to the balding, distinguished-looking man in front of him.

Skye looked briefly discomfited but recovered quickly and added, "Jackson, this is Gabriel Maddox. He's in real estate."

Jackson Harding hadn't become one of the wealthiest men in the world by being unobservant. His expression indicated that he sensed the underlying tension between Gabe and Skye. Fortunately, he was too much of a gentleman to comment on it. He shook Gabe's hand. "I read an interesting article about your company in the *Times* this morning."

Gabe shrugged. "A fluff piece, which was a nice change of pace."

Jackson's thin lips moved into a sympathetic grimace. "Yeah, I've been there, too. I looked at some online pieces that weren't as kind."

"Hard to get to number one without pissing some people off."

"I know what you mean. Perhaps we could have lunch one day soon."

"I'd like that, sir."

Jackson smiled and glanced over at Skye, who, Gabe

was glad to see, had finally closed her gaping mouth, pretty though it was. Harding didn't need to see Skye's astonishment.

"Skylar, it's good to see you . . . but what's with the bruises?" Harding shot a dark look at Gabe.

Skye's laughter tinkled like a wind chime. She put her hand on Jackson's sleeve . . . a light, brief touch of reassurance. "Silly, really. I mean, I go to Argentina to ski, which you know what a horrible skier I am, right? Well, this time I didn't even get to the slopes to fall down and embarrass myself. I jumped off the lift, skidded, and fell face-first."

While Jackson laughed as she had meant for him to, Gabe felt such an immense sense of pride in her he couldn't do anything but stare. After what she'd gone through . . . Hell, she should be a basket case. But other than the slight paleness to her skin and that one lasting bruise she hadn't been able to completely cover, she looked as composed as if she'd really returned from a relaxing vacation. Skylar James had backbone to spare.

"Perhaps a beach vacation might be more fitting for you."

Another soft laugh and then she said, "Jackson, will you excuse us? I see Senator Mills and I wanted to introduce Gabe to him."

"Of course." He held out a card to Gabe. "Give me a call next week and let's set up a lunch meeting. I'd like to discuss some business opportunities."

Gabe took the card, murmured something meaningless, and moved on. If things went the way he wanted, he'd have pinpointed the bastard by then and would be hundreds of miles away from this city . . . away from Skye. He refused to acknowledge the bleakness of that thought. He had come here for only two purposes: one was to find the bastard responsible for Kendra's disappearance and rescue the girl, the other to keep an eye on Skye. Once the first was accomplished, he'd no longer be needed for the second.

That was the way it had to be. It was what he wanted. And at some point soon, preferably in this lifetime, he'd start believing that.

"Skylar? I didn't expect to see you tonight . . . though I am delighted that you finally left your apartment."

Jeremiah James's voice was one he'd just as soon not hear ever again. Gabe turned to the silver-haired man glaring accusingly at him. Damned if he was going to put up with this man's arrogance tonight.

Gabe gave the man a look that had caused lesser men to shrivel. But Jeremiah James was tougher than most. Moving closer so no one would overhear him, Gabe said, "If you got a problem with me being here, I suggest you leave."

James jerked back. Most likely he'd never been talked to that way. About time someone told him what an arrogant prick he was.

Skye's soft voice penetrated the cloud of anger fogging his brain. "Gabe, now isn't the time. Dad was just surprised to see me. I've not been out much since I returned from my trip." She looked pointedly at her father, "Isn't that right, Dad?"

"Yes, it is, but I can't say I like your attitude, Mr. Maddox."

Gabe snorted. "James, I don't give a fu—"

"Both of you, stop it." Skye's furious whisper cut off Gabe's response. "There are at least ten people staring at us, wondering what's going on. I refuse to be a headline tomorrow just because you two can't behave civilly to each other."

James looked vaguely ashamed. "I'm sorry, Skylar.

You're right. I was just surprised to see you. How are you feeling?"

"I'm better, Dad."

"Why aren't you resting? You still look pale . . . you've been through so much."

"I have rested, Dad. Besides, I told you, Kendra is missing. There's evidence that someone in—"

Gabe touched her elbow in warning. Jeremiah James didn't need to know the details of this case. "Skye, I don't believe your father is interested in our efforts to find your friend."

James puffed out his chest. "I'm interested in anything that concerns my daughter."

Skye's face flickered with acknowledgment of his warning. The creep they were looking for was probably someone James knew. The less he knew, the better.

"I know you're interested, Dad. But Gabe and I need to work on this. Once Kendra's found, I'll explain everything."

"Are you still angry with me, baby? About the—"

"Of course I'm still angry. Did you expect I'd just forget what you did?"

"I'm sorry. I did it for—"

"If you say you did it for my own good again, I'll shout this place down and then everyone will definitely have something to talk about over breakfast in the morning." She darted a look around at the dozens of people milling about. Several were making no attempt to pretend they weren't trying to eavesdrop. "We're still attracting too much attention. When this is over, you and I are going to have a heart-to-heart about your interference. Until then, let's just pretend everything's okay."

James shot a hard glance at Gabe. "Who is Mr. Maddox supposed to be? Your new love interest?"

"You got something to say about that, James?"

"Gabe, stop it." When she moved closer to Gabe, an unspoken message that they were indeed pretending to be lovers, Gabe put his arm around her shoulders. The warm, creamy skin beneath his hand was almost his undoing. He'd done his best not to touch her bare skin, and now all he could think about was how much he wanted to run this hands up and down her entire body, explore every curve, rediscover new territory. That elevator stunt she'd pulled to distract him had worked, though not in the way she might have expected. Fire thrummed through his veins and Skye was the only one who would be able to extinguish the blaze.

Gabe clamped down on his teeth. With his claustrophobia, dislike of large crowds, wearing a damn monkey suit, and Jeremiah James's arrogant sneer, having a hard-on in the middle of a mass of people should be impossible. Trust Skye to be the one to make him forget everything but how much he wanted to be inside her.

"Isn't that right, Gabe?"

He jerked himself out of his fantasy. Hell. He was on a job.

"Sorry, I missed that."

Skye gave him an odd look. "I was explaining to Dad that we're telling everyone that we met at a ski resort while I was vacationing in Argentina."

"Yeah. I assume you saw the article about me in the *Times* this morning."

James's eyes narrowed with disapproval as he nodded.

Skye said, "I was going to ask you about that. I didn't know anything about it until Jackson mentioned it. How did you manage that?"

Gabe lifted a shoulder. "LCR has some influence."

"Enough that they'd print something blatantly untrue?" James's mouth twisted in a self-righteous smirk.

Gabe couldn't hold back a dry laugh. "Yeah, like everything that's printed these days is the truth. I've seen complimentary articles about you, James, so I know they lie."

Huffing out an exasperated breath, Skye grabbed on to Gabe's arm and began to pull him away from her father.

"If all you can do is snark and snarl at each other like rabid dogs, let's go mingle. That's the reason we came, isn't it?"

Hell, she was right. This job was his priority. His antipathy for Jeremiah James should not even come into play.

Soft music, glittering lights, fake laughter, and the chattering of too many voices clamoring for attention created a cacophony of too much sound, too much confusion. Suddenly the tightness in Gabe's chest pressed deeper. He took several long, even breaths and plastered an innocuously pleasant look on his face. Taking Skye's hand, he let her lead him through the mass of brightly dressed people and introduce him to several more of New York's elite. He'd had tough assignments before. This was just one more.

Skylar moved from one introduction to the other with her mind only half aware of what she was doing. The meeting with her father had actually gone better than she'd anticipated. It hadn't been pleasant, but no blood had been spilled and no one had ended up on the floor, so she was counting it as a win.

Besides, her mind was still in shock mode as her body continued to reel from the elevator incident. She had instigated the small seduction scene to take Gabe's mind off his claustrophobia. And he had turned it around on her. The body that she'd put on deep freeze for eight years had melted. Like an iceberg on an open fire grill, she'd been like liquid in his arms the moment his mouth touched hers.

Despite the circumstances of why he was here. Despite the fact that she knew he didn't love her and yes, dammit, despite the fact that she was still hurt from what she considered abandonment on his part, she wanted him with a desperation she barely recognized. Gabe had once been a gentle, giving lover. The new Gabe was neither gentle nor, she suspected, giving, but his rough, sensual kiss had given birth to a wildness inside her. A wildness she wanted to explore . . . but only with Gabe.

"Skylar?"

She whirled around at the sound of the familiar masculine voice. The tall, elegant man in front of her usually had an air of amused boredom. But not tonight.

"Should we have this discussion here or somewhere in private?"

Oh hell, he was angry. She so did not need this. "Ben, I told you—"

Grasping her arm, he pulled her toward him. "I know what you said on the phone, but I still want an—"

Gabe's dark head pushed between them. He kept a smile on his face, which impressed her since she could feel rage roaring through him. "Either you remove your hand from her or I'll remove it for you."

Too used to getting his own way, Benjamin Bradford was not easily intimidated. Unfortunately. He shot Gabe an arrogant, challenging look. "Are you threatening me?"

"Let's just say you and I are about to get acquainted in a way you're going to really dislike."

The smile had dropped from Gabe's face and a cold, menacing mask stared down at Ben. If Skylar didn't know Gabe so well, she would've been terrified. He looked murderous. Benjamin must have realized the same thing, because he pulled his hand away from Skylar and stepped back.

Breathing out a shaky relieved sigh, she said, "Ben, I'd like you to meet Gabriel Maddox. Gabe, this is Benjamin Bradford . . . my friend." She raised a challenging brow with her last words. Damned if she'd allow Ben to indicate anything different to Gabe.

Ben was smart enough to realize he had seriously pissed off the couple in front of him and he'd better either move away or make amends. Being a well-brought-up gentleman with an Ivy League education, he chose the latter. "My apologies. I saw Skylar and allowed my emotions to get the best of me." He held out his hand to Gabe. "Mr. Maddox, I hope you'll forgive my rudeness."

Gabe looked down at his hand and then, with deliberate slowness, took it and grasped it hard. Ben's face twitched, indicating Gabe was giving him an unspoken message. Gabe's words weren't much nicer. "Apologize to Skylar and I'll consider it. However, you ever lay a hand on her like that again, your head will be up your ass. Got it?"

Eyeing the man in front of him as if he were a dangerous, unknown species, Benjamin nodded. "Of course." He turned to Skylar. "I'm sorry, love. I forgot myself. Forgive me?"

Never able to stay angry with him long, she gave his arm an affectionate pat. "You're forgiven. Now, do you still want to talk?"

With an uneasy glance at Gabe, he said, "Perhaps we could talk later."

"Why don't you come for breakfast in the morning. Say eight-thirty?"

He nodded and backed away. "That would be fine."

As Ben disappeared into the crowd, Skylar was thankful that other than a few of the nosiest guests, most everyone was too polite to keep staring at them. She turned to Gabe, but before she could say anything, he grumbled, "What the hell do you see in him?"

She'd told him several times that there was nothing going on between her and Ben. Now, in the middle of a crowd that included some of the biggest busybodies of New York society, was not the time to remind him again. Resisting the urge to roll her eyes, she took his hand and headed toward one of her favorite people. "Let me introduce you to one of my father's best friends. He's also my godfather."

She reached the portly, smiling man who stood waiting for her. Though he was a few years younger than her father, she'd known him since she was a baby. He held out his arms and she went into them for a big hug. The familiar scent of his aftershave tickled her nose. He'd worn that scent for years and it always made her sneeze. Which it did again.

She giggled. "Uncle Bill, you know that stuff always makes me sneeze."

He blushed. "I know, sweetie, but Betsy gives it to me every Christmas. I can't disappoint her by not wearing it."

Smiling, she shook her head. "Someday someone's going to nominate you for the Father of the Year award."

Beaming at the compliment, he said, "I hope so." Then he looked up at Gabe, who stood towering over both of them, watching their display with interest. "And who's this new young man?"

Skylar smiled up at her husband. "Gabe, I'd like you

to meet one of the nicest men you'll ever meet and one of my most favorite people in the world."

"High praise indeed." Gabe held out his hand. "Gabe Maddox, good to meet you, sir."

His eyes alight with interest, the older man held out his hand to Gabe. "William Harrington III, but you can call me Bill."

sixteen

Gabe watched Skye sink back into the leather seat of the limousine with a huge sigh. It was almost three in the morning. She had to be exhausted. And though she might be a bit paler than she'd been, she really looked no different than when they'd left her apartment seven hours ago.

He shifted his big shoulders inside the jacket. And damned if he wasn't almost as tired as if he'd worked a double shift at the mines. He'd done that on occasion in his younger days and still remembered the bone-deep exhaustion.

"Have a good time?" Cole Mathison's deep drawl shook him from memories he'd just as soon not revisit.

Skylar flashed a relaxed sleepy smile at Gabe and said, "I think it depends upon who you ask."

"You had fun?" Gabe couldn't keep the disbelief from his voice. All they'd done all night was either sit and talk or roam around and talk about who had gone where for the summer, who had been seen at some artsy film festival in Paris last week, or even worse, what the fall fashions looked like. It all amounted to a bunch of nothing in his estimation.

"Gabe caused quite a stir."

He jerked at that news. "I did?"

"Didn't you see all those women staring at you?"

Yeah, he had. They'd made him damned uncomfortable, as if he were a piece of meat. Not wanting to admit how out of place and uncomfortable he felt, he said, "I'm sure if anyone was staring, they were looking at you."

A smile played around her mouth as if she knew exactly what he was thinking. Skye had always been able to see through him. Even though it had been eight years since they'd been together and it had been just a brief period even then, she saw beneath his bravado. It had been one of the reasons he'd fallen for her so fast. She had seen him for who he was and it hadn't bothered her in the least.

Gabe closed his eyes and rubbed the bridge of his nose, where a slight tension headache was forming. He needed to get his mind off the past. He might not have died as she thought he had, but they needed to treat the situation as if he had. They had no future together, and bringing the past into the here and now would only create a hope that couldn't be realized.

"Headache?" Skye's soft sympathetic question brought his eyes open.

"No."

Skye rolled her eyes and shook her head at his denial.

Hell, what was the point in pretending with a woman who could see right through him? He needed to get back to the real reason he'd just put himself through seven hours of torture.

"You come up with any leads, Cole?"

"Yeah. Several. I'll go over them with you and then contact Noah for some background work. How about you?"

Gabe glanced at Skye, and as usual, she knew what he was thinking. "Don't be hesitant to talk about any of these people to me. Some of them may be my friends, but I know people aren't always what they seem."

He acknowledged her words with a nod. "There were three in particular." He took a breath. Despite what she'd said, he knew she wouldn't like what he was about to say. "Benjamin Bradford, Samuel Pickens, and William Harrington III."

As he had expected, he heard a gasp. However, all she said was "I'm surprised that out of all the men you met tonight, there were only three who interested you."

Gabe shrugged. Explaining how he was able to get a feeling about people wasn't something he could describe. When he didn't go with his gut, he always ended up regretting it.

"I'd say out of the hundred or so men I met, ninety-nine of them are keeping secrets they'd rather the rest of the world not know about. However, the men I mentioned were the only ones that I felt could actually be hiding something of this magnitude."

LCR had given him an opportunity for training that few people had experienced. Spotting lies and subterfuge had become one of his best talents. Last year, he'd seriously screwed up with Shea and sincerely regretted his error. Other than that one time, Gabe could, without ego, claim to be an expert in spotting a liar. And he was damn good at spotting evil, too.

The men he'd mentioned to Skye were all hiding something. He didn't know what yet. Evil? Perhaps. That would take more time.

"I'll call Noah. Ask him to assign someone to watch Pickens. Cole, you keep an eye on Harrington."

Skye eyed him curiously. There was one other man he'd targeted. Hell, there was no point in denying his intense curiosity about the man dating his wife.

"Bradford is coming for breakfast in the morning. I'll zero in on him and see what I can find out."

A small, enigmatic smile played around her beautiful

mouth, but she didn't dispute or argue with his plans. She might disagree with his assessment, but thankfully appeared to be willing to trust his judgment.

The limo glided to a stop in front of her building. They waited until Cole got out and went around to open the door. And again, Gabe felt like an idiot. As if he couldn't open his own damned door. Appearances might be important but he didn't care. He was pretending to be a self-made man. That meant he went against convention. Before Cole could open the door, Gabe shoved it open and stepped out.

"Impatient?"

Cole's amusement earned him a glare. Then Gabe turned and surveyed the well-lit street and sidewalk. Only two photographers lurking. He turned back and said to Cole, "Take Skye up, will you?"

A flicker of compassion crossed his friend's face. "I'll see you in a few minutes."

Skye stepped out of the car with a graceful elegance that defied description. She gave Gabe a brief look, waved at the photographers snapping their photos, and then allowed Cole to lead her into the building.

Glad to see the photographers get into their cars and drive away, Gabe took one more glance around and then headed inside. He might be as tired as an old dog, but he'd be damned if he got back into that elevator with Skye.

Cole believed it was because of his claustrophobia, and while that was a huge reason, it wasn't the biggest. Having Skye try to distract him again as she had before wasn't something he could afford. She might not have known it, but he had been within a second of unzipping his pants and shoving himself inside her. The distraction had worked but damned if he could afford another incident.

This was a job and nothing more. After Cole left, he would explain that to her. And now, he had forty floors ahead of him to convince himself.

Skylar eyed the giant man standing beside her. She wasn't used to big men. Most of the men in her family were of average height. Benjamin stood a little over six feet and was the tallest man she'd ever dated. Not counting Gabe . . . whom she'd never really dated. She'd fallen in love with him, slept with him, and married him. But she could never say they'd dated.

Gabe was tall . . . very tall. When he was a skinny youth in his early twenties, he'd been tall but not muscular. But now . . . she smiled dreamily as she remembered what those muscles had felt like under his tuxedo jacket tonight. How she'd wanted him to make love to her.

A hard hand grabbed her arm. "Skylar?"

Skylar opened her eyes and stared up at Cole Mathison's concerned face. She'd almost collapsed at his feet.

"Sorry, guess I'm more tired than I thought."

His hand still holding her as if he was afraid she'd fall, he said, "You zoned out for several seconds."

A deep breath revived her. "I'm okay now. It's just been a tough few weeks."

Cole nodded. "And you really haven't had a chance to recover from all the trauma you've gone through."

"So you know about Gabe and me?"

"That you're married, but you thought he'd committed suicide?"

She grimaced at his accurate and succinct answer. "Yeah."

"Yes. He told me. That must have been quite a shock."

"You LCR people are masters of understatement, aren't you?"

A small smile tweaked at the corner of his mouth. She got the impression that this man rarely smiled. Gabe's smiles were rare, too, but Cole had a grimness to him as if he'd seen something so horrible that smiling was foreign to him.

"How long have you known Gabe?"

His eyes on the elevator doors in front of him, he shrugged. "Two or three years."

"Do you have a family?"

"No."

The short, harsh words cut off any other questions. Apparently realizing how he'd sounded, he softened his expression slightly as he looked down at her. "LCR is my family now."

"It's a good organization."

"The best."

Thankfully, the door slid open. Skylar's natural curiosity and Cole's reticence to talk about himself didn't make for a good combination. Though she'd always been good at small talk, her mind was whirling from exhaustion, limiting her ability to come up with anything to say. Not that it would do any good. LCR was a well-known organization, but they were almost as famous for keeping secrets as they were for the work that they did. Their employees knew how to keep those secrets.

With a relieved breath at being in her own home, Skylar walked through her living room to her bedroom. "I'm going to change clothes. Tell Gabe I'll be back in just a moment."

Just as Skylar shut the door to her bedroom, she heard the front door open. Cole's amused voice grumbled, "Hell, did you run?"

A barely winded Gabe answered, "Had some energy to expel."

With a slight smile, Skylar unzipped the side zipper on

her gown and slid it off. Despite her exhaustion, anticipation zinged through her. She knew the real reason Gabe had taken the stairs. His claustrophobia might have been partly the reason, but it wasn't the only one. He'd wanted to avoid a reenactment of their earlier elevator encounter. Hence his need to expel some energy. Gabe wanted her but he didn't want to want her. Tough. She was married to the man. If she wanted to kiss him, then she damned well had the right.

Knowing Gabe and Cole would have no compunction about starting their meeting without her present, Skylar quickly slid into a comfortable pair of pants and button-down cotton shirt. She slipped her tired feet into her favorite sandals and pulled her long hair up into a twist, sticking a long pin through it to hold it in place.

As she expected, she opened the door to hear voices in the living room already discussing Cole's findings. She rushed through the door, determined to lend information and a hand where she could. She might well relish the sexual play between her and Gabe, but she would never forget her real cause. Kendra was out there somewhere and had to be found.

"Get up. It's time for your bath."

Kendra snuggled into the soft pillow and shook her head. No, she'd been having the most wonderful dream. She didn't want to let go. In the dream, she'd been sitting with Skylar in the little Chinese restaurant where they met and had lunch every Thursday. They'd just ordered moo shu pork and Chinese vegetables. Her mouth watered and she could almost smell the spicy fragrance wafting through the air.

"I said get up, bitch. This is the only bath you'll get this week. You'd better take the offer while you can."

Kendra rolled over and looked up at her current

tormentor. A young woman, probably no more than a year or two older than Kendra, looked down at her with the coldest, meanest expression she could imagine.

"Please let me go home."

Why she said it, she didn't know. This girl didn't care about her. She had a job to do. How many times had Kendra asked the same thing, only to get the response she got now?

"Get up, bitch, before I show you what your disobedience will cost you."

Kendra sprang from the bed, as the woman knew she would. Anything to keep from having to watch another torture or rape. Every time she remotely resisted, she was punished by being forced to witness a brutal act. She couldn't handle another one.

"Get in the tub."

Shivering from exhaustion and dread, Kendra walked into the bathroom. A large tub of water awaited her. Fighting tears, Kendra lifted her foot and put it into the water, jostling the ice cubes that had been added to it. Frigid, ice-cold water instantly chilled her.

"Get in before I push you in."

Her lips bleeding from biting them from the pain, Kendra slid her body into the water and sat down. Ice-cold water rained down on her as buckets of freezing water were poured over her head. Crying in agony, Kendra forced her mind back to the restaurant with Skylar. The meal sat in front of her. Kendra picked up the chopsticks, speared a sizzling piece of pork, and put it on her tongue. *Heaven.*

Pain searing her scalp pulled her from her dream. The woman screamed at her, but Kendra didn't understand what she was saying. She was beginning to feel warm and cozy again. Lassitude stole over her and she closed her eyes.

Another tug on her hair and Kendra woke to her body being patted down. Long past caring that strangers' hands roamed all over her body, she felt tears pour from her eyes as needles of pain prickled the feeling back into her frozen body.

"You have a meal waiting for you." The evil voice, filled with mocking amusement, continued the torture. "Grilled steak, fresh vegetables, baked potato covered in sour cream and chives. Chocolate cake for dessert. Yum."

Despite the knowledge that it would be just another horrific event of temptation and denial, her empty stomach twisted, then growled in hopeful anticipation.

Someone put a robe around her, while another person towel-dried her hair. She wasn't allowed to do anything for herself. She no longer protested, no longer resented their hands. No longer paid attention to who did what. This had become her life. She didn't know the reasons behind their actions. Didn't know who was responsible. Her only release, her only comfort, was to imagine that someone would rescue her. In her mind, that someone was often Skylar. Occasionally her mother. Her father sometimes, too, even though she hadn't seen him in years. One time it had even been Calvin. But mostly it was Skylar. She cared about Kendra. She would find a way to save her. Kendra knew she would.

"Come on, bitch. Let's go have dinner."

Kendra shuffled toward the room where she knew a meal waited for her. A meal that would no doubt be denied to her. Even knowing that, she somehow prayed that at least this time, they'd allow her to eat.

As promised, a meal sat on the table in the middle of the room. The fragrance of grilled meat permeated the air and Kendra almost doubled over from the growling emptiness in her stomach. *Just a little. Please, God, please. Just a little.*

They made a big production of seating her at the table. Kendra looked up in hope. Surely now that she was seated, they'd allow her to eat.

One of the men leered down at her. "If you're not hungry for steak, I got something else you can eat." He rubbed his crotch.

Bile rose in her throat, even while her mouth watered in anticipation that she would actually be allowed a meal. Ignoring the three men and two women who surrounded her, watching her as if she were an animal in a zoo, Kendra picked up a fork and took a bite from her potato. Thick sour cream and creamy potato melted on her tongue. Her stomach leaped for joy. She took another bite, and then another.

The steak, tender and cooked to perfection, cut easily with a fork. Kendra placed a succulent piece on her tongue and moaned in delight. She took another bite and then . . . the plate disappeared from her sight.

"That's enough."

"No!" Kendra jumped up. Fork in hand, she jabbed at the nearest woman. The woman sidestepped the weapon and landed a blow to Kendra's temple. She felt herself falling. As she landed face-first on the floor, the last thing she heard was a man screaming, "You bitch! He'll kill you for that."

Hoping that the man was talking to her, since death would mean blessed peace, Kendra descended into a welcoming darkness.

William winced at the creak of the stair beneath his feet. The entire household was still asleep. And he should be, too. But it was almost five o'clock and he had a standing breakfast meeting at eight, barely giving him enough time for full enjoyment, but he couldn't wait any longer. He'd tossed and turned most of the night in anticipation.

Visions of what she would look like, how she would be posed, how the shadows and the light would surround her nude body, revealing, then hiding that glorious silky skin, had been torturing him all night.

The DVD had been delivered yesterday evening just before he and Margo had left for their evening out. It had taken every bit of willpower and self-discipline he had not to cancel the night.

His wife would have understood and supported his decision. She knew about his needs, even if she didn't really know what they were. She knew he had secrets, but as long as he was happy, she didn't care to know the details. That was one of the many reasons he loved her. His secret life kept him satisfied. Kept their marriage secure.

William was a family man. He loved his wife and children. Saw to their welfare, supported them in their dreams and desires. Margo fully supported his need to find his happiness wherever he chose to find it. A loyal and supportive wife such as his Margo was a prize beyond rubies.

But he could no longer hold back the desire. A live recording was a poor substitute for the reality of being able to touch and caress that beautiful body, but it was so much better than the still shots he'd had to be satisfied with the last few days. It was a process of progression . . . for him and his subject. The anticipation built for both of them. Though she didn't realize what the crescendo would be. William understood it . . . after all, he'd devised this training method. Had been using it for years and it hadn't failed him yet.

He slipped into his office and closed the door, locking himself and his secret delights inside. His hands shaking with excitement, he unlocked the door to his vault. Picking up the DVD he'd left on the table beside his recliner, he held it to his nose, pretending he inhaled her scent.

No longer able to wait, he slid the DVD out of its sleeve and inserted it into the player. After taking a towel from the cabinet beneath the large-screen television, William seated himself in the recliner across from the screen. Unzipping his pants in preparation, he hit the play button on the remote, placed the towel at the correct position, and then settled back to enjoy himself.

He groaned at his first sight of her. Silky, beautiful perfection. Yes, she was thinner . . . all a part of the process. Soon that would change. He would feed her, clothe her, cosset her. She would love it . . . love him. He still saw a bit of defiance in her pose, in those pretty hazel eyes. But it had diminished. She was changing, refining, becoming . . .

How had he gotten so fortunate to find one so fresh, so beautiful . . . so malleable? Skylar, of course. She had brought the girl to his attention several months back. He remembered that day clearly. He'd been standing in the midst of some of the most powerful people in New York, but the instant she'd walked in, he'd stopped listening, mesmerized. As if a beacon had shone down on her, he'd known in an instant she would be his next jewel.

Though Skylar had introduced the girl to hundreds of people that day, he was the only one who'd sought her out when Skylar had been occupied talking with someone else. The only one who had seen her potential . . . her need to belong. After learning about the girl's goal of becoming a model, he'd developed the perfect lure.

He must remember to thank Skylar. Perhaps later, after he recovered from his pleasure, he would send his goddaughter a gift of flowers or a box of candy in appreciation for the special gift she'd given William. Even if she didn't realize it.

seventeen

Gabe placed a sleeping Skye on the bed. He had to give it to her, she'd been a trooper. As he and Cole threw names around, she'd listened intently, those lively, intelligent eyes of hers gleaming with interest and determination. She'd even thrown in some tidbits of information neither he nor Cole would have been privy to. Then, when they had Noah on the phone, she'd hung in there as they discussed who and why they felt certain people deserved more scrutiny.

And despite the fact that two of the people they were very interested in were her boyfriend and her godfather, she hadn't protested. Other than the slight furrow of her brow indicating she'd like to defend them, she'd kept out of it. An investigation would have gone on whether she had protested or not, but it was good they didn't have to argue the point with her.

It wasn't until after they hung up with Noah and were making plans for the day that he noticed Skye had literally sunk into the sofa. Though she was still sitting up, she was sound asleep.

Ignoring Cole's knowing look, Gabe had scooped her into his arms. As he carried her into the bedroom, it was all he could do not to hold her closer and pretend he had every right to carry her to bed and love her awake.

He sat beside her on the bed and allowed himself the

luxury of staring at her. When she was awake and aware, he couldn't let his guard down. She could read him like a book.

Gently, so as not to wake her, he pushed back a strand of hair from her forehead. How could someone so innocent and sweet be one of the most famous women in the world? It defied logic.

A whispered sigh that sounded like his name came from her soft lips. Desire thrummed through him. Years ago, their lovemaking had been awkward and sweet. Their passion a new and pleasurable pastime. They'd made love for hours . . . four short days of bliss. But he hadn't savored her as he would now. If given just one more opportunity to make love to this woman, he knew it would be the most meaningful physical connection he could ever have.

He stood before temptation got the best of him. The regret-filled sigh he breathed penetrated his soul. Slipping off her shoes, Gabe drew a blanket from the edge of the bed and covered her. He had to get out of here before he did something supremely stupid.

He was halfway across the room when her soft words stopped him.

"We're still married. You don't have to leave."

Turning, he swallowed hard . . . the tempting picture she made was almost more than a sane man could handle. And with Skye, his sanity was seriously in question. Long mahogany hair swept over a slender shoulder as she propped herself up on her elbow, somehow managing to look both provocative and innocent at the same time.

Gabe hardened to an almost bursting moment of desire. It didn't help that Skye's eyes lowered and stared at his hardening cock.

"Dammit, Skye. Don't look at me like that."

"Why, Gabe? You know we both want it."

"Because it would be stupid."

"It would be wonderful."

Her voice, soft and low, held both arousal and promise. And it was almost his undoing. Gabe spoke between clenched teeth, "And then what, Skye? Once we find Kendra, get the bastard who has her . . . what then?"

She stared at him several seconds as if searching for something. Gabe tensed as he waited for the answer he shouldn't want or expect.

Finally she offered him a tentative smile and said, "Do we have to overthink it? Can't we just live for what we have now? Can't we rejoice in finding each other again?"

Steeling his resolve, Gabe gave her the truth. "I always knew where you were."

At her flash of pain, agony seared him. Dammit, he'd said it to make her back off. He'd achieved that goal and then some. He'd hurt her.

She dropped her head onto the pillow and whispered, "Touché."

Forcing himself to ignore her pain, since if he stayed they'd just hurt each other even more, he said, "Get some sleep. We have a full day ahead of us."

He closed the door and then leaned against it. Gripping his hands into fists until he could almost feel the blood pour from them, he snarled at the tender emotions threatening to rise again. Any love he'd felt for her was long gone. He couldn't allow it to come back. He'd fallen in love with a dream. She might have been his dream girl, but he wasn't her dream man.

They were from different worlds. As much as he resented her father for his interference and as wrong as he'd been about so many things, he'd been right about one thing. He and Skye never would have been happy together. Better to acknowledge that now so when temptation overwhelmed him again, as he fully expected it would, he'd be prepared.

So why the hell didn't he feel better about his decision?

Remembered pleasure still strumming through him, William ran up the steps to his club with the energy of a teenager. Amazing what a beautiful young thing like that could do for a middle-aged libido. The knowledge that very soon he'd be touching that nubile body for real was almost more than he could comprehend. Anticipation zoomed through him.

With the deference that William expected, the manager gushingly greeted him. "Mr. Harrington, so very good to see you, sir. Mr. James is waiting at your table."

Unable to contain himself, he felt so damned good, he handed the man a hundred-dollar bill with his handshake. "Thank you."

His eyes wide with surprised pleasure, the manager quickly pocketed the money. "Thank you, sir!" William wasn't known for his generosity. The man probably thought he'd done something to deserve it. Wouldn't he be surprised that William's generous heart stemmed from one of the most satisfying sexual experiences he'd had in years?

With a grin and nod, William headed to the small private table he had been dining at for years. Many things had changed over time, but some traditions had to stay. One being his standing breakfast meeting with his old friend Jeremiah James. They'd been meeting every Tuesday since before Skylar was born.

William came to an abrupt halt when he spotted his friend. The man looked years older than he had this time last week. The deep creases around his mouth and eyes indicated something dire had happened.

"Jerry? Why so glum, my friend?"

Jeremiah looked up, and though his mouth moved upward into a smile, William could tell his heart wasn't in it.

"Hello, Willie."

Jeremiah was the only man William would ever allow to use that nickname. Seating himself quickly, he leaned forward in concern. "What's wrong?"

His friend shook his head. "I've made some terrible mistakes." Tears filled his eyes. "I don't know if Skylar will ever forgive me for them."

Before William could respond, their waiter came with their coffee and juice. Since they never deviated from what they ordered, no unnecessary conversations had to take place.

William acknowledged their drinks with a nod. When the waiter disappeared, he said, "What did you do?"

His friend drew in a breath and began to explain what had transpired eight years ago. William sat back in his chair, enthralled at the drama and exquisite deception. He was as close to Jeremiah as anyone and never suspected a thing. What a remarkable secret.

And how incredibly brave and inventive of his friend to create such an elaborate deception. Despite how Skylar might have been hurt by it all, it had been the correct thing to do. The young man's rough upbringing along with his questionable mental stability would have been much worse for Skylar than merely grieving for a dead husband. This was something William could see himself doing for his own children. A father had every right to protect his children from such trash.

"Skylar may not see it now, but you did the right thing. Thankfully, she recovered and has turned into a beautiful and responsible young woman. But why is this suddenly weighing so heavily on you now?"

Looking furtively around to ensure their privacy, Jeremiah leaned forward and shared another secret. As he spoke, alarm quickly replaced William's earlier happiness. Skylar had been abducted while searching for her young friend. Had barely escaped with her life. Her young friend was still missing.

Not once had his people indicated they'd had any difficulties in procuring his new addition. Had they taken Skylar, thinking to use her in the same way? William shuddered at the thought.

"Poor Skylar. How did she get away?"

"I hired Last Chance Rescue. You know, that organization that rescues kidnapped victims? It turns out that when the people who took her recognized who she was, they sold her to another man who specializes in the kidnappings of high-profile people."

They had profited from Skylar's abduction. That's why they hadn't mentioned it. Money had been made by selling her. Someone would pay for that deception.

"So these Last Chance people rescued her?"

"Yes. Turns out that Mr. Maddox, Skylar's estranged husband, works for this organization."

"So are he and Skylar back together again?" He had a hard time keeping the disapproval from his tone. Admittedly, Gabe Maddox cleaned up quite nicely, but he had a rough edge that couldn't be erased with expensive clothes. William had recognized that last night but was too polite to mention it. And now that he knew the man's common background, he was even more convinced. Gabriel Maddox wasn't good enough for Skylar.

Jeremiah gave an emphatic shake of his head. "No, I don't believe they're getting back together."

"Then why was he with her last night? And why the elaborate story of him being a wealthy entrepreneur she met while on vacation?"

"They're still looking for her friend. They didn't say it, but I got the impression that for some reason they believe someone in our circle might be involved. Absolutely ridiculous, of course." He paused for a second and looked around again. "But that's just between you and me, Willie. I'm sure I'm not supposed to mention that to anyone."

William felt his frozen mouth mutter, "Oh, of course I would never say anything. I do hope they find the young girl." Sick dread soared through him. Gabriel Maddox was looking for him. Everyone would find out. He would be ruined. His reputation destroyed. His family would be forever tainted. And they would lock him up, preventing him from enjoying his newest acquisition. He would lose everything!

"William, are you all right? You look quite pale."

Patting his face with his napkin, William nodded. "Yes, yes. I'm fine. It's just the news of Skylar's ordeal. You know how I love that girl as if she were my very own."

"You're a good friend, Willie."

As he finished his meal, William murmured platitudes to his friend and all the while panic beat inside him. There had to be a way to get Maddox and Skylar to stop looking for the girl. He couldn't let her go . . . he hadn't even begun to develop their relationship. Had yet to enjoy the sweetness that waited for him.

But something had to happen, because Maddox didn't seem the type to just give up.

As ideas sprang to mind, a plan began to emerge. They needed to believe there was no reason to look for the girl anymore. That meant they needed to believe there was no hope. Yes, that would work.

And, sadly, if his idea didn't work, William knew he

might have to take more drastic measures. He couldn't let the girl go . . . and he couldn't kill her. He already loved her too much.

Skylar was like a daughter to him, but she'd gotten mixed up with some very bad company. Though he hated for her to die, a man had to do what a man had to do. Protecting his family and the Harrington name was the most important factor.

If his first plan didn't work, eliminating Maddox and Skylar would be his only other option. And despite the fact that Jeremiah would lose his daughter, William couldn't help but believe that the man would somehow understand.

A man had to protect those he loved.

Skylar woke with a pounding headache and her eyes so swollen from crying, she could barely open them. Great. Not only had Gabe stuck a figurative knife in her heart, he would see the results of his devastating blow.

The sunlight coming through the skylight and the large window beside her indicated it was late . . . very late. She peered at her bedside clock and then shot out of bed. Four o'clock! She'd slept the day away. She had so much she needed to do. And Ben wanted to talk . . . Ben! He was supposed have come for breakfast. How could she have forgotten? Had he come? Why hadn't Gabe woke her?

She dropped back down onto the bed. Her mind was blurred and she felt grimy and disoriented. In no shape to handle the bruised feelings of a fake boyfriend, much less the hard-hearted amusement of a husband who might as well be fake.

Whether Ben had showed up or not couldn't be changed. She couldn't face Gabe looking and feeling like this. She felt fragile and worn. If he said the slightest thing to set her off, she wouldn't be responsible for her actions. She would shower, dress, and put on her makeup of steel. Then she would face the only man who had ever managed to crush her twice in a lifetime.

Under the hot pulsing shower, on her tenth silent rendition of "I'm Gonna Wash That Man Right Outa My Hair," Skylar, at last, felt more grounded and in control. Gabe was alive . . . that was something to be happy about. She might have fantasized about that a million times, but she had never dared believe in the reality. That was cause for celebration, not sorrow. So what if he didn't love her . . . probably never had. He was alive and that was a miracle in itself.

Besides, Kendra should be her only focus. Last night's discussion had been difficult to hear. Two people she thought very highly of were suspects. Questioning Gabe on why he felt the way he did would be useless. Not only wouldn't he share, Skylar got the feeling he might not be able to explain it. She knew all about gut feelings. Sometimes you had to go with them, despite all evidence to the contrary. Besides, her faith in the people she knew had taken a near-lethal blow. Never would she have believed the father she adored could lie to her and betray her as he had. What did she really know about the people she loved?

Half an hour later, wearing a soft lavender summer dress, her makeup flawless, long hair tumbling over her shoulders with a carefully designed casualness, Skylar opened the bedroom door. She heard no one.

Deciding a strong cup of coffee would arm her even more, she bypassed the small office Gabe had commandeered the first night. He was most likely in there working. After a fortifying dose of caffeine and maybe a piece of toast for her roiling stomach, she'd face him.

She pulled to a stop when she found him in the middle

of her kitchen whipping up what looked like an omelet. He turned and that mouth she'd fantasized about even when she thought he was dead lifted in a small smile. Dark blue eyes offered an unspoken apology. He knew he had hurt her and felt bad. Not bad enough to take the words back, though. She needed to remember that.

"I guess I missed breakfast."

Gabe stared at her for several long seconds as if searching for something. Apparently satisfied, he turned and Skylar was finally able to breathe.

"Ben showed up at eight-thirty; we had a cup of coffee and a nice little talk. He left with another apology for his behavior last night."

Skylar examined Gabe. Not a hair out of place. His thick, silky black hair was one of her favorite features. She'd often grabbed on to it when he'd pulled her to him for a kiss. Once she'd held on to his hair as she'd wrapped her legs around him and ridden him till they'd both climaxed. It had to have hurt him but he'd never uttered a word of protest. They'd both been so hot for each other.

"Skye?"

She shook herself from the lustful memory. "Sorry. Guess I need some coffee." She went to the full carafe of coffee and poured some into a cup beside the coffeemaker. Taking a bracing swallow, she turned and said, "I'm assuming the discussion was civil?"

"I thought I handled things damn well . . . considering."

"Considering what?"

"Considering the man is dating my wife."

Damned if she'd let him get away with that. "I'm not your wife, Gabe. I think we established that last night, didn't we?"

His back was to her, so she couldn't see what he might be thinking. Just because Gabe was easy to read didn't mean she always knew how he felt. When he turned, she was surprised to see a tender expression on his face.

"You and Ben aren't lovers."

"I told you there was nothing going on between us."

"Why, Skye? You thought you were a widow. Why haven't you ever married again? Why have you been having a fake affair all these years?"

She absolutely refused to let him feel sorry for her. "Ben isn't the only man I've dated these last few years, Gabe. If you think I've martyred myself in your memory, you're wrong. I created a mutually beneficial relationship with Ben so I could have a life. Being able to sleep with someone else without the press knowing about it is very freeing."

Before Gabe could respond, the buzzer sounded, alerting her she had a visitor. Gabe shoved a plate filled with an omelet and toast toward her. The glare he shot as he passed by said their discussion wasn't over. "Eat. I'll find out who it is."

He stomped out the door, leaving her questioning her sanity. It was one thing to deny she'd been pining away for Gabe, but to claim affairs that had never existed was stupid. He'd see through her ruse and then she'd have to either come up with some fake men or admit the truth. After Gabe's supposed death, she hadn't been able to have a normal relationship with a man. Hadn't wanted one. Damn, how pathetic did that sound?

His words before he'd left last week took on new meaning. She hadn't been able to have another relationship. Had Gabe felt the same way? Had he, perhaps, been pining away for her, too?

Gabe appeared at the door. The grim look on his face told her something terrible had happened. "We need to talk."

Skylar dropped her plate on the counter, the clatter a distant sound underneath the thundering of her heart. "What happened?"

Gabe's chest tightened at Skye's expression of fear and dread. More than anything in the world, he wanted to go to her and hold her.

"What?" She began to walk toward him. "Tell me."

"Cole spoke with one of our contacts on the police force."

She closed her eyes. "Kendra?"

"A young woman's body has been found. Kendra's size, hair color . . . But . . ."

Her eyes popped open. "But what? They're not sure it's her?"

"The body washed up on the shore of the Hudson. It's in bad shape."

"Bad shape? How?"

"You don't need to know the details, Skye. But it'll take some time to identify the body."

"Tell me, Gabe."

Dammit, he was trying to protect her. Knowing she was stronger than she looked, he said, "Much of the body, especially the face, was badly beaten. And the body's partially burned."

"Oh God." She sank to the closest chair.

Unable to see her like this without touching her, Gabe squatted down beside her. "I'm sorry, Skye."

"If they can't identify her body, maybe it's not her."

"Don't get your hopes up. They know it's a female with her general coloring. No one else has been reported missing with those physical characteristics. Chances are good that it's her."

She blew a shaky sigh. "I won't believe it's her until they absolutely prove it. Has her mother been told?"

"No reason to tell her anything yet."

"Good. She doesn't even believe Kendra's been abducted."

"This is still off the record, but they need some kind of DNA to determine if it's Kendra."

"She sometimes stays with me. There's a hairbrush in the guest bathroom she's used. Will that work?"

"Probably. I'll take it to them and see."

She straightened her spine and asked, "So what now?"

"We keep looking. Seems damn coincidental that the day after we start on a round of parties, looking for the creep, a body conveniently shows up. One so badly damaged it can't be immediately identified."

"You think we met him last night and he somehow figured out we were looking for him?"

"I don't know. There's no reason why anyone would think we were. But I'd say we keep on until we can pinpoint the bastard." His eyes locked with hers. "This could get dangerous. I don't want you in danger. That means we're together until this creep is caught. No going out on your own."

When she barely acknowledged his warning, he realized the impact of her friend's possible death was hitting her. Tears welled in her eyes.

"We'll find him, Skye."

"I just never believed it would come to this. Even though I knew she was probably going through a horrific experience, I never doubted that we would find her."

Unable to watch her hurting without comforting her, he stood and pulled her into his arms. She rested her head against his chest and Gabe closed his eyes at the sensation of rightness. No woman had ever felt as right in his arms as Skye did.

After several seconds, she pulled away from him. The

brave but watery smile she gave him made him admire her all the more.

"If we're going out again tonight, I'd better take a look at the invitations and make some decisions."

The effort it took to let her go astounded him. How the hell was he going to say goodbye to her forever when he didn't even want to let her out of his arms? Gabe couldn't even begin to contemplate how that would feel. For the here and now, they were together and he had a job to do.

"While you do that, I'll take the hairbrush to the police."

She nodded and turned to leave. "I'll go get it."

"Skye." Gabe said her name before he could stop himself.

She looked at him over her shoulder.

Unable to let her walk away with that look of hopelessness in her eyes, he said, "Don't give up hope. It could very well be a ruse to distract us."

A smile lifted her perfect mouth. "Optimism from Gabe Maddox. Now, that's cause for celebration."

She walked away, leaving Gabe with a thudding heart and a flood of feelings he refused to acknowledge.

eighteen

Kendra woke screaming the name of her faceless rescuer. She couldn't remember the name, but the dream had been so real. She had really believed it had finally happened. A glance around the four stark walls of her prison told her that once again it hadn't happened. And each day, the longer she was here, the more she realized it probably wouldn't happen. No one was going to rescue her. No one was going to be her savior. It was all up to her.

It was all up to her.

The freeing thought took hold, gained substance. All of her life, she'd depended on others to get her out of the jams she'd gotten herself into. First her mother, who'd finally washed her hands of her daughter after years of digging her out of trouble. Calvin with his money. Roommates and friends who had all the right connections to help her out of a current problem. And then Skylar, who she had depended on probably more than anyone. She'd waited for Skylar to do things for her . . . give her the life that she wanted. The life of a model.

Kendra didn't let herself think that the one time she'd tried to do something for herself, she'd ended up in this shithole. The important thing was, she'd gotten herself into this jam and she damn well needed to get herself out of it.

Raising her head farther, she looked around. The walls

were plain vanilla; no pictures or even a mirror adorned them. A small, narrow window close to the ceiling allowed the only natural light in the room. A bright fluorescent light over her head was kept on day and night. A small camera in the corner filmed every movement she made.

Escape would be difficult, if not impossible, but she refused to believe she couldn't do it. If she were Skylar, she would probably already be away from here. Even though Kendra fully intended to escape on her own, she couldn't help but think about what her friend and mentor would do. How would Skylar escape? She refused to believe her friend wasn't safe. Skylar would have found a way to escape those people who'd bought her. Now Kendra knew she must do the same.

Placing her feet on the floor, Kendra pushed herself slowly to stand. She held on to the bed railing as the room whirled around her. Besides having a pounding headache, she was weak from lack of food. The odd treatment puzzled her. Based on the pornographic photographs they'd taken of her, she had assumed some pervert was getting off on them. But why starve her?

She took a breath to center herself, then shuffled to the small toilet against a wall. She was long past feeling embarrassment at relieving herself in front of cameras. If these sick fucks got their kicks this way, that was their problem. She needed to concentrate on what she could control. Which, right now, was absolutely nothing. But she intended that to change.

Just as she was washing her hands, the door swung open. The demon photographer and one of his female assistants stood in the doorway.

His eyes swept over her nude body. "You need to eat." He shot a look at the woman beside him. "Think you can hide the bruises?"

The woman's leering, cold expression was scarier than the man's. "I think so. You can film her at different angles to avoid the darker ones."

"If we can't, it's your ass."

"Hey, I'm not the one who hit her."

"No, she's been taken care of, but he's not going to be happy if he sees the damage the bitch did to her. Even when I tried to pretend it wasn't that bad, he got pissed enough to order her death. If he really sees how bad it is, we're in deep shit."

"Then I suggest you film it so he won't see."

The man looked behind him and said, "Give her the meal. A full plate this time, let her have all of it. Call us when she's finished."

The man turned back with a final warning. "Eat, bitch. I know how to inflict pain without causing bruises."

If she'd had any extra energy, Kendra would have laughed in his face. Did he think she was going to refuse to eat as some kind of protest? If she was going to escape, she would need all the strength she could get.

Her mouth already salivating, a delectable fragrance tickled at her nose. Her heart kicked up in anticipation as a plate of grilled salmon, rice pilaf, and grilled vegetables was placed on a table beside her bed.

Kendra wasted no time. He'd said she could have a full meal, but she didn't trust him. Fearful they'd take it away from her as they had so many meals before, she plopped down on the bed, picked up her fork, and shoveled the food into her mouth. In two minutes, maybe less, the entire meal had been demolished; not a crumb was left on her plate.

And not once did she consider what her delicious dinner might have been laced with.

* * *

Gabe growled out a foul-mouthed expletive at the cover of a tabloid magazine. Being considered Skylar James's new boy toy was bad enough, but to have his picture plastered across magazines and newspapers disturbed him on a level he could barely fathom.

Two frigging weeks of this crap. Photographers and reporters on their ass every second, shouting asinine questions he refused to answer. If he weren't almost certain they were close to pinpointing their suspect, he'd say to hell with all of it.

But they were close. He could feel it. After a lengthy discussion with Cole and Noah this morning, he was more sure than ever. Problem was, they still had nothing concrete. It was all still supposition and theory. And until they had something more, he would continue with this charade.

Since he refused all press interviews, the vultures had enjoyed creating their own stories. Speculation on his relationship with Skye ranged from the story they'd created of a whirlwind romance at a ski resort to something more far-fetched, such as that he was the father of Skye's illegitimate child, whom she'd given up for adoption when she was a teenager. Now, how the hell they came up with that one he had no idea.

Skye had only laughed. His sense of humor didn't extend that far.

"What's wrong?"

Gabe jerked his head up to see Skye in the doorway, wearing one of the multitude of designer dresses she never seemed to run out of. This one was sky blue, the color of her eyes. And dammit, why did every one of them have to emphasize the areas he wanted to uncover and explore? Every time he saw her, he wanted to rip the clothes off and be the only thing to cover her.

Uneased and unending desire caused him to snarl out his answer, "How the hell do you put up with it?"

A slight frown wrinkling her smooth brow, she came closer. "Put up with what?"

Gabe grabbed up one of the offending magazines. This one had a half-page photograph of Skye and him arriving at one of the many parties they'd attended this week, and below the picture was some inane caption about their relationship. Throwing the magazine at her feet, he said, "Shit like that."

Leaning over, she scooped up the magazine. The V of her neckline revealed her generous breasts in all their creamy perfection to his ravenous eyes.

"And dammit, why do you have to wear stuff like that?"

Sparks of temper gleamed in her eyes. "One thing at a time, Gabe. Which argument do you want to go with first?"

"I don't want to argue, I just—"

"No. You just want to pass judgment like some kind of self-righteous holier-than-thou idiot."

"I'm not passing judgment, I just—"

She advanced into the room, temper flushing her cheeks. "Let me show you a few things about this 'shit,' as you so kindly called it." She pulled a stack of invitations they'd received earlier in the week. "You're so damn busy denigrating my lifestyle, you don't bother to consider that some of these things are actually worthwhile."

"Yeah, I'm sure we're saving the world by chowing down on lobster and drinking five-hundred-dollar champagne."

For the first time, he saw contempt in her eyes. "Most of the food and drinks are donated, because unlike you, these people understand the importance of these causes."

She threw an invitation at him that fluttered to the floor.

"This charity dinner made over three million dollars last year to fight AIDS in Africa." Another invitation landed at his feet. "This one gave two million to inner-city schools. This one raised a million dollars to refurbish an old school and turn it into a youth center. And this event sent two million, three hundred thousand to help rebuild a town in Kansas that was destroyed by a tornado."

As she continued throwing invitation after invitation at his feet, railing at him with the facts and explanation of the good they did, he began to feel like the lowest of slugs. When she came to the last invitation, she crumpled it in her hand.

"So that's why I put up with it all. You think if people are wealthy, they're worthless. Real worth doesn't come from someone's bank account, Gabe." She pounded her fist against her chest. "Real worth is in here."

Gabe pulled her into his arms before she could stop him. Pressing his mouth against the top of her head, he whispered, "I'm an ass."

Leaning her forehead against his chest, she sniffled and said, "No argument there."

With a quick kiss to the top of her head, he let her go and looked down in apology. "Forgive me?"

"Maybe. If you do something for me."

"What?"

"Don't laugh at the event we're going to this afternoon."

"After what you just showed me, how the hell could I laugh?"

She glanced down at the crumpled invitation in her hand. "I like turtles."

Tilting her chin so he could see her face, he repeated, "Turtles?"

She gazed up at him with an expression that was in

equal parts guilty and defiant. "The tea this afternoon . . . it's a benefit to save a special kind of desert turtle."

Gabe burst out laughing and pulled her back into his arms for a hard hug. "Then let's damn well go and save as many of them as we can."

The clank of silverware against fine china covered Skylar's whisper to the man beside her. "Do you think we're making any progress at all?"

In the process of cutting into his chocolate torte, he glanced up at her and answered in a voice so low she had to lean forward to hear. "More each day."

"Really?" She cast a furtive glance around and then her eyes went back to him. "How?"

"While you're charming the socks off of people, I'm listening and observing. They're so busy staring at you, no one pays attention to me."

She stifled a snort. That was most definitely not true. They had yet to attend an event when she hadn't had to pull Gabe from the clutches of some overeager woman who just had to talk about a piece of property she was considering selling or buying. More than one of them had indicated a desire to show him the property and much more if he was so inclined.

"What exactly have you learned?"

"Not anything we can talk about here, Skye. We can talk when we get home."

"But who—"

"Skylar, I didn't know you'd be here."

Skylar twisted her head at the sound of the dear, familiar voice of her godfather. "Now, that makes two of us." She chuckled. "Don't tell me you're a turtle lover, too."

William shook his head. "Leanne is, bless her. She begged me to come and save the poor creatures from extinction. As if I could do it on my own."

"That's because all daughters think their dads are heroes."

He beamed down at her. "I guess you're right. And I wouldn't have it any other way." He shot a bright smile at Gabe. "And what about you, Mr. Maddox, are you a turtle admirer or are you just enamored of our dear Skylar?"

"I'd have to choose the second answer. I've always had a fondness for turtle soup."

Skylar whirled around. "Gabe, that's not funny."

Gabe grinned unrepentantly and said, "Why don't you join us, sir?"

William looked back at his table and then said, "Well, perhaps I could for a little while."

He pulled out a chair left vacant by a guest who'd already departed, his portly figure sinking into it with an audible plop.

"So tell me, Mr. Maddox, are you in the city to stay or is this just a working vacation for you?"

Gabe shrugged. "Hard to say." He shot a warm look at Skylar. "There are attractions here that can't be found anywhere else."

Instead of smiling as Skylar thought he would, William leaned toward her, his face full of earnest concern. "Your father told me about your friend, my dear."

Wishing her father had kept his mouth shut, Skylar nodded. "She's been missing for several weeks now."

"I told Skylar she should just forget about her, since from all accounts she's probably just run away again," Gabe said.

William nodded. "It's hard not to worry about the young people of today, especially when you know they're making mistakes." He gave Skylar a strange look. "Sometimes it's best to let them go and let them learn from their mistakes."

Gabe took a giant bite of his dessert and chewed with

obvious enjoyment. He pointed his fork toward Skylar. "Exactly what I told her. How can you learn from your mistakes if people keep bailing you out?"

Somewhat startled at Gabe's unusual eagerness to get involved in the conversation, Skylar found herself sitting back and playing Gabe's normal role of quiet observer.

Winking at William with one of those obnoxious "we think alike because we're men" kind of looks, Gabe said, "I've seen pictures of the girl. She's a sweet young thing . . . sexy, too. Her skin looks like cream satin, smooth as silk. Full, plump mouth makes a man think all sorts of thoughts of what it could do. And that body . . ." Gabe made a disgusting, lecherous sound she never imagined she would hear from him.

He gave a small smile to Skylar. "Sorry, sweetheart, you know I think you're the most beautiful woman in the world, but I have to say, when you showed me pictures of her, my first thought was someone has probably bought the right to touch that smooth, supple skin."

Even though she recognized he was acting, Gabe's words still riled her. "You act like she's a piece of meat."

Gabe guffawed and winked at William again. "If she were, she'd be prime rib, eh, William?"

As if he was embarrassed by Gabe's vulgarity, William's smile was a bit tight. He stood and said, "I think Leanne is waving at me. Looks like she's ready to leave." With an affectionate pat to Skylar's shoulder, he nodded at Gabe and moved away.

"What the hell was that all about?"

"Let's go," Gabe said.

Throwing her napkin on the table, Skylar stood.

Holding herself stiffly, Skylar walked through the mass of people sitting and standing around, chatting, drinking, and laughing. She smiled when necessary but kept her eye on the door. Her goal was to get out of there without having to stop and speak with anyone.

She pulled away when Gabe grabbed her elbow.

He tightened his hold and said quietly, "Behave."

Knowing eyes were following them everywhere, she flashed her famous fake smile and said with the proper amount of sugary sweetness, "Darling, you have no idea how much I'd love to slug you right now."

Gabe snorted a surprised laugh and guided her out the door. As usual, the press were camped outside the restaurant and gave a collective, appreciative shout as Skylar paused on the steps, allowing them to take pictures.

"What the hell are you doing?" Gabe asked.

"Pissing you off," she muttered under her breath.

He huffed out an exasperated sigh and grumbled, "Hell, Skye, you know me better than that."

He was right. She did know him better. It was just that his words had reminded her of how some men thought about her. She could put up with almost any kind of attitude but that. Gabe wasn't like that. He might hate her money, but he was actually very respectful of women.

Flashing him a genuine smile, she said, "You're right. I'm sorry."

His face registered surprise at her apology. "Let's get out of here before I have to kiss you in front of everyone for being so damned sweet."

Now it was her turn to look surprised. Ignoring the questions being screamed at her, she allowed Gabe to nudge her into the limo that Cole had waiting for them.

Sinking into the soft leather seat, she waited until the door was closed and then said, "Okay, tell me why."

Excitement gleamed in his eyes. "Did you see Harrington's face?"

"What do you mean?"

"He was flushed."

"Gabe, he'd been drinking. A lot of people get flushed when they drink, that doesn't prove—"

"He got redder the more I talked about Kendra. And sorry to sound so crass, but when he stood up, the man had a definite boner."

No, that didn't make any sense. "There's no way that Uncle Bill would—"

He took her hand. "You need to look beyond what you know about the man."

"Gabe, it's not possible. I've known him since I was a baby." Tears filled her eyes. "He used to sneak Tootsie Roll Pops to me because my mom wouldn't let me eat sugar. I used to hide them under my pillow and eat them when I went to bed."

"I'm sorry, sweetheart. If it's not him, we'll prove it."

"But you think it is, don't you?"

Gabe didn't answer but his look said it all. Her godfather, the man she would have trusted her life with, was some kind of pervert.

No, she couldn't accept it.

"What about all the other people you suspected? Since starting your investigation, you've identified as least ten other men. Why do you think it's William?"

"We've already eliminated eight of those ten. We've got someone still watching one of them."

Gabe glanced out the window and then gave her a solemn, sad look. "I was going to wait until we got back to your apartment to tell you, but LCR has found some offshore money of Harrington's. A substantial amount."

"That's not that unusual. William's a wealthy man."

"True. But this money doesn't appear to be coming from any of his known businesses or investments. The majority of it isn't in his name, but we've followed the money trail and his name keeps popping up."

"Maybe he's doing something else illegal." As much as she didn't want William to be guilty of anything, she'd rather him be guilty of almost anything other than what he was being suspected of.

Resignation flooded through her at the certainty in Gabe's eyes. And though she hated for this to be true, she trusted his instincts.

"Sorry to interrupt," Cole said. "Got a message from McCall. There's something at the apartment you need to see."

Gabe didn't take his eyes from hers as he said, "What is it?"

The long pause had both of them turning their gazes to Cole.

"It's a streaming video . . . of Kendra."

"What kind of video?"

"I haven't seen it. Noah says it's pretty explicit."

Her horrified eyes went to Gabe. "Like a sex tape?"

Gabe squeezed the hand he still held. "Happens all the time. A special website is set up. People can go there, see just about anything."

"But that makes no sense. Why would he want others—"

"No, you're right. I suspect he wouldn't want to share. This one's probably set up just for him."

Cole maneuvered around a slow-moving car in front of them and said, "Our Web-watchers found it."

Shock and exhaustion swamped Skylar. She sank back into her seat, barely hearing the rest of the conversation between Cole and Gabe. Everyone she thought she could trust was turning out to be a liar.

A more horrendous thought slammed through her; bile surged toward her throat. "I introduced them," she whispered hoarsely.

Gabe leaned forward. "What?"

"I took Kendra around to a few benefit events. William was at one of them. He was standing in the midst of a group of people. Since they seemed to be in a serious discussion, I just made a sweeping introduction, then moved on." She closed her eyes briefly as the horrible realization took hold. "I wanted her to meet some influential, respectable people. Instead she met the devil."

"Skye, it's not your fault. There are hundreds of people at those events. You can't blame—"

She shook her head. "He never would have seen her without me bringing her there. . . . I brought her to his attention." Her stomach roiled. Oh God, she was going to be sick.

"Pull over, Cole."

Gabe's voice penetrated her misery. He recognized her need before she could say anything.

The limo pulled to a stop and Gabe opened the door, allowing Skylar to hang her head out and vomit. And all the while, he held her hair back and whispered to her. She couldn't understand the words, but the soothing tone of his voice calmed her.

Her stomach now empty but still roiling, she took a breath and sat up. A cold, wet cloth wiped at her mouth and face, giving her instant relief. She opened her eyes to find Gabe's expression a hard grimace of concern.

She traced the lines at his mouth with her finger. "You frown too much."

Instead of responding to her, he said, "Let's go before a photographer shows up."

Wouldn't that be a pretty sight in tomorrow's paper? Her mind still on the horror of her discovery, she closed her eyes and lay back against the seat. And not once did Gabe let go of her hand.

nineteen

William sat in his chair and stared longingly at the beautiful image on the giant screen across from him. Tears poured down his face even as he rubbed the aching flesh between his legs. He tried not to think about what he had to do. This was his pleasure. His only pastime. His outlet. A man had a right to a hobby.

Gabriel Maddox suspected him. He'd seen it in his eyes. When Maddox had started talking about his jewel, he hadn't been able to control himself. The vision of that supple, soft flesh had appeared in his mind. The more Maddox talked, the more aroused William had become.

Skylar had looked shocked to hear Maddox talk like that, but soon she would know, too. He had to stop them. He couldn't allow his family to be destroyed. His reputation would be in shreds. His family was one of the oldest families in this country. He couldn't bring shame to them.

His hand still on his aching crotch, William kept one eye on the beauty undulating before him simulating the sex act as he pressed speed dial. He needed this done as quickly and painlessly as possible. He didn't want Skylar to suffer. After all, she was his goddaughter . . . he loved her.

Maddox, on the other hand, he'd liked to choke and torture, but it had to be done quickly, which meant it had to be done while they were together. Since they were never seen anywhere without each other, his choices were limited.

The man picked up on the first ring.

"The job we discussed last week. It's a go. Just make it as fast and painless as possible."

"Money," the toneless voice said.

"Half will be transferred now. Half when it's done."

The phone clicked. The line went dead. William sobbed as he continued to stare at the beauty on the screen and rubbed himself even harder. A man had a right to a diversion. Why couldn't anyone understand that?

Skylar emerged from the steam-filled bathroom. As soon as they'd entered her apartment, she'd headed straight to the shower, stripping her clothes off as she went. She had to get clean. . . . She needed to be alone. Thankfully, Gabe seemed to understand those needs and hadn't tried to stop her.

"Feel better?"

Drawing the towel around her tighter, she whirled around. "Yes . . . a little. Sorry I lost it like that."

"You have nothing to apologize for, Skye. Kendra isn't the only victim here."

Thickness increased in her throat as she asked, "Did you look at the website?"

"Yes."

"Is it as bad as you thought?"

The expression on his face didn't require an answer, but he gave one anyway. "It's obvious she's drugged. Her eyes are dilated and vacant." He blew out a sigh. "And it's explicit and vulgar."

"Is she . . ." She swallowed. "Was she raped?"

"No. Apparently that's not what does it for him. She's alone. Simulating sex."

Skylar closed her eyes against the tears springing up again. "Can you tell how old the video is? Is it live?"

"No, it's not live. It's set up where he can go to it and watch it anytime he wants. And we were right. He's not making it public. Even though we've got people watching the Web 24/7, we were lucky to find it."

"So Kendra could still be dead and this was made before her death."

Gabe shook his head with certainty. "No. I don't think so. I definitely think that was a diversion. After seeing his face today . . . his reaction . . . I don't think he'd let her die."

"So you're saying he had someone killed to throw us off."

"Yeah."

"My God, what kind of a monster is he?"

"There are all kinds of monsters in the world, Skye. Some are just more obvious than others."

She drew in a trembling breath. "So what's our game plan?"

"The plan is for you to get some rest."

"Dammit, Gabe. I have to do something."

"Sweetheart, there's nothing to do. We can't prove a damn thing. It's still all supposition. If I went to the police and told them what I think and why I think it, they'd either lock me up or laugh at me."

"Then what—?"

"LCR's people are trying to track where the website feed is coming from. Cole is following Harrington everywhere he goes. We're tracking as much of his banking and real estate business as we can get our hands on, hoping it leads us somewhere."

His hands grasped her shoulders and gave her a bracing squeeze. "Believe me, we're doing everything we can.

The bastard won't get away with this. . . . It's just a matter of time."

"I just can't imagine what she's going through. What this is doing to her."

"We'll get her help when we find her. The most important thing now is to find her."

Gabe was right. Everything that could be done was being done . . . except one thing. "What if I go to him and tell him what we know? Shame him . . . threaten to go to Margo or his kids unless he confesses. We've always had a good relationship."

Though Gabe's head started shaking the instant she'd started talking, she continued, "He's been like a second father to me, Gabe. I'm sure I can get him to tell me the truth."

"Skye, your own father kept a terrible secret from you for eight years. William's number one priority will be protecting himself. If you confront him, there's no telling what he would do. I don't want you anywhere around him."

Helpless tears sprang to her eyes. "But I—"

Gabe pulled her into his arms. "Skye, baby." The words sounded tortured and strained as he breathed them against her hair.

Skylar closed her eyes. "I used to dream about you saying that."

"Saying what?"

" 'Skye, baby.' "

She looked up at him, smiling at the sweet memory of the first time he'd said them. The first time they'd made love. The most beautiful experience of her life. How incredibly tender he'd been. So wonderfully loving.

Gabe held her tighter. She felt his arousal. Knew he wanted her and she wanted him. Making love to him would be totally, absolutely one of the stupidest things she could imagine doing. But she wanted him. After denying herself for so long, she refused to deny herself this. Gabe was her husband, one she thought she'd lost long ago. How could she not want to relive, if only for a brief time, those glorious moments?

Skylar stood on her toes and kissed the small dimple in his chin.

"Skye." Gabe swallowed hard and said again, "Skye." Then he whispered, "Skye, baby." And lowered his mouth to hers.

With a groan of surrender, of need, Skylar wrapped her arms around him and opened her mouth, allowing his tongue inside.

Oh. Sweet. Mercy. She'd forgotten his taste. Tart and delicious, he stirred desire to a fever pitch of longing and need. She heard moaning, told herself to stop and couldn't. It had been so long . . . eight long, lonely years. How often had she fantasized about this? Dreamed of his hard, masculine body pressing against her.

Gabe pulled away and asked softly, "Are you sure?"

"Yes," she whispered.

With one sweep of his hand, Gabe pulled the towel away and dropped it to the floor. Then, as if he were seeing heaven for the first time, his eyes devoured her body. Goose bumps spread everywhere those hot midnight blue eyes roamed. Throbbing began deep inside. A throb of longing. Hot. Intense.

"Your nipples are peaking as if I've already been sucking them."

Skylar closed her eyes at the sexy growl in his voice. How could she have forgotten? When Gabe made love, he talked . . . narrated. He'd realized early on that his sexy talk turned her on, and when they made love, he used his voice to arouse her even more.

"You want me to suck them?"

"Yes . . . please."

A husky groan and then his hot breath bathed her breast in heat. Skylar could feel her nipple harden further in anticipation of his hot, moist tongue. But then, instead of sucking, he moved to the other nipple. She cried out her disappointment.

"Just a minute, sweetheart. I want both of them to know what's coming."

His mouth breathed on the other one and then his tongue licked lightly.

"Gabe."

His name was a moan of need and he recognized it as such because his mouth closed over her nipple and sucked hard . . . then harder. Skylar cupped her hands to his head and fed him her breast. He pulled away slightly, licked again, sucked again, biting gently. Skylar gasped at the sensation. A hot moist pool of desire settled between her legs, throbbing, wanting, anticipating.

Just when she thought she couldn't handle any more, he switched and went to her other breast and gave it the same treatment.

Suddenly her hands needed to be all over him at once. She ripped at his clothes and the husky "Yes" he gave told her he loved her enthusiasm. When her hand met the smooth velvet flesh of his penis, she slowed down. This . . . she wanted to savor. And remember.

But it was not to be.

He pulled away from her and dropped to his knees. His eyes glittering with a scorching lust, he growled, "Hold on to my shoulders."

Unable to refuse him anything now, Skylar complied.

Masculine lips moved over her stomach. Skylar groaned at the sensation of his beard stubble scratching her soft skin. The throb inside her deepened. Unable to stop herself, she took one of her hands off his shoulder and pushed his head toward the part of her dying for his kiss.

Groaning his approval, he placed a kiss on her mound. Skylar pushed her hips forward, letting him know she wanted more.

Laughing blue eyes looked up at her. "Put your hands back on my shoulders, sweetheart. You're going to need something to hold on to."

When she once again complied, he issued another instruction: "Spread your legs for me."

Barely able to hear from the lust roaring through her head, she forced her legs to move apart.

For the longest time, he just stared at her sex. The longer he looked, the hotter she got. Skylar was almost to the point of begging him to take her, when he looked up at her again and gave her the sexiest, most tender smile she'd ever seen. "Do you remember the first time I put my mouth on you?"

She shuddered at the memory. "I screamed."

"And then you came. Remember that, Skye? You exploded in my mouth . . . on my tongue." He pressed a soft kiss just above the deepest throb. "The sweetest taste in the world."

"Gabe, do it again."

"With pleasure."

Sliding his hands from her hips, he used his thumbs to open the folds of her sex and then . . . sweet, merciful heavens, the pleasure. He licked, sucked, and then went deep.

Without conscious thought, her body began to ride his tongue. A growl from his mouth vibrated against her clit and she sighed out a gasping sob. Gabe pulled away abruptly. Dazed from the exquisite need building inside her, Skylar looked down . . . surely he wasn't stopping.

Hot eyes locked with hers, he lifted one of her legs, placed her knee on his shoulder, and said, "Open for me, Skye."

With a groan, she arched toward his mouth. Using both thumbs, Gabe opened her folds again and delved deeper. Closing her eyes, Skylar was no longer aware of anything other than what was happening between her legs. Pleasure swamped her as Gabe swirled his tongue, licking, sucking . . . eating at her. Sobbing with needs she barely knew existed, she rose on her toes and then came down again. Gabe's tongue slid outside her, licked, and then went back inside, thrusting, plunging, retreating, and then thrusting once again.

Skylar's fingers dug into his hair as she rode against him. Groaning sounds came from his mouth and vibrated against her. Tension built . . . a scream rose inside her. Skylar opened her mouth on a silent scream and flooded his tongue.

As she came down to earth, her body shaking and almost collapsing from the insane pleasure, she looked down at the dark head between her legs. Gabe continued to nuzzle, lick, and thrust . . . gently, sweetly. Heat rose again, but as much pleasure as his mouth had given, she wanted something else inside her even more.

Pulling away slightly, she whispered, "Take me to bed."

Gabe straightened; lifting her in his arms, he turned around and walked the few steps to the bed. When he placed her on the edge, she thought he meant to join her there. Instead he dropped to his knees in front of her.

"Gabe, I want you inside me. Now."

As if he hadn't heard her, his hands cupped her butt to pull her closer and his mouth was on her again. He muttered against her clit, "You taste even better than before. Give me just a little more."

Unable to deny his command or herself the pleasure, Skylar spread her legs wider and allowed that diabolical tongue to sweep inside and have its way. Her hands went to his head, her fingers tangled in his hair, and she was once again riding, thrusting against him. A blast of heat speared through her and this time she screamed his name.

While she continued to throb and spasm, Gabe stood and turned. She looked up to see him grabbing something from his pants. A condom. She hadn't even given that any thought. Thank heavens he had.

Scooting toward the middle of the bed, she watched him approach her. Eyes glittering with heat, his face held a fierce, sexual expression that might have frightened her at one time. No more. This was Gabe, her husband, her lover. Her eyes dropped lower. She shivered in delightful anticipation as the throb inside her renewed and intensified. With no hesitation or embarrassment, Skylar opened her arms and her legs in welcome.

With a groan, Gabe came over her and, without any further preliminaries, was inside her. With a sob, Skylar threw her arms around his shoulders and wrapped her legs around his hips and lived out the hot, beautiful fantasies that had kept her warm these last lonely years.

His mind blurred with passion, Gabe ignored the stinging reprimand in the back of his mind. The one that said he was doing something so asinine and stupid, he'd never recover. It no longer mattered. Not right now. He was exactly where he wanted to be . . . where he wanted to stay.

"I'd forgotten how good it felt," Skylar gasped beneath him.

Raising up on his knees, firmly embedded deep inside her warmth, Gabe gazed down at the beauty before him. Never had she looked more lovely. Her face, her entire body, was flushed a beautiful glowing shade of pink. The deep rose of her nipples, taut and distended, lured him. No breasts in the universe could ever be as luscious as Skye's. He thrust harder and watched her eyes dilate. Her breath hitched as she arched up off the bed, thrusting him even deeper inside her heat.

Gabe lowered his body, groaning with a need he'd never imagined. It had been eight damn cold lonely years, but Gabe didn't regret a moment of not touching any woman since Skye. And in that silent, stark place where true knowledge existed, he knew no other woman would ever replace Skye. In his heart or in his bed.

Almost sobbing with her need, Skye wrapped her legs tighter around him as she undulated beneath his body. His mouth roaming over her face, neck, and chest, he couldn't stop the words even if someone had threatened death. He remembered how she loved to hear him talk when they made love, and he wanted to give her everything she wanted. Could deny her nothing.

"You are so damn beautiful, Skye. No one could ever be more beautiful." When he felt her inner muscles tighten around him, pulling him deeper, complete sentences were beyond him. "Yeah . . . take me . . . deeper. That's it . . . Just. Like. That."

And then, with a small scream, she arched her body and clenched him, milking his cock. He allowed himself the freedom to let go. With a guttural "Sweet, Skye," Gabe thrust harder, plunging, pounding. Lightning zipped down his spine; flashes of color exploded behind his eyes. With a groan of ecstasy, Gabe followed Skye into oblivion.

twenty

Kendra stared at the blank wall before her. Voices floated around her. Familiar and unfamiliar, male and female. She didn't know who they were. Didn't care. She was empty.

"How long has she been like this?"

"Since that last dose you gave her. I think with the lack of food in her system, we dosed her too much."

"Dammit, he's asking for another show."

"Hell, she's done four this week. What's the perv's problem? He can watch them over and over."

"Apparently he has . . . over and over. With these kinds of creeps, it's never enough. He's wanting more now."

An excited male voice asked, "Is he wanting the real thing?"

"Hell no. He'd kill anyone who got to her first. He sent a box of sex toys he wants her to use." He paused for a second and Kendra felt a hand touch her chin, raise her head. She blinked groggily up at the man in front of her. He wavered into a tall, dark blob . . . a featureless image of evil.

"She's so out of it, there's no way in hell we'll be able to pull this off."

For some reason, the disgust in his voice penetrated the dull cloud in her mind. Disgusting . . . yes. It was disgusting. She was disgusting. Her head dropped to her chest and she closed her eyes. Sleep. She just wanted to sleep.

"Wake her up. Give her some food, coffee . . . whatever it takes. Once she's sober, we'll have to shoot it."

"You want me to give her something else?"

"No, she'll have to do it without the drugs. Bring one of the girls in here. If she sees what'll happen if she doesn't obey, we should be able to get enough footage to satisfy the bastard this time."

"When's he going to be ready for her?"

"I think he's been ready for her . . . she just wasn't ready for him." A hand tilted her head up. "She's close . . . another couple of days and he'll want to claim her."

The voices began to fade as they walked away from her.

"He must be one sick fuck."

Someone laughed . . . sounded like a woman. "To each his own. Whatever rocks his boat is fine with me as long as he pays us for it."

The voices disappeared and Kendra was once again alone. Without will, her body dropped to the soft surface of her mattress. Burying her face in the soft pillow, she closed her eyes and drifted away. . . . Finally, at last, she had peace.

"Where are you going?"

Skylar turned from her desk and smiled up at Gabe. "Good morning."

Instead of returning her smile, he looked grumpy. Her smile grew bigger. How could someone who looked like he'd just as soon chew gravel as smile look so damn sexy?

Folding his long arms over the broad chest she'd nuzzled all night, he asked again, "Where are you going?"

"My dad called. He wants me to come for lunch."

"Why can't he come here?"

"Well, for one thing, I haven't been to the market in days. I have nothing to feed him."

"Fine. I'll get dressed."

Skylar bit her lip. Here was the sticking point. "He asked me to come alone. I think he wants—"

"Skye, I don't care what the man wants. You're not going anywhere by yourself. Now, you can call your dad and tell him to come here or I go with you. Your choice."

"Gabe, don't go all he-man on me. It's my dad, for heaven's sake."

The obstinate set to his face told her he wouldn't back down. His words proved it. "Those are your choices. Until we get Harrington behind bars, you go nowhere—and I mean nowhere—alone. Not even to your dad's house. Is that clear?"

"Don't treat me like an imbecile. I'm getting into a taxi and getting out at my dad's. Then I'm coming right back home. There's absolutely no reason—" She cut off her words when he turned around and started walking away. "Where are you going?"

He didn't bother to turn around. "Apparently your choice is to have me go with you. I'm going to get dressed."

Skylar watched his retreating back. It would do no good to argue. When Gabe went into protective mode, changing his mind was impossible.

A glance at the clock told her she had fifteen minutes before she had to leave. Plenty of time for him to get dressed and plenty of time for her to give careful consideration to the conversation she wanted to have with Gabe when they returned home.

She wanted a real marriage with him. Last night had been everything she could have wanted. Gabe had been passionate and tender. In equal parts giving and demanding. When he'd told her that he hadn't made love to a woman since they'd parted, she hadn't been sure she believed him. A man as highly sexual as Gabe going without sex for that long seemed impossible. After last night, she believed him.

Seven times . . . they'd made love seven times. She didn't even know that was possible. In all the books she'd read, men couldn't respond like that. Gabe had had no problem. And though she was impossibly sore and achy in places she had forgotten existed, every particle of her body had a tingling, glowing feel. She'd had no problem keeping up with Gabe's seven times.

They hadn't talked a lot, other than those oh-so-sexy passages he knew turned her on. Eventually those had morphed into the most rudimentary words, such as "Feel good?" "Want more?" And a whole lot of yesses and pleases from her.

A glow of happiness permeated her entire body. Oh yes, it had been a very good night.

Now that their passion had been eased, it was time to talk about the future. And she prayed with all of her might that there was one. After last night, she had no doubt that Gabe had strong feelings for her. And though she had tried to deny it, she had never stopped loving him. Yes, there had to be a future for them.

"Ready?"

Skylar came out of her worried thoughts to find Gabe standing before her. And despite the fact that she'd spent hours in his arms last night, there was nothing she wanted more than to go back to bed and make more memories.

"When you get that look on your face, you know there's only one thing I can do."

Already knowing, she cocked her head and said softly, "Oh yeah . . . like what?"

Growling low in his throat, Gabe pulled her quickly to him and covered her mouth with his.

Sighing into his mouth, Skylar gave herself up to the passion that only this one man had ever been able to ignite.

Misty rain shrouded the air. Giant umbrellas covered busy New Yorkers as they scurried along the crowded sidewalk. The few fortunate enough to be able to hail a cab ran quickly to the opened door of their ride.

Gabe stood at the doorway of Skylar's apartment building. Since Cole was busy trailing Harrington, they needed to rely on taxis. Why the hell hadn't he called one before they left? He knew the answer to that . . . he'd been too damn busy feeling up his wife. That's what he got for taking his mind off the job and being stupid to boot.

"We should have called a cab," Gabe said.

Skylar peeked around his shoulder. "Let's start walking. We'll find one."

"No, it won't hurt to be late for lunch. Let's go back in and call one."

"Don't be ridiculous, Gabe." She reached up and wiped at his mouth, smiling as she pulled away a finger stained with her lipstick. "We're already almost an hour late." Holding out her hand, she said, "We'll find a taxi within a block. Betcha ten bucks."

When Skylar gave him that smile of innocence and sensuality combined, Gabe went to mush. He took her hand. "Fine. Stay right beside me, though."

Rolling her eyes at him, she pulled him with her down the street. Neither of them had thought to bring an umbrella, and Skye's hair was already getting damp. Cursing his lack of professionalism and foresight, Gabe walked beside her, his eyes open not only for an available cab but also for any kind of threat.

Halfway down the block, she said, "I win. There's a cab

right there." She raised her hand to hail it. The roar of a car engine caught Gabe's attention. His head jerked around. A black Toyota sedan with its window open drove slowly by. *Window open . . . in the rain.* He pushed Skye to the pavement. Bullets whizzed by his ear. In one simultaneous motion, Gabe pulled his gun and threw himself on top of Skye, covering her completely.

The car roared past them. Screams and shouts filled the air. Thousands of things went through Gabe's head but he could focus on only one question. Why wasn't Skye moving?

"I'm fine, Gabe. I promise."

His face was pale and his eyes were blazing with fury. Skylar was more worried about him than the slight nick on her shoulder and the bump on her head. If Gabe hadn't pushed her down when he did, she'd be dead. And, most likely, so would he.

"I'm going to kill the bastard."

"You don't think it was Bill, do you?"

"Not personally, but yeah, he hired someone."

"Gabe, we don't know that. People are always targeting celebrities for one reason or another. We can't just assume—"

"How many people have tried to kill you?"

"Well, none that I know of, but—"

"But nothing, Skye. This is beyond just a coincidence."

Wrapping her arms around herself, Skylar faced facts. As much as she would have liked to argue with Gabe further, she couldn't. A deep hurt penetrated the numbness. The man she'd known all her life, would have trusted with her life, was not only torturing Kendra and possibly other girls, he'd hired someone to kill her and Gabe.

Gabe dropped to his knees in front of her. "Let me call a doctor. You're as pale as death."

"I'm fine, really. The EMT checked my shoulder. It's barely a scratch."

His finger softly grazed the bruise on her forehead. "What about this bump?"

"I don't have a concussion."

"You lost consciousness . . . you had the hell scared out of you. You could be in shock."

Skylar shook her head. "I'm not in that kind of shock. If anything, I'm furious I didn't really believe you. You're right. It's too coincidental that the day after you made those statements to him, someone tries to kill us."

"He's getting desperate."

"Shouldn't we tell the police at least something? They bought the story of a random shooting . . . but if we tell them—"

"What, Skye? That one of the wealthiest and most influential men in the country is the head of a sex-trafficking ring? That he's holding at least one young girl captive and making her do vile things for his amusement? That he hired someone to kill us because we're onto him? And oh, by the way, we have no proof of any of this but please believe us anyway?"

"But LCR has influence."

"Influence, yes. But even LCR has to have proof before we go about slandering someone's name. If I went to them, it's his word against mine."

"Against ours."

Gabe smiled and touched her cheek gently. It was already sore from her fall onto the pavement. Stupid really, but she'd knocked herself out briefly when she hit the concrete. And had scared Gabe to death. He thought she'd been shot.

"I know you have influence, Skye, but the man has managed to hide this for years. He may well have contacts in the department we're not aware of. There's no way in hell I'm bringing them in until I have positive proof."

Her fingers smoothed his hair that was still damp from the rain. "I'm sorry I didn't listen to you."

He shook his head. "My fault. I should have called a taxi. Or hell, I shouldn't have agreed to this anyway."

"I need to call my dad. It'll be all over the news soon, if it isn't already. He'll be worried."

Gabe stood and grabbed the phone from the table and handed it to her. "Assure him you're all right. Tell him what we told the police. And that you can't see him right now . . . that you need to rest. Until we figure out how to get to Kendra and get Harrington, I don't want you going anywhere."

Skylar drew in a breath as she hit speed dial for her dad. She'd wait a while before she told Gabe her idea. He wouldn't like it, but she was determined to convince him. They needed to get information on William Harrington, and what better way to do that than brave the devil in his own home?

twenty-one

"Take your clothes off."

Kendra gritted her teeth but didn't move. He wanted her clothes off, he could damn well take them off. She'd woken this morning, clearheaded for the first time in days, and determined she would no longer be their puppet. She'd had a full meal, and though she still felt lethargic and weak, she was lucid enough to know what was going on. Damned if they'd get any more cooperation out of her.

She couldn't remember what they had made her do . . . she only knew that even in her drugged-out haze, she'd felt shame. For what, she didn't know. She remembered lewd words. She remembered male and female laughter. She remembered pleasure, pain, and all the while, she'd felt the shame. She'd been hot and breathless, as if she were burning inside and out.

Never again.

"I said, get your clothes off, bitch."

She raised her head and glared. "Go to hell."

Shocked silence followed her cold, hollow statement.

A face, flushed red with anger, appeared inches before her face. "You either get them off or I'll give you a show you'll never forget."

She knew what he meant. They would bring another young girl in and do vile things to her as punishment for Kendra's defiance. And as blackmail. She no longer cared.

Let them do their worst. She was determined to survive no matter what. They wanted to torture another young girl? Let them. To survive in this world or any other, you had to look out for number one. *Number one.* That would be her mantra from now on.

The man turned to someone behind him. "Strip her, but don't leave any marks he can see. I'll be back."

Two sets of hands pulled at the thin nightgown she wore. Kendra sprang into action. Skylar had offered to take her to some self-defense classes. Kendra had refused, but she remembered Skylar's advice. Her fist bopped the woman in the nose. She yelped a curse and cupped her hand over her face. Kendra kicked her in the stomach. The woman bent double, gagging as blood gushed onto the floor.

The man grabbed for Kendra's hair. She swung her forearm to block him, then punched him in the eye. He shouted and reached for her again. She swung her fist up and jammed it hard into his crotch.

Kendra ran for the door. Both of her assailants were on the floor howling in pain, but probably not for long. And that other bastard would be back soon. She had to get out of here as soon as she could. She ran through the opened door and found herself in a narrow, well-lit hallway. There was a door at both ends. Would either one of them lead to freedom? She didn't know, but she had to try.

Her heart pounding with fear and hope, Kendra took off.

"That's about the dumbest, most asinine suggestion I've ever heard from anyone."

Hands on her hips, Skylar advanced toward the stubborn, glaring man standing in front of her. "You may not like my idea, but you don't have to insult it."

"Fine, it's a brilliantly stupid idea. That better, princess?"

Resisting the urge to stomp her feet like a five-year-old, she snapped, "And stop calling me 'princess.' "

Rolling his eyes, he said in a controlled, toneless voice, "Skylar, the idea you gave, while it has merit, is not feasible and would not be prudent to pursue. Therefore, my answer is: Hell. Fucking. No." He raised an arrogant brow. "That sophisticated enough for you?"

She drew in a breath. Just blurting out her idea hadn't been the wisest course of action. Gabe blamed himself for her almost getting shot. Suggesting that they brave the lion's den as if nothing was wrong had him questioning her sanity.

Her chin set with determination, she ticked off the reasons why it was their best bet to find Kendra. "Think about it, Gabe. We can't involve the police, because they won't believe us without proof. LCR still can't find where the webcam is streaming from. Cole has already admitted that by following William around, he hasn't uncovered anything worthwhile." She held out her hand to deliver her final point. "We're running out of time. The longer we wait, the more Kendra will suffer."

"Then I'll go . . . you stay here."

She swallowed a soft snort. "You're not invited and he's not going to let you in without me. This is an annual event. My family is invited every year. My dad and I are usually the only people in my family to go. William can't cancel, because it would cause speculation. And he can't call me and tell me not to come."

His eyes searing her with heat, Gabe walked slowly toward her. "You've thought this through?"

"Yes."

"And if it means putting yourself in danger?"

"I'm willing to take the risk."

As Gabe reached her, he took her hand and drew her to him. "I'm not."

Though his words were still saying no, she saw acceptance in his eyes. He knew this was their best shot, perhaps their only shot, to find something on William. Staying at his home for a long weekend would give them ample time to explore. If he had something there that would incriminate him or help them get information on Kendra, then they would find it.

Tucking a strand of hair behind her ear, he said, "He'll have people watching us, night and day."

"There will be over a hundred there at any given time. He may have people watching us, but I'm betting you'll find some way to create a diversion or two."

His grin sexy and dangerous at the same time, he nodded. "I might be able to think of something."

Unable to be this close to him and not kiss him, she stood on her toes and kissed his chin softly. The rasp of his beard stung her lips and Skylar shivered as she remembered last night when he'd buried his face between her legs and the stubble had created the most erotic, pleasurable feeling she'd ever known. She'd woken this morning with stubble burn on the inside of her thighs. And every time she moved, the sensation was a reminder of how delicious it had felt.

"You want me to kiss you?"

"Mmm?"

"You get a look in your eyes when you want me to kiss you," he said.

"Don't ask," she whispered. "Take."

With a groan, Gabe lowered his head and complied. Covering her mouth with his, he pressed deep, seeking entrance. Skylar opened her mouth and let him in. His tongue thrust hard, then retreated quickly. Skylar groaned and chased his tongue, wanting his taste back in her mouth.

Gabe spoke against her lips, "Slow down, Skye."

Slow down? She was burning for him. Had years to make up for. Ignoring his words, she grabbed his hair and pulled him back toward her. Gabe resisted.

"Gabe," she protested softly.

His smile filled with sexual male heat, he held out his hand and said, "Let's go to bed."

Holding her hand in his, Gabe led Skye to the bedroom, and for just a brief instant, imagined what life would be like if he could do this every night.

Skye's smile was shy yet sexy, innocent yet bold. Gabe's heart floundered for a regular beat. This one woman was the only one who'd ever made him forget how to breathe, how to exist outside of her arms.

Gabe shut the door, closing out the world and everything that told him he was crazy for even entertaining the idea of staying married to the beauty before him. It was a dream . . . but one he wanted to indulge for as long as possible.

Drawing her close, his mouth grazing hers, he whispered, "Will you do something for me?"

"What?"

"Strip."

Her eyes widened with just a hint of uncertainty. Then he saw what he wanted to see. The fire . . . the need to please blended with the intense desire to excite. Hell, little did she know that Skye just breathing excited the hell out of him.

A slow smile spread across her face. Pointing to a chair in the middle of the room, she said, "Sit over there . . . and watch."

Gabe was in the chair before she even finished talking.

Her husky laughter at his speed spread fire throughout his body and then settled south. He throbbed with an erection so immediate and hard he figured he'd explode before Skye even got her blouse off.

She started with her hair, which was held in a clip at the nape of her neck. Swaying to music only she could hear, she reached up and released the thick mass, allowing it to fall around her shoulders like a dark cloud of satin.

Then her fingers went to her blouse. As she slid each button through its opening, his heart rate quickened. At last the blouse hung loose and Skye's beauty showed through the sheer lilac bra she wore. Her nipples were hard and distended . . . already aroused. His mouth watering, Gabe had to grip the arm of the chair to keep from going to her and putting his mouth on the sweet berries.

Her eyes stayed on his as she unzipped the skirt and let it slide slowly down her silken legs and pool at her feet. Gabe groaned as she kicked the skirt away, then in a move that surprised the hell out of him, she tore her blouse off and threw it to him. He caught it with one hand and held it to his face. Skylar. It smelled of his Skye. The most beautiful fragrance in the world.

Still swaying to her own music, she was now clad only in a see-through lilac bra, barely-there matching bikini panties, and her heels. Gabe swallowed hard. An almost nude Skye in heels was a sight to behold. A vision beyond his imaginings. And she knew it. Gone was the shy, innocent look she'd first given him. A sweet, sexy vixen had emerged.

Continuing her dance, a smile of sensuality on her beautiful face, Skye skimmed her hands over her body the way his hands ached to do. Slender fingers ran over her breasts, circled the beautiful, erect nipples pressing against the material of her bra. Nipples he longed to taste. Delicate, slender hands caressed the soft skin at her waist, her taut belly, and then moved lower. Gabe's heart stopped.

As if she knew exactly where he wanted her hands to go, that sexy mouth tilted as she veered her hands back up. His cock almost burst when he saw the damp evidence of her desire against the cloth of her panties. Skye would be hot, moist . . . delicious.

Pulling his eyes away from her sex, he watched as her hands moved up to her breasts again. He held his breath as she unclasped the front opening of her bra and, without warning, pulled the bra completely off. Then, as if her hands were her lover's hands, she caressed her breasts, plumped them up as if in offering and then . . . and then she tweaked her nipples and closed her eyes on a gasp. Gabe groaned, sure that soon he would fall from his chair to his knees.

Her eyes opened now and locked with his; her hands were on the move again. They smoothed down her sides and hooked her fingers into her panties. Then slowly, surely, she drew them down. Gabe lost sight of her hands. His eyes zeroed in on her sex; he could see moisture . . . Skye's essence. He braced himself, ready to come to her, taste her.

She raised her hand and stopped him. "Wait."

Gabe dropped back into his chair. Probably best anyway. He wasn't sure his legs would hold him.

Then Skye, his lovely, wondrous Skye, began to dance in earnest.

She swayed like a willow in a strong wind, bending and moving in impossible ways but never too far. It was a dance of beauty. A dance of elegance and grace. And it was all for him.

Unable to wait any longer, he growled, "Come here."

Her smile one he would take to his grave, Skye gracefully walked toward him. Inches from where he sat, she lowered herself to her knees, placed her hands on his thighs, and ran her fingers upward.

His hand went to unzip his pants; her hands were there to stop him. Then, with slow deliberateness, she unzipped his pants and took him out. They both looked down at his cock. Had he ever been this close and not exploded? He was hard . . . the color almost purple with the pulsing of blood just beneath the surface. And Skye knew it . . . she knew what she was doing to him. Still wearing that smile of knowledge, she bent forward and swirled her tongue around the crown. Before he could gasp or groan, she opened her mouth and took him in . . . to her throat.

Unable to stop himself, his hands grasped at her hair and he moved her head back and forth . . . showing her what to do . . . what he liked. From the sounds of her moans, she liked it, too.

Gabe pulled his hand away from her head and reached for her breasts. And as Skye sucked and licked, Gabe leaned his head against the back of the chair, closed his eyes, and played with her beautiful breasts.

He waited. The pleasure was immense . . . unbelievable. He didn't want it to end. . . . A red haze of lust built . . . blazed hotter. Her mouth tightened around him . . . sucked harder. And then it was too much. He jerked from her mouth; grabbing her under her arms, Gabe picked her up and seated her fully on him. Thrusting upward, he went impossibly deep; they both groaned at the sensation.

She was slick . . . more turned on than he'd thought. As close to explosion as he was. Holding her hips, he lifted her up and down quicker and quicker. Her eyes locked with his and then, just when he didn't think he'd live another moment, they exploded together. She milked him and he thrust deep, hard . . . wanting to reach so deep inside her, she would never leave him, never deny him . . . always want him. Forever.

Skylar woke to heaven. Wrapped in a cocoon of warmth, she lay on her side and savored the feel of Gabe's long, hard arms surrounding her. How many nights had she woken from this dream and cried when she realized it wasn't real? But this was real and she cherished every single second. Gabe's deep, even breaths told her he was sound asleep. She smiled at the knowledge that she had tired him out.

How she'd gotten the courage to strip in front of him, she would never know. The heat in his expression . . . that sensual, knowing look he always wore when he looked at her had empowered her. She'd seduced her husband and felt pretty damn good about it.

Never would she have thought she could behave the way she had. But when she saw Gabe's eyes and his more than obvious arousal, something had been set off inside her, freeing her from all inhibitions. Lightning and dynamite coming together. She'd wanted to turn him on, to please him until he exploded from the pleasure. And he had . . . several times. As had she.

Despite the glory of being in his arms, doubts assailed her. When this was over, when they found Kendra, what would happen between them? Gabe hadn't said and Skylar still hadn't worked up the courage to ask. How did you ask your husband if he'd stay with you when for eight years he apparently hadn't wanted to?

She loved Gabe. In every way possible. Growling, grumpy, caring, loving, and arrogant. All those traits were Gabe. She recognized that the man he had once been—the idealistic young man she'd adored—was still inside Gabe.

And now she had fallen in love with the man he had become. Together they made up the man she would love forever. But how did Gabe feel? She knew he desired her . . . that was no longer in question. But lust didn't mean love. He said he hadn't been with a woman in eight years. A whole lot of lust could build up in eight years. She was living proof of that. But her lust was deeply intertwined with love. Was Gabe's?

Odd, but in every other area of her life, she had tremendous self-confidence . . . sometimes to her detriment, since she had a tendency to be overly optimistic. That wasn't the case with Gabe. Even years ago she'd been unsure and vulnerable with him. Maybe she had realized he had the power to hurt her unlike anyone ever had.

The arms around her tightened as Gabe gave a long, quiet sigh. She smiled at the sound of contentment. Pressing a kiss to his arm, she wiggled her bottom up against him and felt the hardening of his erection against her.

"Be still," he growled.

"Why?"

"Because that sweet ass of yours distracts the hell out of me."

"What's it distracting you from now?"

"Just holding you, Skye . . . just holding you."

The emotion in that one sentence was almost more than she could take. Gabe's feelings were strong. But were they strong enough to overcome the bitterness of his past? The insecurities that hampered him . . . ones that he would most certainly deny?

She drew in a silent sigh. Gabe had always been so honest, so open, but there was one thing that still weighed heavily on him. One thing he'd never really been able to talk about with her. Could she break that last barrier? Would it help him or hurt him even more? Sending up a silent prayer that she wasn't doing something she'd regret, she said, "Tell me about Brandon."

His entire body stiffened instantly and he stopped breathing. Then, just when she thought she had indeed made a major mistake, Gabe released a ragged breath. "I think I told you that Dad married my stepmother when I was four . . . Brandon was two." Skylar felt his shoulder shift as he shrugged. "For some reason, from the minute we met, we were brothers. He followed me everywhere and something inside me loved being a big brother . . . even at that young age."

"What was he like?"

"The total opposite of me in almost everything." She could hear the smile in his voice. "Medium height, maybe about five-nine or so, and skinny. We used to laugh at him because he'd shovel food in but never seemed to gain weight. He had reddish blond hair, kind of a fair complexion and freckles. Lots of freckles. And he had a grin that got him out of every bind he ever got in. Everyone loved Brandon. He had a charm about him and the kind of sunny, optimistic attitude that just made you feel better to be around him."

Tears stung her eyes. Gabe, the dark one, with the serious personality—no wonder he'd felt so responsible for his kid brother. He'd been like a dark guardian . . . his brother's protector. And when Brandon died, Gabe felt as though he'd failed him.

"What's your best memory of him?"

Without hesitation he answered, "His acceptance into Yale."

More tears came to her eyes . . . Brandon had never made it to Yale. He'd died under a mountain of coal while his big brother lay beside him trying to keep him alive. That much she knew. Gabe had been able to share a little of the dark stuff. It was the happy memories he'd never been able to speak of.

"What was he going to study?"

Gabe snorted. "Law."

"Why the snort?"

"Because he was always in so much trouble . . . nothing bad or anything, just innocent pranks. With that charm of his, he could get out of it so easily. I told him he'd better work for the good side. If he'd defended criminals, the world would be more dangerous than it already is. He would've been able to get anybody off."

"Tell me about that day."

There was no need to explain what day she meant.

"It was summertime. Brandon was due to leave for college that fall. Both of us hated the mines, but that's what we did each summer. Dad was a coal miner. All the men in my family had been miners. It's just what we did."

"Weren't you in college by then?"

"Yeah. I was in my second year at UWV, but I was home for the summer. Brandon and I always tried to work as much each summer as we could to help the family out."

"What happened?"

"A lot of it is a blur. Doctors told me I'd probably never remember it all. We'd been underground for about an hour. Brandon and my dad were working over in another part of the mines, not far from me. I heard Brandon crack a joke . . . heard my dad's deep chuckle and then a monstrous thundering sound. Like the entire world had caved in.

"I don't know how long I was unconscious. I woke up . . . heard moaning. I managed to crawl toward the sound. It was dark as death. The air had a thick film that burned my eyes, my lungs. I remember gasping, coughing, and wheezing my way toward the sounds. I tried calling their names but no one answered. So I just kept crawling till I stumbled upon a foot. He swallowed hard. It was my dad's. His lower body was buried, trapped under a giant rock. Brandon was beside him. My dad was unconscious."

Gabe stopped for a second and Skylar hurt for him. "Brandon was awake . . . but in pain. God, he was hurting so bad and there wasn't a damn thing I could do for him. A giant boulder was wedged between us. I could hear him. Couldn't see him."

"Weren't you hurt, too?"

Another shrug. "A few busted ribs, couple of broken bones. Nothing serious. Nothing like Brandon or my dad."

"Were you able to talk to him?"

"Yeah. I couldn't stop talking. Afraid that if I stopped, he'd stop living. Stupid, I know, but I couldn't reach him and thought if the sound of my voice could keep him alive, then he'd damned well hear it forever."

"And you talked to him for five days?"

"I tried . . . got hoarse after a couple of days. Lost consciousness a few times." His voice thickened. "I don't know when he died. Even though I could barely hear myself, I wouldn't stop talking. I couldn't. They said my dad probably died within an hour . . . he never regained consciousness. The other six, in another part of the mines, died instantly. Brandon." Another hard swallow. "They did an autopsy on Brandon . . . told my stepmom when he most likely died. I didn't want to know. I was his big brother . . . I should've protected him. And in the end, I couldn't do a damn thing for him except talk."

Tears poured down her face at the unspeakable pain in his voice.

"Gabe, your words—the words of the brother he loved—were the last ones he remembered. The last ones he heard. He took those words with him. You gave him that."

Gabe's silence told her he disagreed. There was nothing she could say that would ease his pain. At some point she hoped he would forgive himself for something that was most definitely not his fault.

"Why have you never tried calling your stepmother?"

"Let it go, Skye."

"No, Gabe. It's been twelve years. Don't you think it's time you put the past to rest?"

"It is at rest, Skye. I told you she remarried. Her new husband had a couple of kids. She has a new life. She doesn't need me bringing back all the bad memories."

"But they weren't all bad, Gabe."

He didn't answer.

"Don't you think she'd like to see you?"

"No. When I left, I swore I'd never go back. Having an entire town stare at you because you survived when their loved ones didn't isn't something I want to relive."

"But your stepmother—"

"My stepmother lost her son and her husband. It was only natural that she resent me."

"There's nothing natural about that at all."

"I understood it."

He understood it because he blamed himself, too. Survivor's guilt could play hell with your life . . . she should know. She'd experienced her own brand for the eight years she thought Gabe had killed himself. The guilt had at eaten at her like a cancer. As had Gabe's. It didn't take a genius to figure out why he went to work for Last Chance Rescue. He hadn't been able to rescue his brother and now rescuing was his life.

Apparently wanting to end their discussion, Gabe pulled his arms from around her and rolled her over on her back. His fingers touched her wet face with a gentleness that made her want to cry all the more. There was such gentleness and goodness in this dark, brooding man she adored.

"Don't cry for me, Skye. I'm living the life I chose."

No. She would not let those words hurt her. The life he'd chosen was working for Last Chance Rescue. It had nothing to do with their marriage. That was still to be worked out.

"Did you ever think about going back to Africa?"

A harsh frown wrinkled his brow. "The village was destroyed. There was nothing to go back to."

Skylar released a silent sigh. Yet another betrayal by a woman he loved. After leaving his West Virginia home, Gabe had joined an altruistic group who built houses for impoverished villagers around the world. He'd been sent to a small African community. In the midst of building homes and helping the villagers, he'd fallen for the daughter of the local missionary. And he'd thought his affections were returned until the village was attacked by a neighboring band of thugs. His captors had taunted him with the truth. The woman he loved had sold the village out in return for money to go back home.

And the moment Skylar had met him, she'd betrayed him by not being truthful. Not telling Gabe had been a stupid, selfish thing. And she'd paid dearly for it. They both had.

"I'm sorry I never told you who I was, Gabe."

"Don't, Skye. I understood."

The way he said the words had her questioning them. "Just what did you understand?"

"A famous, beautiful woman fools around with a poor country boy? The press would have had a field day."

"I didn't fool around with you. I fell in love with you."

Lowering his body over hers, he skimmed his lips over her face. "Let it go, Skye. It's over."

Pain speared through her . . . followed quickly by cold determination. Hell no, it wasn't over. Grabbing his head, she brought his lips to hers and kissed him fiercely. If she had to seduce forever out of him, then that's what she'd damn well do.

She and Gabe had waited too long for their happy ever after. Once Kendra was rescued and William was in jail, Gabe Maddox would learn just how ruthless his wife could be when she wanted something.

Skylar refused to acknowledge the little voice inside her that whispered, *Just because you want forever doesn't mean Gabe does.*

twenty-two

Kendra swallowed sobs as she ran down the hallway. They would be after her soon. She had no idea where she was going . . . hadn't been out of that room since she'd been here. She had to try, though . . . She had to find a way out. Rescue would not come. She had to find a way to rescue herself.

Lungs burning, her limbs trembling and weak, she stopped at a door at the end of the hallway. Where it led, she didn't know. She eased it open and stuck her head through. A stairway . . . she must be in the basement. Half crawling, half running, terror providing adrenaline, she dashed up the stairs. At the top was another door. Easing it open, she peeked in. A modern-looking kitchen, thankfully empty. On silent feet, Kendra ran through the kitchen, her head turning at all angles. At some point very soon, someone would see her. She had to find a door.

Standing in the middle of living room, she noted locks on the windows. She spotted a door and ran for it, tugging at the doorknob. It was dead-bolted. Refusing to give up, she ran from room to room. She found two more doors. Both dead-bolted. The windows were locked. Taking an awful chance, she picked up a heavy vase and crashed it against the window. She didn't care if she was cut to pieces; she'd crawl out of the damn window. Better to die bleeding to death than stay in this hell any longer. The vase shattered; the window didn't even crack.

Sobs of desperation threatening to explode, Kendra turned and started running again. Each room was furnished in a nice, respectable décor. Good God, was she in someone's home? She skidded to a halt when she saw a miracle. A cellphone lying on the coffee table.

Grabbing it, Kendra did the only thing in her muddled, terrified mind that made sense to her. She pressed in Skylar's number.

Skylar groaned at the irritating buzz beside her ear. Gabe growled beside her, "Skye, it's your phone. Want me to get it?"

Mumbling "No," she stretched her hand out and felt for the phone. Only her family and close friends had this number. Without looking at the display, she opened it and held it to her ear. "Hello."

"Skylar! Help me! Please!"

Skylar shot up in bed, all drowsiness gone. "Kendra! My God . . . Where are you?"

A sob. "I don't know. Some kind of house. They won't let me out. Please, Skylar, help me."

Before she could answer, Gabe grabbed the phone. "Kendra, I'm a friend of Skylar's. Can you tell me if you're still in New York?"

"I don't know. I haven't been outside."

"How many are holding you?"

"I don't know. Maybe three men . . . two women."

"Where are they now?"

"I got away from them but—"

"Can you get to a door?"

"They're all locked. Please help—"

"Can you see outside the windows?"

"Yes, I think so."

"What do you see?"

A small, desperate sob and then, "Trees. And a driveway. I think I'm in someone's house. Please, God, help—"

"You little bitch! Give me that phone," a man shouted. And then there was silence.

Skylar had heard every agonizing word. She locked eyes with Gabe, who looked both horrified and furious. He bounded out of bed, pulled his jeans on, grabbed his shoes and shirt. Phone in hand, he headed toward the door. "I'm going to try to trace the call. I'll be back in a few hours."

Before she could respond, he ran out the door. Seconds later, she heard the elevator ding. And then there was silence. Skylar was left alone with the sickening knowledge that at this very moment, Kendra was being tortured or worse and there wasn't a damn thing she could do about it.

Hours later, Gabe opened the door to Skye's apartment. Defeat dragged at him. It had been years since he'd felt such a sense of hopelessness. The only thing they'd been able to get from Skye's phone was that the call had come from the New York area. Yeah, it was great that she was still in the state. But they had already deducted she was still in the area by having pinpointed Harrington.

And New York was a big freaking area to cover.

He threw the phone and apartment keys on the table beside the door. A slight sound brought his head around. Skye stood at the entrance to her office. Ghostly pale, the only color in her face was the bright blue of her eyes. As he drew closer, he saw that her eyes were swollen. She looked like she'd been crying for hours. She probably had.

Though he'd called her the second he learned of the

failed trace, he hadn't been here to comfort her. But he was here now.

He held out his arms, and with a small sob, Skye ran into them. Holding her tight against him, he breathed in the beauty of Skye's fragrance.

"I'm sorry, sweetheart. I'm so sorry."

Soaking his shirt, harsh sobs tore through her. The only thing Gabe knew to do was hold her and try to be as positive as possible. Hard as hell to do when he felt so damned little hope himself.

Scooping her into his arms, he carried her to the couch and sat down with her in his lap. The sobs had slowed to soft little gulps of air. He smoothed the hair off her forehead, pressed kisses to her head, and whispered, "We'll find her, Skye. I know we will."

She pulled her head back to look up at him. "But will it be too late?"

Sitting back deeper into the couch, Gabe held her tighter. "Let's look at the positives. We know she's in New York. We know William doesn't want to get rid of her or he would have already."

Her husky voice interjected, "And we know who's got her."

"And I'm betting she's close. Not at his house, but close enough so he can see her when he wants to."

"But Cole said he rarely goes anywhere alone."

"Maybe that doesn't do it for him. The website he's got set up—maybe that's his particular perversion. But he's going to want her close. With these kinds of freaks, the need escalates. At some point, he'll want more than just being able to watch. He'll want her close so he can get to her."

Skye shuddered against him and pressed her face against his chest again. "I can't imagine what she's going through now."

"Don't try. You'll only drive yourself crazy."

"You're right, I know." Pulling in a deep breath, she sat up in his arms. Though she looked as though she'd been through a windstorm, she was still beautiful. And then her chin tilted and Gabe recognized that determined expression.

"The party at William's house is this weekend. I accepted the invitation months ago."

"Skye, I don't want—"

She pressed fingers to his mouth to stop his protest. "I'm going, Gabe. And I'm going to find a way to get to Kendra. Are you coming with me or not?"

As much as he hated to admit it, this crazy idea of hers could well be their only hope. Cursing himself for not setting his foot down and saying hell no again, Gabe did the only thing he could do. He pushed her till she lay on the sofa and came over her. Knowing she could read the answer on his face, the acceptance of her plan in his eyes, he grazed his mouth over hers and said, "New rule. No one leaves this apartment today without a minimum of ten orgasms each."

He could feel her smile under his lips as she whispered, "I'm three ahead of you. Let's get started."

Groaning his approval, Gabe covered her mouth, his tongue thrusting deep. This was one area he would never argue with her about.

Gabe threw some wadded clothes into his duffel bag. "I still can't believe I let you talk me into this."

Knowing his words came from worry for her, Skylar silently nudged him away and pulled the clothes from his bag. Taking her time, she folded them neatly and returned them to the bag.

"We're not going," he said.

She turned and resumed packing her own bag. She

wouldn't change her mind—Gabe wouldn't go without her.

"Did you hear me, Skye? We're not going."

"Yes we are, Gabe. You know this is the only way to find anything on William. He works out of his home. Any files or information will be there."

"That doesn't mean we'll be able to get to it."

She stopped packing and turned. "The bastard has had Kendra for over a month now." Tears filled her eyes as she remembered that heartbreaking phone call. "The damage he's done to her already might well be irreparable. We have to take the risk. She's depending on us."

Gabe continued to glare for several seconds but didn't speak. How could he when he knew it was the truth? Finally he pulled her to him and wrapped her in a strong embrace. "We'll find her, Skye. I'm sorry I'm such an ass."

She pressed a soft kiss of reassurance to his mouth. "I'll be careful, I promise." Then, before it could turn into something else and delay them further, she pulled away. "Is Cole resuming his job as chauffeur?"

"Yeah. Since his prime target will be at the same place we'll be." Gabe shot a glance at his wristwatch. "He should be here in just a few minutes." Turning around, he pulled something from one of the dresser drawers he'd been using and said, "Come here."

Skylar moved closer and saw a jewelry box in his hand. "What's that?"

"I had this made for you."

Her heart kicked up to a gallop. Other than the fish T-shirt and her wedding ring, Gabe had never given her a gift. A warm glow spread throughout her body.

Opening the box, Skylar gasped. It was beautiful. An old-fashioned silver locket shaped in the profile of a woman. Skylar leaned closer in . . . the woman looked an awful lot like . . .

"I used one of your pictures and had them design it."

She reached out a finger and traced the edge of the locket. "It's beautiful." Tears sprang to her eyes. Too embarrassed to let him see what this gift meant to her, she immediately whirled around and said, "Put it on for me."

Gabe placed the chain around her neck and closed the clasp. He picked up the fragile chain that she already wore. "You want to take this off?"

Skylar froze. She had never shown him what she wore around her neck. Since they'd become lovers again, she had stopped wearing it, too afraid of the questions he'd ask and the reaction he would have at her answers. But this morning, feeling nervous because of what lay ahead of them, she'd put the chain on for comfort.

"Skye, you want me to unclasp this one?"

"No . . . that's okay. It's fine. I'll wear them both."

"Is it new? I've never seen you wear it."

She took a step to move away. "No, it's not new."

His hand pulled on her shoulder, turning her around. His eyes quizzical as if he knew she was hiding something, Gabe pulled the chain up from beneath the blouse that covered it.

Skylar couldn't look at him. If he looked the least bit disturbed, or worse, amused, she wouldn't be able to handle it.

His hand looked even larger as he held the two objects and fingered the gold bands.

"You kept them." His words sounded gruff, almost strained.

"Yes."

"Why, Skye?"

When she didn't immediately answer, he tilted her

chin with a finger, turning her face up to him. "Why, Skye, baby?"

"Because I—"

"Hey, Gabe." Cole's voice boomed from the living room. "You ready to go?"

Skylar breathed out a long breath, unsure if she was grateful for the interruption or resented it. If she had told him the truth, what would have happened?

Gabe pressed a kiss against the small bands and placed them back under her blouse. He stared at her the longest time. Skylar so wanted to ask him what he was thinking. How she hated this insecurity. This man was the only person who'd ever brought it out in her, and she resented the fact that, as her husband, he was the one man she should be able to feel the most secure with.

Either unwilling or not ready to know why she kept their wedding rings, Gabe picked up their bags and headed to the door. Stopping at the entrance, he turned to look at her. "When this is over . . . we need to have a serious talk."

A sinking wave of despair washed over her. The words had sounded like a promise, but his eyes revealed the truth. Gabe didn't want to stay in the marriage. Her question had been answered. These last couple of weeks had been about lust and nothing more.

To Gabe, their marriage had ended years ago. It had just never been legally finalized. As soon as this job was over, their marriage would be, too.

Propped up against the wall, Cole watched Gabe emerge from Skylar's bedroom. Used to his friend's dark moods, he shouldn't have been surprised by the expression on Gabe's face, but he was. The last two weeks, since Gabe and Skylar had become intimate again, those dark looks had all but disappeared.

Not that Gabe had told him that they were lovers, but it didn't take a rocket scientist to see the evidence. He'd dropped in one day for a quick review of the case. Though both Skylar and Gabe had been fully clothed and in the midst of eating dinner, he'd seen that expression way too many times on his own face. Having once been a happily married man, Cole had lived those sensual moments of wedded bliss. Gabe's mouth had a relaxed sensuality and his eyes had followed Skylar wherever she went with the look of a satisfied but still-hungry tiger.

Skylar's demeanor had been even more telling. She was flushed, beautiful, and had a vitality about her that had been missing up until then.

Now, however, it looked like there was definite trouble in paradise. Cole knew Gabe didn't want Skylar involved in the case any longer; maybe that was why he looked both angry and tortured.

Skylar came through the door seconds later. And once again, her face revealed much more than Gabe's. She was hurting, almost in tears.

Resisting the urge to clock his friend for hurting the woman he so obviously loved, Cole asked, "Everyone ready?"

Gabe nodded and stalked out the door. As was their way if Cole was around, Gabe took the stairs and Skylar got into the elevator with Cole.

Skylar seemed to be in another world. She'd yet to say anything and she stared at the elevator doors with a sad, almost desperate look. Dammit, he really didn't like to get involved, but he hated to see two people screw up so badly. Having once had the kind of happiness that every man longs for, he hated it when people were too blind to see it for themselves.

"If it makes you feel any better, men in love often act like idiots."

She gave him a sideways glance and he was relieved to see her mouth turn up slightly. "You sound as though you've had experience in that area."

"Yeah."

"You told me you didn't have a family. You're divorced then?"

As was usual, pain shot through his head and his heart at the same time. But he was the one to start the conversation, so he owed Skylar an answer.

"Widower."

A soft gasp. "I'm so sorry."

He only shrugged. Anything he said would be trivial.

"Do you have children?"

A deeper slice of pain slashed through him, and despite himself, he winced. "I did."

"My God, what happened?"

"Home invasion. They came looking for me. Settled for my wife and daughter."

"Who? Why would anyone . . . ?" She seemed unable to finish the sentence.

His dry, cracked laugh held nothing but bitterness. "I was their history teacher . . . gave them a failing grade. They got kicked off the football team."

"My God."

Thankfully, the elevator stopped and the doors slid open. He hated talking about the past. It wasn't until recently that he'd even remembered that he had one. And there was still so much he didn't remember. Damn stupid drugs.

A couple of minutes later, Gabe met them in front of the elevator. He gave Cole a nod and Skylar a long look. Then, flanking her, the two men led Skylar outside to the waiting limo. All three solemn. All three strangely silent. All three hurting in their own way.

twenty-three

William nervously chewed his lips as he waited for his wife to join him. Their guests would be arriving any minute now. Those guests would include Skylar and Gabe Maddox. Both healthy and both, more than likely, looking for any opportunity to bring him to his knees.

The moment after hiring a hit on them, he'd suffered a pang of conscience. Especially knowing that he would be causing his dear friend Jeremiah James a great deal of grief. Then, when they'd escaped with barely a scratch, fury had replaced the guilt. Quickly followed by stark terror. They would know it hadn't been a random shooting. They would know!

He hadn't given up. They still had no proof of his involvement. Going to the police would be pointless. Not only would they be laughed out of the building, he'd have his attorneys filing a defamation claim within the hour. Now it was a chess game.

His lovely jewel had recently been moved to her permanent residence. And a few days ago, he'd made his very first visit to her. Having her so close, only a good brisk walk away, was heaven and hell. Heaven because he could see her so often; hell because he wanted to be with her all the time. It was always like this at the beginning. An obsession. He would glut himself on his new acquisition until the enormous lust he'd built up inside him had been released. And then, usually two or three visits a week would suffice. Somehow he thought this one might be different. She was so very special.

Unable to stop himself, William dropped into the nearest chair and relived those moments of perfection.

She was dressed in virginal white. Oh, he knew quite well she wasn't a virgin. At least not in the regular sense of the word. But she was a virgin to his desires . . . a virgin to the lust that only she could appease.

Sadly, they'd had to drug her a bit. Apparently she'd become quite violent the last time they filmed her. He'd seen a portion of that video and, despite himself, had thoroughly enjoyed those moments . . . probably more than he should have.

When he entered the room, she raised her head from the bed the instant she realized she wasn't alone. Her hazel eyes were slightly dazed and out of focus. Not too much, though. He wanted her aware . . . wanted her knowing.

He started walking toward her and her smooth forehead wrinkled slightly in confusion. Yes . . . she was trying to remember him. She knew him . . . yet she did not.

"Hello, my dear."

He watched her slender white neck move as she swallowed nervously. "Who are you?"

"I've come to save you, Kendra."

She struggled to sit up, her eyes squinting slightly as if she was having trouble focusing. Then she got to her knees. Oh, what a pretty picture she made. Her nipples, dusky and dewy, pressed against the material as it tightened against her lovely breasts.

"But who are you?"

"You remember me, don't you?"

He stayed in the middle of the room. Let her come to him . . . let her seek him out.

Throwing her slender legs over the side of the bed, she

stood. Then she began to walk toward him, albeit a little unsteadily. The closer she got, the harder he grew. Oh, she was delectable . . . even more beautiful than he remembered.

"You do look familiar. Are you really going to save me . . . take me away?"

"Yes, my dear. I'm taking you away from all of this."

Grateful tears pooled in her eyes. "Who are you?"

"I'm William."

Recognition came fast, followed by immediate joy. "You're Skylar's friend!"

"Yes."

"Did she send you?"

His smile was gentle, compassionate . . . loving. "Yes, Skylar sent me here to save you."

The gratitude and sheer happiness in her expression hit him as it always did, but this time it was even stronger. A surge of immense lust mingled with power. Unbelievable power. He felt omnipotent, invincible. She would do everything he told her to do. He was her savior, her rescuer. Having the connection of Skylar between them would make what they had even stronger. This might well be his most meaningful, fulfilling relationship ever.

That look of appreciation and gratitude lasted through the sumptuous hot meal he gave her. He fed her himself, insisting she was too weak. She accepted each bite of food like a little bird, her eyes gleaming with gratitude. After dinner, he ordered a warm bath for her, scented with the fragrance of gardenias. She seemed hesitant about him being there, but he told her he feared she was too weak to bathe herself. It had taken all of his considerable willpower not to bathe her himself. That would happen soon, but not yet.

Just when he thought she might be getting concerned,

he provided clothing for her. Real covering for her body. She hadn't been clothed like that in weeks. Though there were still questions in her eyes, she was too grateful to ask them. She felt safe, warm, happy. Content.

And then, when he had her where she needed to be in her mind, when she knew he was her only hope, her destiny, he'd painstakingly, but lovingly, showed her how to express her gratitude. Revealed to her what her real purpose in life was. Of course the tears had fallen again, but this time those tears had bathed his naked skin. Remembered pleasure shuddered through him.

"William, are you all right?"

Returning to reality was a slam to his senses. William blinked up at his wife of thirty-three years. "Yes, I'm fine. Just waiting for you, my dear."

Taking Margo's hand, he walked down the stairs with her. His eyes roamed over the enormous entrance of his home. Five generations of Harringtons had lived here. His family was one of the oldest and most esteemed in the country. He had children he adored, a wife he loved, and employees depending upon him. He had too much to lose to allow his minor indiscretions to become public.

As much as he hated to do it, especially with Jeremiah in attendance, another incident would take place. And this time he would make sure that neither Skylar nor her low-class husband recovered from it.

Skylar stepped out onto the small balcony of their bedroom. The lush scenery before her and the elegance of the bedroom suite behind her indicated they'd been given preferential treatment.

Despite the seriousness of their mission here and the knowledge that Gabe didn't want to stay married to her, she still couldn't stop the little thrill of delight as Gabe came up behind her and wrapped her in a hard, warm embrace. He was here with her, and until that changed, she would take whatever joy she could get, for as long as she could get it.

Snuggling her back to his front, she was gratified to feel the erection pressing against her butt. It was his usual reaction when he was this close to her . . . and one she wholeheartedly shared. The man could turn her on with a smile. Having his body pressed against her could quickly send her into sexual overdrive.

Gabe's hand moved her hair off her shoulder. When he pressed a kiss to her bare skin, Skylar shivered.

But in spite of his iron-hard erection and warm embrace, his words indicated he had more serious things on his mind than making love to her.

"I checked the room for bugs and cameras. It's clean."

"Does that surprise you?"

"Worries me more than anything."

Unwilling to pull away from his arms, Skylar twisted her head slightly and look up at him. "Why does it worry you?"

"He should want to know what our plans are."

"And the fact that he doesn't tells you what?"

"That it doesn't matter what our plans are . . . his plans are to get rid of us either way."

Skylar shivered again, this time in fear. How could a man she'd known most of her life really be planning on having her killed?

"I should never have agreed to let you come."

"You didn't have a choice, Gabe. You wouldn't have been invited otherwise."

He blew out a sigh. "You're right. And as much as I don't want you here, it could very well pay off. The man's obviously got some damn good security. Outside and inside. He's got things here he doesn't want anyone to know about."

She turned in his arms to look up at him. "But you still don't think she's here at his estate, do you?"

"No. That'd be too dangerous."

"Gabe, the properties around here are owned by some of the wealthiest and oldest families in the country."

"And your point is?"

"There aren't any abandoned houses or empty buildings where he could be holding her."

"Doesn't mean he doesn't own another property . . . under another name. She's close, Skye . . . I can feel it."

Being a woman who believed in gut instinct and one who had total faith in the man in front of her, she drew in a long, controlled breath, trying her best not to get too excited.

"So what are we going to do?"

"You're going to stick to me like flies on a watermelon."

She giggled. Gabe rarely used one of his homespun analogies, but when he did, she was delighted. And it had broken a bit of the tension, as he had planned.

"Am I the watermelon or the fly?"

His eyes darkening to midnight blue, he said, "You're definitely watermelon. Sweet. Syrupy. Delicious." His mouth covered hers.

Skylar groaned under the scorching kiss. Timeless moments passed as they blocked out everything but the burning passion that could ignite so quickly between them.

Breathless and glowing, she finally pulled away and said, "Once this is over—Kendra's safe and William's in jail—we're going to talk about the future."

The words were out before she could stop them. How stupid. She'd seen the truth in his eyes earlier. Why open up the gaping hole in her heart again? *Damn idiotic optimism.* The blank expression that slid over his face was like another stab to her heart . . . one that had been damaged too much already.

Pulling out of his arms, she put as much distance between them as the small balcony would allow and turned away. It was lousy timing, but suddenly she had to know for sure. And cowardly it might be, but she couldn't face him as she said, "You don't want a future with me, do you, Gabe?"

His ragged sigh gave her fair warning that his words wouldn't be what she wanted to hear. Not that she really needed the warning.

"This isn't the time to talk about the future, Skye."

Willing herself courage, she whirled and said, "Answer the question, dammit. At least have the guts to say goodbye to my face this time."

"I'm not saying goodbye. And what do you mean, have the guts to say it to your face? I wasn't the one who destroyed everything eight years ago."

"No, not yet you're not, but you've made it pretty clear that when this is over, we're over." She straightend her spine and gathered her courage. She'd never said anything to him about this. It was time she did. "You knew where I was, Gabe. For eight years. That phone call and letter might have deterred you early on, but you had years when you could have gotten in touch with me. You never tried."

His jaw clenched, he snapped, "I tried and got my ass kicked. I told you that."

"You work for an organization that can infiltrate almost any company, any agency, so don't tell me that in eight years you couldn't get to me. I'm not buying it. Don't act like an innocent victim. You abandoned me."

Ice couldn't be colder than the expression on his face. "Blame me all you want, sweetheart. You're the one who started it all with your lies."

Despair washed through her. He was right about that.

She had started it all. But there were no longer any secrets between them and he still didn't want to be married to her.

"You're right, Gabe. I've apologized several times already. Here's one more . . . but it's the last one." She drew a breath. "I'm sorry . . . sorrier than you'll ever know . . . that I didn't tell you the truth. And if it makes it easier for you to blame me for everything, then go right ahead. I'm a big girl; I can take it."

Before she could belie those brave words by crumpling at his feet and sobbing her heart out, she glanced down at her watch. Though her eyes swam with tears, she could just make out the time. "We'll be late for dinner if we don't go down now."

She went to walk past him. In her peripheral vision, she saw his hand shoot out to stop her. She almost stopped on her own, but waited for his touch. It never came. He dropped his hand and said, "Stay close to me, Skye. Don't let your anger put you in danger."

A thick, mountainous lump of emotion prevented her from speaking. She merely nodded and took another step toward the bedroom. The reminder had been appropriate. So what if she now had an empty space where her heart used to be? Saving Kendra and putting William away were the reasons she was here. The reasons Gabe was with her. When that was done, they were done.

"One more thing. The necklace I gave you. Keep it on at all times."

She jerked around at his request. "Why?"

"It has a GPS device. If we somehow get separated, I can track you."

Nodding numbly, Skylar escaped back inside the room before he could do any more damage. He'd already ripped her heart out by his rejection. How could he hurt her any more? But she couldn't deny that he had. A gift she thought was given to her out of affection had actually been just a device to keep up with her. The protection might well be necessary but it didn't prevent the crushing blow of the truth.

His hand at her waist, Gabe led Skye into the enormous dining room of the Harrington mansion. Though only a hundred or so people were supposed to be in attendance, to Gabe there seemed to be a thousand times that number. The crowd pressed in on him, causing his pulse to race and his breathing to increase. *Dammit, not now!*

"Are you all right?"

Despite how he'd hurt this woman and her worry for her friend, she was concerned for him. Skylar James had more courage than most people had in their little finger . . . including him.

"I'm fine," he said.

Damned if he'd allow his weakness to mess up this operation. Skye had called him a coward earlier and she'd been right. He was too afraid to try to make a future with her.

She'd been right on the money that he could have gotten to her. He should have . . . if nothing other than to end their marriage. But he had been cowardly in that as well. Because despite the fact that they hadn't really had a marriage, if he'd sought a divorce, ended things permanently, that would have been a finality he wouldn't have been able to face.

Now he had no choice but to end it. The difference in their backgrounds couldn't be rectified. Skye wanted him now, but what would happen when all this excitement had passed? When her normal life resumed? When she had to start telling people the truth about him? He couldn't face her disillusionment when she realized her mistake. Better to face it now, before it totally destroyed both of them.

"Would a drink help? Or do you want to go outside?"

Get your head out of your ass and do your job. The snarling inner lecture centered him. He was here for a reason. Personal problems had to be put on the back burner.

"No, let's mingle awhile. Then we'll see if we can do a little exploring."

Her smile was one he'd seen her adopt when she wanted to appear happy and serene, but Skye's eyes told a different story. Concern for him, worry for Kendra, and heartbreak. Nevertheless, she knew her priority. She gazed around at the crowd and murmured, "Are we going to talk with William?"

William and his wife, Margo, had greeted them when they first arrived. Both had acted as if they were welcoming honored guests to their home. No hostility, nothing clandestine. Which put Gabe on alert even more. Harrington thought he had all his bases covered.

"Let's not seek them out. If William wants to come see us, we'll let him. If not, we'll just socialize for a few minutes. Then we'll pretend we're so into each other we need to be alone for a while."

Her smile a bit strained, she said, "Sorry you have to pretend."

Gabe allowed a flash of his inner feelings to emerge. He could at least give her that. "I've never had to pretend with you, Skye. Never."

A shuddering breath and then that amazing smile reappeared. "Let's go mingle."

Standing on the other side of the room, pretending an interest in a conversation about a new play opening next month, William watched Skylar and Gabe Maddox as they moved through the room. He had to give them credit for having the guts to come here. Of course, they believed they would find something incriminating on him. They wouldn't. And even if they did, they would never leave the estate alive. He'd made sure of that.

Though he nodded his interest, his eyes moved to a bulky figure standing in a shadowed corner. One of seven newly acquired bodyguards who had only two purposes—keeping William safe and doing away with Maddox and Skylar.

He didn't anticipate it would be easy. Gabe Maddox was a trained professional. Just one look at that hard face sent shivers through William. The man had a lethal edge that scared the hell out of him.

And Maddox had come with some formidable company. That mountainous man who claimed to be Skylar's chauffeur was most likely cover as well. Between the two of them, his men would have their work cut out for them. But they were well trained, too. And they were missing something he suspected Maddox and the fake chauffeur had. His men had no conscience.

He'd taken them to his little hideaway and tested them. If they hadn't performed correctly, he would have had them killed. That hadn't been necessary. They'd behaved splendidly and appropriately . . . like rabid dogs. The girls they'd entertained themselves with would eventually recover, but they would never forget. And neither would his precious jewel, who'd been made to watch. She'd been gratifyingly obedient after the exhibition had ended.

Yes, once Maddox and Skylar met their end, life would once more be exceedingly pleasant.

"You there?" Cole kept his voice low as he spoke into the tiny microphone hidden behind his shirt collar.

The almost invisible earpiece Gabe was wearing should have been working flawlessly. When he didn't get an immediate answer, Cole straightened from his semi-relaxed pose against the brick retaining wall and headed toward the back entrance of the mansion. Gabe not answering meant major problems.

"Yeah, I'm here. Sorry. Was in the middle of a group. Had to step away."

The grim tone of Gabe's voice told Cole more than his words. The man was on edge in more ways than one.

His eyes on the lookout for more threats, Cole said, "I spotted an interesting-looking character hanging around outside. He seems awfully interested in me and I don't mean in the 'I want to be your BFF' way."

"Yeah," Gabe muttered. "At least two more in here. One's attached to Harrington's ass. The other has zeroed in on me."

"Want me to go ahead and take care of my guy?"

"If you can do it without attracting attention, go ahead. Let me know when it's done. I want to get what we can and get Skye out of here as soon as possible."

"Will do."

Keeping up his pretense of a bored employee with nothing to do but meander around the outside of the small apartments that housed the servants who'd traveled with their employers, Cole strolled toward a pathway he'd discovered earlier. The path, hidden by shrubbery, would be the perfect spot for him to take the gorilla by surprise. If he chose to follow him.

The thud of oversized feet behind him assured Cole that the man indeed had an interest in him. And judging by his lack of finesse, the man was not only dumb, he was overconfident. His favorite kind of prey.

Cole paused at the edge of the path and looked left and right and then entered into the dense shrubbery and disappeared from view. A *clomp, clomp* came from big feet as they crashed through the bushes. The guy had most likely been told not to lose sight of his target.

A big head and beefy shoulders entered first. Cole swung an upper cut to the guy's jaw and an immediate but controlled kick to his too soft belly. While the man was hunched over, gasping for breath, Cole brought his knee up and connected with his nose. A satisfying crunch immediately followed.

With a roar, the man jerked his head up. Blood slung everywhere. Cole stepped back a few feet to avoid the spray. "I get your attention?"

"Son of a bitch!" The man rushed him. Cole sidestepped him, turned and kicked. His foot connected with the side of the man's head, dazing him. While he wobbled, Cole took advantage and jumped on his back, taking him to his knees. The guy swung a giant fist behind him, trying to knock him off. Cole hung on, squeezing the oversized neck until he went still beneath him.

Getting to his feet, Cole took plastic ties from his pocket and bound the man's feet and hands together. Then he pulled him deeper into the bushes. And because he didn't want to see or hear from him again tonight, he pulled a roll of tape from his pocket, tore off a strip, and slapped it on the man's mouth.

From another pocket, he pulled out a white handkerchief and wiped at the blood he hadn't been able to avoid. Feeling reasonably clean, Cole stepped back through the bushes and headed back to the mansion. On his way, he gave his mic a click and said, "I'm done."

No answer. Adrenaline surging, Cole took off running. He didn't see the man step out of the shadows until it was too late.

twenty-four

Skylar tapped her foot underneath the table, the only nervous gesture she could get away with. Gabe had left her at the table with her father and a few of his friends with the excuse of needing to go to the men's room. She didn't believe him for an instant. Something was up.

"Did your mother get in touch with you today?"

She twisted her head slightly for a quick glance over at her father, unwilling to take her eyes off the door Gabe had gone through for more than a second. What if something happened to him? What if he didn't come back?

"Skylar, did you hear my question?"

Not taking her eyes from the door, she said, "Sorry, Dad. Yes, I heard your question. And no, Mother didn't call me today. Why?"

When he didn't answer her, she risked moving her eyes for an instant to give him another glance. His mouth was pursed with disappointment. Sighing, Skylar faced him and said, "No, Mother didn't get in touch with me. Why? What does she need?"

"She's planning a trip to Europe and wants you to go with her."

Spending an afternoon with her mother was about as much as Skylar could handle. Going to Europe with her was a torture she refused to inflict upon herself.

She shook her head. "I don't think so, Dad. I have too

much to do here." She twisted around again, her eyes searching for the tall, dark figure of her husband. Where could he have gone?

"Skylar, is he that important to you?"

That brought her attention back around to him full force. "What are you talking about?"

Suddenly her father looked old, almost elderly, and so very sad. "Is Gabe Maddox that important to you?"

Unable to give him anything but the truth, she answered softly, "He's everything, Daddy. He always has been."

Tears filled his eyes. She had seen her father cry only twice before. At her grandmother's funeral and the day Gabe returned her home from her abduction. And now.

"I'm so sorry, Skylar. For so many things. I caused you such heartache."

Speechless, Skylar could only stare at him. What could she say? Other than agree with him.

"If you love him, Skylar, that's all that matters."

She shook her head, confused and angry at this odd turnaround. "Not that I need your approval, but what changed your mind?"

"I've never seen love like that between a man and a woman before. I saw him looking at you earlier, when you were talking to the mayor. His feelings were written all over his face. The man adores you. I never should have interfered in your life. I thought I knew what was best for you. I didn't."

Once again, she was speechless. Not because she didn't know what to say, but because she knew it wasn't true. If Gabe had looked like he loved her, he'd been acting. Their conversation earlier proved that. He wasn't interested in being married to her.

But she was happy about one thing. At least her father

understood the depth of the pain he'd caused both her and Gabe. Not that it did any good now.

"I don't know what will happen between us, Dad. But I'm glad you feel that way. I—"

"Skye, let's get something to eat," Gabe murmured in her ear.

Relief flooded her as Skylar whirled around, her heart leaping for joy. She swallowed a gasp. Gabe had a split lip and tiny specks of blood on his white shirt. "What happened?"

"I'll tell you later." He offered a cool nod to her father, who seemed as speechless as Skylar had been earlier.

Walking beside him as they headed to the buffet line, she whispered again, "What happened?"

"Needed to get rid of a couple of Harrington's men."

Skylar skidded to a standstill in the middle of the room. "You went after them by yourself?"

Taking her by the elbow, he urged her forward. "I'm fine, Skye."

She jerked away from him. "That's not the point. You could have been killed." A mass of emotions swept through her, fury leading the way. "What would have happened if they had killed you?" She stopped to glare at him. "Dammit, don't you dare do that again!"

Taking her arm once more, he led her to the buffet table. Standing behind her as they waited in line, he whispered so only she could hear him, "I'm sorry I scared you."

Unable to help herself, knowing that soon he'd be leaving, that soon she'd never feel his warmth against her again, Skylar leaned back against his hard body.

Gabe, apparently not caring that dozens of eyes were on them, wrapped his arms around her from behind and pressed a kiss to the back of her head. He held her for several seconds and then said, "Let's get something to eat. Handling those bozos worked up an appetite."

Skylar picked up a plate and began to pile food on it, not caring what it was. Eating food while all these feeling churned inside her seemed impossible. Still, they needed to act normal, as if nothing was wrong.

She nodded her thanks to the server who poured dressing on her salad, smiled at the man who carved a slice of prime rib for her, and even managed to say "Thanks" to the bartender who handed her a glass of wine. She turned to look behind her and gasped as Gabe grabbed her arm.

"Where are we going?" Skylar whispered out of the corner of her mouth. One moment she'd had a drink in one hand and her plate of food in the other, the next moment he'd taken both from her, handed them to a wide-eyed servant, and said, "Let's go."

Stumbling a little to keep up with him, she smiled serenely at the people she passed, who seemed equally surprised to see her normally controlled companion acting like a caveman.

Finally reaching the hallway, she jerked at his hand and whispered furiously, "What's the matter with you?"

"Both your drink and your food were drugged."

"What?"

"The dressing on your salad . . . the drink you picked up that the bartender took back to wipe the bottom. Both times something was slipped into them."

"Gabe, I didn't see a thing."

"Because you weren't looking."

She couldn't argue the point. Her mind had been occupied with a thousand other things. "So you think William's trying to poison me?"

His big body vibrating with tension, his eyes roamed the area, as if a threat could come from anywhere. "Drugs to incapacitate you. The killing would come later."

Skylar eyed the furious man in front of her. Was this

just his overprotectiveness coming out, or was everyone on William's staff out to do away with them?

Apparently sensing her doubt, Gabe never stopped looking around for a threat as he said, "I don't hallucinate, Skye. Whatever we eat or drink this weekend is likely to be spiked. We need to get this shit over with and get out of here tonight."

Wrapping her arms around herself, she refused to get nervous now. Their plan had been to take the weekend to snoop and find something incriminating. Other than the timeline being moved up, nothing had changed.

"So what do we do?"

He put his fingers to his ear as if waiting to hear something. She knew he wore a wire and a hidden microphone so he and Cole could communicate.

"Sounds like Cole's taking care of his guy." He led her deeper into the hallway, out of sight of any guests, his eyes continuing to search around him as he reached inside his jacket. Pulling out the gun that was never far from his hand, he turned and gave her a fierce stare. "You stick by me at all times. If I say run, you run. If I say duck, you—"

"Duck?" She cut in, her dry tone and arched brows a reminder that she wasn't stupid.

Ignoring her sarcasm, he took her arm and started down the hallway. "I scoped out the house while you were with your father earlier today. Cole did some questioning of the servants. We pinpointed an area to target. With Harrington's men out of the way, we should have some time to explore."

They headed down the long, elegant hallway. Portraits of long-dead Harrington ancestors looked down upon them as if in disapproval. Skylar shivered. Had other Harringtons shared William's perversions? She hoped not.

Gabe stopped at a massive oak door and handed her his gun. "Keep it pointed down the hallway."

"What are you going to do?"

His hand went inside his jacket again and this time pulled out a slender leather case. "Open the door."

Wrapping both hands around the gun, Skylar turned and kept an eye out for anyone who might head their way. She could only hope she saw no one, since she was quite sure explaining why she held a gun in her hand would be one for the record books. She had no clue what she would say. Especially since guns terrified her. Just the feel of this one in her hand caused that cold pit of dread inside her stomach to deepen.

Her ears alert, the click behind her was a welcome sound. Keeping the gun pointed in the other direction, she glanced back to see Gabe easing the door open.

"What about cameras?"

He shot her a smile, and despite the fact that she was holding a gun and scared out of her mind, a thrill zipped through her. Gabe's smiles were not only rare, they were beautiful.

"Taken care of." He shot a look around and said, "Let's go."

Skylar came in behind him and released a relieved breath when she heard the door close.

"Okay, what now?"

It took all of Gabe's self-control not to grab Skye and kiss her until neither could remember their name. The sparkle in her eyes and flush in her face told him that despite the danger and seriousness of their mission, she was enjoying herself.

"Look for any place he could hide documents, photographs, DVDs. It won't be obvious . . . most likely hidden."

He watched her for a few seconds and was glad to see

she went for some areas he would have looked if she hadn't. Figuring it was useless, Gabe nonetheless switched on Harrington's computer and tried to access the man's personal accounts. He wouldn't leave incriminating information out for anyone to find. Gabe quickly clicked keys, tried various passwords and gave up. They had little time . . . no use wasting it on this.

He turned to see Skye crawling beneath a table. Ignoring the way her shapely ass wiggled enticingly, he turned to the massive desk. Each drawer opened easily and held nothing more dangerous than the usual office supplies. Nothing to hide here. His hands felt under each drawer, hoping to find a false bottom. No luck.

"Anything?" Skye asked.

"No, I—" When he moved away slightly, his foot landed on an area of the carpet that felt different from anywhere else. Going to his knees, Gabe felt around until he came to a patch of carpet that felt loose under his hand. He pulled until the thick material lifted. Underneath was a small metal door, with a keyhole. His heart kicked up a beat.

"I found something."

Skye was beside him in an instant. "What?"

Taking his lock tools out again, Gabe set to work. Apparently, William felt quite sure that his secret hiding place could never be found, because it was ridiculously easy to unlock the door. Several folders, along with what looked like a packet of photographs, were crammed into the small area.

"Pay dirt."

Together they pulled the folders from the compartment.

"Look through everything as quickly as possible. Ignore the photographs unless there are buildings you might recognize."

"What are we looking for?"

"Anything that indicates a location."

Gabe shuffled through piles of filth—photographs, perverted passages of loose text, writings and ramblings that were apparently William's attempts at writing his own pornographic short stories. But no clue as to buildings or properties where Kendra might be stashed. When Skylar's breath caught, he figured she'd come across a vile photograph or comment. "What?"

"It's a deed."

"To what?"

"A house and property . . . not far from here." She glanced up at him, excitement gleaming in her eyes. "It's got to mean something . . . why else would he have it hidden if it has no significance?"

"Good question, my dear Skylar. Would you like me to answer that before or after I kill you and your husband?"

Cursing himself for his inattention, Gabe grabbed the gun from the desk and pointed it at the man at the door. William Harrington, dressed in a tuxedo that probably cost enough to feed a small country for a year, stood unarmed. His flushed face revealed excitement but not a hint of fear. Of course, the two goons at his side had a lot to do with that. Both held .357 Magnums. And both guns were pointed at Skye.

"Mr. Maddox, please drop your gun on the floor and kick it forward."

Gabe didn't move. "You'll never get away with it, Harrington. You think killing Skylar James won't bring you a boatload of trouble?"

"Mr. Maddox, I really don't want to kill Skylar. After all, she is my goddaughter. Her life is entirely in your hands." His waved his hand to indicate the men beside him. "Hank and Tyler have silencers. No one will hear them shoot. She would be dead in an instant and it would be your fault. Now, I suggest you put your gun on the floor as I requested. I'm not known for my patience."

Two choices and both of them sucked. Shoot one man but the other would no doubt shoot Skye. Or drop the gun and look for a way to take both men out. Not willing to risk Skye's life, Gabe dropped the gun and kicked it toward Harrington.

Harrington's smug smile had no effect on Gabe. The man was confident, which meant he would make mistakes. Gabe planned to be ready when that happened.

"So what now?"

Harrington nodded at a large portrait of Margo Harrington hanging on the wall. "My darling wife indulges my need for privacy, so in her honor, I used her portrait in a way I know she would approve." His gait that of a cocky penguin, Harrington waddled over to the portrait and pressed an edge at the bottom. The wall separated, revealing an opening.

Turning, he gave a small shrug. "My most private of places. On occasion I've considered bringing one of my jewels here but was afraid I'd like it too much. Having them that close, at all hours . . ." His smile was a bit chagrined. "I fear I'm not strong enough to resist that kind of temptation." He shot a glance behind him and then smiled broadly at Gabe. "And besides that, it's a bit too closed in and small."

Gabe already recognized what was coming. Somehow Harrington knew about him. Knew his biggest weakness . . . his biggest failure. *Shit.*

Skylar had stayed still and quiet, taking in all the nuances of their situation. But when she saw the room, saw the smug grin on William's face, she knew exactly where this was headed. And she knew exactly who had told him about Gabe's illness. *Her father.*

Once again, the things she'd confided to her father in

her grief over Gabe were coming back to haunt her. And for whatever reason, he had given that information to William, providing him an advantage none of them had predicted.

"If you would be so kind, Mr. Maddox, as to enter into my private sanctuary."

"Like hell," Gabe growled.

"Possibly. It's certainly dark, but not nearly as hot." He looked at his men. "Why don't we give Mr. Maddox some encouragement?"

Her heart in her throat, Skylar watched as Gabe began to walk slowly toward the opening. He stopped abruptly. Both men raised their guns, now pointing them at him. Gabe held his hands up in an act of surrender and turned to Skylar. He said nothing. He didn't have to say anything. His look was one filled with promise. He would escape and he would find her.

Unsure if he could read her as well as she could read him, Skylar gave him the words. "I believe in you."

His answer was a gentle, beautiful smile and a small wink. Then he turned away from her and shouted, "Duck!" He sprang into action, throwing himself at the two men. Both men had lowered their guns slightly when he appeared to be surrendering. Caught off guard, they raised their guns the instant they saw him coming. It was too late; Gabe managed to hit the hands holding the guns. Shots pinged across the study.

On the floor, Skylar stared in horror as Gabe took on the two men. Unable to watch and do nothing, she jumped up and grabbed a lamp from the desk. Yanking the plug from the socket, Skylar swung the heavy brass lamp toward the head of the closest man.

He merely grunted, turned, and swung at her; knocking her to the floor. Only slightly dazed, Skylar jumped back up.

Gabe had managed to knock one man out; the one who had hit her was heading toward Gabe's back. Skylar screamed, "Watch out!"

Gabe moved so fast, Skylar could barely comprehend his movement. He whirled, his arm and leg hitting the man simultaneously. The man fell backward; Gabe leaped on top of him, wrapping his hands around his neck. The distinctive pop Skylar heard was unmistakable. The man was dead.

She took a running step toward Gabe and then came to an abrupt halt as another man barreled through the door and picked her up.

Gabe growled and sprang toward her. *Ping!* A bullet barely missed Gabe's head. He turned to William, who held a gun steadily in his hand. "I suggest you stop right there, Mr. Maddox. As you might guess, among other things I'm very good at, I'm also an excellent marksman."

The man holding Skylar lowered her feet to the floor, but refused to let her go. She watched helplessly as Gabe's eyes darted between William and the man who held her.

"You'll never get away with this, Harrington."

"They always say that in movies."

"Because it's usually true."

His smile was supremely confident. "Not always, though."

As if he didn't care a gun was pointed directly at his heart, Gabe stalked slowly toward William. "I promise . . . you will not get away with this."

"Mr. Maddox." William's voice sounded a bit less self-assured as Gabe approached him. "I congratulate you on being able to take down two highly trained men. You're obviously very strong. However, will you be able to save Skylar?"

At William's words, the man holding her tightened his

arms around her chest and squeezed. Bracing herself on to the man's arms, she used both heels and kicked back at him. He tightened his hold even more. The pressure on her ribs was unbearable . . . her chest felt as if it would explode. Unable to breathe, Skylar knew she was within seconds of passing out. If he held her any tighter, he would soon be breaking bones.

"Dammit. Stop it."

Gabe's furious voice penetrated the roaring in her ears.

"You have the power to stop him, Mr. Maddox. All you have to do is obey my instructions." William nodded toward the opening in the wall. "If you don't, Skylar will die and you'll be responsible."

Adrenaline still erupting like a volcano, Gabe forced a calm. Skye's color had returned to normal but the bastard holding her could kill her in an instant. Her fragile bones couldn't stand up to that kind of pressure.

He tried to reason once more with Harrington. "She's your goddaughter. You've known her since she was a baby."

"Don't bother trying to appeal to my emotions, Maddox. I may have a certain fondness for Skylar, but not enough to allow her to ruin everything I have."

Fighting a helplessness he hadn't felt in years, Gabe looked at Skye. Though tears filled her eyes and he knew she was in pain, she never said anything. Just stared at him with that amazing faith she seemed to have in him. Damned if he would let her down again.

"How the hell do you—"

William huffed a small laugh. "Mr. Maddox, I know you're wanting to keep me talking so that fake chauffeur of yours can come in and save the day. I'm afraid he's been taken care of . . . and you have no weapon. All I have to do is say one word and Skylar will die. And then

I will shoot you." His smile pure evil, he nodded again to the wall opening. "This way is so much more appropriate. Now, be so kind as to step into the room."

It was the most difficult move he'd ever had to make as he walked toward the dark entrance of William's secret room. Despite Harrington's assertion that he would kill his goddaughter, Gabe was taking the chance that he wouldn't. His only option right now was to do what he said. Gabe didn't question why Harrington didn't just go ahead and shoot him. He was just glad as hell that he didn't.

He would escape. Skye was wearing the necklace he gave her. Gabe would be able to pinpoint her location and save her. He refused to believe anything else.

Before the door closed, Gabe gave her a promise, this time verbally. "I won't let you down again, Skye."

Her smile brightened the encroaching darkness already slithering inside him. And then the door slammed shut, closing him into the smothering black pit and the gut-wrenching terror he swore never to feel again.

twenty-five

Kendra rolled over on the bed, pretending the drug she'd been fed had taken effect. Since that vile bastard had taken over her care, she'd been fed and clothed like a pampered slave. As long as she performed appropriately, she got everything she wanted. Warm baths, clothing, privacy in the bathroom, and, of course, food. Delicious, plentiful, and, as she'd discovered too late, drugged.

After they'd caught her calling Skylar, they'd filled her with drugs. How long she was out, she had no idea. But when she woke, she was in a different room . . . a new prison. This one was nicer. The walls were painted a pale peach, she even had a small private bathroom. But she still had no bedclothes; nothing had really changed. Until he came.

How stupid to believe that Skylar had sent him to rescue her. Skylar had sounded concerned; the man she had talked to on the phone, Skylar's friend, had sounded concerned, too. He had tried to help her, but he couldn't. No one could help her. She had to help herself.

Once she realized that everything she was given, no matter how small or insignificant-looking, was laced with a small amount of the drug, she'd made provisions. No one knew what she did with the food after she consumed it. The privilege of privacy in the bathroom had afforded an opportunity to purge.

The drugs were still in her system, but not like they

believed. She was still groggy and lethargic, but she was also aware. And being aware, she could act as drugged as she wanted.

The things that vile bastard had made her do were fogged and blurred in her mind, but she remembered enough. Enough to know that she would never allow it to happen again. More than anything, she remembered what he had made her watch. The brutal and repeated rapes of three young women. He had made her stay in the room. Listen to their screams, their pain and humiliation . . . and the disgusting grunts and laughter of the animals who attacked them. And then he'd made her do things with him.

At that time, she'd been helpless and too out of it to do anything but comply. But no more. She was getting clear-headed. Yes, she was weak from lack of nourishment, but she was a damn sight stronger than she had been. And soon, very soon, she would escape, and when she did, she would find those other victims and they would all escape together. This she vowed.

Cole ran to the north entrance, where Gabe and Skylar were to meet him. A few guests were scattered around the large patio, but not the people he was looking for.

He tried his mic again. "Gabe, you there?"

"Cole?"

Relief flooded him. Gabe's voice sounded muffled and odd, but at least he was alive. "Gabe, you okay? I can barely hear you."

"What happened?"

"Sorry, got sidetracked by another of Harrington's goons. Where are you?"

"Can . . . get . . . my . . . room?"

"Yeah . . . why?"

"Harrington . . . Skye."

"Did you say Harrington has Skylar?"

"Yes," came Gabe's muffled reply.

"Shit. How'd that happen?"

"GPS. Hidden . . . duffel."

Since he could only make out about every third word, Cole went on instinct. Harrington had Skylar. The GPS monitor that could trace her was in Gabe's duffel bag. How this had happened he'd worry about once he got the monitor.

Gabe not only sounded like he was a thousand miles away, he also sounded breathless and weak. However, Cole knew Gabe's first priority would be Skylar. Best thing to do was get the monitor and then find Gabe.

Despite his lack of formal clothing, Cole walked with the confidence of a man who knew exactly where he was going. Few people questioned a man his size with a "don't piss me off" expression. The bruises on his face, along with the rip in his shirt and the speckles of blood on it, most likely gave them pause. A couple of people glanced at him oddly but their eyes flickered away when he shot them a challenging stare.

Taking the stairs three at a time, he rushed to the bedroom suite. He burst through the door, then stopped abruptly. Bureau drawers were hanging open, the closet door was open, and pieces of clothing were scattered about the floor. The room appeared to have been ransacked or as if someone had left in a tremendous hurry. The man standing in the middle of the room holding Gabe's duffel in one hand and a gun in the other no doubt knew why.

"Who the hell are you?" Cole growled.

His jaw clenched, Gabe ignored the wheezing sounds coming from his lungs. Skye's life was in danger. Nothing else mattered but that.

Refusing to give in to the agonizing weight pressing against his chest, he continued to search for a way out. Apparently, Harrington used this room for his private stash of porn. Gabe couldn't see the magazines, but he'd knocked several around as he stumbled in the darkness.

Right after Harrington had closed the door, he had found the light switch. Unfortunately, it didn't work. Most likely it had been dismantled. The bastard had been prepared for this.

"Stupid" and "arrogant" were the least of the insults Gabe hurled at himself as he followed his hands, feeling for some kind of opening. He'd been overconfident of his ability to read Harrington's mind. Had thought by disabling the cameras in the hallway this afternoon, taking out the three bodyguards, and having Cole as backup, that would have ensured them enough time to find what they needed. He hadn't expected Harrington to have hired an army.

Damned if Skye would pay the price for his carelessness.

Since it was pitch dark, he could rely only on his sense of touch. Hands in front of him, Gabe crept along the walls, using his fingers to methodically search every square inch. There had to be a release or opening somewhere.

Cole would get the GPS monitor. Once they had that, it should be easy to trace Skye. He hadn't told Cole about his situation. Wouldn't do a damn bit of good. Finding Skye had priority over anything else.

Until then, he'd just keep looking. He could hear Cole running, most likely going up the stairs. Five, ten minutes at the most and they could start looking for Skye.

"Who the hell are you?"

Gabe halted his search as he heard Cole ask the question.

"What's going on?" Gabe growled in Cole's ear. He didn't expect an answer. If the man was confronting the enemy, he needed all his wits. However, if he could give an identity, Gabe might be able to shed some light.

"I asked you a question, buddy. That gun you got pointing at me makes me think this isn't a friendly meeting."

Gabe closed his eyes. *Shit.*

"William, don't do this."

"Skylar, I'm hurt. You've always called me Uncle Bill."

Her hands on the steering wheel of William's car, Skylar took her eyes off the road to shoot a killing glare at the man she'd once been so fond of. The man who now held a gun in his lap, pointed directly at her head. "You ceased to be Uncle Bill when I learned you kidnapped and raped innocent women."

Instead of looking insulted, he appeared to be amused. "Innocent? Oh, my dear, those poor girls haven't been innocent for years. They're just doing what they would have eventually done anyway . . . we just helped them along. With their experience and background, they're extremely trainable and obedient. And they've finally found their place in life." Something odd flickered in his expression. "And really, isn't that what life is all about? Finding your place?"

Ignoring his asinine question, Skylar glanced in the rearview mirror. The road was deserted. Not that she would try to attract anyone's attention. If she did, William might shoot them. She refused to be responsible for another person's misery. Besides, they were headed in the direction she believed William was holding Kendra. If that was the case, then she would go with him. And she would find Kendra.

And Gabe would find her.

She refused to think how Gabe was suffering. She'd seen the effect of his illness just in a short well-lit elevator ride. But no matter how difficult it was for him, she didn't doubt that he would escape and find her. Gabe wasn't invincible, but he was resourceful and as brave as they came. He would come for her. She knew he would.

In the meantime, she hoped to find out where Kendra was. Would William tell her? It was worth a shot.

"Where are we going?"

"Don't play dumb with me, my dear. It really isn't becoming. You saw the deed to my little hideaway. You must know that's where we're headed."

"Is Kendra there?"

"There is a young girl who looks like Kendra. The Kendra you knew no longer exists."

Grief tore at her; Skylar shoved it back down. No matter what Kendra had gone through, Skylar would make sure she recovered. She would get her the help she needed.

"You're one sick, fucked-up bastard, aren't you?"

The back of his hand flew at her face. Skylar screamed and jerked the steering wheel. The car crossed the line, careening toward a car coming at them from the opposite direction.

William caught hold of the wheel, straightened the car out, and said calmly, "Take the wheel, Skylar. If we attract attention, I'll have to kill someone else. And I really don't want to have to do that."

Her jaw and eye stinging, Skylar wrapped her hands around the steering wheel. Swallowing past the pain, she said, "Did you know I was kidnapped, too?"

"Yes, my dear, I knew. But not until your father told me. If it makes you feel any better, the men who took you were severely reprimanded. I would never have had you taken."

"Gee, that makes me feel so special."

He ignored her sarcasm and addressed her statement with utmost seriousness. "You are special, Skylar. That's why I'm so torn. I really don't want to kill you, but I can't have you revealing my secrets, now can I?"

"It doesn't matter what you do with me. You won't get away with this. The people at LCR know all about you. Even if you get rid of me and Gabe, a hundred more will come after you."

The hearty laughter surprised her. "You sound so tough, my dear. I don't think Mr. Maddox has been good for you. It's not at all becoming. And I'm not concerned about this LCR you think so highly of. There's no evidence I'm involved in any of this. If there were, you would have already gone to the authorities. Yours and Mr. Maddox's disappearance will be a small, unsolvable mystery for a while. With your fame, I'm sure there will be television specials . . . maybe even a movie. Your fame will live on."

She didn't argue with his assessment. There was a lot of truth in his words. If there had been proof that William was involved, he would already be in prison where he belonged.

"Turn here, Skylar."

Skylar turned in to a private drive. Giant trees obscured everything but the narrow drive. The headlights picked up a medium-sized house behind a brick wall.

"Drive around back," William said.

As she drove to the back of the house, the adrenaline she'd carefully suppressed had returned with interest. She needed to disarm William and disable him before they went inside the house. Other people would no doubt be there. Without William, she could sneak in and try to find Kendra.

She pulled the car to a standstill. Her hand on the door, Skylar prepared to get out. With a gun pointed at her head, she had no choice but to pretend she would follow his instructions. But once they were out of the car, the tables would be turned.

"Hold on, my dear. Before you get out, I have one more thing I want to say to you."

Furious at his smugness, Skylar turned to face William, about to give him a scathing reply. She never got the chance. The gun smacked into the side of her head, and agony speared through her as she slumped into the seat.

William blew out a tired sigh. Really, for a man his age, he'd gone through some extraordinary events today. Exhaustion pounded on him but it wasn't yet over. He still had to figure out what to do about Skylar.

Poor dear. She'd had a bad day herself. Watching her lover get locked into a dark, airless prison he could never escape from and then being bashed in the head by her godfather. No, it hadn't been a good day for either one of them.

But things were finally coming together. He'd sent his bodyguard to gather Maddox's and Skylar's things. When people started looking for them, it would simply appear as if they'd left the estate without telling anyone. And they would never be seen or heard from again. Simple. Uncomplicated. Easy.

Of course, he still had a few dead bodies to dispose of, including that pesky chauffeur. He would call the bodyguards as soon as he was inside and instruct them to dump them together somewhere until the party was over. Perhaps the wine cellar, where it was relatively cool. Explaining the stench of dead bodies to his guests would be inconvenient, not to mention embarrassing.

After this weekend, once all evidence of this drama was gone, everything could go back to normal. And he'd earned himself some extra time with his precious jewel. Would she appreciate what he'd had to go through to keep her? Probably not . . . but he would make sure she rewarded him appropriately.

Opening the passenger door, William pulled himself from the car. Walking around to the other side of the car, he looked down at the unconscious woman. Skylar was by no means a large woman, but he was long past the days when he could pick up an unconscious body, slender or otherwise. Besides, that's why he had loyal employees. Pressing a key on his cell phone, he spoke quickly: "We have a guest. Please come to the back and retrieve her."

An odd urgency suddenly hit him. One he couldn't put a finger on. There was no way Gabe Maddox could escape from his tomb. Not only was it impenetrable, but his claustrophobia would incapacitate him and soon all the air would be gone. And even if by some miracle he did escape, he'd never be able to find Skylar. She hadn't been able to show him the papers to the house before they were caught. And William now had those papers in his jacket.

No, he was safe. He had all his bases covered. Nothing could go wrong.

"Get up, bitch."

Her eyes wide open and alert for the first time in weeks, Kendra kept her face buried in her pillow and waited. *Let him come to me.*

The man expelled a huge sigh and stomped closer. "I said, get up!" A hand touched her . . . not hard. He knew he couldn't hurt her or he'd pay a heavy price. She was counting on that.

"Come on. I don't have all day." The hand nudged her again.

In a quick full-body roll, Kendra swung her arm up. In her hand, she held a glass she'd been able to hide under her mattress. The thick, heavy crystal made a satisfying thud against his temple. He dropped to the floor with a thump.

Kendra jumped from the bed. There was no time to waste. Cameras were on her. Someone would be here any second. She quickly searched the pockets of the creep on the floor. No weapons, but a key ring held some interesting keys. She grabbed them and ran to the door.

Opening the door, she stuck her head out. Footsteps were running down the hallway. She took off in the opposite direction, hoping to find the other girls and get them loose before they were found. Hopefully, they weren't so drugged that they couldn't help. If they banded together, they could overpower the freaks in the house and get out of here.

The footsteps drew closer, and now people were shouting. Any second now, she would be discovered. Spotting a doorway, she ran to it and turned the knob. Locked. Taking the keys, she tried three . . . the third one worked. Twisting the lock, Kendra opened the door and ran inside. She closed the door. Holding her breath, she heard footsteps running past. Her breath coming out in a ragged sigh of relief, Kendra turned around. She swallowed a scream.

"Hello, my jewel. Were you as eager to see me as I am to see you?"

Grinning with delight, there stood her tormentor. And sitting in a chair behind him was the woman who had introduced them. Skylar . . . the woman she'd once called friend.

Oh God. Oh God. Skylar's sob was one of both relief

and sorrow. Relief that Kendra was alive; sorrow because the young woman was almost unrecognizable. Gaunt and hollow-eyed with an emotionless, empty expression on her face. William had been right—Kendra Carson was no more.

Skylar had woken seconds ago and found herself slumped in a chair, her hands tied behind her back. The incessant throbbing of her head was but a distant, irritating pain. The obvious abuse that Kendra had gone through made any pain she felt shrink to insignificance. Now she just needed to figure out a way to help them both.

"Kendra?" Skylar said softly.

The girl moved toward her as if she were in a dream. Was she still drugged? Her eyes looked dead, but not dazed . . . just empty.

"Kendra, I'm so sorry . . . I didn't know."

And finally Skylar saw emotion in her eyes. With a sob, Kendra dropped to her knees and wrapped her arms around Skylar. "I knew you would come . . . I knew it. And I know you had nothing to do with this." She raised her head and glared at William. "You son of a bitch. I know everything."

"Really, my dear. So dramatic." His adoring smile was both terrifying and revolting. "I'll make sure you apologize appropriately when we're together again."

The door opened behind him. Two men stood in the doorway. "About time you found her." William nodded toward Kendra. "Give her an extra dose this time. The vein in her foot . . . between her toes, like we've used before. Make sure she's ready when I come for her."

Skylar screamed when the man pulled at Kendra. But Kendra wasn't going without a fight. She turned and punched the man in the face. He grabbed for her again. Kendra ran toward William, and Skylar could see the emotion in his eyes. Amazingly, he looked as though he believed Kendra was running to him for protection. There was delight and pride in his face. Before Kendra reached him, he held out his arms in welcome. Taking advantage of his open-armed, unprotected stance, Kendra raised her foot and kicked him deep in the balls. With a howl, William grabbed his crotch and dropped to his knees, gagging and crying.

The man behind Kendra grabbed her and threw her over his shoulder. Skylar jumped to her feet and ran toward them. Kendra kicked and screamed, pounding against the man holding her.

Though Skylar's hands were tied, she had every intention of stopping the bastard from taking the girl. A hand grabbed Skylar's hair and pulled her back, throwing her to the floor. The man holding Kendra walked out the door, closing it behind him.

Skylar sprang to her feet, bypassed the bastard who'd knocked her down, and went toward William, who was still on the floor, apparently in agony. She shouted, "William!"

He raised his head and Skylar registered tears streaming from his eyes. Her foot connected with his face. Blood spurted from his busted nose.

Holding one hand to his crotch, the other to his nose, he screamed at the other man, "Dammit! Take her! Give her the drug. Not enough to knock her out. I want her awake when you kill her. And I want to be there to watch."

Screaming, Skylar bit the arm that reached for her. Blood filled her mouth. He yelped and backhanded her, knocking her to the floor.

"Shit, that hurt," the man said.

Still on the floor, his hand holding a handkerchief to

his nose, William's voice was muffled as he screamed, "Get her out of here! Now!"

The man grabbed for her again, avoiding her mouth. Skylar kicked at him. He remedied this by pressing his big foot on her throat. Struggling for breath, her vision dimming, she saw William's bloodied face glaring down at her and then nothing more.

twenty-six

A crushing weight pressed in on Gabe's chest. No wonder William had looked so smug when he locked him in. The room was actually a vault. No air circulated. The dizziness he'd felt could no longer be ignored. He'd assumed his stupid-assed sickness was just having a field day, but now he knew the dizziness came from lack of oxygen in the room.

The last words he'd heard from Cole weren't promising. Was his friend even still alive? The microphone in his ear had picked up enough grunts, curses, and growls to fill twelve rounds of a wrestling match, and then there had been total silence. After several minutes of calling his name, Gabe had given up. If Cole was alive, he would have answered. Already he felt the grief at the loss of a good friend.

His breath hitched unexpectedly as if the air were being sucked out of him. How long did he have before the air completely disappeared?

For an instant, he was back in the mines, listening to his younger brother breathing his last breaths of life. The helplessness and grief almost overwhelmed him. How he'd loved that kid.

And Skye. God, how he loved Skye. He'd been so stupid. So incredibly blind. He loved Skylar James Maddox. Soul deep. Unstoppable. Forever.

What did his insecurities matter? His idiotic, stiff-necked pride? He loved her . . . and he knew without a doubt, despite his stupidity in the way he'd treated her, that she loved him, too. She knew him inside and out and she still loved him. What a freaking idiot he'd been.

With superhuman strength, Gabe got to his feet. He'd found the small crevice where he believed the door was. There was no movement to indicate it would open, but since this was the only opening he'd felt in the entire room, this had to be the door. However, it felt as solid as if a steel bar was in front of it. That didn't matter. Whatever breath and strength he had left he would use to bust out of this prison. Skye's life was in danger and he'd be damned if he let her down again. She'd almost died because of his mistakes before. Never again.

Taking a controlled breath from the remaining air in the room, Gabe backed up and took a running start to the door. He was six feet four inches and 220 pounds of determined male. As he slammed into the wall, pain slammed back.

Refusing to give up, Gabe backed up and slammed again. Again. Then again. The wall felt slippery and he didn't question why. He'd busted his hand on the second slam. His face on the third one. Didn't matter. Wouldn't stop.

With a roar, Gabe went at it again and then again. Something moved. Backing up, barely able to think straight, he tried to pull in a breath and couldn't find one. The air was almost totally depleted. An inhuman growl came from deep within . . . Gabe took one more slam and heard a wonderful sound. *Craaack!*

Giving it all he had, Gabe backed up, took a running leap, and slammed against it again. And found himself lying face-first on the floor of Harrington's office.

Lungs burning and breath wheezing, Gabe got to his feet and staggered to the door. He opened it. His gait shuffling and wobbling, he ran toward the stairway. Muted music came from the party that apparently was still going strong.

He heard a scream and didn't bother to look around. Probably looked like he'd been through a wood chipper. Didn't care. Just had to get to Skye.

Halfway up the stairs, his legs went out from under him. Gabe crawled the rest of the way. On the landing, he took a deep breath to steady himself. Passing out would do Skye no good. Feeling slightly better, he put one foot on the floor. Two big hands grabbed him. Growling an obscenity, Gabe jerked his head up, ready to kill whoever was planning to try to stop him. Instead he looked up into the battered but very alive face of Cole Mathison.

Despite his bruised and bloodied face, Cole smiled and said, "Hell if I know who's the ugliest one now."

Gabe drove while Cole read the monitor. It was picking up the signal perfectly. Skye was close . . . even closer than Gabe could have hoped for. Now pray God she was still alive.

A van with four more LCR operatives followed behind them. They wouldn't assist unless Gabe and Cole found it necessary. With hostages involved, going in stealthily, with as few operatives as possible, was LCR's way. Taking down the bad guys was secondary to making sure all hostages came out unharmed.

"How do you want this to go down?" Cole asked.

"You mean Harrington?"

"Yeah."

"Even if Kendra's at this house, he's responsible for more than one girl's disappearance. Do your best to keep him alive. We need him talking."

Cole nodded. Gabe couldn't help but appreciate that

Cole had asked. After the hell the man had gone through last year, he'd made no secret that killing wouldn't be something he'd ever willingly do again. After being used as a personal killing machine for a maniac, who could blame him? The guilt of the death of one innocent man weighed heavily on Cole's shoulders.

"Slow down. We should be just about there," Cole said.

Gabe slowed to a crawl and the monitor started a rapid blink. A few feet farther and the dot was solid red . . . no blink. Skye was here.

"There's a narrow path," Cole said. "Barely big enough for a car. Bet there aren't many people who even know there's a house here."

Not wanting to alert anyone to their arrival, Gabe drove past the driveway a few yards. A small clearing on the side of the road gave him the perfect spot to park. The car was dark green, and unless a light shone directly on it, no one would see it.

Both men got out and went to the trunk. Pulling a Kevlar vest on over his damaged shoulder and ribs barely caused Gabe a blip of pain. Skye was in that house—nothing could faze him now.

Working silently, they slid their guns into the holsters at their sides and ankles. Taser guns and knives went into a belt at the waist, along with rope and other necessary tools of their trade.

Once set, they gave each other a look—one filled with purpose and the knowledge that they may not come out alive, but they'd do their dead-level best to make sure that any victims they found would.

With a small nod of acknowledgment to the operatives parked a few yards away, waiting for further instructions, Gabe took off at a run, Cole at his side. They had both changed into black T-shirts and pants. The night was as black as pitch; no one would see them coming up the path.

The drive was graveled but held deep ruts as if heavy traffic had been on it for years. Harrington probably didn't want to have it repaired since that might call attention to what went on only a few yards away.

At the end of the drive, Gabe held up his hand. Compared to the other houses in the area, this one was small. Still, it did have two stories . . . and most likely a basement. It would take some time to go through each room.

"Let's stay as invisible as possible until we don't have a choice."

Cole nodded his agreement.

Going low, they ran to the back door. Standing to one side of the door, Cole turned a knob and pushed it open. On the other side, Gabe peered in. A laundry room . . . empty.

Giving Cole a signal of his intent, Gabe went through the door. Cole followed.

Not since the dark days when she first thought Gabe was dead had Skylar felt such sadness. Only by concentrating on the need to save Kendra and Gabe was she even able to think with any kind of coherency. The drug, of course. A depressant, designed to take away all will and hope . . . it was doing its job. She fought it with a vengeance. She had so much to live for . . . so much to do. She tried to ignore the demons of doubt that reminded her that Gabe didn't love her. That there was no hope. Kendra had been raped and tortured. William had made it clear he intended to have Skylar killed. And Gabe might well be dead.

Pulling herself to her knees, Skylar squinted around the room. The dim light cast shadows over a chair in the corner. The big flat surface she saw across the room was a bed. She pushed herself to her feet and stumbled toward the chair. Halfway there, her legs gave out and she fell.

Sobbing weakly, she lay there for several seconds, once again fighting the overwhelming hopelessness. A dim voice in the back of her mind began to shout at her. She ignored it. The voice grew stronger, screamed at her and called her names. Told her to get off her ass and fight.

Skylar pulled herself up and crawled to the chair. Finally reaching it, she lay her head on the chair cushion and rested. The voice wouldn't stop. Insistent, irritating, and belligerent, it told her to get up and get the hell out of there. This time, Skylar recognized the voice. It was hers. She stood, straightened her shoulders, took a breath, and made herself walk to the door. She would find Kendra and they would escape. There were no other options.

Her hand on the door, she took another bracing breath and opened it. A man stood at the entrance—a battered-looking but very alive Gabe.

With a sob of thanksgiving, she threw herself into his arms. He held her close, whispered gruff words she couldn't hear for the roaring in her ears. With a soft sigh, she let unconsciousness take over again.

His heart in his throat, Gabe scooped Skye into his arms. Myriad emotions came to the surface, not the least of them was panic. Had she passed out from fear or something more deadly? Stalking back into the room, Gabe laid her on the bed.

"Is she all right?" Cole called from the doorway.

Pressing his fingers to the pulse at her neck, he sighed. "Yeah, I think so. Her pulse is slow but steady."

"You need me to stay?"

"No. Go see if you can find Kendra. I'll hide Skye and be right behind you."

Gabe heard the door close as Cole moved on. Brushing the hair from her face, he noted a multitude of new bruises on her creamy skin. Harrington would pay for each and every one of them.

Still uneasy about her unconsciousness, Gabe lifted her eyelid. Her eye was slightly dilated and glazed. The bastard had drugged her.

"Skye, can you hear me?"

She moaned slightly and whispered his name.

"That's right, Skye. It's me. But I need you to wake up, sweetheart. I need to find Kendra and Harrington. I need your help."

As if her eyelids were weighted, Skye blinked slowly. Gabe could tell she was struggling to wake up and whispered encouragement to her. "Help me, Skye. We need to find Kendra. Wake up, baby."

Her eyes opened halfway; his heart flipped over when she whispered, "I thought I'd lost you again."

Pressing a soft kiss to her bruised mouth, he whispered, "Never again. I promise."

Her eyes widened more as if she realized what had happened. She struggled to sit up. Gabe held her shoulders to help her.

She leaned against the headboard. "I saw Kendra. The bastard took her away again. But she's alive."

"Good. Any idea how many people Harrington has here?"

"I've seen three, but there may be more."

"Cole's looking for Kendra. I need to go help him. I'm going to leave you here and lock you in. You'll be fine until—"

"No, Gabe. I'm going with you. I need to help."

"Like hell. You're injured and have drugs in your system. I'll be able to work better knowing you're safe."

He squatted down so he could get closer to her face. "Promise me, Skye. Promise you'll stay here."

She blew out a sigh and nodded. "Okay."

With one last kiss to her lips, Gabe stood. Pulling a gun from the holster at his ankle, he handed it to her. "If anyone other than Cole, myself, or Kendra comes in, don't hesitate. Don't ask questions. Shoot. And I mean to kill. Go for the biggest target. The chest. Got it?"

She nodded again and whispered, "Please be careful."

Gabe stalked to the door and then stopped for one last glance at the most beautiful woman in the world. "I have a lot to live for, Skye." He opened the door slowly and looked out. Saw nothing. He turned the knob and closed the door, locking Skye inside. If someone wanted in, the lock wouldn't hold them. But it would give Skye enough time to raise her gun and shoot.

"Cole, you there?"

"Yeah." Cole's voice came as a whisper. "I'm on the second floor. Took two out, a man and woman. No sign of Harrington or Kendra."

"Okay. I'll finish the first floor, then I'm headed for the basement."

"I'll meet you there once I'm through."

The layout of the house was a choppy array of rooms. The furnishings were scarce in most of the rooms, nonexistent in others. Apparently those who lived here didn't care about the finer things of life like sofas and television sets.

Gabe came to the kitchen and stopped abruptly. A man standing in the middle of the room held a milk jug to his mouth and was gulping sloppily. A bag of cookies sat on the table in front of him. His gun pointed directly at the man's big gut, Gabe gave him an opportunity to get a mouthful and then said, "Got milk?"

Milk sprayed everywhere as the man sputtered and spewed. His eyes wide as saucers, he made a grab for the gun sitting beside the cookies.

"Touch the gun and we're going to have a milk-and-cookies mess all over the floor."

The man drew his hand back. "I don't have anything to do with what goes on here. I just got hired last week."

"Sorry to put you out of work so soon." Gabe waved his gun at the refrigerator. "Get over there."

The man gave a longing glance at his gun and then went to stand in front of the fridge.

Pulling handcuffs from his pocket, Gabe tossed them at the man. "Handcuff yourself to the handles."

The man caught the cuffs, inserted them through the double door handles of the fridge and freezer. Then, wrapping them around his wrists, he clicked them shut.

Gabe took the gun from the table and slid it in the small of his back. "How many are here?"

"Two or three. People are coming and going all the time. It's hard to keep up."

"And how many girls are here?"

The man's eyes skittered away guiltily. Like hell he didn't know what was going on here.

"I asked you a question."

He shrugged. "Two, maybe three girls."

"Where are they?"

"If I tell you, will that get me some kind of immunity?"

"No. What it'll get you is one less bullet hole in your leg. Now, tell me."

The man's mouth crimped; apparently deciding he'd just soon take his chances on not talking. Gabe cursed himself. Honesty was rarely the best policy with scum. He should have promised full immunity or whatever they said on television shows to get people to talk.

Gabe knew he wasn't much for subtlety. Pulling his

knife from its sheath at his belt, he stalked over to the handcuffed man. "Okay, I can't really shoot you because it'd be too loud. However, I don't mind slicing you up a bit."

He eyed the knife nervously, swallowed audibly, and said, "You wouldn't dare."

Wrong words to say to a man who'd had a fairly shitty day. Pulling tape from a pouch hooked to his belt, he ripped off a piece and slapped it over the man's mouth. His hand wrapped around the handle, Gabe thrust the knife into the meaty part of the guy's upper thigh.

A muffled scream of pain and rage quickly followed.

"You believe me now?" Gabe asked quietly.

Tears poured from the man's eyes as his head nodded in frantic little jerks.

Gabe pulled the tape halfway off so the creep could talk. "Where are the girls?"

"In the basement," the man gasped out.

"And how many men are there, really?"

He sobbed pitifully, "I told you, three or four. I don't really know."

"Uh-huh, you told me two or three. Want me to go for the other leg . . . maybe a little higher up this time?"

"Okay . . . well, I'm telling the truth now . . . three or four."

When Gabe pulled out his knife again, the man swallowed and said, "I'm telling you the truth, man . . . really."

"Okay, I believe you. If I find out different, I'm coming back. Next time I won't be so nice—I'll be cutting off one of your favorite parts. Got it?"

The man gulped some air and said, "Okay . . . well, maybe there's two or three more men and one woman. As I said . . . it's hard to keep up with all their comings and goings."

Gabe gave his a nod of approval. "Good."

He slapped on another piece of tape and stalked out the door. "Cole . . . you hear that?"

"Yeah, I've got two more rooms to check and then I'll meet you down there."

Gabe turned to a door connected to the kitchen and opened it. A stairway led downstairs. He turned back and looked at the man, who was doing his best to jerk the handle from the refrigerator door. Figuring he'd be pulling the tape off and screaming his head off, Gabe went back to him.

The man's eyes widened; he probably thought Gabe was going to live up to his promise to cut something off. Feeling no need to reassure him, Gabe raised his gun and conked the man on the head. The guy slumped over.

Satisfied he wouldn't be making any noises for a good while, Gabe headed down the stairs. Gun at the ready, he reached the bottom and peeked around the wall.

Blood boiling and gut churning, he was in the middle of the room before he even realized it. The horror of what he saw there was almost more than he could comprehend.

twenty-seven

Skylar paced back and forth. The drugs were almost gone from her system, and all the anger and determination to save Kendra and help Gabe had returned. She'd promised him she would stay put, but something told her she needed to leave. That gut feeling she'd learned to heed told her something was going down and someone needed her help. Kendra or Gabe? It didn't matter. She had to help.

Holding the gun securely the way Gabe had showed her, Skylar put her ear to the door. She heard nothing. Unlocking it as silently as possible, she opened it slowly and peered out. Heard no noises . . . saw no one.

Praying she wasn't making a major mistake, Skylar closed the door behind her and headed in the direction she'd heard Gabe take.

The house was ominously quiet. She stopped in the kitchen and sighed. An unconscious man was handcuffed to the refrigerator. Somehow she got the idea that her husband had been by this way. A door on the other side of the kitchen stood open. Tiptoeing toward the door, Skylar peeked inside. An empty stairway leading downstairs.

Both hands wrapped around the handle of the gun, Skylar crept down the stairs.

An odd noise hit her ears. She froze at the sound. Someone crying? Taking the steps quicker, she came to the bottom step and listened intently. Yes, crying . . . and more than one person. Sticking her head around the wall ever so gingerly, Skylar peeked. And lost all breath.

The basement was one gigantic room. There were six queen-sized beds, three on each side of the room. Thick curtains hung in between the beds, but they were all pulled back, revealing rumpled bedclothes and their occupants. Young girls. Haggard. Drugged. Ravaged.

And there was Gabe. Squatted down, several feet away from two young girls who were holding each other, sobbing pitifully. She heard his voice, low and soothing, as he apparently tried to comfort them. His distance from them indicated he was afraid to get too close in case they deemed him a threat.

Skylar must have made a sound, because Gabe's head jerked up. In his eyes, she saw a myriad of emotions. Compassion. Fury. Determination.

"I told you to stay put." Gabe's voice was a low sound. He obviously didn't want to startle the girls.

Skylar shook her head as she made her way toward him. "I couldn't, Gabe. Not when I thought I could help."

His eyes roaming over the room, Gabe said, "Thank God you don't obey worth a damn. I have no idea what to say other than I'll kill the bastards who did this to them."

"There's not much to say. Other than we're getting them out of here and they'll be safe."

Nodding, he stood and said, "Stay here with them." Giving her a stern look, he added, "And this time, please do what I say. I'm going after Harrington."

"Oh, there's no need for that, Mr. Maddox. I'm right here."

Skylar and Gabe whirled around to find William Harrington once more pointing a gun at both of them.

"I must admit, I'm a bit flabbergasted that you escaped my vault. I had it designed so air could be withdrawn to preserve my most precious belongings." His eyes turned cold. "You should have died."

Gabe glared and started walking toward him. "You first."

William's laugh came out like a long, dry hiccup. He was terrified and doing his best not to show it.

Skylar backed away slowly as Gabe drew closer to William. They both had a gun. She looked down at her shaking hand. Make that all three of them had a gun.

"I'll give you two choices, Harrington. Drop your gun and surrender quietly or I'll shoot you."

"I really don't care for either choice, Mr. Maddox. How about I give you the same choices."

"I'll admit, I'm not a math genius, but you've got two guns on you. In my estimation, that makes you doubly screwed."

"Look again," William said softly.

Suspecting a trick, Skylar dared a look behind her out of the corner of her eye. Now she knew why William had begun to look more confident. Two of the young girls held guns. One gun was pointed at Gabe, the other at Skylar.

Gabe didn't look surprised. Only angrier. "So you brainwashed these children into helping you."

"Children?" William snorted and jerked his head at the girl who held the gun on Gabe. "I picked Missy up in a whorehouse in Vermont. She was only too happy to move to nicer accommodations. And I got Lana off the street in New York. She took a bit more persuading, but she eventually came around."

Fury ignited within Skylar. Both girls couldn't be more that nineteen and looked emaciated to the point of death. "You mean after you raped them a few times?"

He shuddered delicately. "I've not touched these girls."

"What about Kendra?"

An odd, eerie expression flashed in William's eyes. Skylar's stomach roiled at that look of absolute evil.

"She's special. A reward for the hard work I've put into this business. My jewel stays with me . . . pampered and treasured. The others are only here for training. Once they're ready, they'll go out and fulfill their real destiny."

"Training that includes raping and drugging them?"

"Skylar." William's voice sounded as though he were instructing a not-too-bright child. "Nothing has been done to them that they haven't let a hundred other men do."

"Other than taking away their right to choose."

"Rights? Oh my dear, you are so very naïve. Rights are only for those who have earned them."

Without conscious will, Skylar raised the gun in her hand and pointed it at the man she'd once thought of as a second father. "You are such a disgusting pig."

"I'm no different from any man trying to make it in this difficult economy. Times are tough. Taking care of my family is my primary responsibility. One I take very seriously."

"Do Margo or your children know about this?"

William looked shocked that she would even ask such a question. "Well, of course they don't, Skylar. I handle the finances for the family."

"How do you think they'd feel if they knew that their father was no better than a slave trader and a pimp?"

A slight shrug. "Your insults have no effect on me. I'm much tougher than what you might think. Margo and my children know I do what I deem necessary to take care of them. And before you become so sanctimonious about these girls, think about what their life would be if

I hadn't found them. They have it better than if they were on the streets."

"You act as if you're running some kind of charity."

"Oh no, my dear. There is no such thing as charity. We all pay a price." He motioned at Lana, the girl who held a gun on Skylar. "Take the gun from Skylar."

Skylar knew only one thing. She could not give up her gun. Unsure how to go about that without hurting Lana, she shot a helpless glance at Gabe.

Gabe gritted his teeth. What a fucked-up mess. Skye wouldn't shoot the girl. Gabe didn't want to shoot her either, but if she hurt Skye, he'd have no choice.

Apparently, Harrington believed it was just Gabe and Skye in the house. Since the man's back was to the stairway, he couldn't see the size-fourteen shoes sticking out on the last step. Cole was there, waiting for Gabe's signal.

Now he just needed to figure out how to handle the situation without Skye or any of the girls getting hurt. All the girls, including the ones holding guns on them, were victims. If anyone had to die, it was going to be Harrington.

Needing to get both girls unarmed, Gabe began to walk to Harrington again.

Harrington backed up as his gun went higher. "Don't come any closer."

Gabe stopped and held his hands up. "Guess you have us outnumbered after all." Without taking his eyes off Harrington, Gabe said, "Skye, drop your gun, honey."

"But Gabe—"

He dared a glance at her, nodded and gave her an encouraging smile. For an instant, her expression held both surprise and confusion. Gabe wasn't a man of encouraging words and smiles. Snarls and glares were more his style. Once again, her faith in him humbled him to his soul as she stooped and dropped the gun onto the floor.

Harrington nodded in approval. "Wise move, Skylar." He jerked his head at Gabe. "Mr. Maddox, please kick your gun over to Lana so she can retrieve it."

Gabe kicked the gun so hard it flew past Harrington and landed behind him.

Harrington glared. "Not funny." He turned to Lana. "Pick up the gun."

Lana passed by Harrington and stooped to get the gun. With an almost unworldly quietness, Cole yanked her up and pressed a hand over her mouth and a hand on her neck just hard enough to cause unconsciousness. With utmost gentleness, he placed her on the stairway, out of sight.

As if wondering why she was so silent, Harrington glanced back. Gabe flew toward him. At the same time, Cole reached Missy, who seemed frozen in shock.

Gabe landed hard on Harrington and they crashed to the floor. The man held tight to the gun in his hand. Without any compunction, Gabe twisted his wrist until there was a loud bone pop.

Harrington howled.

Rage and glee combined into a surging mass of emotions as Gabe sat up and pummeled the man's face and gut.

Skylar's soft voice in his ear finally penetrated the haze. He stood and looked down at the bloodied, unconscious man. Never in his life had he wanted to kill someone as much as he wanted to kill this bastard. Harrington had done despicable, vile things. He deserved death for each and every one of them. But for daring to hurt Skye, Gabe wanted to tear him from limb to limb.

"Are you okay?"

After what she'd been through, she could ask him that? He held out his arms and Skye flew into them. Holding her close, he said a prayer of thanksgiving that she was safe.

"Everyone okay?"

Keeping Skye at his side, Gabe turned to Cole. "About as well as we can be. Did you find Kendra?"

"Yeah. She's in a room upstairs. She's pretty out of it."

"Anyone else around?"

"No. There were only three men and a woman upstairs. None of them the bodyguard type. More the weasel type. One of them was the photographer."

Skylar pulled away from Gabe's arms. "We need to get these girls some help."

They all turned to look at the young girls who were now all huddled together on one bed. Arms around each other, they formed a small, sad group. But they were alive. And now they would be free.

"Our backup is coming in. Authorities have already been called. I'll go back and check on Kendra," Cole said.

Taking some plastic ties from his pocket, Gabe headed to Harrington. "I'll tie the scumbag up." He turned to Skye. "Why don't you see if the girls will talk to you?"

Skylar turned and looked at the young girls. What could she say to them to make them feel better? It would take years of therapy for them to overcome what they'd been through.

She heard Cole stomp up the stairs. She began to walk to the girls and then stopped at the sound of an odd noise . . . like a soft grunt. Skylar turned. Time went into slow motion.

William was back on his feet and holding a gun. He stood over Gabe, who was slumped down on his knees.

Skylar saw blood pouring onto the floor. Somehow he had injured Gabe. And by the expression on William's face, he had every intention of finishing Gabe off with the gun.

Her only thought being to save the man she loved, Skylar dove for the gun lying only a few feet away from her. Harrington looked up at the movement. In one fluid move, Skylar grabbed the gun, rolled onto her knees, and pointed it at Harrington. Without hesitation, she fired.

Harrington dropped the gun and clutched his chest where the bullet hit. He fell face-first onto the floor.

With a sob, Skylar ran to Gabe. Pulling him up to face her, she let out a small scream. Blood poured from his throat. He'd been stabbed . . . an artery. *Oh sweet God, an artery.*

"Cole!" Skylar screamed.

Cole was beside her in seconds. He shouted for someone to bring him a towel. Skylar never looked up as she kept pressure on the gushing blood pouring from Gabe's throat. His eyes were closed. She didn't know if he was conscious. She only knew one thing, she could not lose him again. Please God, not again.

"Lift your hand, Skylar. I'm going to press the towel down and try to slow the bleeding."

Her hand pressed against the wound, Skylar couldn't let go. If she did, even for a second, she would lose him. She couldn't lose him. Not again.

"Let go, Skylar."

Cole's even, cool voice calmed her. She lifted her blood-soaked hand and watched Cole apply pressure. In the background, she heard someone talking on the phone. Were they calling an ambulance? Would it be too late?

"Skylar. Look at me."

Raising terrified eyes to Cole, she said the only thing she had in her mind. "Please don't let him die."

"He's not going to die. The gash is deep. Looks like it nicked an artery but it's not severed. We just need to get him to a hospital. Okay?"

Her head felt like it weighed a thousand pounds as she tried to nod. She could not lose Gabe. Not now. Not again.

twenty-eight

Ten days later

Dressed in a tailored black suit, her hair pulled back at her nape, Skylar looked appropriately somber as she walked out of the police station. She had just given another statement, hopefully her last, on the death of one of the city's most prominent citizens.

Despite her name recognition, city officials were not happy with how things had developed. It was a media nightmare and every television station around the world had reported on the famous Skylar James shooting and killing the powerful and wealthy William Harrington III. The circumstances were sordid, which made the press love it all the more.

William's employees had been rounded up and were going through extensive questioning. It was everyone's hope that the extent of Harrington's business could be gathered from them and all of his victims over the last ten years identified. Gathering this information would have been easier if William had lived. And while Skylar regretted that his death made the investigation more difficult, she refused to feel guilty for killing the perverted bastard. Hopefully, he was in hell enjoying all the rewards he so richly deserved.

Margo Harrington and her children had retreated to their vacation home in Portugal. Margo claimed to not know about William's illegal activities. Skylar would have liked to believe that was true, but wasn't so sure. On leaving the police station earlier in the week, she'd passed by Margo. Since she'd had no idea what to say to the woman, she had just looked at her. The expression on Margo's face indicated antipathy and hatred, but absolutely no shame for what her husband had done. William had said that his family would understand why he did what he did. Perhaps he was right.

Exhaustion tore at Skylar from every angle. The young girls William had held were being treated at a privately funded women's health clinic. Kendra was there, too. All the girls were not only traumatized, but also suffering from various addictions and malnutrition. They would require extensive care and counseling. Somehow, Skylar thought that Kendra might need it more than any of them.

Kendra still hadn't spoken to Skylar. Wouldn't even look her in the eye. And even though Skylar understood why, it still hurt so much. She had introduced that monster to Kendra. It didn't matter that she didn't know what he was. She'd brought Kendra to his attention and for that she would never forgive herself.

The counselors had said Kendra needed time. Skylar understood, but God, it still hurt so much.

"Hey, Skylar, are they going to charge you with anything?"

"Skylar, look over here. Did you know William Harrington was a pervert?"

A small pocket of reporters gathered around her at the bottom of the steps. She had successfully avoided them for days. And had hoped with her dark glasses and somber dress, she could escape their attention once more. It wasn't to be.

"Are you and Ben getting back together? Didn't he visit you yesterday at your apartment?"

If her mouth didn't feel so frozen with pain, she would have smiled at the question. The reason Ben had come by would be laughable if it didn't infuriate her so much. His "Gabe sent me to make sure you were all right" almost got him a punch in the face.

When she'd asked the obvious question, "Why the hell doesn't Gabe find out for himself?" he'd grimaced and had been stubbornly silent.

Ben was the fifth person Gabe had sent to make sure she was "all right." First there had been Cole, who'd assured her he was merely following orders to make sure she was eating and sleeping.

Then, of all people, her father had come by, again at Gabe's request. Seemed that her dad was now warming up to his son-in-law. Not only had Gabe saved his daughter's life once again, but her father was seriously reconsidering his opinion on a lot of things. After all, his best friend, the man he'd known for years, had been a human trafficker and sexual predator. Jeremiah James's faith in his own judgment had been shaken to the core.

Then, just this morning, Noah McCall and his wife, Samara, had come by . . . with Micah, their beautiful little boy.

Noah and Samara had perhaps been the most helpful, though still not as forthcoming as Skylar needed. While Micah dozed on the couch, his head propped on Noah's thigh, Samara had explained that Gabe had issues to resolve. And that each person at LCR, at some point, had to deal with them in their own way.

Issues? What was she? Chopped liver?

All the people Gabe had sent to check on her had been kind. All had been helpful. But none had told her what was going on or where Gabe had gone. It had taken every bit of her stamina not to scream at them: *If Gabe*

Maddox is so concerned for his wife, then why the hell doesn't he come see for himself?

If only she knew where the man was, she'd . . . what? What would she say to a man who'd made her love him all over again and then once again abandoned her? "Go to hell" didn't seem appropriate—she'd only run into him because she was already there.

For four days she'd sat by his bedside. Four days when, because of his blood loss, along with two cracked ribs, a partially collapsed lung, and a dislocated shoulder, she hadn't been sure he would make it. The doctors had assured her he would. She hadn't believed them. She'd needed to see for herself.

And then, when she'd gone home for a few hours to change clothes and grab a nap, what had he done? He'd woken, discharged himself against doctor's orders, and disappeared. Without one word to her . . . he'd disappeared.

"Come on, Skylar. Give us some news! What did Ben come see you about? Are you going to get back with him? What about that real estate man, Gabe Maddox? Did you two break up? What happened?"

And finally she'd had enough. After years of allowing inappropriate, stupid questions, putting up with these people hounding her day and night, taking photographs, nosing into her business for no good reason other than a story they could sell for their own benefit, it was just too much.

Her eyes roamed the four photographers and five reporters who shouldered one another as they tried to get the best spot. She zeroed in on one of the reporters. The one who was always following her, always asking the rudest questions.

When she began to advance toward him, his expression was one of excitement. But it quickly changed to fear.

She could see the questions in his eyes. After all, she'd recently killed one of the wealthiest and most influential men in the country. Maybe she wasn't completely sane.

Skylar stopped within inches of the man's face. She was well aware that the photographers were snapping shots left and right. She couldn't stop that, but she could damn well turn the table on the questions.

Hands on her hips, she snarled, "What gives you the right to ask me about my life?"

His cocky bravado no longer apparent, the man swallowed audibly and said, "The people want to know."

"What people?"

"The public."

"And what right do they have to know about what goes on in my private life?"

"Well . . . I . . . they . . ." He swallowed again. "You're a public figure."

"And that gives you the right to ask anything you want?"

"Well . . . I . . ." The man glanced around for help, but his gaze only met faces that looked as astonished as he did.

"Let me ask you a few questions. Are you married? Do you sleep around? What did you have for dinner last night? Are you breaking up with your girlfriend?"

Gabe stood a few yards away from the small group of astounded reporters and photographers and enjoyed the show. Never in his life had he seen a more beautiful, exciting, or wonderful woman than this lovely creature he was married to. How the hell had he gotten so lucky?

He knew she would be furious with him. She had every right. But during the time when he had been locked up in that hellhole of Harrington's, he'd faced some home truths. Every man has defining moments in his life. Moments that change, reshape, and re-form opinions about life and about himself. Gabe had thought he'd had his share.

Lying beside his dying brother and father in a collapsed mine. Being held captive in a foreign prison and treated like an animal. Those two events had hardened and toughened him, but they hadn't been the mind-altering, soul-shattering experience he'd had in Harrington's vault. Not knowing if Skye was alive or dead . . . if he would ever see her again . . . had transformed him.

Rarely does life give another chance. In the eight years since he'd been separated from Skye, despite his inability to end it completely, Gabe had believed there was no chance in hell for them.

But in those moments of stark terror for Skye, Gabe had questioned everything and had come up with one definitive truth: he loved Skylar James with a depth he hadn't known existed. Nothing else mattered but that. And if given another chance, he would do everything within his power to save her, make her his, and be with her for all eternity.

When he'd woken in the hospital, he'd known there were things he had to put to rest before he could come to her a whole man. So, despite the doctor's strong discouragement and the knowledge that Skye would be hurt, he'd left to get those things done.

And now it was time for a new chapter. A very long chapter and one he planned to spend the rest of his life on, perfecting, refining, and thanking God he'd been given another chance to make it right.

Now he just needed to see if Skye was going to give it to him.

He sauntered over to the small group, where Skye was continuing her tirade on the right of people to be informed versus the right of privacy. The stupefied faces that surrounded her told him they'd stand there all day and listen to her. She'd even collected a few passersby who'd stopped in the middle of the sidewalk and stared, seemingly mesmerized.

Poor Skye probably thought they were learning a well-needed lesson. But Gabe had seen that expression on men's faces before. Hell, it was on his face every time he looked at this beautiful woman. Fascination and adoration. Awe. These people were loving the hell out of being this close to a real-life goddess.

Time for an intervention.

Gabe shouldered between two photographers who were knocking against each other, trying to get the best shot. One of them whined, "Hey, who do you think you are?"

They didn't recognize him. Every time they'd seen him before, he'd been clean-shaven and dressed in designer clothes. His worn jeans, black T-shirt, and scruffy face looked totally different. But this was the real Gabe Maddox.

One person recognized him, though. The only one he cared about. She stopped in the middle of her lecture and just stared at him. Her expression one of uncertainty, hope, and not a little anger.

"Who are you?" a reporter asked.

His eyes on the amazing woman in front of him, he admitted to the world what he'd hidden for so long. No longer wanting to keep it a secret. Proud to be able to say it.

"I'm Skylar James's husband."

Her eyes brimming with tears, Skye flew into his arms. Holding her tight, Gabe swung her around, glorying in the knowledge that he had indeed been granted one more chance.

* * *

Lying beside her husband, his arms locked around her, hearing him breathe the slow, easy breaths of deep sleep, Skylar knew she'd found true peace. They hadn't taken a moment to talk yet. The instant she'd let go of him, reporters had started clamoring with even more questions. Cameras had clicked furiously.

Gabe had grabbed her hand and started running. He hailed a taxi, they jumped inside, and then she was back in his arms, his mouth on hers. No words had been necessary. She'd seen the truth in his eyes. Whatever demons had been eating at him had been slayed. This time, Gabe was here to stay.

They'd rushed into her apartment building and she'd almost suggested they use the stairs. Gabe never gave her a chance. The instant the elevator doors had opened, he'd pulled her inside and his mouth had been on hers again. If this was his way to handle his problem with enclosed spaces, he would get no complaints from her.

Now, hours later, secure in the knowledge that she and Gabe were indeed forever, she needed to get a few things out of the way.

"I can hear your mind working."

She smiled at the gruff growling voice in her ear. "And here I was trying to think quietly."

Gabe drew her earlobe into his mouth and bit gently. Skylar shuddered with arousal. Soon, very soon, she was going to seduce her husband into exhaustion. But not yet.

"Why, Gabe?"

There was no need to explain what she meant.

His arms tightened around her as he sighed. "I'm sorry, Skye. I needed to go back home and see Ruth before I could go forward with you."

"You saw your stepmother?"

"Yes."

"Was it difficult?"

"It was until I saw her face. You were right. I should have gone back a long time ago."

"What happened?"

"She cried a lot, apologized, which I told her she didn't need to do."

Skylar disagreed with him but she wasn't going to argue the point. Gabe had punished himself for surviving a horrific accident. And while she could understand his stepmother's grief, she would never understand how she could have treated Gabe with anything but gratitude that he had survived. Gabe had needed someone to be happy that he'd lived. The entire town had failed him.

"How is she doing?"

"She's good. Both of her stepchildren are in college now. Her husband is semi-retired. She looks happy. I hope she is."

"Did you see anyone else?"

"No, not really. Went back to my old high school and looked around. Took a walk to the old cabin my dad, Brandon, and I used to camp out at. Visited their gravesites."

"And what did you find?"

"Peace, Skye. I found peace."

"I'm glad." She paused for a second. "I missed you."

"I know, sweetheart. I'm sorry. I won't do it again."

"Do what?"

"Leave you."

"Ever?"

"Ever."

"Promise?"

"Promise."

"So where do you want to live?"

Gabe's arms tightened around her again. "Wherever you like."

She smiled at his words. Even as much as he hated the city, he was willing to live here if this was where she wanted to stay. It was about time the man knew just who he had married.

Rolling over to lie on top of him, Skylar propped her elbows on the bed and gazed down at the love of her life. "You would do that for me? Live here, in the city?"

There were no shadows, no subterfuge, no doubts. He was telling the truth. He would actually live in what he considered hell just to be with her. The fact that he loved her that much amazed and humbled her.

"What if I want to live in Florida?" Skylar asked.

"Where in Florida?"

"Where do you live now?"

He grimaced. "Sweetheart, I live on a very small island. Alone. No restaurants, theaters, or shopping. Only the occasional gator and a few snakes for company."

Skylar swallowed hard. She could live without the restaurants, theaters, and shopping. The gators and snakes she wasn't so sure of.

"How many gators?"

His eyes narrowed. "How many would it take to scare you off?"

The truthful answer was one, but she smiled bravely and said, "I could live with two or three."

His chest rumbled beneath her as he laughed. "Baby, you don't live with gators. They have a tendency to want to eat you."

"Well, then—"

"How about a compromise? Noah called me yesterday. He wants to open an LCR branch in East Tennessee. Asked if I'd be interested in co-running it with a couple of other operatives."

Her eyes searched his. Was he curtailing his LCR activities for her? "How do you feel about that?"

"Good, actually. The other two operatives are Ethan and Shea Bishop. They're good friends of mine and already live in East Tennessee. I think you'll like them."

"And you promise you're not doing this just for me?"

"Doing what?"

"Taking a desk job?"

"I won't deny that coming home to you every night would be a huge incentive. But it's not as much of a desk job as you might think. I'll still be working ops. Maybe not as many, but I'll still be out there. How do you feel about that?"

"I can't say I won't be worried, because I'd be lying. But I truly believe in what you do. I wouldn't want you to be anything other than who you are."

"And what about who you are, Skye? You're one of the most famous women in the world. How will you feel about leaving all of that behind?"

"Famous I can do without. I would like to maintain a residence here so we can have a place to stay when we visit. I'm not giving up on Kendra."

Gabe cupped her face in his hands and brought her down for a soft kiss. "She'll come around, sweetheart. She just needs some time."

"I know. I just want to make sure she doesn't think I've abandoned her. I'll stay in touch with her counselors, and the instant they think she's ready, I want to be here for her."

"What about your mentoring and charity work?"

"I've enjoyed that and would like to continue it in some form, if possible."

"LCR has a lot of different opportunities . . . if you're interested."

Pressing a soft kiss to his scruffy chin, she whispered, "I'll think about it. But for right now, I think I'd like to seduce my husband."

Gabe rolled her over onto her back. The chain holding their wedding rings lay between her breasts. His midnight blue eyes as serious and solemn as she'd ever seen them, he unclasped the chain at her neck and pulled the rings off. After sliding his ring onto his left hand, he took her left hand in his and whispered, "With this ring, I thee wed. I love you, Skye. This time past forever. I promise," and slid the ring on her finger.

With a small sob of happiness, Skylar threw her arms around her husband and allowed him to seduce her instead.

acknowledgments

Sincere and heartfelt thanks to the following:

My husband, Jim, who amazes me with his love and support, makes me laugh with his dry wit, and generally makes my life so much happier simply by being in this world. And to the two precious creatures that sleep at my feet, keep me company, and bark excitedly when I share my lunch with them.

My mom and sisters, who are my biggest cheerleaders.

Romance Writers of America, especially the wonderfully talented writers and friends in my home chapter, Southern Magic.

Special thanks to Callie James and Carla Swafford for brainstorming this book with me on the way home from the Heart of Dixie Readers Luncheon. You both helped tremendously.

Danny Agan, for technical assistance and advice.

Gill, for his help with things that have engines that I know absolutely nothing about, and his wife, Tammie, who sends me lovely notes of encouragement when I need them most.

The awesome neighbors on my street, especially Laurie, Kent, Susie, and Steve, who threw me such a fabulous book-signing party.

My wonderfully talented editor, Kate Collins, whose vision and enthusiasm for this book made it so much better, and all the amazing people at Ballantine who have been so incredibly helpful and kind.

My agent, Kim Whalen, whose support, encouragement, and professionalism keep me focused and sane.

And to the readers of the Last Chance Rescue books: your support, kindness, and encouragement have meant the world to me.

Read on for a preview of

SECOND CHANCE

the fifth novel of sexy suspense and thrilling adventure in Christy Reece's *Last Chance Rescue* series!

A female shriek, loaded with drunken laughter, ripped through the air. *Oh yeah.* The Saturday night crowd at Bug-n-Booze was alive and kicking. The aroma of the roasted peanuts covering the floor blended with the lusty smells of women who only wanted two things—to get drunk and to get laid.

Wesley's Tuttle's mouth slid up in an easy smile . . . his favorite kind of woman.

"Are you listening to me?"

With deliberate slowness, Wes turned back to his companion. She'd asked to meet him hundreds of miles from Fairview; least she could do was let him enjoy himself for a little while. This was his first time here and Wes already knew it wouldn't be his last.

Wes eyed the woman sitting at the table with him. With her upper-crust, snooty attitude and expensive clothes, she looked as out of place here as a possum would at a pie-throwing contest. It was all for show; everything about her was fake. He knew more than most anybody about this particular rich bitch. Those clothes might make her look high class, but when she had a little liquor inside her or needed a favor, she could make a Saturday night slut look like a nun.

He gave her the smile he reserved especially for her, knowing it'd piss her off. "I want the woman, too."

Shock reflected on her face for barely a second, then a skinny, manicured hand waved dismissively. "Don't be ridiculous. If you make this more complicated, it will never work. You'll get more than enough for the kids."

He stared hard. This point was non-negotiable. If she wanted him to do the job, she'd come around.

Her eyes skittered away from his face. Good. She might be his employer for this particular gig, but she was scared of him. Just the way he liked it.

She chewed at her lower lip, smearing scarlet lipstick over her teeth. "What do you want her for? Ransom?"

A grin tugged on his mouth. "You know money ain't the reason I want her."

Jealousy dripping from every word, she said, "What is it with you men? Her ass is the size of a double-wide and those boobs are freakishly large."

It was all he could do not to laugh in her face. "If double-wide trailers were shaped like her ass, I wouldn't mind living in one the rest of my life."

The woman continued her rant. Wes ignored her, as he did most of the time. When she said something he wanted to hear, he'd tune in again.

She was pissed he wasn't still trying to get into her panties. He'd been there and done that more times than he liked to count. Every time he made the return trip, he always swore he'd never go back again, but when he was horny, sometimes he needed the itch scratched without preliminaries. Given the proper incentive, this bitch was always willing.

"Are you listening to me?"

"I will when you say something worth hearing."

Eyes flashed with a haughty fury; she reared back as only her kind could.

Wes snorted, not one bit impressed with her high-brow attitude. "Listen, we may be in business together, but I ain't taking no shit off you. You tell me where I can nab the brats and the woman. I'll take care of the rest. That sure as hell don't mean we gotta be bosom buddies." Wes swallowed another snort. Like she had any kind of bosom he could buddy up to. Hell, she barely had anything up top at all. Another reason she was so jealous of the woman. The difference between them was like an ocean to a mud puddle.

The anger in her eyes seemed to dim for the moment. Talking business was one way to keep that jealousy under control. "They'll be hard to get to; she barely lets them out of her sight. And it'll have to be done somewhere out of the house. It'd take a tank to get inside that estate."

Wes shrugged. "So? Find a way to get all of them out in the open. I can get rid of anybody who sees me."

"No, I don't want anyone killed. That would attract too much attention."

He cackled. The bitch was dumber than he thought. "Hell, you don't think kidnapping two little girls with that last name in this state ain't going to cause an uproar? Especially after what happened to their daddy? FBI's gonna be on it like flies on chicken shit."

A small bit of fear flashed in her eyes and then she shrugged. "You do what I tell you to do and no one will ever find them . . . it doesn't matter who's looking for them."

Man, she sure hated the woman. Wes wasn't one to question other people's motives. Most times he didn't care. If he got money for it, there wasn't a lot he wouldn't do. He'd always prided himself on having no limits. Took balls of steel and major smarts to do what he'd done most of his life and not get caught. He eyed the woman again. Hell, might as well make the offer. It'd be some extra dough and no skin off his nose. "If you hate her that much, I can off her once I'm finished with her."

Her eyes widened with what looked like genuine shock. "I don't want her dead, you idiot. I don't want anyone killed." She leaned forward, her eyes darkening to an ugly mud brown. "Understood?"

Fine with him. He sure as hell wasn't going to do extra stuff he wouldn't get paid for. "Fine. I'll wear a mask or something. Don't know why you're so against killing all of a sudden. You sure didn't seem to have a problem with it when you got rid of her husband."

Her face went still for an instant and then her mouth tilted in a smirk. "Now, what makes you think I had anything to do with that?"

" 'Cause I saw you right after they got married. Never seen you so pissed before. Besides, it sounds like something you'd do."

She pressed a hand against her heart in fake outrage. "I can't believe you think I'd be so vindictive." The slight humor he'd seen in her eyes disappeared and the ice-bitch look returned. "Despite all the evidence that pointed to her, she was barely even considered a suspect."

"Well, least you got the money for it."

She waved a negligent hand. "Money is inconsequential."

Spoken like a woman who had it to spare. To Wes, money would never be inconsequential. "What'd you have him kidnapped for then?"

A skinny, haughty brow lifted. "I never said I did."

Wes swallowed a guffaw. Wasn't no use denying it. He knew what the bitch was capable of. "Bet the outcome really honked you off, too. She got the money, the mansion, and got rid of a cheating husband to boot. I'd say you got screwed."

"The only reason they believed her is because of her looks. Idiot men take one look at her and start thinking with their dicks. It's disgusting."

Unable to resist needling her, Wesley quipped, "Thought you said she wasn't good-looking."

Her mouth tightened at the reminder, but she stayed focused on business. "One hundred thousand to snatch both of them, plus the money you get from each buyer." She slid a piece of paper toward him. "Here are the names, phone numbers, and addresses." A blood-red nail tapped on the paper. "The dark-haired one goes to these people in Florida; the blonde to this couple in Pennsylvania. As soon as you make the delivery, they'll give you the money. It's all yours."

Like he needed her telling him how to conduct business. Whatever she said didn't mean squat. He'd do it his way. He already had a buyer set up for the blond one and would be getting a whole hell of a lot more than the twenty-five thousand the people in Pennsylvania were willing to cough up. The dark-haired one might have to go to the Florida people, though. The blond one would be easier to pass off as his till he could drop her off; the dark-haired one looked too different to be his.

She continued with her instructions. "You'll need to get out of town immediately after you take them."

He knew how to take care of his business. Just 'cause she'd started the process didn't mean she was going to run the show.

Once he got rid of the kids, he'd keep the woman for as long as he wanted, then drop her somewhere when he was through. Using her brats as leverage would ensure she'd do everything he told her to do. Wes squirmed in his chair as he thought about all the things that plump pink mouth would do to him.

Putting those needs on the back burner, he leaned forward, eager to get things into motion. The sooner he got the plans in place, the sooner he'd be getting what he'd been wanting for years. "Here's what you're going to do."

Her face lit up and became more animated than he'd ever seen it.

Man, if she really hated Keeley Fairchild that much, why the hell didn't she want her dead?

Two weeks later
Fairview, South Carolina

A gurgling giggle caused Keeley to smile. Even without looking, she knew the giggle belonged to Hailey. It had a tinkling, musical quality to it. Her sister Hannah's giggle was softer and sounded more like a wind chime.

"Mommy, look at me!"

She turned and grabbed Hailey's waist just in time to pull her down from the monkey bars she was trying to climb. The little knot on her head from last week's adventure was barely gone. "Hailey, I told you not to go up there."

She sat her daughter down on the ground and tried for a hard look. When her angel just looked at her with an innocent, adorable grin, Keeley figured she'd failed the stern-mother-glare test. With her light blue eyes and fair complexion, Hailey looked so much like her father that Keeley felt that familiar painful twist to her heart.

Going to her knees, Keeley brushed a blond curl from her daughter's forehead and gave her button nose a gentle tap. "No climbing . . . promise Mommy."

Another gap-toothed grin was her response. Keeley held back a sigh. How on earth had she managed to create a daredevil daughter? Hailey wasn't happy unless she was doing something she knew her mother would definitely not want.

"Mommy, can I have some juice?"

She pressed a kiss to Hailey's forehead and twisted around to Hannah, Hailey's sister. Though the girls were twins, they were as unalike as if they came from different parents. Hannah was a miniature version of Keeley—light olive skin, ebony hair, and black eyes. Her personality was easygoing and pleasant. She could be entertained with a book for hours; her sister might hold out for five minutes.

Sometimes it amazed her how these two precious little girls had come from something so disastrous as her marriage to Stephen. Not that she'd known how bad it was until just before he died. But the gifts of her daughters more than made up for the other things. No doubt about it, they were heaven-sent.

Pulling out a large thermos, she poured a small amount of apple juice into a plastic cup. She dropped a kiss onto Hannah's silky head and then handed her the juice. "Here you go, sweet-pea."

Smiling her thanks, Hannah headed toward her sister, her tiny hands wrapped tight around her cup as she sipped her juice. Little Miss Careful never wanted to spill a drop.

Keeley turned to grab another cup from her bag, knowing once Hailey saw her sister with juice, she'd want some, too. She was pouring the juice when she heard the first scream.

"Mommy!"

Keeley whirled around. In an instant, she dropped the cup and ran. A man in a black ski mask had both her babies in his arms and was running down the sidewalk toward the parking lot.

Her heart was pounding as her feet flew toward the monster. "What are you doing? Stop!"

Her eyes focused on her children, Keeley barely noticed when another masked man ran up beside her. He threw his arm around her waist, picked her up and started carrying her. Her only instinct to get to her babies, Keeley kicked and beat at him until he dropped her to the ground.

Terror exploding inside her, Keeley was back on her feet in an instant and running. Her babies were screaming for her; the man carrying them never looked back.

A hard arm grabbed her from behind. "Come on, bitch." The voice sounded breathless and angry.

Barely pausing, Keeley slugged the man in the face and kept on running. She screamed, "Don't you take my babies!"

"Bitch!" The second masked man was beside her again. He made another grab for her and missed.

Keeley didn't spare him a glance. Their faces red and puckered with fear, her babies screamed, shouting for her. With a gasping sob, Keeley stretched her hand out and managed to claw at their abductor's sleeve.

He glanced back, wrenched his arm away and sped up.

Oh God, don't let him get away. "No!" Keeley screamed.

He reached the parking lot and ran toward the opened side door of a white van. Keeley took a leap and sprang toward him, her arms outstretched. Once again she felt the brush of his jacket on her fingertips. He pulled away sharply and Keeley felt herself falling. Pain slammed into her as she smacked face-first onto the concrete pavement. On the edge of consciousness, the last sound Keeley heard was the cry of her babies screaming "Mama!"

Wes glanced in his rearview mirror at the two sleeping kids. Seeing them with their arms wrapped around each other for comfort and warmth kind of tugged at his heart. They'd been so upset he'd given them orange juice laced with Valium to calm them down. They'd fallen asleep almost immediately. Had he given them too much? Maybe he should check and make sure they were still breathing.

Damned if he needed anything else to go wrong with this job. He had two kids, hopefully alive, but no woman. The bitch had double-crossed him; the grab hadn't gone down like he'd instructed. The email he got on his BlackBerry just seconds ago indicated that as far as she was concerned, the job was finished: "Your money's at the P.O. box. Get out of town and don't come back."

Like hell.

Wes turned down the gravel path to his cabin. First thing he needed to do was get off the road. He'd paid Fletch the money he owed him for his help, though not as much as Wes had promised him. Hell, even if the setup wasn't right, the bastard should've been able to grab Keeley. That'd been his only job. In Wes's estimation, if a man couldn't take down a woman, he wasn't much of a man. Stupid prick.

Wes parked in front of his cabin and turned the ignition off. Twisting around, he eyed the unconscious kids. He reached out a hand and touched the pulses at their necks. Yeah, both still beating. At least that was one thing that hadn't got messed up.

Weird that they were twins when they didn't even look related. One had blond hair; the other one had black hair . . . the color of her mother's. The dark-haired one would be going to some people in Georgia. He'd found somebody who was willing to pay five thousand more than what the Florida people had promised. Thirty thousand had a nicer ring to it than twenty-five.

The blond one was going to bring him more than double what the dark-haired one had. With the hundred thousand he'd gotten for the grab, he was going to be sitting pretty for a long time.

First, he had a call to make.

Wes pressed a key on his cellphone. She answered on the first ring in that haughty voice he hated. "I told you not to call me."

"You're going to pay. Nobody double-crosses me and gets away with it."

She laughed. The bitch had the nerve to laugh at him!

"I did pay you. With that kind of money, you can find plenty of women to do anything you want. And I got what I wanted. We're even."

His teeth ground so hard his jaw ached. "We ain't even and you know it. I'll be back. You're going to get me what you promised or else."

He ended the call before she could say anything else. Wouldn't matter what she said. He wanted what he wanted. And he had wanted Keeley Fairchild for years.

In high school, she'd been focused on other things, never dated. Not that he'd ever asked. She wouldn't have anything to do with him or any of the other boys who'd panted after her. She was always too serious, had her head in a book, or was busy practicing for track. But her body . . . Wes hardened at the mental image. Keeley's hot-damn body was the kind boys dreamed of and men salivated over.

After high school, he'd tried a few times to get her to go out with him, but she'd always turned him down. She'd always been nice about it, though, and he figured she was just shy. Then what she'd do but up and marry that rich bastard Stephen Fairchild. Whatever good feelings he'd had about Keeley had been lost. Most everybody knew Fairchild couldn't keep his pants zipped. Wes figured Keeley had gotten what she deserved.

Things were different now. Fairchild's ass was ashes, and Wes had been dreaming and salivating way too long. When he got back to town, the waiting would be over.

First things first . . . get rid of her brats. Other than getting a nice chunk of money, the only satisfaction this job gave him was the knowledge that the double-crossing bitch would be pissed he hadn't dropped the kids where she'd told him to go.

Wes snorted. Like he was going to take orders from a woman.

Once he took care of his transactions, he'd lay low and enjoy his rewards for a while. Let the bitch get comfortable, think he'd forgotten about her. He'd be back and show her that nobody double-crosses Wesley Tuttle and gets away with it. She'd either pony up the other part of the bargain or he'd be announcing to the world just who was responsible for Keeley Fairchild's misery. Wouldn't the good citizens of Fairview be surprised?